The
Secret
Diary

BOOKS BY ANNA STUART

The Berlin Zookeeper

The Secret Diary

ANNA STUART

bookouture

Published by Bookouture in 2021

An imprint of Storyfire Ltd.
Carmelite House
50 Victoria Embankment
London EC4Y 0DZ

www.bookouture.com

ISBN: 978-1-80019-515-8
eBook ISBN: 978-1-80019-514-1

This book is a work of fiction. Names, characters, businesses,
organizations, places and events other than those clearly in the
public domain, are either the product of the author's imagination
or are used fictitiously. Any resemblance to actual persons, living or
dead, events or locales is entirely coincidental.

For my supper club friends – Anne, Fiona, Johanna, Kate, Kate, Louise and Zoe. You've got me through so many of the ups and downs of motherhood for the last nineteen years and truly are my very own gunner girls!

Prologue

Nancy sets down her hairbrush and looks at herself curiously in the elegant triple mirror. Three faces stare back but she isn't sure if she recognises any of them. Who is she now? Is she Nancy the gunner girl, battling with her crew to keep the enemy from invading their skies? Nancy the new wife, fighting for a place as a gamekeeper at her husband's side? Or Nancy the young mother, keeping a happy home for her growing family?

She feels like all three of them at once, but the world doesn't seem to want to allow that. Why can't a woman operate outside the kitchen? Why can't a wife work? She thought that when the war ended, the fighting would be over, but it seems that for her, and so many women like her, it's only just starting.

With a sigh, Nancy looks down at the red leather book on the dressing table – a solid, forthright rectangle amongst the curvy hairbrushes and perfume bottles. She bought it just after VE Day to record her married life with the beloved husband she finally knew would come home from submarine-haunted seas. She'd felt such joy that day, such optimism, but peace hasn't turned out to be quite as simple as she'd hoped.

War has changed them all. The things they've seen, the things they've done, the secrets they've shared. The world is different now, and you can't just pack the past away with your gas mask and your ration book and 'go back to normal', because normal is different too.

Nancy picks up the book and strokes its cover. She's loved recording the last year in this diary, however up and down it's been, but she fears she's been too frank. There's a secret in here she agreed to keep – for her own sake and the sake of the rest of her fellow gunner girls. She doesn't regret what they did in the darker corners of the war, but she doesn't want it known either. It's locked in their hearts and that's where it should stay.

Opening the diary, she scans the entries, reliving events, shaking her head at the things she's been through. Her hand pauses on the final pages and she sighs. She shouldn't have made this particular entry. It was foolish, reckless.

There's only one thing to be done.

Gritting her teeth, Nancy takes hold of the last few pages in one hand, braces the other against the spine, and tears. The pages come away cleanly and she looks at the torn remains against the leather, feeling ashamed at defacing the precious book.

No matter. Worse has been lost in the last six years than a few idle scribblings. Setting the papers down, she opens up the left-hand drawer, nudging her lipsticks and compact aside to find the tiny lever and release the compartment beneath. She places the diary gently inside and then, on an impulse, drops a kiss onto her index finger and touches it to the red leather.

A noise somewhere in the house beyond makes her jump, and she hastily closes the compartment and sweeps the lipsticks back across it with a cheery clatter. She stands and all three reflections merge into one Nancy. Giving herself a little nod, she picks up the torn-out pages and looks to the bin, but instinctively her fingers tighten around the papers, around the words – around the secret. Somehow, she can't quite bring herself to throw this away.

She doesn't want her wartime secret known right now, but maybe some time in the future, when the suffering is less raw and people are more forgiving, there will be the space for it to come out. She looks around the lovely annex tucked away at the back of the gamekeeper's cottage she's proud to call home, and smiles as she spots the perfect hiding place. There is always, it seems, more than one place to keep a secret…

Chapter One

Lorna Haynes climbed slowly out of the car and looked in astonishment at the stunning cottage in front of her. Her mum had said her new home was 'rather sweet', but she hadn't mentioned that it was chocolate-box perfect. She grabbed her phone and checked the address again. Yep – The Gamekeeper's Cottage, just like the plaque on the wooden gate said.

'Whoa! Is that where we're staying?' Nine-year-old Charlie tumbled out of the back of the car. 'It's like something out of the olden days.'

'It is,' Lorna agreed, taking in the beautiful house before them.

The Gamekeeper's Cottage was a golden, sandstone building with a pebbled path leading up to a rose-covered porch, and gabled windows nestling beneath an actual thatched roof. It was the sort of place that Lorna had dreamed of as a child; the sort of place that had fuelled her interest in the past and eventually led to the job she loved as a history teacher. Or rather, the job she *had* loved until all interest in anything, past, present or future, had been knocked out of her by the dreadful phone call.

She forced her thoughts back to the pretty house, trying desperately to be positive.

'Isn't it fantastic, Charlie?'

'It's OK, yeah, though it better have Wi-Fi.'

'I'm sure it will,' she said, ruffling his hair.

He looked at her sceptically.

'*Minecraft* doesn't work without Wi-Fi, Mum.'

'Granny has Wi-Fi, Charlie. Remember, she FaceTimes you.'

'Yeah, but that could be on mobile data.'

Lorna shook her head at her son's knowledge and was grateful when little Stan emerged, rubbing his eyes where he'd fallen asleep on the journey. Her five-year-old crept up to her, wrapping his hands around her leg, and she hugged him close.

'Pretty,' he said, pointing to the rose that climbed over the porch. Then: 'Are we staying long?'

Lorna's heart faltered. She'd been so sure about coming here until now. She thought of her best friend, Aki, clasping her hands a few hours ago and saying, 'Why not go to your mum, Lorna? Why not let someone look after you for a change?' It had sounded so simple, so very appealing, and she'd made the hour-long journey from Norwich on autopilot, willing herself just to get here. Now she'd made it, though, this beautiful house suddenly felt more daunting than comforting. Should she have come?

'Lorna! Oh, my sweet one, I'm so glad you're here.' Suddenly there was her mum, Mary, running down the path in an elegant jersey dress to scoop all three of them in her arms. 'It's so wonderful to see you. I'm so happy you're here.'

Lorna took a deep breath, drawing in the pleasingly familiar scent of the L'Air du Temps her mum had worn for as long as she could remember and feeling it steady her. Mary drew back and looked into her eyes.

'My poor darling. I can't tell you how much my heart aches for you, for all of us. I'm so, so glad you've come at last. It's been tearing me apart not being able to do more for you.'

Lorna smiled.

'Aki told me to come.'

'Aki is very wise.' Mary tenderly kissed her forehead. 'Come along in, darling. David's popped out for a bit of shopping, but I'm sure he'll be back any minute.'

Lorna glanced down the road for her stepdad. Her own father had made for the horizon the moment he'd found out about her foetal existence, so Mary had brought her up alone, rarely even dating. Lorna had liked it as just the two of them when she'd been young but had started to worry about her mum as she'd got older, and so she'd been delighted when Mary had tentatively told her that she had 'met someone rather nice'. She'd married David last year in a quiet but very happy ceremony. On the few occasions Lorna had met him, he'd seemed lovely, but she didn't know him all that well and just hoped he didn't mind them invading his beautiful home. There was no sign of him yet, though, and she looked back to the boys as Mary bent down to speak to them.

'I told Grandpa David you like to eat cabbage, beetroot and snails – is that right?'

'Granny! Yu-uck.'

Mary winked at her grandsons.

'Well, maybe Jaffa cakes, pizza and Haribo then?'

'Yay!'

Lorna watched as they chased her up the path, enviously easily distracted. She went round to the boot to fetch the bags, taking a little time to herself as Mary absorbed her sons' constant energies. Perhaps Aki had been right after all.

It had been a desperate six weeks since the phone call telling her that Matt, her husband – her best friend – had been snatched from them. She'd been sitting in the bustling swimming pool café whilst the boys doggy-paddled up and down when the picture of a smiling Matt had popped up on her screen. She'd rolled her eyes to the ceiling, sure he was calling to say he was stuck at work.

'Don't tell me you're going to be late, babe?' she'd purred into the phone. 'Or I'll have to punish you like I did last time!'

The awkward silence should have told her something, but it had been noisy in the café. Then: 'Mrs Haynes?' It had been a woman's voice, clipped and formal. Lorna's blood had run cold.

'Who is this?'

'Mrs Haynes, this is PC Patel. Where are you, please?'

'Why does it matter? What's happened? What's wrong?' she'd babbled. Then: 'Where's Matt?'

'Is there another adult with you? Or someone you can call?'

'Why? Please – what's going on?'

'I'm afraid we need to ask you to come to the Norfolk and Norwich hospital, Mrs Haynes. There's been an accident.'

'Matt? Is he alive?'

There'd been no mistaking the pause this time and Lorna had collapsed right there in the middle of the café, amongst the lattes and the muffins and the pervasive smell of chlorine, and screamed.

She could remember little else of that terrible day except Aki, her best friend since teacher-training college, arriving to collect her and the wailing boys and take them home. Mary had arrived later and held Lorna's hand as she'd stood by a blank slab in the bowels of the hospital and seen Matt's precious face unveiled as if she were in some stupid TV programme. Except that no one had called 'cut' and eventually she'd come to realise that he wasn't coming back. Not this evening, not tomorrow – not ever.

The funeral had been a blur of tears in which Lorna had been able to do little bar clutch Charlie and Stan close and pray that doing so held her together as well, but afterwards she'd insisted Mary and Aki and all the other well-meaning friends let her get on with it. She'd wanted space to breathe, however hard that had felt, but perhaps she'd been mad to think they could get through the worst time of their lives alone. Then, today, she'd tried to send the boys back to school. It hadn't gone well.

She'd been looking forward to a day alone and had started out fine, with a nice relaxed coffee and an online yoga class. It was when she'd decided to sort Matt's things that it had all gone wrong. The soft, familiar jumpers had smelled so achingly of him that she'd ended up just crawling into the wardrobe to burrow amongst them. It was only when Aki, who was the headteacher at the boys' primary school, had called her at lunchtime to tell her how they were getting on, that she'd admitted she was stuck in a cupboard. Aki, bless her, had been there like a shot.

'You shouldn't be alone, sweetie,' she'd said, once she'd finally coaxed her out. 'Why not go to your mum's? You're signed off till September, aren't you?'

'Yes, but the boys aren't.'

Aki had stroked her back softly.

'There's less than two weeks to the summer holidays, Lorna, and they're only young – what does it matter?'

'Aki Sato – you can't say that.'

'Not officially, maybe, but I can to you. In fact, as their head-teacher, I'm authorising their absence. What they need now is time and space, and so do you.'

'Really?'

Lorna had looked into Aki's burnt-chocolate eyes and seen nothing but care.

'Really, Lor! Mary's been offering five times a day, so take her up on it. It's not weakness. It doesn't mean you can't cope. It just makes sense to let someone else share the burden, and who better than your mum?'

'Who better than my mum?' Lorna echoed now, yanking the big suitcase out of the car, and heading for the pretty gate.

Part of her wished that she was retreating to the house she'd grown up in, going back to the safety of her childhood, but truth be told, that had been a cramped suburban terrace and not a patch on the beautiful cottage before her. Plus, as soon as she stepped in the door, she smelled a familiar scent of home baking, washing powder and flowers, and felt the tension in her shoulders physically release. Looking around the cosy hallway full of coats and wellies, she noticed the same photo that had always hung in her old house and was comforted.

The picture was of her and Mary on a double swing, both with their heads flung back, laughing their happiness up to the blue skies above, and it was hard not to smile when you saw it. It also, to Lorna, summed up her childhood – just her and her mum against the world.

'It's a lovely picture.'

Lorna jumped at the low voice and swung round to see her new stepdad standing in the doorway. He had a supermarket bag in each hand, incongruous against his slim, corduroy-and-cashmere-clad frame. She straightened automatically.

'David. Hi. Thanks for having us to stay.'

He dropped the bags.

'Nonsense! We're delighted to have you. I'm so, so sorry for your loss, Lorna. May I?' He held out his arms and, surprised, she nodded and stepped into them. His grip was warm and strong, and he smelled of Imperial Leather and fresh grass. 'You poor child. It's so cruel.'

That was so exactly what it was, and she hugged him back gratefully. She should have known her mum would marry someone nice, but it was good to see it for herself all the same. The knowledge that Mary now lived in David's house had perhaps been part of her concern about coming here; a concern that was rapidly dissipating.

'Let me take that to your room,' he said, reaching for her suitcase. 'Would you like to come and see it?'

'The boys…' she said faintly.

'Are fine with your mum, really. She's bursting with grandmotherly energy, so let her take some of the slack and give yourself a little time to rest. I imagine you need it.'

'No, I—'

'It's allowed, you know. In fact, it's vital – that's professional advice.'

He gave her a kind wink. He was a retired GP so she supposed he knew what he was talking about, but it was still hard to believe. The boys had lost their father; surely they needed her more than ever.

'Maybe a quick look,' she agreed, glancing down the corridor to where she could hear Charlie and Stan chattering to her mum in what must be the kitchen.

'No problem. We thought you could go in the annex so you'd have a little space from us oldies, but if you'd rather be in the main house that's totally fine too.'

'Annex?'

Lorna looked around curiously. She'd specialised in homes and their interiors in the third year of her history degree, and the cottage had all the squinty angles and low beams she would have expected from an eighteenth-century building. It didn't seem the place for anything as modern-sounding as an annex.

'It was built between the wars,' David told her, 'back before anyone worried about little things like planning permission. This way.'

He led her towards the kitchen but turned right into a square hallway. Oak doors on either side stood open to a cosy living room and a wood-panelled study, but the white-painted one dead ahead was shut. David reached for the handle as Mary appeared behind them, the boys in tow, and Lorna looked quizzically at her.

'You'll love it, darling,' her mum said. 'It's been kept almost totally as it was in the forties. It's like stepping into history.'

She nodded keenly at her and Lorna looked obediently back to the white door. This was the sort of thing that would normally have the historian in her salivating, but since Matt had died it had been hard to taste the world in the same way. It all seemed so dull and lifeless. She battled to summon up a smile, and followed David inside.

'Wow!'

'Isn't it amazing?' Mary gushed, as the boys darted past Lorna and raced around the space, touching everything as if it were an interactive museum. It might as well have been. The living area had a parquet floor, softened by a swirly rug, and was furnished with low art deco armchairs and coffee table. The fireplace was cast iron with red tiles, and on the mantelpiece sat an ancient walnut wireless.

To one side was a bright kitchenette with a Bakelite oven and open shelving fronted with faded gingham curtains, and to the other, a door stood open to a luminously pink bedroom. The double bed was covered with a shiny, pale pink eiderdown, and had a slim wardrobe to one side and an art deco dressing table to the other, complete with a big triple mirror. The walls were papered in garish cerise roses. The whole effect was startling.

'It's…' Lorna started, but she couldn't find the right words.

'Do we have to sleep in there?' Charlie demanded, pointing disgustedly into the pink room.

'No, Charlie. These are for you and Stan.'

Mary indicated a set of bunk beds against the right-hand wall.

'Cool! Bagsie the top one.'

Charlie flung himself up the ladder. Stan watched him thoughtfully, clearly deciding whether this was a privilege worth fighting over, then gave a little shrug and climbed happily into the cave-like space of the bottom bunk. Lorna's heart ached with love for them both.

'Are those bunks usually there?'

'No,' Mary admitted. 'We brought them from upstairs after you called and I popped out for some new linen. I hope they like it.'

'*Minecraft*! Cool covers, Granny!'

'They do,' Lorna said, her heart throbbing with gratitude. 'You didn't need to do this, Mum.'

'I know that, Lorna, but I wanted to. If I can't spoil you three, who can I spoil?'

Lorna swallowed. *You three.* That's what they were now – not a nice, solid square of a family but a spiky triangle.

'It's very kind,' she managed.

'Well, I thought you'd like to be in here for, you know, the history. It's been like this since just after the Second World War.

David rents it out for TV and that. It's been in all sorts of programmes. Do you like it?'

Lorna looked around, desperately wanting to like it. Some dispassionate, academic part of her historian's brain was definitely impressed, but she couldn't summon up anything more.

'It's great, Mum,' she said flatly.

'Oh, Lorna.'

'It is, really. I just…' The ever-ready tears threatened again and she strode into the pink bedroom, fighting them hard. 'I just don't seem to have the energy to love stuff like this at the moment. I don't have the energy to love anything. Well, apart from the boys of course, and you and, and…'

Now the tears were coming. *Matt would have thought this place was hilarious*, was all she could think as she looked around at the ludicrously pink bedroom. The fact that she'd never, ever be able to show it to him threatened to overwhelm her. She sank onto the bed, battling for strength, and was dimly aware of David saying something about showing the boys the garden, and her mum sitting down next to her and taking her hand. She clutched tightly on to it, scared that she might float away on this endless tide of grief.

'I miss him so much, Mum.'

'Of course you do, darling. Of course you do. We all miss him. I've often woken myself crying in the night, remembering all the happy times we had together, so I can't begin to imagine how awful it is for you. I wish I could do it for you, Lor. I wish I could take it from you.'

Lorna squeezed her fingers.

'You're doing loads already, Mum. It's good to be here, really it is. The annex is amazing. I just can't seem to find any enthusiasm for the past at the moment, or the present for that matter. As for the future…'

She choked up on the word, for the future felt like one great big gaping hole, waiting to suck her into its dark centre.

'Sleep,' Mary said firmly. 'That's what you need.'

'If only it were that easy.'

'I know, darling, but everything is a little bit easier with some rest and some food. Are you hungry?' Lorna shook her head. 'I bet the boys are. Why don't I go and feed them their tea and you can slide into that bed and have a little nap?'

She looked at the pink bed.

'Are those forties sheets?'

Mary laughed.

'Lord love you, no. Brand new, I promise. So, what do you think – a little lie-down? We've got all summer to do things, so let's take it a day at a time, shall we?' Lorna nodded and, feeling like a little girl again, let her mum tuck her under the sheets and kiss her forehead. 'Take as long as you need.'

'Thanks, Mum.'

Mary tiptoed out and Lorna lay there, fearing that she needed more time to get over losing her husband than she would ever have. She and Matt should have been celebrating their tenth wedding anniversary next month. They'd been planning a week away, just the two of them. Matt had emailed her a link to an amazing-looking apartment in Genoa the very morning the lorry had ploughed into him. She'd bookmarked the link, and she called it up whenever she particularly wanted to torment herself with what would now never be. That was no way to think, was it? She had to be strong, positive, thankful – all that crap.

She closed her eyes, willing her tortured brain to let go, but it wasn't having any of it. All she could see was pictures of Matt the day they'd met. She saw him desperately trying to steer his sledge sideways as he came careering towards her at the bottom of a snowy slope in the local park one beautifully cold winter; she saw his blue eyes looking into hers as he offered to buy her a mulled wine in the nearby pub to make up for scaring her; then his warm lips soft against her own as, much, much later that night, he'd walked her home. They'd been almost inseparable from that moment on, and had married two years later. Now he was gone.

Anger rippled through her and she threw back the covers, pacing the little room in an attempt to keep it at bay until, catching sight of herself in the triple mirror, she stopped. This way madness lay. Taking several deep breaths, she sat down on the stool and considered her reflection. God, she was a fright – her eyes were etched with red, her skin as pale as if it were November and not a sunny July, and her chestnut hair looked like something might be nesting in it. Perhaps she'd have a haircut. That was what people did, wasn't it? That was part of the 'cycle of grief'. Her mum was bound to have some lovely salon in the area where she could have it cut short. If nothing else, it would be less work to look after. For now, though, it needed a good brush.

She reached for the handle of the left-hand drawer in the art deco dressing table. It rattled open and she paused, then bent and looked inside. There was no hairbrush, or indeed anything else, bar a lining cut from some ancient, embossed wallpaper. That, however, was no longer what she was looking for. Lorna had written her dissertation on 'The Secrets in the Furniture – A Study in Hidden Panels through History', and she was sure she recognised this drawer style from her research. If she wasn't mistaken, you just had to lift out the lining and reach down the central side for a small lever.

Click.

Lorna froze. It had worked. It had actually worked. She ran her hands along the base of the drawer for the ridge of the secret panel and prised it open. It was a slim compartment, big enough for a few jewels or papers, or maybe…

The book was small and bound with dark red leather, tied shut with a matching cord. 1945 was written onto a cream panel on the front in a careful hand. Lorna reached in and lifted it out, her heart pounding with something other than grief for the first time since that hideous phone call six long, dark weeks ago. Untying the cord, she opened it up and read the first line: *Saturday, 16 June 1945.*

'A diary!' she gasped.

It was like a gift – a little bit of joy from a world that had only thrown her pain for far too long. With trembling hands, Lorna took the diary back to bed and opened it up. *So this is it*, she read. *I'm here at the Gamekeeper's Cottage and it's ten times as pretty as Joe led me to believe.*

She stared at the words. Seventy-six years ago, another woman had come to the Gamekeeper's Cottage and written those words, presumably in the very bed Lorna was now lying in. They were housemates across the ages and it seemed that, even if she couldn't enjoy her own life right now, she could at least escape into someone else's.

Chapter Two

So this is it. I'm here at the Gamekeeper's Cottage and it's ten times as pretty as Joe led me to believe. Ten times as grand too. I can't believe this is going to be my home now, my home as Mrs Nancy Wilson proper after a crazy year as a half-wife. The Gamekeeper's Cottage – our family home, the place where we'll live and work, the place where we'll be man and wife, the place, I suppose, where we'll be mother and father. It's exciting but it's terrifying too.

Nancy Jones – Wilson now, she had to remember that – stared up at the Gamekeeper's Cottage in disbelief. It was beautiful, like something out of a fairy tale, and a world apart from her own family's cramped terrace up in Chester. Was she really going to live here? Work here? She stared at the thatched roof, gabled windows and rose-covered porch.

'It's lovely,' she cried, fumbling her diary back into her bag.

The two men sitting in front of her in the borrowed motor car turned and smiled, and for a moment she saw how very similar they were. Father and son were distinguishable only by the lines time had etched into Ted's weather-beaten face, and the scar on Joe's temple where he'd been hit by debris as his boat went down at Anzio. Her heart turned over with love.

It was still so hard to truly believe she was here. She'd been stationed on the anti-aircraft gun at RAF Langham just up the road for the last three years, so she knew the area well, but this would be different. This time she would be part of the village. She could still so vividly remember Joe walking into the local pub back at the start of 1943, looking so handsome in his naval uniform, with his brown hair cut short and his hazel eyes alight with the joy of being home. She and the other gunner girls had been about to head back to base but, seeing Joe, a rich energy had run through Nancy's veins and she'd persuaded the others to stay on for one more.

Heading to the bar, she'd engineered bumping into him, but had executed her nudge a little too enthusiastically, sending his pint splashing down his front. Her frantic apology had, thankfully, turned into a conversation which had rapidly become a flirtation and then the sweetest kiss Nancy had ever known. It had been his last night of leave before he'd had to report to the south coast to set sail for the Mediterranean, so she'd sent the others back to base without her and defied curfew to sit up all night beneath the stars with him, talking and kissing.

Twice more he'd made it home to Langham, but the fourth time, in the spring of '44, he'd not been allowed to travel more than ten miles from his ship in case the D-Day orders came in. He had been in port fresh from surviving the sinking of his ship at Anzio, and Nancy, desperate to see for herself that he was whole and well, had fought to get leave and find a train south to Portsmouth. It had been a hard trek but worth it; she'd found him full of tales of the friends he'd lost to the deep and talk of the inestimable preciousness of having a future. She'd barely been with him an hour before he'd swept her into his arms and said, 'Marry me, Nancy,' and she'd replied, 'Yes.'

They'd been at the registry office with their special licence two days later, both in uniform, the only bridal touch the bouquet of roses she'd nicked from the park. They'd had two blissful days in a boarding house just down the coast, and then Joe had sailed for France and Nancy had gone back to shooting German planes out of the sky. They hadn't seen each other again for nearly a year and she'd spent too many long, terrifying days waiting for letters confirming he was alive, forever dreading the summons to the office that would mean the worst of news.

'At least now you're his wife, you'll hear first if he's killed,' Peggy had said, as they'd lined up the guns one wet and miserable night back in March.

'Peggy!' Connie and Dot had protested, but it had been the truth and Nancy had watched out for this dubious privilege like a hawk, her dreams perpetually haunted by fears of enemy submarines and mines hunting down her precious groom.

The telegram, thank God, had never come. Instead there'd been more and more good news, of Allied advances and German retreats, and then, as if every flower in the land had burst into bloom at once, VE Day had arrived and with it the knowledge that Joe was safe down in the Mediterranean, no longer war-torn. Now, after a week's glorious reunion in a scruffy hotel in the back streets of London, they were on the threshold of the rest of their lives.

Climbing out of the car, Nancy looked again to the Game-keeper's Cottage, noticing that the thatched roof was sitting at an angle she was sure wasn't natural, as if it had got tired and slid down a little. She tilted her head, considering it, but at that moment the door of the beautiful cottage was flung open and a rounded lady came rushing out. Betty Wilson had a head of wild grey curls, barely contained by a pink headscarf, and a substantial bosom straining at her floral housecoat. Dark pink slippers completed the cosy look and she enveloped Nancy in a lavender-scented hug.

'You must be Nancy. Welcome, dear, welcome. I've been so excited to meet you. Oh, and Joe. My dear, dear Joe.' She let go of Nancy to fling her arms around her son. 'Truly I thought this day would never come. Isn't it wonderful that we're all safe and those horrible Germans are defeated?'

'Wonderful,' Nancy agreed.

'My Joe saw them off, didn't you, lad?'

'Not single-handedly, Ma.'

'I know, I know, but you did your bit, boy, and we're proud of you.'

Nancy stood back a little to take in the sight of her new in-laws as they fussed over their only child. She'd known that she should go and introduce herself to Ted and Betty Wilson once she'd married their son, but without him at her side it had felt odd and she'd gratefully used the busy final year of the war to excuse herself from the task. Now, she would be living with them in the Gamekeeper's Cottage and working with them on the estate. It was a lot to take in.

'Nancy did her bit too,' Joe said, reaching for her hand to pull her into the family group. 'She's been shooting Jerry out of the skies these last three years.'

Betty clasped her hand to her bosom.

'So brave of you, dear. You must have been terrified.'

'Well—'

'Let's hope you never have to do anything like that again.'

'War was awful, of course,' she agreed, 'but I'm hoping to still use the skills I learned.'

Betty squinted at her in confusion and Nancy looked to Joe, who ducked away to grab their suitcases. Her heart squeezed. He'd talked so eloquently to her of the Langham estate and his gamekeeping job with Ted. He'd told her of their pheasants and deer, of all the work that went into managing the land, and he'd also told her that, when peace came and he brought her home with him, she could help out. The family were contracted to Lord Langham to manage the estate, but how they divided it between themselves was entirely up to them. 'You'll be one of us gamekeepers' had been Joe's exact words, but had he neglected to discuss this vital inclusion with his parents?

'I'm very much looking forward to learning about the estate,' she said to Betty.

Her mother-in-law frowned. 'The estate?'

'Yes. Joe's been telling me about the work he does here. I can't wait to learn about managing the hedges and the birds, shooting the pests and—'

'You can't possibly want to handle a nasty old gun again, Nancy?'

'Well, actually—'

But Betty was fussing over their suitcases and didn't seem to hear. Nancy looked behind her, away from the pretty cottage and across the fields to where she could just make out the tops of the airfield buildings. The base was still functioning, albeit in a limited capacity, and as if on cue a plane took off into the blue sky. Nancy fought to hold in a sigh. There was no way she'd rather be there than here, in her beautiful new home, and yet a guilty part of her already missed her life as a gunner girl.

She'd never known such adventures as she'd had with her crew, or such ready laughter either. Anti-aircraft crews had come and gone from Langham, learning how to aim the guns in the state-of-the-art training dome, but she, Peggy, Dot and Connie had been the only gunner girls actually stationed at the airfield and they'd become like sisters. Then, of course, there'd been that dark night towards the end of the war that had bonded them even closer. Nancy swallowed and reached out for the little picket fence, suddenly feeling giddy.

'You're tired, Nancy,' Betty said, instantly solicitous. 'No wonder, with silly me keeping us mithering on the doorstep! Come you in. I've made scones.'

'Scones!' Joe exclaimed, sliding his arm around Nancy's waist and guiding her up the path. 'With cream and jam?'

Betty batted at his arm.

'Of course. Wouldn't be scones without, would they now, boy? We've got a lovely exchange going with Mrs Barker at the farm – her cream and butter for our eggs – and the fruit's grown aplenty, war or no war.'

Joe looked to Nancy in delight and she forced herself to push her foolish concerns aside. She couldn't have asked for a warmer welcome, and no doubt Joe would soon talk to his parents about her working on the estate. In the meantime – cream and eggs! Wait until she wrote to her family – they'd never believe it.

She stepped under the roses and in through the front door, taking in the low beams and sturdy furniture. Betty hustled them into a formal front room, painted in muted colours that made her stand out like a large, exotic bird.

'We eat in the kitchen normally,' she confided, 'as it's cosier, but let's do it proper for this first time.'

'Can I help?'

'Oh no, dear, not today. After this, yes. Once you've settled in. Can you cook?'

Nancy remembered all those lessons at her mum's stove, mainly in how to make the ingredients stretch further.

'I can, but I've not done it in years.'

'Oh, you'll soon pick it up again. You look like you've a strong arm for a mop and a mangle. I do struggle with the mangle!'

'I'd love to help,' Nancy forced out, looking to Joe. He knew she didn't want to be chained to the house, so surely he needed to say something now? But his mouth seemed firmly shut so she added, 'I bet Joe's good with a mangle too, aren't you, Joe?'

There was a shocked silence. Then Betty said, 'I couldn't let *Joe* do the mangle.'

Nancy should shut up now, she knew she should, but she still heard herself say, 'Oh, I'm sure he wouldn't mind. If I can turn a gun handle, he can turn a mangle.'

'Course I can,' Joe said brightly. Too brightly.

'But he won't,' Ted said firmly. 'Now, Bett, where's the tea?'

The moment passed in a clattering of cups and a serving up of scones, and Nancy concentrated on eating hers, trying to enjoy the delicate sweetness of them and banish the hint of sourness on the warm parlour air.

Take it steady, girl, she told herself. *Be patient and get to know them.*

'Don't forget that my parents haven't had the enlightenment of life in the forces,' Joe had told her on the train up here, and she supposed he was right. She'd just forgotten, that's all. Three years as a gunner girl had warped her sense of normality.

Not warped, the voice in her head nagged, *improved*, but she shouldn't rush to judge. Joe understood her. Joe said he'd fallen in love with her 'fire', and he knew she didn't want to be stuck behind a mangle. They'd sort it together but it might take time.

'Delicious scones, Mrs Wilson,' she said.

Betty beamed, instantly mollified.

'Thank you, dear, and it's Betty, please. I've allus wanted a daughter, you know. We lost a little girl. Did Joe tell you?'

'No.' Nancy leaned in. 'Oh Betty, I'm so sorry.'

Betty patted her hand.

'Thank you, dear, but it was a long time ago. She only breathed a few hours, my Rose. We tried to have more, but I was in a bit of gyp after her birth and it wasn't to be. Not that it matters. Our Joe is enough for any parents, isn't he, Ted?'

'He is,' Ted agreed gruffly, adjusting his tweeds over thickset thighs.

'And now we have you, Nancy. I'm sure we'll rub along very well. I'll learn you how to make scones and you can tell me about these guns of yours, how's that?'

That was not really what Nancy had had in mind. She'd married Joe to have a life with *him*, not his mother, but it was a kind offer and she squeezed Betty's hands and nodded as, thankfully, Joe spoke again.

'The house is looking a little… squint, Pa.'

Ted grimaced and fidgeted at the well-worn pipe that seemed to hang perpetually from his lip.

'The truth of it is that the roof's falling down. We've patched her up a few times but it needs redoing. I've asked Lord Langham about it as often as I dare, but it's not like anyone's got any money, is it?'

'Not as yet, but it'll come, and now I'm here perhaps I can help.'

'That would be grand,' Betty said. 'And you'll be glad to know that your annex is fine.'

'Annex?' Nancy asked Joe.

'Didn't I tell you? Oh, Nance, you'll love it – our very own bedsit at the back of the house.'

'Bedsit?'

Nancy sat up, intrigued, and Betty clapped her hands happily.

'The previous Lord Langham had it built when Ted and I moved in with his parents just after the Great War. Very forward-thinking, it was. New couples need a bit of time alone, don't they? You don't want to be hanging around with us old folk all the time. Come and see, come and see.'

Nancy felt her spirits lift as she followed Betty out of the parlour and down a narrow corridor. Pausing to check they were all behind her, Betty threw open the door with a flourish.

'Ta-da! I've had it decorated specially, so it's modern for you youngsters.'

She ushered them keenly inside and Nancy found herself stepping into the sweetest room. There was a big living area with a smart sofa and chairs, and what had to be a brand-new wireless.

'Look, Joe!' She rushed over and turned the dial. It crackled and then, as she adjusted it, let out a run of lively jazz, as clear as if the band were right there in the room. 'That's amazing! We can dance.'

'Dance?!' Ted gasped, as Joe swept Nancy into his arms and jived her around their new home.

'Oh, come, dear,' Nancy half heard Betty say over the beating of her heart against her husband's. 'We used to dance. We should do it again, with the war over'n all.' Ted coughed gruffly and Nancy self-consciously tugged Joe to a standstill, though she was already looking forward to stepping into his arms again once they were alone. Betty smiled at them both and took her hand. 'Come you into the bedroom, Nancy.'

She pulled her into the separate room at the far corner and Nancy had to stop herself putting up a hand against the glare, for the room was done out in unrelenting pink, from the pale eiderdown to the floral walls to the checked curtains.

'How... pretty!'

'Isn't it?! I'm so glad you like it. I thought about waiting so you could choose yourself but I wanted it fresh for you. Who wouldn't like this? A bit of colour after those nasty army quarters, hey?'

'Pretty,' Nancy said again. 'Isn't it, Joe?'

Her husband looked from her to Betty.

'It's very pink, Ma,' he said eventually.

'Course it is, love. You've got a wife now.'

He smiled and put an arm round Nancy.

'I have, haven't I? Lucky me.'

'And it's a new bed too, son – a double. Your father was horrified, but I told him it's quite the thing for couples to sleep together these days.' Nancy had no idea where to put herself and Betty flushed. 'Did I do right?'

Joe leaned in and gave her a kiss.

'You did right, Ma. Thank you.'

An awkward pause followed, then Betty cried, 'Kitchen!' and hustled them all out, though not before Joe had time to throw Nancy a wink and a nod towards the bed. She raised her eyebrows cheekily back at him, already hoping their journey here would count as excuse enough to retire early, but she couldn't let herself get too distracted as Betty was keen to show her the Bakelite stove and the neat units.

'I made the curtains myself,' she said.

'Where did you get the fabric, Mrs... Betty?'

'Oh, don't ask, dear. It's amazing what people will find you in exchange for a rabbit or two!'

'Right. Well, er, thank you. Thank you so much.'

'Course, it's only a tiny kitchen, for occasional meals. We'll eat together, won't we? As a family. I hope you'll think of us as your family, Nancy?'

'I'd be honoured, Betty.'

'Honoured!' Betty pulled a tissue from her housecoat pocket and dabbed at her eyes. 'Hear that, Ted – honoured. How lovely is that?'

'Lovely,' Ted agreed, shifting across to his wife and patting her arm.

'It'll be strange for you at first, love, I know,' Betty went on, 'but we'll rub along very well. Very well indeed. Now, how's about you and I take these dishes through to the kitchen and leave the boys for a smoke?'

Nancy looked to Joe, longing for him to stand up and lead her into their little annex so she could take all this in, but he sent back an almost pleading gaze towards the kitchen. Squashing down an instant annoyance, she looked away again and picked up the cake plate. It was their first day here; it wouldn't hurt to be polite.

Sunday, 17 June 1945

So I've had a day here, at the Gamekeeper's Cottage. Home. Lord, that sounds strange. It's a beautiful house and we have an 'annex' all of our own, bigger than our whole downstairs up in Chester, and it's just for Joe and me. It's quite posh, whatever Joe said, but his folk are lovely. Ted seems a bit severe but Betty has been proper welcoming, bless her.

It feels very… domestic, but then anything would after army life, right? And I'm going to fit in here, I swear it, even if the housecoat Betty has given me feels itchier than my stiff army uniform, and our bedroom makes me want some of those dark glasses the GIs used to wear, and I so wish the damned mangle was a great big gun. Any stupid reservations are just me being ungrateful, foolish even. How can I hanker for the stark, harsh, scary life of the ATS when I have the comforts of the Gamekeeper's Cottage? It's a madness, that's all, and it will surely – pray God – pass.

It's odd to be back in Langham though. Joe wants to take me down the Blue Bell but it'll be so strange being there without the others. Perhaps for the best, mind you. Who knows what the talk'll be at the bar, and we made a pact, the girls and I. We made a pact we have to keep and that'll be easier on my own. I'm Nancy from the Gamekeeper's Cottage now, not Nancy from the airfield, and the sooner I learn that, the better – for us all.

Chapter Three

Lorna woke with the now usual tug of sadness and lay still as if perhaps, if she didn't move a muscle, the swirl of black thoughts and broken dreams wouldn't be able to find her. She hated this dark void in the middle of the night when everything seemed at its most bleak and minutes stretched into hours. With a sigh, she reached for the edge of the covers and, feeling the silky touch of the 1940s eiderdown, forced her eyes open.

'What the...?!'

She looked around her. The cerise roses on the wallpaper were as violently girlie as she remembered, but what surprised her most was that she could see them. She turned to the window and, sure enough, sunlight was creeping around the edges of the predictably pink curtains. For the first time since Matt's death, she had slept through the night, and the sheer relief of it gave her a strange shiver of something like joy. She sat up in bed, looking around the funny little room and listening – it was not only light, but silent. Were the boys still asleep?

Creeping out of the bedroom and into the living area, she found the bunk beds empty, the treasured *Minecraft* duvets flung aside, and Charlie and Stan both gone. The door stood open and when she went up to it, she could hear the chime of young voices in the main house. She drew in a long, slow breath and, after just a moment's hesitation, sat down in one of the armchairs to enjoy a few minutes more alone. She was shaking off sleep now and she felt good – a little lighter, a little less tense.

Mum was right, she thought, rolling her eyes to the Artex ceiling, *everything does feel easier with some sleep.* What had released her to – she glanced at her watch – ten full hours of rest? Had it perhaps been the very nice wine David had served with her mum's signature beef bourguignon? Or the pleasure of chatting on afterwards with the boys safely tucked up? Or the feeling that, under this roof, someone else was responsible, that everything didn't fall on her shoulders?

Or perhaps the fact that she'd gone to bed with Nancy Wilson's life rolling around in her head instead of her own?

Lorna looked around the little annex and smiled, unable to believe that David had kept it this way for so long. Had Nancy sat in this very chair? Had she cooked on that stove and lit that fire and danced to that beautiful wireless? She got up and went to it, turning it on and fiddling with the dial to try and catch a station, but she could find nothing more than static. Her eyes alighted on the painting above – a curiously dark landscape that seemed at odds with the bright décor of the rest of the room. She thought it might be a Turner – well, a copy – and wondered who had chosen it and why.

'Did you like this, Nancy?' she asked out loud, and then felt foolish.

She didn't believe in ghosts, and had relentlessly resisted looking in the shadows of even the darkest part of the night for Matt's. It was too painful to contemplate talking to him, so what was she doing chatting to some woman from the past? She probably just needed some breakfast.

Pulling on her dressing gown, she went through into the house, taking time to look around the lovely rooms with the morning sunlight streaming in. She heard Stan laugh upstairs and padded quietly up onto the landing. Through the open door of her mum and David's bedroom, she could see Stan and Charlie tucked up in bed with Mary, all three of them staring intently at the tablets clutched in their hands. They were tipping them this way and that in some sort of game until, with a cry of triumph, Charlie said, 'Got you, Granny.'

Mary groaned.

'You boys are too good at this. Go again?'

'Yeah!'

Lorna smiled. She had no idea what they were playing but they were happily engrossed, so she tiptoed back downstairs and went through to the kitchen to find the kettle. David was sitting in an armchair reading the paper by the big French windows that definitely weren't part of the original cottage, and she sidled in a little shyly, aware she must be interrupting a well-established morning routine.

'Morning, David.'

'Lorna! Good morning.' He leaped up. 'Did you sleep well?'

'Surprisingly well, yes, thank you. Please don't get up.'

'It's no bother. Cup of tea?'

'I can get it.'

'OK, great. Tea's in the caddy, mugs up above. Help yourself, please – to anything.'

'Thanks. D'you want one?'

He looked into his mug.

'Yes, please. I seem to have drunk this all up.'

He set the mug down by the kettle and went back to his chair, picking up his paper and sitting quietly as she set about making the tea. She appreciated the lack of fuss and pottered happily around the kitchen until the kettle boiled.

'Here you go.'

'Lovely. Have a seat.' He indicated a second chair on the other side of the window, then hastily added, 'If you want to, that is.'

'I'd love to.'

She sank into the comfy chair and looked out down the pretty garden. It was surprisingly large, with beds bursting with flowers on either side and a vegetable patch at the bottom. It was the sort of garden she'd love to tend, if she ever had the time. Hers back home was a rough patch of lawn, offering nothing more glamorous

than a football net and a few battered shrubs. She suddenly saw
Matt out there, goalkeeping for Charlie as the little boy peppered
him with shots, and grief, robbed of its usual middle-of-the-night
rampage, hit her with a near knock-out punch.

'Lorna? Are you OK?'

She hadn't realised she'd closed her eyes until she had to open
them to see David crouching before her. She grimaced.

'I'm OK. It's just, you know, memories.'

He nodded and sat down again.

'I do know. You think you're doing so well, getting on with
things, and – bang – they hit you out of nowhere.'

Lorna looked at her stepdad curiously.

'You know?'

'I know. My first wife, Sue, died eight years ago. We'd been
married thirty-five years.'

'I'm so sorry.'

'It happens. She was older than me by a couple of years – we
used to joke that I was her toy boy – but it was still unexpected. She
didn't even make it to seventy. Cancer, I'm afraid – murdering git.'
He gave her a lopsided smile. 'So, if it's any help, I do know what
you're going through, and I do know that it gets better – eventually. I also know that right now you're probably thinking that you
don't want it to get better, that you don't want to betray Matt in
that way?' Lorna nodded – he was painfully accurate. 'Can I ask
you something, Lorna?'

'Of course.'

'If it had been you, how would you have wanted Matt to be?'

'What?' She thought hard. 'You mean, if the lorry had taken
me out?'

'It sounds rather stark like that but, yes, I suppose so.'

'I'd have wanted him to be happy. I'd have wanted him to get
on with life and have fun with the boys and, eventually, I suppose,
find someone else.'

David leaned over and patted her knee.

'Let's not worry about that bit right now. The being happy thing is key. And it's OK, you know. Happiness comes from all sorts of sources and just because one of them – albeit a really big, important one – has been taken away from you, doesn't mean you're not allowed the others.'

Lorna smiled at him.

'You're very wise, David.'

'Not wise. Just old. I've been around the block a few times and seen a few things. Not just myself but my patients.'

'You were a GP, right?'

'That's right. I was part of the practice here in Langham for thirty years until your mother persuaded me to retire.'

Lorna looked at him. She knew from long experience how persuasive her mum could be.

'Did you not want to?'

'Oh God, yes. I'd wanted to for a while but until Mary came along, I didn't really have a reason to. Through my grief, work was the one thing that kept me sane. I needed the routine of it, not to mention the focus it gave me on other people's lives rather than my own. Once I fell in love with your mother, however, I could see a thousand things I wanted to do with her and that gave me the impetus to hand in my notice. She's been a great blessing to me, Lorna. I loved Sue with all my heart but the heart, it turns out, is a rather miraculous organ – it always seems to have room for more.'

Lorna smiled at him.

'I'm so glad. Mum's a lucky woman and I'm delighted she's found you too. Bringing me up alone seemed to stop her finding someone for far too long.'

'Well, selfishly, thank the Lord it did! More tea?'

'Please!'

Lorna could hear the noises upstairs growing louder and suspected they were going to be invaded by hungry boys at any moment. Her arms ached to hug her sons good morning, but she could wait. On Sundays, when the boys didn't have school or football, she and Matt had taken it in turns to have a lie-in, and these moments held a tang of the pleasure of lying luxuriously in bed, hearing them play and not having to find the energy to be a part of it. Grief hit at the memory, but not as hard as it had earlier and she absorbed it.

Watching David make tea, humming to himself, she considered this man who was now, it seemed, a part of her family. He had been very frank with her and she appreciated it. Plus, it was good to talk to someone who truly understood. One thing he'd said about needing a focus on other people's lives had particularly chimed with her and she thought it over now, remembering the diary on her bedside table – the diary she was already thinking of as her personal treasure. But of course, she'd found it in David's house so it belonged to him. A little voice came down the stairs, clear as a bell – 'Granny, I'm hungry' – and she knew the boys would be upon them any moment. She cleared her throat.

'David, did you know there was a diary in your annex?'

He turned.

'A diary? No. Where?'

She bit her lip.

'In a secret compartment in one of the dressing table drawers.'

'Really?' His eyes sparkled. 'How exciting. How on earth did you find it?'

'I'm a bit of an expert in old furniture.'

'Of course. You're a history teacher, right?'

'Right.'

'And you've found a little slice of history in my annex?' Put like that, she supposed she had. 'Do you know whose it is?'

'Someone called Nancy?'

At that David visibly jumped.

'Really? Nancy was my mother. I mean, that figures, seeing as she and Dad lived in the annex when they first came to the cottage, but even so… When's it from?'

'1945.'

His jaw dropped.

'The year the war ended? That's pretty cool, right?'

'Right,' Lorna agreed. 'I read some of it last night. It's about her being demobbed and coming to live here with Ted and Betty.'

'My grandparents.'

'I suppose so. Did they talk to you much about that time?' David rubbed at his jaw, clearly trying to remember. 'Or the war? Did your mum talk to you about what she did? It sounds like she manned anti-aircraft guns.'

'She did, yes. She had some lovely friends that she always referred to as her gunner girls. They were posted right here, in the village. Well, at the airfield.'

'It must have been very scary.'

'Must it?' David shook himself. 'I mean, yes, of course it must. Hard too, I suppose.'

Lorna looked at him curiously.

'Did she really not talk to you about it?'

David contemplated this but eventually said, 'She really didn't. How awful is that? Mum was doing this amazing work to help defend our country and I know almost nothing about it. I feel terrible now. I should have asked her, shouldn't I?'

'She could have just told you.'

'I suppose so, but I don't think the people who were actually in the war liked to talk about it much afterwards. They were just glad it was over.'

'Understandable.'

'Maybe, but later, once I was an adult, I should at least have been curious. I'm supposed to be an intelligent man.'

David looked devastated and Lorna smiled at him.

'I'm guessing you were too busy looking after people in the present to worry about the past.'

'Maybe, but still – my own mother! Actually, hang on, I do remember her and her friends saying one thing about the war – they said it taught them to run their worlds, their ways.'

'Really?' Lorna considered this, remembering Nancy's worries about being allowed to work on the estate. 'Well, that's good then. Let's hope the diary can tell us a bit more about how that came to be.'

'Yes! Good point, Lorna. It's as if we can still talk to her, isn't it?'

He looked delighted and she was pleased, really she was. It would be great for him to have this account of his family, but she couldn't help wishing that she'd at least waited until she'd read it before mentioning it.

'I could fetch it for you,' she suggested, trying to keep the reluctance from her voice.

He looked at her, really *at* her. Was that a look he'd perfected with his patients, she wondered, or did it come from being a father to three kids? She'd met them at the wedding – two daughters and a son – and as far as she remembered they'd been lovely, but she and Matt had spent most of the day chasing after their own over-excited boys and she'd not had time to get to know them properly. She imagined, standing here before their clever father, that they hadn't got away with much as teenagers.

'I think you should read it first,' he said, interrupting her thoughts.

'You do?'

'Definitely. You're the historian after all and, besides, who knows what it'll say. I've heard about girls' diaries and I'm not sure I'm strong enough for all those intimate confidences, especially from my own mother.' Lorna laughed at the thought of the confessions she'd already read about Nancy and Joe's love life. The sound of it surprised her – she'd not laughed for far too long. 'Now I *know* I want you to read it first,' David said.

He grinned at her but heavy footsteps were sounding out down the wooden stairs and, glancing down the corridor, he expertly braced himself just before Stan shot into the kitchen at bullet speed and crashed into his legs.

'Thanks, David,' Lorna said to him.

He started to reply, but his words were blocked out by Stan's delighted cry of 'Mummy!' And then her little boy was in her lap, kissing her face all over, and she had to laugh again. Two laughs in one morning – perhaps life was looking up at last. She hugged Stan close and smiled gratefully at David over his soft head.

'Was Mum pleased to come here?' he asked her.

'Seems to have been, mainly. There were some worries over the roof, I think. It was…' She frowned, trying to remember the word Nancy had used. *Ah yes.* 'Squint. She said it was squint.'

'Squint?' David laughed, tickling Stan. 'Doesn't sound good. I think they had the roof mended not long after the war actually, around the same time they took on full ownership of the house.'

'Did they?'

'I had to have it repaired about two years ago and Kyle, the local builder, said it was a miracle it had lasted as long as it did. The 1946 craftsmen did a bang-up job apparently.'

Now it was Lorna who frowned.

'That's odd. Nancy specifically says there wasn't any money to do it.'

'Looks like they found some and thank heavens for that, or we might not be living in here now.'

'Thank heavens for that,' Lorna agreed, because it was certainly a blessing for her this summer. But her dormant curiosity was even more piqued now and she couldn't wait to read more.

Chapter Four

Joe wants a baby. I mean, of course Joe wants a baby, and so do I. One day. I'm just not sure I'm ready for it quite yet. There's no money, for a start, and whatever there is will have to go on stopping the roof sliding off above us, so how will we afford a baby? Plus, mean as it might sound, nothing keeps a woman in the home more than a baby on her hip, does it?

I'm a bit scared, if I'm honest. It's stupid really, as I truly thought I'd never be as scared again as I was the night that plane screamed overhead, flames pouring from its engine, but I was wrong because I'm scared now. Not of death this time but of life – of a dull, empty, domestic life. Is that unnatural? I think it might be, but it's how I feel all the same.

'You ready then, Nance?'

Was she ever! Nancy hastily stowed away her diary and all but skipped to the door of the Gamekeeper's Cottage. Today Joe was going to show her around the estate and she couldn't wait. The sun was shining down on the rolling green fields, the lambs were springing around as if they were on pogo sticks, and flowers were bursting out beneath the hedgerows. It was a perfect English summer's day and she wanted to take in every glorious bit of it.

'Sturdy boots?' he asked her as they headed down the path.

'Of course.'

She lifted a foot and he shook his head.

'Army ones, Nance?'

'They're all I've got. What's wrong with them?'

'Nothing, but you're not in the army now. We'll have to get you some proper walking ones, and some country clothes too, so you fit in on the estate.'

'Yes, please.'

He bent and kissed her, and she pressed herself against him.

'Ooh, love's young dream!' she heard someone coo, and pushed reluctantly away from Joe to see two older ladies tottering past. She'd been introduced to them at church on Sunday, she was sure, but she was damned if she could remember their names. There'd been so many people there keen to meet Joe's 'soldier wife'.

'The army, dear – how brave!' they'd all said, as if she'd been the only woman in the country to join up.

The inhabitants of the village of Langham, it seemed, had been either too old or too married to go to war, despite having an airfield right on their doorstep. It was, perhaps, little wonder. No woman with children had been called to serve and, as far as Nancy had been able to ascertain, every girl here got pregnant straight out of school. She'd found herself wondering if the local boys queued at the school gates to snap them up the moment they were handed their leaver's certificate, and had reprimanded herself for being catty. Most girls were hitched by twenty and even she, who'd waltzed off to fight, had managed to end up a married woman. And very happily married too.

'Morning, Miss Snales, Miss Richardson,' Joe called, and Nancy made a mental note of their names as they paused at the gate.

'Morning, Joe, Nancy. Off somewhere nice?'

'I'm showing my wife around the estate.'

'So she can see where you work?'

'So I can—' Nancy started, but Joe cut her off.

'That's right. Beautiful day, isn't it, ladies?'

'Beautiful,' they both agreed and moved on.

Nancy looked to her husband.

'Why did you cut me off, Joe?'

'Sorry. It was just easier. They'd gabble on all day if you let them and I've got loads to show you.'

'Oh. Right.'

'So, shall we?'

She took his arm and he guided her up the drive at the back of the Gamekeeper's Cottage. It stood on a three-way junction with Langham to the right, the airfield to the left, and the Hall up the slope ahead. The bulk of the estate proper was to the right of the drive, where pastures gave way to arable fields on the lower slopes and woodland on the rise. Thankfully, she thought to herself, it wasn't the same woodland in which the events of that terrible night had taken place. Then she guiltily remembered that she was meant to be pushing all that from her mind and, shaking herself, tucked in close against Joe as he cut right to head for the trees.

'It's so good to be out, Joe.'

'Isn't it?' he agreed. 'When I was huddled on the ship, scanning for the beep-beep of a mine just waiting to blow us all up, I'd close my eyes and picture exactly this walk we're doing now. I'd take myself up the hill and into the woods, and the birds would be singing and the deer grazing and the sun shining, exactly as they are today.'

'That's nice, Joe.'

'Yes.' He looked down and gave her a sudden cheeky grin. 'Course, once I'd met you I had even nicer things to picture in the tough times.'

'Joe!'

He grabbed her hand and pulled her in for a kiss.

'But look, now I've got you *and* my favourite view! I must be the luckiest man in the world.'

'And I the luckiest girl.'

'Creep. Did you picture home when the guns got bad, Nance?'

She considered.

'I'm not sure I had time. We weren't stuck waiting around as much as you. There were quiet nights, for sure, but then I'd just chat to the girls. I learned a lot about *their* homes – Dot living it up in Norwich, Connie in her parents' fancy mansion down south somewhere, and Peggy all over the place with her army husband.'

Joe smiled.

'Maybe girls are better at asking questions of each other.'

'Maybe. Then when the planes did come, we were far too busy to think of anything but aiming and firing. Some nights would pass in a flash.'

He shook his head.

'Did you hit many Boche?'

A shiver went through Nancy at the harsh word. *Scum!* voices screamed in her head suddenly. *Boche scum!*

'We preferred to think of it as hitting planes, not pilots,' she told him, sounding prim even to herself. 'We were stopping the bombs, not killing the men.'

Joe frowned.

'I suppose so, but the pilots died all the same.'

Images crowded in on Nancy and she looked up to the leafy trees above, fighting to see peace in their pretty patterns.

'Not many of them,' she said tightly. 'They could get out.'

'If they had time.'

'Yes.'

'Nance? Are you all right?'

She grabbed his hand.

'I always found it hard, if a plane came down, not to picture a British pilot crashing onto German land. They're not so very different, surely?'

'Save that they were attacking and we were defending. That's a big difference.'

'I suppose. They had conscription too, though, Joe. Somewhere over in Germany there'll be gamekeepers just like you who had to go and fight whether they wanted to or not.'

He sighed.

'Then let's hope that, like me, they've got home again.' He pulled her into his arms. 'I'm sorry this country forced you into the army, Nance. I'm sorry you had to work with the nasty, dirty, dangerous guns. I'm sorry—'

She put up a hand to stop him.

'Please don't be sorry, Joe. I'm certainly not. I loved it.'

'You loved shooting guns?'

'Too right. You know I did. I told you about it. It's the one good thing this bleeding war did. If I hadn't joined up, I'd never have met Peg and Connie and Dot. I'd never have learned how to do all the things we did, and I'd never have found out that I can be brave and strong and, and, resilient. I was a real wet dishcloth before the war.'

Joe laughed.

'That I do not believe.'

'I was! I wanted to be a hairdresser back in Chester. Can you imagine?'

'Your hair always looks very nice.'

He reached out to stroke her dark locks and she squinted up at him.

'Thank you, I think, but so what? It's not important, is it?'

'Well—'

'Not compared to freedom.'

'No! No, not compared to freedom.' He looked momentarily confused then perked up again. 'But hey, Nancy, now we can have both freedom and nice hair. Isn't that wonderful?'

'Wonderful,' she agreed because of course it was, but she knew one thing – if she had to go back to her eighteen-year-old self, sweeping up hair all day and fretting over fripperies like curler designs, she'd go mad with boredom in a week. But she didn't have to go back, she reminded herself; she had a new life as a gamekeeper.

'Come on, Joe,' she said, 'show me these pheasants.'

She let go of his hand and raced up the hill, grateful for the space and the fresh air and the chance to properly move. Joe had wanted to take her out yesterday, but Betty had sucked in her breath and protested that it was Monday.

'So?' Joe had said.

His mother had rolled her eyes.

'Monday is laundry day, Joseph.'

'Oh! Of course. That's fine then, I'll take Nancy out on Tuesday.'

There'd been nothing she could say, so Joe had headed out with his father straight after breakfast and she'd been left to put Ted's not-so-smalls through the mangle. It hadn't been hard and Betty had been sweetly grateful, but she'd had little to contribute to the conversation over supper as the men had jabbered away about hedgerow repairs and game feeders, so she couldn't wait to see it all in action.

'Oh!' She stopped dead as they headed into the woods and came to a clearing. The open area was fenced off with fine mesh barriers, and within them maybe a hundred little brown chicks were pecking corn from metal feeders and cheeping merrily at each other. 'Are they pheasants?'

'Certainly are.'

'Can I hold them?'

Joe frowned.

'Best not. We try to keep them as wild as possible so they can have a natural life.'

'Before we shoot them?'

'Well, yes. All the more reason to keep them happy, don't you think?'

'I suppose so.' She peered at them through the fencing which she couldn't help noticing, now she got up close, was patched with twine and tape. 'Is that safe?'

Joe made a face.

'It's the best it can be. No money for the pheasants' home either, I'm afraid.'

Nancy bit her lip. The Wilsons really needed money to get this place going, and Ted had explained to them last night that Lord Langham's funds were all used up on running the Hall as a hospital, both during the war and, even now, for those still gaining enough strength to travel home. He'd very generously offered to gift them the cottage if they took on the repairs themselves but lord knows how they were meant to do that. She wished she could do something, but her family hadn't two pennies to rub together so she was helpless – save that she could graft. She *would* graft.

'Do people really pay to shoot these, Joe? They're uglier than I'd expected. Sorry, birds!'

The birds looked supremely unconcerned and Joe laughed.

'They'll grow into beauties, you'll see, especially the males.'

'Lucky them.'

'Not so lucky. They get shot first. We only need one cock for every hundred hens to breed next year's lot.'

'Wow! Good job humans don't operate like that.'

'Very good job,' he agreed, catching her around the waist and kissing her deeply. 'Though some girls might need to share after this war.'

'Joe!'

'What? You're lucky you bagged me, wife. We're a rarity these days, us fit young men.'

She laughed and hit out at him but he was right. Too many women had lost husbands and fiancés and would struggle to replace them, though none of her gunner girls, thank the Lord.

Young Connie had received plenty of letters from soldiers with double-barrelled surnames so would surely have someone to go back to. Peggy's husband was an officer and had survived, albeit with a limp in his left leg, and Dot… Well, Dot hadn't exactly pinned her affections, or her favours, on one man, but Nancy didn't think she'd struggle to find a husband. She wasn't conventionally pretty, but she laughed a lot and men flocked to her wherever she went. Nancy, though, had definitely got lucky.

'I won't argue with you there,' she told Joe and kissed him back. His hand sneaked up her top and he pushed her against a tree. 'Joe!'

'What? They're my woods, sort of, and you're my wife.'

Her body tingled. She looked around but only the chicks looked back.

'Where's your pa?'

'Up behind the Hall, mending the tractor. There's no one about, Nance. No one but you and me…'

His hands found her bra strap and unhooked it, caressing her gently. She ran her hands up round his neck, teasing at the brown hair that was finally growing out of its army crop, making him look more handsome than ever. Hot for him now, she grabbed at his belt and he hitched up her skirt.

'Oh God, Nancy, I want you so badly.'

He lifted her up in his arms and she wrapped her legs around him, inviting him in. Then she thought of something.

'Joe! Protection.'

'What?'

He was nuzzling at her neck and it felt so good, but this was important.

'Have you got any protection?'

He pulled back a little.

'Why?'

'You know why! So we don't have a baby.'

He frowned.

'Surely that doesn't matter now? We're together, Nance, for always. We're free of worrying about all that.'

'But...'

Then his mouth was on hers, silencing any protest, and he was driving inside her and it felt so good. Something about the position was doing amazing things to her. Sensations shot through her body and she gasped and clutched him tighter as they took over all her senses, even drowning out the little voice saying, *I don't want a baby yet*, because what she did want was Joe, now, here.

'Oh God, yes!'

Her own arousal ignited his and, as the last waves of indescribable pleasure ebbed from her, he cried out in joy.

'Oh, Nancy, Nancy darling, that was so good.'

'It was,' she agreed breathlessly. She'd always enjoyed making love to Joe, but that had been something else. It was hard, though, not to worry about the results. 'Do you have a handkerchief?'

'What? Oh, of course. Sorry. Shall I...?'

'No. Thank you.'

She turned away to clean herself, trying not to obviously scrub as much away as she could. She'd been standing upright, so surely that meant she was unlikely to get pregnant? That's what a girl in the barracks had said. Mind you, all sorts of such stories used to circulate regularly and none of them had been guaranteed, save that, as far as Nancy had been able to tell, those who were the most desperate not to get pregnant were the most likely to do so. Maybe it was similar to the way cats always made a beeline for those who disliked them? And if so, did that mean that she should hope for a baby to put the sperm off? It didn't seem sensible.

'Nancy? Are you all right?'

'Yes! Sorry, Joe, yes, of course. Just a bit... dazed.' She swung back round and kissed him, stuffing his hanky into her skirt pocket. 'I'll wash this.'

'Not with Ma.'

'No!'

He grinned at her.

'Come on then, and I'll show you how we plash a hedge.'

'How you *what*?!'

But he was off and she had no choice but to run after him. They spent a fascinating time weaving across the estate towards Langham Hall, looking at plashing and coppicing and pollarding, and by the time they found Ted – or at least the bottom half of Ted poking out from under a big tractor – Nancy's head was spinning with the new information.

'Hey there, Pa, how's it going?'

Ted's feet scrabbled at the ground and he emerged, dirty and smeared with engine oil.

'Joe! Just who I need. We've got a leak in the radiator, son, and my fingers are too darned thick to reach it. Can you help?'

'Course I can, in a minute. I've been showing Nancy round the estate.'

Ted looked to Nancy for the first time.

'Do you like it, lass?'

'Oh, yes! It's very interesting. I especially liked—'

'Good. That's good. Has she seen it all, Joe?'

Nancy stopped, mouth still half open, as Ted addressed himself once more to Joe.

'Well—'

'Only we could really do with getting on with this.'

Nancy crouched down and peered under the big vehicle.

'I have slim fingers, Ted.'

'Sorry?'

'If you need someone to reach the radiator.'

'You?!'

'If you'd like. I learned a bit about fixing machines on the gun. Ours was always breaking down and—'

'I couldn't possibly let you under a tractor, Nancy.'

'Oh, I don't mind. I quite like—'

'It wouldn't be right. It wouldn't be proper.' He'd gone very red in the face and fought to stand up. 'You're a lady.'

'A woman maybe, but I know a bit—'

'No.'

'Ted—'

'I said no, Nancy. No daughter-in-law of mine is dirtying herself beneath an engine. Besides, wasn't that midday just struck? It'll be dinnertime soon.' Nancy gaped at him. 'Betty's on her own in the kitchen,' he said, nodding furiously at her like some sort of kid's toy. But this was no game. Nancy looked to Joe.

'I do know what I'm doing, Joe.'

'I'm sure you do, but…'

But what? she wanted to scream. *But just because I'm a woman, I have to make pies and wash pants instead of mending pipes?* She'd shocked Ted enough for one day though, so she bit it back.

'Right. Well, I'll leave you two men to it then, shall I?'

'Nancy—' Joe started, but Ted cut him off.

'I think that'd be best, lass. Thank you.'

Then he pulled Joe down with him and, before Nancy had taken even ten heavy steps across the yard, all she could see of her husband were his two feet alongside those of his father.

I hope you fail, she thought bitterly, as she headed down the long drive to the Gamekeeper's Cottage. *I hope you fail to mend your stupid tractor, and I hope you fail to mend your stupid squinty roof.* It was mean, she knew, but not half as mean as they'd been to her.

Turning slowly, she looked over the estate to the airfield beyond. It was almost a mile away, but the land around here was very flat and she could just make out the tops of several planes standing on the long runways waiting to fly. It felt almost as if they were taunting her – *Look at us, free to zoom off and go* – but that was surely madness? She'd only just got here; she didn't want to go. She'd been praying to be with Joe ever since their snatched wedding a year ago, and it was wonderful having him at her side every day; it was just going to take a little time to adjust to civilian life, that was all.

She dropped her eyes away from the temptation of the airfield and noticed a herd of deer grazing gently at the long grass down the slope. There was something so calm, so unhurried about them, that she felt her restless soul settle. Standing very still, she watched as they worked their way quietly across the meadow, the hinds in a little clutch and the stags, antlers only half grown, moving around them.

Then suddenly one of the planes beyond hit the runway with a roar of its engines and the nearest stag, spooked, broke into a run. Instantly the whole herd was up and off, moving with quiet, bouncing grace until they had headed over the rise and were lost from her view. Nancy sighed. How could she possibly wish herself back in the noise and chaos of RAF Langham when she could have the peace of her new home? Resolutely, she turned her back on what was left of the airfield, and headed for the Gamekeeper's Cottage and Betty's warm, cosy, mildly restrictive kitchen.

Chapter Five

'Dinner's nearly ready.'

Lorna looked up guiltily from the little leather book in her hands to see David standing before her, a flowery pinny wrapped unselfconsciously around his slim waist.

'I'm so sorry, David,' she gasped. 'I should have been helping, I just got so engrossed in your mum's diary.'

David smiled and placed a gentle hand on her shoulder.

'And it's wonderful to see. Please don't worry, Lorna, we like taking care of you and it's great to see you enjoying it. Is it very salacious?'

Now it was Lorna who smiled. She stroked the soft cover of the red volume fondly.

'Not really. It does seem that your parents were, shall we say, making the most of being together, but mainly so far it's about Nancy trying to fit into civilian life after being on the air base. Is there still an RAF Langham now?'

'Not any more,' he said, as Charlie and Stan shot past the door on their way to the table. 'Shall we?' He ushered Lorna through to where Mary was settling the boys into their seats and waved her to her own, before going on. 'I remember planes flying out of it when I was a kid, but it was closed down in the sixties and sold to Bernard Matthews as a turkey farm.'

'Seriously?'

''Fraid so.'

'How funny. Land round here is obviously good for birds. I've just been reading about Nancy being introduced to the pheasant hatcheries. She seems to have been quite keen on them, though she says they were rather run-down.'

'That's odd.' David looked curiously at her. 'Mum used to tell me that before Langham Hall was sold to a hotel chain, their hatcheries were the best around.'

'Well, in 1945 they were just about held together with twine.'

She and David looked at each other as Mary dished up a delicious-smelling casserole.

'So, Mum found the money for a new roof and new hatcheries?' David said.

'It seems so.'

'In the years just after the war? When the economy was up the spout and everyone was scrabbling to make ends meet?'

He frowned and Lorna bit her lip. Put like that, it did sound a bit odd.

'I'm sure there's a perfectly reasonable explanation.'

'Did they have the lottery then?'

She shook her head but now Stan was tugging on David's arm.

'Turkeys like at Christmas?' he asked.

David turned to him.

'That's right,' he agreed, switching topics with practised skill. 'Surprisingly fun birds, apparently. People used to throw balls into the field for them to play with.'

'Balls for turkeys?!'

'They loved them! Or so my kids said.'

'Your kids?' Charlie demanded, looking around suspiciously. 'Where are they now?'

'They're all grown up and living their own lives, Charlie. Helena is a doctor in a hospital in London, Rob works in a bank in Singapore, and Tilly… Tilly just does her own thing.'

Lorna instantly liked the sound of Tilly.

'What sort of thing?' she asked.

'Travelling mainly. She works wherever she can and then travels around. She was out in Singapore with Rob for a bit, but she soon moved on into Thailand and Vietnam. Now she's in South America. She's a wonderful girl but… restless. Perhaps it was being the littlest and following the other two who were, frankly, every bit as swotty as their father before them.'

'Charlie is swotty,' Stan said solemnly.

'Am not!'

'Are too. He does reading till really late.'

He screwed up his little face in disapproval and Lorna leaped hastily in. 'That's a very good thing to do, Stan. There's nothing swotty about reading.'

'And there's nothing wrong with being swotty,' Mary added. 'Not if it gets you a good job.'

Stan pouted.

'I'd rather go twavelling.'

Lorna ruffled his blond curls.

'You can do both, Stan. If we're being honest, I was a bit swotty too, but I had a year travelling after university.'

'With Daddy?'

'No, with Aki.'

'Miss Sato?' Charlie asked, looking at her askance as if he couldn't believe his headteacher capable of anything quite so fun.

'The very same. We stuck rucksacks on our backs, got on a boat across the Channel, and worked our way right around the world.'

'Cool!'

Charlie regarded her with new awe and she had to admit she liked it. She remembered David saying that he'd not spoken to Nancy about her earlier life, and vowed to make sure she told the kids a bit about her pre-mum self. For now, though, it was Nancy on her mind.

'You said your mum worked at RAF Langham in the war?' she asked David.

'That's right. She met my dad in the Blue Bell pub here in the village when he was on leave at the start of 1943. It was love at first sight by all accounts, but I never asked more. She was shooting planes down less than a mile from where I've always lived, and I never talked to her about it. Isn't that awful?'

He looked to Mary who grabbed his hand.

'I never talked to my mum either, love. Turns out, she worked in a munitions factory in Sheffield and was on shift when a bomb took out half the place – luckily not her half.'

'A bomb?' Charlie exclaimed. 'Cool!'

'Not cool,' Lorna said sternly. 'Lethal and painful and devastating. How did you find out, Mum?'

'There was an article on it in a local paper and one of her old mates sent it to me. My mother was listed as one of the survivors with a bit about how she rescued two other girls. God, I wished I could talk to her about it all, but she was gone by then.'

'Gone where?' Stan asked.

'She was dead, Stan,' Mary said gently.

'Like my daddy?'

Pain shot through Lorna and she gripped at the table, but her mum stayed calm.

'That's right. It happens to us all some day.'

'But not Mummy?' The little boy shoved back his chair and ran to her, panic all over his face. 'You're not going to die, are you, Mummy?'

'Of course not,' Lorna promised, gathering him onto her lap.

'You could though,' Charlie said, his lip wobbling dangerously.

She pulled him towards her too and for once, with no friends to impress, he flung his arms around her neck to hold her close.

'I will do my very, very, very best not to, Charlie, OK?'

He nodded against her hair and she realised anew how fragile her quiet older child was, and cursed all the fates for doing this to him. To them all. She swallowed back the hard lump of grief that had lodged in her throat and tried to focus on the here and now.

'So, you can't see anything of the airfield now?' she asked David.

'Oh, I didn't say that. The runways are still visible, and of course Langham Dome is open.'

'Langham Dome?'

'It was where they trained the anti-aircraft fighters. They used pioneering camera technology to project images of the planes onto the underside of the dome, to simulate real flight and practise shooting them down.'

'Like Nancy did?'

'Who's Nancy?' Charlie demanded, pulling back from Lorna.

'My mum,' David told him.

'Your mum shot pretend planes? Like an old video game?'

'Like the first video game ever,' David told him, and Charlie's eyes widened. 'And that was training to shoot real ones.'

'Real planes? Out of the sky? Mega-cool!'

Lorna sighed. Her anti-violence campaign wasn't going well, but then, the boys had so much of it on their gaming stations that it was a hard battle anyway. And at least if they saw real-life situations, it might bring some of the cost of fighting home to them.

'Can we visit the dome?' she asked David.

'You can. It was renovated a few years ago. One of my mates from the village was involved in the project. He did ask me to join the team, but I was still working then and didn't have the time. I'll text him now.'

He tapped away, as Lorna focused on getting the boys back in their places and eating their dinner. Before they were halfway through their helpings, he looked up again.

'Richard says they're having an open day this weekend. There's going to be a band and food and a fly-past of old fighter planes.'

'What d'you think, Charlie?' Mary asked. 'Sounds fun, right?'

Charlie considered.

'What sort of band?'

'A girl group, I imagine,' Mary said, winking at Lorna. Lorna rolled her eyes – the 'girl group' would most likely be in uniform and singing about bluebirds over white cliffs – about as far from the likes of Little Mix as it was possible to get.

Charlie wrinkled his nose.

'Will it be good food?' he queried.

'Burgers,' David said promptly. 'And hot dogs.'

Charlie nodded approvingly.

'OK. I'll go. So will Stan, won't you, Stan?'

'I like bands,' Stan said obligingly. Lorna kissed him.

'It sounds great, David,' she said. 'I'll look forward to it.'

And for the first time in ages that was actually true.

'There it is!' Stanley squealed. 'Over there. It looks like aliens have landed in the field.'

'It really does, Stan,' Lorna agreed, taking his hand to stop him running off to the big white dome.

It was a sunny morning, so plenty of people had turned out for the Langham Dome open day and she didn't want to lose him. Ever since the terrible phone call, she'd been paranoid about harm coming to either of the boys, and she had no idea how she was going to cope once they were teenagers and wanting to head out on their own. Instantly, she felt panic rise within her and could almost smell chlorine on the wind, as if she were back in that awful swimming pool listening to a PC crack her world apart.

'Not now,' she muttered furiously.

She was nowhere near a pool; she was in a bright field in North Norfolk with music and barbecue smoke wafting tantalisingly into the soft air. Straight ahead of her was the curious dome where Nancy had apparently trained to shoot German planes out of the skies and, if she paid attention, she might find out more about her to complement her late-night diary reading. There was no need to panic at all.

Normally Lorna would absolutely love this sort of thing, and she dug deep to try and find the geeky history teacher inside, but she was proving remarkably elusive. The other night she had played with Nancy's wireless for ages, as if the past might speak to her out of the little grille, yet she'd got nothing but the same sort of static that seemed to fill her own mind these days. She hated the fact that the wretched lorry had robbed her of even the simple pleasure of studying history, as if it had ploughed not just into her husband but deep into her very being. The only bright spot was Nancy's diary, which felt less like history than the life of a friend, and she was holding on to that with all she had.

'The dome looks fascinating,' she said, though clearly not very convincingly as her mum took her arm and gave it a gentle squeeze.

'I'm sure it will be. Now, how about some sweeties first, boys? Look – there's an old-fashioned sweet shop over here and they're selling fruit wines on the side. Just what we need, hey, Lorna love?'

Lorna squeezed her mum back. She'd largely avoided alcohol recently, scared of the doors it might open up in her torn mind, but she had to admit that a little something might help quell the strange nerves that this large – if very happy – gathering of people seemed to be setting loose inside her.

'Lovely. Blackberry for me, please.'

The wine was rich and sweet and rather strong. She sipped at it gratefully as the boys agonised over the choice of pear drops, barley twists and cola cubes. To one side the 'girl group' – four women smartly dressed as WAAFs – were singing 'Pack Up Your Troubles in Your Old Kit Bag' and Lorna watched them, wishing she could do just that, though she feared it would take more than one bag.

'David!'

A smart older man in the uniform of a World War II officer came striding towards them, holding out his hand to David who shook it eagerly.

'Richard. Great to see you.'

'And your lovely wife! Mary, looking radiant as always.'

'Richard, you flirt!'

Mary's blushes, at least, made Lorna smile. To be fair to the new arrival, her mum did look radiant. Marriage clearly suited her, which made Lorna a little sad that she'd never known its joys when she was younger. She remembered Mary dating occasionally, especially once she was a teen, but she'd always come home early, saying simply, 'Lovely man, but not for me.' Lorna had suggested once that she should perhaps try a woman instead, and Mary had thrown back her head and roared with laughter.

'Never say never, darling, but it's not the equipment that worries me.'

Lorna's teen self had been mortified at the time, but the memory made her smile now.

'Richard,' Mary said, 'meet Lorna, my daughter.'

She stepped forward and shook his hand.

'She's every bit as beautiful as you, Mary – and that's saying something.'

Richard, clearly loving the old-fashioned persona that matched his World War II uniform, took her hand and kissed it extravagantly. David stepped in hastily.

'Lorna's very clever too. She's a history teacher, Richard, and has made a brilliant discovery in our very own annex – my mother's diary from 1945. Mum worked up here at RAF Langham as a gunner girl, you know. Most likely trained in the dome itself.'

'Really? That's fascinating.' Richard finally looked at Lorna with genuine interest. 'As part of the ATS?'

'That's right,' Lorna confirmed. 'She and three other women were on a gun crew here towards the back end of the war.'

'How marvellous! The Ack-Ack girls did wonderful work. I've been reading up on them recently, thinking we might do an exhibition on them at the dome – something to grab the attention of the ladies, you know. Maybe we could feature your mum and her chums, David?'

Lorna looked sideways at this larger-than-life man. Had he really just said 'chums'? On the other hand, an exhibition featuring Nancy, Peggy, Connie and Dot would be amazing, so he was probably worth putting up with.

'I'd be happy to share anything I find out,' she said. 'If that's OK with you, David?'

David nodded easy assent and Richard beamed.

'Marvellous, marvellous. Come and look around the dome.'

He strode towards the almost space-age white sphere just across the stall-strewn lawn, beckoning them imperiously to follow.

'There's a bit of a queue,' Lorna said, pointing to the line stretching out from the entrance.

'Oh, never mind that. You're my VIP guests. Step this way.'

He offered Lorna his arm, as if she were some Jane Austen heroine entering a dance. She took it with a look back at her mum, who laughed.

'He's harmless,' she mouthed. Lorna nodded and, checking Mary had the boys by the hand, gave herself in to her old-school escort.

She had to admit she felt pretty lucky to be led past all the other visitors to the very door of the dome, and ushered inside like a princess. Richard, it turned out, was one of the founding members of the Friends of Langham Dome, so pivotal to the renovation project, and as he dropped his flirtation and showed them around proudly, she was drawn deep into the history of this fascinating structure. Richard talked them through all the displays before rounding them up at the gun in the centre.

'And this,' he said, 'was the sort of mock-gun they would have used to practise shooting the planes.' He stepped past the *please don't touch* sign and took a firm hold of it. 'The trick,' he told them, plus the rest of the crowd who were gathering eagerly, 'was to calculate the speed and trajectory of the plane so that you could aim the gun just the right amount ahead of it for the shell and the plane to meet, and then – boom!'

'Boom!' Charlie echoed keenly, and Richard waved him forward.

'Want to try, young man?'

'Yes, please!'

Richard pressed a button on a machine to one side and the dome over their heads lit up. A cartoon plane flew across the top and Richard helped Charlie to line up the gun and 'shoot' it. It blasted into dramatic pieces as the picture shattered over their heads, making everyone gasp. Richard beamed.

'Of course, this is just a simulation. The actual machine was far more complicated to work, which is probably why it was usually manned by women!' There was a female whoop from the crowd and he gave a smart bow to it. 'We hope to get a replica at some point in the future, but for now...'

He trailed off and Lorna leaped forward.

'For now it's excellent, Richard. It's easy for us, safe in the twenty-first century, to think it looks simple, isn't it? The people training on this in the forties were going into real situations against real planes.'

'Quite right, Laura.'

'Lorna.'

Richard didn't seem to hear her, but questions were being flung at him from the crowd and he turned to them, clearly in his element. Lorna was happy to step back and look around, trying to picture Nancy and her friends in this curious dome, preparing to man the anti-aircraft guns that would keep their country safe from invasion. She'd felt the thrill of Charlie's simulated attempt run through her right here, on this cheerful open day, and it must have been fifty times as intense during the actual war. No wonder

Nancy had found it so hard to give up that sort of adrenalin and sense of purpose to become a housewife. It just wasn't the sort of thing you could go back from.

'Lorna, can I introduce you to someone?' David interrupted her musings and she looked round to see a small, neat woman at his side. 'This is Lilian, secretary of the Friends of Langham Dome. She's just persuaded me to join and I wondered if maybe you'd like to as well.'

'Me?'

'David tells me you've found a diary,' Lilian said. She was wearing a pretty forties dress and an eager smile, far more unassuming than Richard – not that that would be hard.

'I have, yes. It's David's mother's.'

'And it details her time here?'

'Not as such, I'm afraid, no. More her time afterwards – her struggles to fit back into civilian life.'

Lilian nodded.

'I imagine that was almost impossible. Just think – one minute you're shooting guns and the next you're expected to be satisfied with standing at the kitchen sink. Nonsense!'

Lorna smiled, liking Lilian.

'Richard said he was keen to do some sort of exhibition on the ATS girls.'

'Did he? He was probably just trying to impress you, but let's hold him to it, shall we?' Lilian gave Lorna a surprisingly mischievous smile, then added, 'Do join us, please. I'm desperate for more women to get involved.'

'I'm only here for the summer, I'm afraid.'

'That doesn't matter. Really.' Lilian gave a sideways nod to Richard, who was still holding forth to the crowd. 'Richard knows his stuff, bless him, and he's very enthusiastic but he's not much of a doer.'

Lorna laughed.

'OK, I'll join. It sounds interesting.'

'Wonderful! This way to sign the form, dear.'

'Now?' Lorna asked, but Lilian was already tugging her towards a table at one side of the dome and producing a pen, and it seemed there was little choice but to sign on the dotted line. Maybe that blackberry wine had been stronger than she thought?

'Look at you,' Matt's voice said suddenly in her head. Closing her eyes, she saw him laughing at her a year ago, when she'd come back from her first ever PTA meeting to rather bemusedly announce that she'd somehow been elected as secretary. 'You always get dragged into this sort of thing. You're just too nice to say no.'

'I've done it again, Matt,' she whispered, when Lilian finally released her and she was able to head back out into the welcome sunshine. The Spitfire fly-past was being announced, giving her an excuse to turn her eyes up to the blue skies, but she wasn't really looking for a war plane. 'Am I mad?'

'Not mad, no,' Matt seemed to say. 'Just you. Just my lovely, enthusiastic you.'

The plane appeared, low on the horizon, and everyone pointed. Lorna bent to share the moment with Charlie and Stan but, in her head, she was still with Matt and for the first time since she'd lost him, that felt like a good place to be.

'Isn't it brilliant?' Charlie said, pointing to the plane as it executed an impressive spiral.

'Brilliant,' she agreed softly. 'Hard, but brilliant.'

Chapter Six

Oh my goodness me, I'm so excited. I couldn't sleep a wink last night, not even after Joe 'settled' me, as he calls it. He says he sleeps much better after lovemaking but I have to say, I find the reverse. Last night, though, it was more the thought of today that was keeping me awake staring at those damned pink roses, and I've rarely been more pleased to see the dawn. I love sleeping at Joe's side, but it does stop you putting on the light and reading. Mind you, I got used to that in the dorms. Dot needed her sleep, Lord love her, and was so grumpy if you shifted around too much. I pity any man who gets her in his bed – if she ever actually falls for one, that is!

Oh, but today I'll get to find out who she's dallying with at the moment because I'm going to meet them, my gunner girls – all three of them. We're going to be together again! It's been over a month since the demob and I know it's a terrible thing to say, with me having a lovely home and a handsome husband and all that, but I've missed the girls so much. I can't wait to hear what they're getting up to, how they're taking on the world.

I really hope they don't think I'm letting them down.

Nancy climbed onto the first bus to Norwich, watching the village children running down the street to school. Would that be her and Joe's little one in a few years' time? They all looked very happy in their pinafores and shorts, calling out to friends and chasing around. It would be a good childhood, she was sure, with all this space to run wild. Even so, as the bus pulled out of Langham, her eyes went to the mothers walking along behind, most of them neatly dressed in pretty frocks and pushing prams, or hitching babies on their womanly hips. They, too, looked happy, chatting away to each other, but something about the relentless domesticity of the scene nagged at Nancy. Had working on the guns taken away some of her core femininity, like so many people had feared?

'Women shouldn't go to war.'

'Women shouldn't fight.'

She'd heard that so many times back at the start of the war. Everyone had been desperate to 'protect' them and, to be fair, they'd been desperate to be protected. Nancy could still remember sweeping up hair in the salon, looking out of the window at the men parading past in their new uniforms and thinking, *Thank God that's not me.* She'd felt safe surrounded by other women with nothing more to worry about than how pretty their hair looked. But then…

Then the war had gone on and on, and they'd quite simply run out of men. When, in 1942, it had looked as if Hitler was going to invade, there had been no choice. They'd had to either shut themselves in their salons and wait for the Luftwaffe to come calling, or go out and shoot them from the sky themselves. Women had had to do their own protecting and it turned out they'd been rather good at it. More to the point, they'd enjoyed it. Was that what everyone had been trying to protect them from all along – finding out how exhilarating it was to be out in the world having an adventure?

Nancy shook herself. She mustn't get bitter. Ted and Betty were lovely, and it wasn't their fault if they were stuck in an era before the war. That's what they'd all been fighting for and, if the battle wasn't quite over yet, she would just have to be patient. For today, at least, she could relax. She looked over her shoulder as Langham disappeared from view. It was good to be getting away and she'd picked the day well. A thatcher was coming to quote for a new roof and Ted, Betty and Joe were fretting about it. Despite Joe's best efforts, the repairs hadn't gone well and it was clear the cottage needed more wholesale restoration. The chance to own the cottage outright was a wonderful one but everyone was worried that the cost was going to be too high and it was making them decidedly grumpy. Yes, it was very good to be getting away today.

'Nancy!'

Dot was there when she pulled into the bus station in Norwich, jumping up and down and waving like a girl possessed. Nancy scrambled down and they threw themselves on each other.

'Nancy! Oh lordie, Nancy, it's so good to see you. I've missed you so much.'

'I've missed you too,' Nancy said, hugging her tight.

Aside from her family, Peggy, Connie and Dot were the people she knew best in the whole world. Joe was getting close, but she still hadn't spent as much time with him as she had with her gun crew.

'And I tell you something else, Nance,' Dot said, clutching her tight. 'I miss the guns. Is that weird? Everyone around here thinks it's weird and I'm sure they're right. It was tough, wasn't it? And scary and all that, but God, it was exciting. Do you miss it, Nancy?'

Nancy felt a rich warmth spread through her. She pulled back and looked Dot full in the face.

'Oh, Dot, I miss it so much.'

Dot let out a joyous laugh.

'Thank God! I thought maybe I was going mad. I've told my new fella all about it. He loves hearing my stories but he gets a bit funny if I say I miss it, and I can see why. It sounds wrong, doesn't it? Obviously I want peace, and obviously I love being with him, but it was a big part of me – of who I am now – and I can't just let that go.'

Nancy took her arm.

'I couldn't agree more, Dot. Honestly, domestic life is driving me mad. But come on, let's go and find the others and you can tell us all about this fella. Where are they?'

'Peggy's coming in on the London train. If we're quick, we can make it to the station to meet her. Connie doesn't finish her lectures for another half an hour, so she's going to join us at the restaurant.'

'She's studying here? In Norwich?'

Connie had written to tell Nancy that she'd decided to take a teaching course, but she hadn't realised she'd actually started it, or that she was doing it right here.

'Yep. Started last week. This way.'

Dot tugged Nancy sideways. Having grown up in the city, she knew it like the back of her hand and wove down side streets like a pro.

'So I guess you can see Connie often then?' Nancy asked, panting after her.

'Not often, Nance. She's got a busy timetable and I'm working a lot of hours too.'

'You are? Where?'

Dot turned her left onto the main street and Nancy saw the station up ahead, scarred by bombs but still with trains puffing happily in and out.

'In the best factory in Norwich,' Dot said happily, coming to a halt at the roadside. 'It's new. Well, not new but converted from an old shoe factory. I was one of the first girls they took on.'

'Converted to making what, Dot?'

Dot beamed at her.

'Handbags! Amazing or what? We get to buy any wonky ones for almost nothing. I've got three new ones already and they're all beautiful. MacLaren's it's called, and I love it. Oh, Nance, you should smell the place! It's so sexy with all that fresh leather. I swear I'd have had it away with anyone after just a few days working there and then…'

'And then?' Nancy urged.

'And then I met Tony,' Dot said. 'But come on, that's the London train – we'll have to run to meet Peggy.'

And she was off, ducking across the road and in through the station entrance. There wasn't time to get platform tickets, but they stood at the barrier, scanning the new arrivals until there was Peggy, tall and elegant in a brand-new uniform. Nancy stared as the oldest of their gang of four walked towards them. Gone was the rough-fitting four-pocket tunic and trousers of the everyday ATS girl, and in its place was a tailored officer's uniform in fine serge with a sharp, A-line skirt. The bronze shoulder title was also gone, replaced by a cap and collar badges to denote her higher rank.

'You've been promoted?' Nancy asked, as she and Dot rushed to hug their friend.

Peggy smiled shyly.

'I have. My Harry's been made a major, so they thought they'd bump me up the ladder too. Only to second lieutenant, but I've been asked to head up a committee to form a permanent Women's Royal Army Corps.'

'That's brilliant!' Nancy said.

'I hope so. There's a long way to go. We've got loads of women keen to join, but the blinking men at the top are kicking their heels. Lots of noise about how marvellous us girls were in the war, but a distinct desire to put that behind them and get back to the good old days when it was just men.'

Nancy laughed bitterly.

'It's not only the army where that's going on,' she said. 'I miss my uniform.'

Dot nudged her.

'No, you don't, you idiot! It was stiff and scratchy and such an ugly dark green.'

'But I felt important in it.'

Dot looked sideways at her.

'And you don't now?'

Nancy swallowed.

'Not so much. Maybe I'm just missing you lot, hey?'

'I get that,' Peggy said heartily, linking arms with them both. 'I seem to spend most of my life surrounded by men. They're great and all, but they're not as much fun as you! I'm so ready for some gunner-girl chat.'

Nancy's heart swelled. That was exactly it. It was wonderful being with Joe, and Betty was really sweet to talk to, but there was nothing like the easy banter of her crew. She happily followed Dot to the restaurant she'd chosen for them, though she stopped nervously in front of the smart exterior.

'Is it expensive, Dot?'

She'd had to ask Joe for money to come out and she'd hated it. He'd been very nice about it, saying they'd have to set her up with an allowance, but she didn't really want an 'allowance'; she wanted a wage.

'Not at lunchtime,' Dot assured her. 'They have special deals on and the food's fabulous. Tony brings me here all the time.'

Peggy swung round.

'Who's Tony?'

'That's what I'm waiting to find out,' Nancy agreed, but now Connie was leaping up from a table in the corner and they all rushed past the maître d' to greet her.

'Ladies,' he protested faintly, but they were too busy squealing out their greetings to notice.

'Sorry,' Peggy said, waving easily around the other diners. 'We've not seen each other since we were in the army together.'

Her smooth words and smart uniform soothed the room and, with indulgent smiles, everyone turned back to their food as the girls hugged each other. Nancy couldn't believe she was here with her crew again, and like an idiot she burst into tears.

'They're happy tears,' she assured the others, flapping at the air to waft them away. 'It's so good to see you all. You look exactly the same.'

That wasn't strictly true. Peggy wore make-up with her uniform now, and had her dark hair in an elegant chignon instead of the hasty buns they had favoured in barracks. Blonde Dot was even more exuberant than before in a polka-dot dress, and Connie, the baby of their crew, looked older somehow, in a smart tweed skirt and russet jumper that set off her hazel colouring to perfection. Their eyes though – their eyes were the same and their voices, as they shared their new lives with each other, rose and fell with familiar cadences and warmed her heart.

They settled into their seats and Dot called for cocktails.

'Cocktails?' Nancy asked nervously, fearing that Dot's take on expensive was a bit different to hers these days.

'On me,' Dot said easily. 'I'm earning loads and Tony pays for everything when we go out, so I have no other way of getting rid of it!'

Nancy looked at her enviously but the others were pouncing.

'Who the hell is Tony?'

Dot giggled.

'He's the manager at my factory. The actual factory manager. He's not old though. Well, not very. Only thirty and that's not so old, right? Any which way, he doesn't act old. He's got the good bits of it – like money and his own house and that – but he's not crusty or anything. Lord no! He loves to dance. Isn't that great, girls? You know how I love to dance.'

'Oh, we know, Dot!' Nancy agreed.

Dot had always been looking for a night out on the tiles, but with nothing more exciting than the Blue Bell on offer in Langham, she'd usually had to kick up her heels in the barracks. Not that she was frivolous, not really. She'd knuckled down like the rest of them; she'd just been able to find fun at the drop of a hat.

'He's a lucky man, this Tony,' Nancy said, squeezing Dot's hand over the table.

'And I'm a lucky girl. I really think he might be the one.'

The other three gawped at her. Dot had had a different man every week all the time they'd known her.

'That's amazing, Dot!' Peggy gasped.

Connie just stared.

'You're so lucky,' she said. Something caught in her voice and Nancy turned to look curiously at the youngest of their group.

'Don't worry, Connie, you'll soon find someone.'

Connie flushed.

'Oh, it's not that.'

Now the other two were looking at her as well.

'What is it then, Con?' Peggy asked.

'Nothing. It's nothing really, a throwaway comment. Sorry, my brain's a bit tired – all this learning, you know.'

She'd gone very pink and Nancy suspected there was more to her protests than she was letting on, but she wasn't about to push her.

'So you're training as a teacher?' she asked.

Connie looked gratefully at her.

'I am, yes. Started last week. There's a scheme to get women into schools. A lot of the blokes are dead, or as good as, poor things, but it's a great chance for us women to step into their place.'

'Quite right, Connie. I bet you'll be a fabulous teacher.'

'Glad *you* think so.'

She looked a little glum and Peggy gave her a nudge.

'Your folks not keen?'

'Not keen at all.' Connie looked around and then let out a bark of a laugh. 'You should have seen their faces when I told them what I was going to do. They were all set for me to go home and swan around with Mother, waiting for the season to start so I could put on a ridiculous extravagance of a white dress and catch myself a husband. Their main ambition was for me to get someone "with all their limbs". Imagine!'

Dot squealed with laughter but Nancy understood.

'I get that, Con. My lot were delighted that I'd bagged myself a husband. They barely asked anything about the guns when I went home. Well, my little brother did, but not my parents. They just wanted to know about Joe, as if he was my main achievement during the war. In fact, they asked more about where he'd sailed with the navy than they did about my work out at Langham. As for Joe's parents!' She rolled her eyes. 'They want me to slot into the kitchen as if the war never even happened. D'you know why they like me?' The others leaned in. 'Because I've got a "good strong arm for the mangle"!'

More laughter.

'Is that why you're doing your training here in Norwich then, Connie?' Dot asked her.

Connie shifted in her chair.

'Are those cocktails not coming?' she asked.

'They take a while to make,' Dot said knowledgeably. 'So…?'

'I guess so, yes. I mean, I didn't want to do it from home with them nagging on about what a waste of time it is for a "girl like me" every evening. I don't know when they're going to get that I'm not a "girl like me" any more – I'm a totally different girl. And I really like her!'

'Quite right too, but how come you're studying in Norwich? Why not London?'

Connie swallowed.

'Expensive. My parents have refused to fund me in this "non-sense", so I'm having to pay my own way.'

'But you're loaded,' Dot burst out.

'Glad you think so,' Connie said tightly, 'but I've actually not got much cash until I come into my trust fund when I'm twenty-one.'

Peggy shook her head.

'You're not twenty-one yet? Lord, Connie, I forget how young you are.'

'Next year,' Connie said defensively.

'And you couldn't wait until then to start your teacher training?'

'Why should I?' Connie snapped. Silence fell around the table. 'Sorry. God, I'm sorry. I didn't mean to be rude, I just…'

'Want to make your own choices without people questioning you?' Nancy suggested.

Connie smiled at her again.

'Something like that, yes. Norwich was where I first saw the advertisement about the training, so it seemed as good a place as any. I've met some lovely girls to share a house with, too, so as long as I can stay solvent it's all working out well.'

'Plus, you can see me,' Dot said, giving her a conciliatory smile.

'Exactly!'

'And me,' Nancy said. 'The bus from Langham is only forty minutes into Norwich.'

'And the train from London only an hour,' Peggy put in.

Connie beamed round at them, her composure fully restored.

'So it was very much the best choice. Ah, cocktails!'

She pushed her chair back to let the waiter place the tray of glasses on the table and they all reached eagerly for one.

'To the gunner girls!' Peggy proposed, and they clinked glasses heartily together and drank.

'Look at us,' Nancy said. 'Not quite RAF Langham, is it?'

'Bit warmer than that gun battery!' Dot laughed.

Nancy pictured it. They'd been stationed out on the end of the runway, a cold, muddy walk from the barracks and right in the teeth of the icy winds blowing the enemy planes off the sea. There'd been nine of them on the crew in total; the four gunner girls to operate the identification telescope, the height and range finder and the predictor – the 'stuff requiring intelligence', as they'd liked to joke – and then five men to load the shells and pull the trigger.

It had rankled with all the women that they didn't get to do that final bit, but those had been the rules and only occasionally, when the men's fingers had been too cold to squeeze, had they been secretly broken. Nancy had stepped up a few times and loved the thrill of actually sending the shell into the sky – of finishing off the job they started. They'd never spoken of it off the battery though. It was just one of those secrets of war.

She shivered at the sudden thought of the other secrets and looked around at her girls.

'Thank God we got out safe and well.'

'Quite right,' Peggy agreed. 'Safe and well and running our worlds our ways, like we swore when…' She cut herself off and took a hasty swallow of her drink. 'Anyway, look at us – I'm getting the women's army going, Dot's taking the handbag world by storm, Connie's masterminding the future of the children of this country, and Nancy's all but a gamekeeper. Not bad for a handful of raw recruits, hey?!'

Dot cheered. Connie smiled. Nancy felt like a fraud. From the moment she'd arrived at the Gamekeeper's Cottage, she'd been waiting for Joe to talk to his parents about her role on the estate. She'd told herself over and over to be patient and let it all come about naturally, but she could see now that wasn't going to happen. The other gunner girls were getting on with sorting out their own lives and she was spending hers in the kitchen.

'I'm nowhere near a gamekeeper, Peg.'

'But you will be, Nance. Show your in-laws how amazing you are and it'll come good. That gun, I tell you, it put steel into all our spines, and we won't be bent back to domestic servitude.'

'I'll drink to that!' Dot said.

As they toasted each other again, Nancy felt warmth rise through her, not so much from the cocktail as from the sheer joy of being with people who truly understood. She'd talk to Joe. She'd remind him of the woman he'd fallen in love with – the active, determined, purposeful gunner girl. She was still that girl, even with the war over, and somehow she had to make him see that before she lost everything she'd fought for.

Chapter Seven

'Swings!'

Stan jerked out of Lorna's grasp and made a run across the park towards the brightly coloured play area at its centre, his little limbs all anyhow in his excitement. Lorna watched him go, envying his ready enthusiasm, then turned to Charlie.

'That looks like a decent spider's web.'

She indicated the giant pyramid of ropes, usually Charlie's favourite bit of equipment, but her elder son just shrugged.

'It's OK, I guess.'

'Are you not feeling like climbing today?'

Another shrug. Lorna tried to take his hand but a group of bigger boys were coming towards them, skateboards slung under their arms, and he pushed her off. Lorna sighed. She was worried about Charlie. Some days he seemed fine, chatting away to Mary and David, eating like a trouper and playing out like normal, and others he withdrew totally into himself. She got it, she really did – she felt exactly the same way herself – but she had no idea how best to help him. She waited until the bigger boys had gone past, then drew him onto a bench. Stan had joined some other children on a roundabout and was happy enough for now, so she had a little time to talk.

'Do you feel sad, Charlie?'

'Don't you?'

'Yes. All the time.'

'*All* the time? Even when you're with us?'

She caught herself.

'Of course not. I love being with you and Stan.'

'And Granny and Grandpa?'

Lorna noted the easy use of 'Grandpa' but didn't comment.

'Them too. You all make me happy, but there's always a sort of sadness underneath because Daddy's not here. Do you know what I mean?'

Charlie kicked at the foot of the bench.

'Yeah,' he grunted. Then: 'I hate it. I hate feeling sad. I don't want to be sad. No one else is. It's not fair, Mum. It's just not fair.'

Lorna's heart broke. She reached quietly for Charlie's hand, and he grasped at it and held on so tight she feared for her fingers, but he could crack every one of them if it would help.

'I hate it too, Charlie,' she said. 'And you're right – it's not fair. Look at all these other people getting on with their lives, having fun as if there's nothing wrong at all.'

They both looked at the families playing in the park.

'They don't know how lucky they are,' Charlie said darkly.

'They don't. I guess that's part of the luck.'

Charlie looked at her, his eyes blue with sorrow and alight with something that Lorna greatly feared was anger.

'Why us, Mum?'

Tears sprang to her own eyes but all she could do was shake her head and say, 'I don't know, Charlie. I really don't know.'

He seemed to accept this. They sat in silence for a little while, watching Stan fling himself around on the roundabout.

'Why isn't Stan sad?' Charlie asked.

'He's only little, Charlie. He *is* sad when he remembers Daddy isn't here any more, but his brain isn't made to hold on to that all the time.'

'So he's lucky too?'

'In a way. But you know what, Charlie, missing someone shows how much you loved them.'

He yanked his hand from hers.

'That's stupid,' he spat. 'I knew how much I loved him already.'

Lorna closed her eyes a moment. She wasn't handling this well at all.

'You're right, Charlie,' she said. 'It was stupid. I'm sorry, I…'

But when she opened her eyes, she saw that he was gone, off to grab a swing and kick himself higher and higher, until his feet were level with the top bar and the chain buckled. She wanted to cry to him to stop, to come down where it was safe, but she feared that the safest thing for him right now was to push his anger down those chains. Slowly, she got up and went over to Stan.

'Fancy a swing, Stan?'

'Yeah!'

She went across with him, choosing a swing on the next set to Charlie's. Her elder son refused to look her way but at least she was near in case he needed her – or, to be more accurate, in case he allowed himself to need her. It was so hard to know what to do for the best.

Matt would have been better at it, she thought suddenly. Matt wouldn't have thrown stupid adult platitudes at their son. He would just have listened to him and hugged him and then taken him out to kick a football around, working through the grief together in a way she didn't seem to be able to manage. She was useless with a football. At any family kickabout she'd always been shoved in the goal, not so much as keeper than as target practice.

She huffed to herself. *Family kickabout!* That made it sound like the sort of aunty-and-uncle-rich gathering that she could see setting up across the park – a tumble of siblings and cousins, joking and laughing and teasing each other. She'd never really had that. Growing up with just her mum, they'd formed a self-contained pair. Her Aunty Jill had moved to Australia and they'd never had the money to visit her, and of course she'd had no dad and, as a result, no paternal family. She'd never really thought much about that until she'd had Charlie and Stan and realised that she had no cousins to offer them, but oh, she really wished she did now.

Matt had two sisters but they were both a lot older than him, and their kids were in their late teens and only interested in Charlie and Stan in a five-minute aren't-they-cute way. They were never going to race to the park with them, or play hide-and-seek in the bushes, or snuggle down for a sleepover. They'd all been hugely kind after Matt's death and she knew they mourned him as she did, but with the concrete link of her happy-go-lucky husband now gone, she could feel the ties slipping and was struggling to find the energy to keep them up.

'Higher, Mummy!' Stan called, and she automatically pushed him harder, registering his squeal of delight even as her eyes slid over to Charlie, still kicking himself fiercely back and forth.

To one side of him, a woman holding a baby was waving madly across the park, and Lorna watched as another woman came running up, pushchair wheels almost squealing on the soft surfacing as she ran to hug her. Their voices drifted across to Lorna:

'Sooo good to see you.'

'It's been too long.'

'Far too long. Look at this little beauty! May I?'

The second woman took the baby and the two cooed over her together, as the toddler clamoured to be let out and join in the fun. Lorna watched enviously. She had friends too, she reminded herself, good friends. There was Aki, who she still saw several times a week. She was the prettiest woman Lorna knew, her Japanese heritage giving her the most amazing almond eyes and the cheekiest smile, but she'd ridden a very rocky romantic roller coaster and, as of yet, her only children were those under her amazing care at the primary school.

Aki loved Charlie and Stan as much as any 'real' aunty would do, and Lorna treasured her support. She had other friends too, though – women from the playgroups and footie clubs and schoolyards that were the inevitable preserve of those with young kids. They'd

been wonderful after Matt's death. She'd had so many messages
of support, so many flowers and cakes and, most welcome of all,
casseroles to keep their bodies together whilst their hearts fell apart.

And I've run away from them, she thought guiltily, then caught
herself. She wasn't running away; she was taking time out. They'd
all be busy as soon as the schools broke up anyway, heading off
on their happy family holidays with little thought for her bar the
odd 'poor Lorna' as they sipped cocktails in a beach bar. Her whole
body clenched at the thought of being an object of pity, but there
was nothing she could do about it. She pitied herself, for heaven's
sake, so why shouldn't other people be allowed to?

'Too high, Mummy!'

Stan's high-pitched voice pierced her thoughts and she realised
she'd been using the swing almost as fiercely as Charlie.

'Sorry, sweetie. Don't worry. Mummy's got you.'

She slowed it down, smiling at Stan as he looked over his
shoulder at her.

'Kick bottom,' he demanded.

'Stan, I—'

'Kick bottom!'

It was a game Matt had always played with him, standing in
front of the swing as if he'd just casually ended up there, positioned
so that Stan's little feet could just catch his bum, at which point
he'd go squealing dramatically forward, clutching it and gasping
in a mock pain that had his son bursting into peals of delighted
laughter. Lorna had never been as good at it as Matt, and she sure
as hell wouldn't be right now.

'Sorry, Stan, it's time to get off. Look, this other little boy is
waiting for his turn.' She waved with relief to a child who'd come
running up. Stan stuck his lip out mutinously and she rushed to
placate him. A scene was another thing she didn't have the energy
for. 'Let's go on the slide. You like slides. Look – it's a really big one.'

Stan followed her finger and, thankfully, liked what he saw. He wriggled to get out of the swing and she was able to lift him up and away.

'We'll be over here, Charlie,' she called.

Charlie gave the smallest of nods. Stan frowned.

'Why doesn't Charlie have to let anyone else have a turn?'

It was a good point, with other kids milling around below him, but life wasn't always fair and for now Charlie needed the swing more than most. She leaned down to Stan.

'Because he's grumpy today, Stan, and we'll have more fun without him.'

Stanley gave a mischievous grin.

'Yay! Come on, Mummy – last one down the slide's a rotten egg.'

Lorna let him drag her across. She glanced back at Charlie and thought she saw him cast her a grateful look, but it was hard to tell when he was that high in the air. She'd have to make an effort when they went back to Norwich. She'd invite people round, sign up for events, maybe join a single parents' group. She groaned. Even thinking about it felt exhausting.

Their life in Norwich had been so bound up with Matt. The parks and play areas were places they'd been to as a family; the house and garden had been chosen and decorated together; her friends were his friends too – so facing it all without him felt unbearably hard. There was time yet, she reminded herself, as she sat on the slide and turned to help Stan onto her knee. It was only July so she could hide here in Langham for a few weeks, cocooned from a world that held so many painful memories.

'Ready, Stan?'

'Ready, Mummy. Wheeee!'

They walked back through the village, Stan trotting happily at Lorna's side and Charlie a few deliberate steps behind. A delicious smell wafted out of the door of the prettiest old chip shop Lorna reckoned she'd ever seen, and she paused in front of it.

'Chips, boys?'

Even Charlie roused himself to agree to that, and Lorna bought them all a bag of chips and took them across to a bench opposite to enjoy the treat. She looked curiously around her. She was on a small green with a smart village sign, just across from the Blue Bell pub, a low, white-walled structure, jauntily painted with blue woodwork to suit its name. A few people were enjoying a sunny pint on the tables outside and, as she watched them chatting together, she thought of Nancy. This was the pub she'd drunk in with the gunner girls, the pub where she'd met Joe and sealed her future here in the village. From the diary she didn't get the impression she'd liked the place very much, which was odd if it had given her Joe.

She looked curiously at the white walls. Matt would have loved it, she thought, and forced away the wash of instant pain. They'd been planning to come to Langham together this summer, guiltily aware that in all the chaos of family life they hadn't seen Mary's new home. She'd been to stay with them often since the boys were born, slotting into the household with ease, but after the wedding to David she'd chattered proudly to them about the Gamekeeper's Cottage and they'd been all set to visit. Now Lorna was glad they hadn't made it, as at least in this little village she didn't have to remember her husband at every turn.

'Nice chips, boys?'

'The best,' Stan agreed happily.

'Not bad,' Charlie grunted, though she noted he'd already polished off most of them.

The thought of Matt had killed her own appetite and she transferred some of hers to her eldest son, who accepted them with a little nod. She looked around again and her eyes were caught by a war memorial in the corner of the patch of grass. It must once have been a bigger green, she thought, noting the new houses behind, and she tried to picture the village when Nancy had lived here.

Getting up, she wandered over to look at the memorial. It was a smart piece of work in white marble, with a simple cross on the top and a list of names on a brass plaque below. She scanned a few of them: Tommy Wright, Norman Hall, Jacob Chapman, Ernest Taylor – they were just names now but once they'd been living, breathing men, sent out of this safe little village into the muddy, blood-soaked warzones of Europe, never to come home again. She sighed.

'OK, Mummy?'

Lorna pulled herself away and went back to her sons.

'I'm OK, thank you, Stan. Shall we go back to Granny?'

'Yes, please,' Stan said. 'I've saved her some chips.'

He held out his chip paper which boasted a handful of scraps, and Lorna laughed.

'She'll be delighted. Let's go.'

They let themselves back into the Gamekeeper's Cottage to the delicious smell of home baking.

'There you are!' Mary said, coming out of the kitchen in a homely apron, a smudge of flour in her immaculately dyed hair. 'Had fun?'

'Yeah,' Stanley agreed easily. 'We had chips.'

'That's good. Charlie?'

Charlie didn't reply.

'He's grumpy,' Stan said.

His brother glared at him.

'I am not.'

'You are. Mummy said you are.'

Now Charlie turned his glare on Lorna, who withered.

'We're all grumpy sometimes,' she managed. 'It's allowed.'

'Is it?' Stan looked curiously at her, then started to try out a range of grumpy faces that would have made her laugh if it hadn't been for Charlie still shooting daggers at her.

'Maybe a chocolate brownie will help?' Mary suggested. 'Fancy that, Charlie?' It was a temptation too far and Charlie nodded, pushing past them to head into the kitchen. Mary looked back to Lorna. 'OK?' she asked. Lorna shrugged. 'Shall I talk to him?'

'Maybe.'

Mary gave a firm nod, then followed Charlie into the kitchen.

'Come on, young Charles,' she heard her say. 'Let's take our brownies into the garden, shall we? If I'm feeling grumpy, I like to go and talk to the worms about it.'

'Worms?'

'That's right. The worms at the bottom of the garden. They love it in the rich soil of Grandpa David's veggie patch, and they're very good listeners. Really. They don't interrupt you or give you advice or anything irritating like that.'

Lorna heard Charlie grunt his approval and sighed. Thank heavens for her mum. She held Stan back a moment to let them escape out of the door and then released him. The brownies were sitting on a stand in the middle of the pine table, still warm and looking unbelievably tasty. Her appetite hadn't been great recently, but those looked tempting.

'Cup of tea with it?' David suggested, turning from the side where he was marinating lamb.

'That'd be great, David.'

She sank onto one of the pine chairs, her whole body suddenly feeling horribly weary. It was pathetic, but grief seemed to be harder on your limbs than marathon running or lifting weights. She'd done a bit of both in her youth and had never felt as knocked out as she did just getting through the days right now. David came over and set a steaming mug of tea in front of her, placing a warm hand on her shoulder as he did so.

'OK?'

She looked up at him.

'I guess so.'

'That good, hey?' She grimaced and he turned to Stan. 'Hey, Stanley, d'you fancy a play on my tablet? It's got Netflix.'

'Yes please, Grandpa!'

David settled him in his chair over by the French windows and came back to sit with Lorna.

'Thanks, "Grandpa",' she said.

'Is that OK?'

'The tablet? Of course.'

'No, him calling me Grandpa. I don't want to tread on toes.'

She smiled at him.

'You're not. It's fine, really. Lovely in fact. The boys need all the family they can get right now, and I appreciate everything you're doing for us.'

He pressed her hand.

'It's nothing, Lorna. You're hardly difficult, and they might get a little more family soon. I heard from Tilly today that she might be heading this way in a week or two.'

'From South America?'

'Yep. She said something about it being time to "do Europe". She's looking for flights and hoping to come and stay for a few days, if that's OK?'

'Of course it's OK. It's great. I'll look forward to meeting her. I was thinking in the park that I needed to connect with friends again, so she'd be the perfect place to start.'

'She's certainly friendly, my youngest. Never a dull moment with Tilly. I swear she's the one who turned my hair white.'

Lorna laughed.

'Sounds fun.' She looked up as her mum came back into the kitchen. 'Where's Charlie?'

'With the worms. He said he had things to talk to them about and I'd say that's a good thing.'

'Worms, though, really? *I* want to help him.'

'You *are* helping him, darling, every moment of every day, but he's a sharp kid and there are a lot of thoughts running around his little head. I'm afraid that some of this he's going to have to work out for himself, and all we can do is be here to support him when he's ready.'

'I suppose so.'

'I *know* so.'

'How?'

'Because I'm having to do it with you.'

Lorna looked up at her mum and her heart pounded, for once not with hurt but with love. She leaped up and drew her into a hug.

'And I love you for it, Mum. Both of you.'

Mary rubbed her back and she caught again the comforting scent of L'Air du Temps.

'You can talk to me you know, Lor.'

'I know, thank you, but sometimes I want to do anything but talk, at least about how I'm feeling. It's so damn dull!'

Mary released her.

'Fair enough. Let's talk about how brilliant my baking is then, shall we?'

'It *is* pretty brilliant. You'll have to teach me how to make these bad boys. Or, better yet, teach Charlie!'

'It's a deal.'

They all took another brownie and sat around enjoying the rich, chocolatey taste in easy silence. Through the French windows Lorna could see Charlie sitting beneath the runner beans, staring intently into the soil, but she fought to leave him to it. He needed friends too, and if for now they were wormy ones, so be it. Which reminded her of something.

'Tell me, David – you said you remembered Nancy's friends from the war. Did you meet them?'

'Oh, yes,' he agreed, 'all the time, their kids too. They were like family really. Whenever they came over, Mum used to giggle like a girl – we thought it was hilarious. We'd stay up, hanging off the balustrade and listening to them laughing the night away.'

'They must have been very good friends.'

'Mustn't they? Actually, they were all keen on that "our worlds, our ways" idea, now I come to think of it. It was almost a mantra for them. They'd say it if any challenges came up, then look at each other and wink.'

'Wink?'

'Yep. I guess it was a solidarity thing – something they learned when they were running the gun. I never thought about it at the time, just rolled my eyes to the other kids and ran off.'

'They stayed with you a lot then?'

'They did. Aunty Dot lived in Norwich so we saw the most of her and her twin daughters, but Aunty Peggy and her son would visit whenever she could and we'd go to them.'

'Did they, er, have big houses?'

'Biggish, I suppose. Why?'

'Just wondering if they had money.'

'They weren't super-rich, if that's what you mean, but they were both pretty well off. Peggy and her husband were on army pay which was pretty good back then, and Dot and Tony's business did really well. MacLaren's was the smartest factory in Norwich, or so they used to say.'

'And that was from Tony's family?'

'I'm not sure. Why?'

'Oh, something in the diary implied that it wasn't only Nancy who was short of money just after the war. Connie, at least, seems to have been struggling too.'

David looked at her curiously.

'Connie?' he asked. 'Who was Connie?'

Lorna stared at him, astonished.

'There were four women on their gun team: Nancy, Peggy, Dot and Connie. According to the diary, all four of them were meeting up after the war.'

Now it was David's turn to stare.

'Well, they weren't later on. I only ever had two gunner-girl aunties. I wonder what on earth happened to Connie?'

It was a very good question, and suddenly Lorna was desperate to get back to the diary. She rose to go, but as she did so the French windows opened and Charlie slid inside.

'Mummy?' His voice was small and young-sounding.

'Charlie, my gorgeous boy.'

'I'm sorry I was grumpy.'

Her heart broke and she rushed forward to sweep him into her arms.

'It's OK,' she said. 'It's so, so OK. You can feel whatever you want.'

His arms went around her.

'I love you, Mummy, you do know that?'

'Of course I do. I love you too, so much.'

'Can we watch *Wreck-it Ralph*?'

'Sounds good to me. Stan – *Wreck-it Ralph*?'

'Now? In the middle of the afternoon?' He could hardly believe his luck.

'Why not?!'

Lorna led the way to the living room, Charlie still pressed tight against her. She was dying to know more about what had brought Nancy and her gunner girls their sudden prosperity, but it would have to wait. Her boys needed her – and she them – and that was the most important thing of all.

Chapter Eight

Saturday, 18 August 1945

Victory in Japan! Thank heavens. Joe and I were so lucky to be demobbed early – a perk of getting married, it seems, as couples were given greater priority in getting home. We avoided anything to do with war in the Far East, but even that's over now. We went to the cinema yesterday and watched the footage of the bombs the Americans dropped. I couldn't believe what I was seeing – a great mushroom of destruction over both those cities. It must have been awful for the people living there, but what could the Yanks do? We had a pilot at Langham who'd been stationed in Singapore and he said fighting the Japanese was like fighting the very devil himself. They just kept coming, he said, hundreds and hundreds of them, and none of them caring about death. It's an honour, apparently, in their country. I mean, it's an honour here too, but not one anyone would seek. We like our boys – and girls – home alive, and now they can be. Proper, total peace. That deserves celebrating.

Mind you, Betty's idea of a celebration doesn't quite match mine. The vicar called a fete for today to celebrate the 'true end of the war', and Betty had me chained to the stove making food to feed the masses. I'm fed up of it, although there've been all sorts of delicious deliveries to the back door – illicit bags of sugar and pats of butter, honeycomb and cream, and great jars of jams and pickles. I've not seen so much good food in years and I'll say one

*thing for the countryside – they know how to grow stuff.
It's fascinating. Every day that I get to go out on the estate
– which isn't anywhere near often enough – I see apples
turning red on the trees, berries growing in the woodland
and crops ripening in the fields. It's like magic. Joe tells me
stuff about pollination and grafting and osmo-something
and I find it all amazing.*

*He keeps pointing me to the kitchen garden, which is
nice, sort of, but I know it's just to keep me occupied and not
fretting at him to take me further afield. Well, tough, I'm not
going to stop. Seeing the girls has hardened my resolve. Next
time we get together, I want to tell them I'm a gamekeeper
like he promised me. But not today. Today is for fun.*

'Oh Nancy, look at it! Doesn't it look beautiful? Aren't we lucky
to be here?!'

Joe pulled Nancy in close against him as they stood together
looking at Langham village green. It did indeed look very jolly.
The green was surrounded with brightly coloured bunting made
out of scraps of worn clothing which fluttered gently in the late
summer breeze. Down the centre was a run of tables, brought out
of every house and laden with more food than Nancy had seen
in a long time.

At the far end, near the Blue Bell, a group of men were standing
around a hog they'd been roasting since daybreak, and the smells
wafted tantalisingly across to them. The doors of the Blue Bell were
flung wide open and the landlord was apparently doing half-price
ale all day long. It would be a party to remember and the whole
village was out to enjoy it.

'It's just like the old days,' Nancy heard someone say, and she
turned to see Miss Snales and Miss Richardson sailing past arm in
arm in their best frocks.

'Only with fewer men.'

They both crossed themselves. Langham might not have been much changed by the war, but the village had had its losses like any other. There were several widows who'd be bringing up children alone now, and one man sat under a tree in the corner, both legs missing. A young woman was circulating with a box, seeking donations for a memorial to honour them. Joe dropped a penny in it as they passed and got a grateful smile, but money was tight for everyone and Nancy feared she would be collecting for a long time, however worthy the cause.

'So sad,' Miss Snales said, and Nancy saw Miss Richardson squeeze her arm.

'It is, dear, it is – but we've long known that women can look after each other, haven't we?'

It was spoken so low that only Nancy heard it, and she looked determinedly the other way. As far as she was concerned, everyone should get their happiness where they could. One of the girls in the barracks had approached her once, suggesting they 'find comfort in each other'. Nancy had appreciated the compliment and turned her down as gently as she could.

'And besides,' Miss Richardson said now, 'I heard the wounded soldiers may be coming down from the Hall, so that'll give the girls something to make them blush, hey?'

They moved off to greet the vicar, all sweetness, and Nancy smiled. Maybe Langham wasn't as staid as it seemed if you knew where to look. Patience – that was all she needed.

She let Joe lead her forward, battling to remember names as people came over to greet them. She spotted Ted and Betty laughing with some of the other villagers and was glad to see it. The roofer's quote had come in last week and it had been even higher than any of them had dared to estimate. Lord Langham had said he could build them a smart new cottage for half that price, but Ted and Betty didn't want a smart new cottage; they wanted the one Ted had grown up in and Joe after him. Nancy could understand that.

She'd only been under the shaky roof for a few weeks and already she was very fond of the pretty place, but what could they do?

'Roll up, roll up!' called a piping voice, and Nancy looked round to see that two young boys had set up a tub of water with an assortment of wooden ducks bobbing about on it. 'Hook a duck, mister?'

One of them proffered Joe a stick with a wire hook fastened on the end of it, and Nancy saw there were loops in the heads of the ducks.

'Why not?' Joe agreed.

'Penny a go.'

'Cheeky!' Joe told him, but he fished in his pocket for a penny all the same.

'Thanks, mister.' The lad's eyes glowed and he turned to his mate. 'I heard Mrs Runcie is getting some sherbet in. Save your coupons and we'll be first in the queue.'

Nancy smiled at Joe as he stood, as ordered, behind a white line painted onto the grass, and lifted the stick.

'You got one minute,' the lad told him, drawing out a big old pocket watch. 'Ready – go!'

Joe confidently reached out the stick, but every time he got close to a duck, the wire hook nudged it and it bobbed away.

'Lord, this is harder than it looks!'

He redoubled his efforts as the boy loudly counted down the last ten seconds, but to no avail.

'Time's up, mister, sorry.'

'Dash it.' He looked at Nancy. 'Maybe I need a pint to, you know, steady my hand.'

'Maybe,' she agreed, 'or maybe you need to let your wife have a go.'

He nodded and pulled out another penny, then handed her the stick. The boys looked delighted and the first one reached for his watch again. Nancy took up her position behind the line and eyed the hooks with care. She'd worked the height and range finder on the anti-aircraft gun. After Dot had identified a German plane with binoculars, it had been Nancy's job to calculate the distance the shell would have to travel to hit it, passing that on to Connie and Peg to feed into the predictor. They'd used a complex piece of kit that had needed a very steady hand, so surely she could manage a bit of simple fishing. Biting her lip, she selected a likely duck, lined up the stick and then, in one swift motion, hooked it straight up into the air. The boys gasped and Joe applauded loudly.

'Nicely done, darling. What does she win, lads?'

Reluctantly they waved to a plate of rock buns on a little table.

'Lovely!' Nancy picked one up, broke it in two, and then handed the boys half each. 'For you.'

'Really? Thanks, missus.'

They both stuffed the treat into their mouths so fast that crumbs spurted everywhere, and Nancy laughed and took Joe's arm again.

'Nice work, Mrs Wilson,' he said to her.

'Told you I'd learned a few things in the war.'

'You're amazing.'

'Can I have a gun then?'

'What?'

'A gun, Joe, to help you shoot crows and that. You did say so on honeymoon, I distinctly remember.'

Joe groaned.

'So do I. You were standing naked at the window of that odd little boarding house on Hayling Island pretending to shoot seagulls, and you looked gorgeous. I could refuse you nothing.'

'So?'

He swallowed.

'So, I'll get you a gun if that's what you really want.'

'It is. Well, a gun and the chance to use it, to help out on the estate.'

'Right. Yes. You still want to do that then?'

She squinted at him.

'Of course I do, Joe. Why wouldn't I?'

He shuffled his feet on the grass. Two kids ran past with hoops and he ducked aside to avoid them.

'I thought that maybe now you'd, you know, got away from the guns you'd feel more... settled.'

'Settled?!'

'With, you know, the...' He'd gone very red. 'The usual stuff.'

'Usual, Joe?'

He looked longingly to the Blue Bell, but she wasn't going to let him off that easily. This was important.

'Traditional,' he tried.

She knew exactly what he meant, and no, she wasn't going to 'settle'. She felt anger rise up inside her. She'd been trying to be patient, as the girls had advised, so she'd buckled down and helped out as best she could. Every day now, Ted and Joe headed out into the fields or the woods after breakfast, leaving Nancy to clean and wash and cook. And every day at 12.30 on the dot, they came back in and dinner had to be on the table ready to eat, or woe betide.

Nancy understood that. Three years in the army had taught her the value of routine. If you had a job to get on with, you needed your meal ready on time. What she hated was that the job was the men's and she was there merely to provide support. Betty seemed to derive huge satisfaction from having the meal ready to serve up the moment Joe and Ted walked through the door. She'd fuss over getting the gravy right and the veg cooked exactly as Ted liked it. She'd pore over menus and eke out ingredients and preside over the table, pouring tea and hovering ready to cater to any additional requests. To Nancy's astonishment, she didn't even eat with them, preferring to wait to see what was left once they were full.

'You need to eat as well,' she'd said to her mother-in-law once when Ted had had seconds, leaving Betty to mop up his gravy with bread for her own meal.

'Oh, not really, dear. They're out doing all the work, after all.'

'You've been on the go all morning, Betty, cleaning the windows.'

'Well, yes, but I don't need so much to eat, really I don't.

And to be fair, Betty wasn't exactly wasting away and would always take a sneaky slice of cake if there was one going, but that wasn't the point. She treated Joe and Ted like kings; which would be fine if they, in turn, treated her like a queen and not a servant.

'Traditional?' she threw back at Joe now, and he squirmed.

'Nancy, please, can we leave this? Just for today. We'll talk about it later, I promise, but it's a party, a celebration of all we achieved, you and I and everyone who fought for this wonderful freedom we have now.'

He cast a hand around the bustling green, the very picture of contentment and peace, and Nancy forced herself to take a few deep breaths and let the anger go. Joe was right; this wasn't the time.

'You promise we'll talk later?'

'I promise.'

'Fine then.'

'Great.' He bent and gave her a slow, grateful kiss. 'Pub?'

She glanced to the Blue Bell and felt a shiver pass through her. *Scum!* a voice called in her head. *Boche scum!* When was that going to go? She couldn't stay away from her local forever, but being in there reminded her of that night when… She shook the thought away. They'd sworn not to talk about it ever again and that ought to include inside their heads. She smiled up at Joe.

'Could you bring mine out, darling?'

'Course I can. Gin and lime?'

'Please.'

He made a dash for the pub, and Nancy watched him go and sighed. He was trying, she knew. He was so happy to be home that he couldn't see anything wrong with life at the Gamekeeper's Cottage, and why should he? Nothing *was* wrong with it for him. As Nancy looked around at the groups of men nursing pints outside the Blue Bell and the groups of women fussing over the food and chasing up the children, however, she truly feared that, for her, 'freedom' had been the war years. Was it all downhill from here?

'Penny for 'em.'

Nancy jumped and turned to see a tall, slim young woman in the most glorious red dress.

'Oh, I was just thinking how, erm, idyllic this scene is.'

'Rustic, you mean!'

Nancy stared at the new arrival and she stuck out a hand. 'Meredith Langham. Back with Mummy and Daddy for the foreseeable, Lord help me! You must be Nancy Wilson, right?'

'Right,' Nancy stuttered.

'The soldier wife.'

She groaned.

'That seems to be what they all call me around here. I was in the ATS, on an anti-aircraft gun.'

'Right here at Langham, I know! Wonderful to have an Ack-Ack girl amongst us. Bit different in the village itself though, hey?'

'Everyone's been very welcoming,' Nancy said cautiously.

'I bet they have, bless 'em. They're lovely people, really they are. Just a bit… last century.'

The laugh burst out of Nancy before she could stop it. Meredith was spot on and it was such a relief to hear someone say so. Joe was coming out of the pub with her drink and she turned happily to him.

'Thank you, darling. This is…'

'Hello, Merry. Didn't know you were back.'

'You know each other?' Nancy asked, but of course they did. Everyone in Langham knew each other.

'Joe and I used to kick about the woods together as kids.'

'When Merry was let out to play with the hoi polloi.'

'Or when I snuck out.'

'As a kid?' Nancy asked.

'Oh, yes. It's a big house so no one ever really knew where I was. I was always at it when we were older. Remember that time we nicked Cook's cider at midsummer?'

'Barely!' Joe said, and they both laughed.

Nancy looked from one to the other, trying not to feel uneasy.

'Was there a gang of you?' she asked.

'A handful, yes,' Joe agreed.

'Sometimes it was just the two of us,' Meredith said, then batted at Nancy's arm. 'Oh, not like that. Lord no, Pa would have killed me. I've got to find myself someone "suitable", if they're not all dead. Still, being heir to that place should give me a bit of a leg-up, hey?'

'You're an only child?'

'Am now.' For a moment Meredith's poise wavered, and then she almost visibly pulled it back into place. 'Have you met Ma and Pa yet, Nancy?'

'A couple of times at church.'

Nancy had been introduced to the lord and lady of the manor and been suitably intimidated. She'd have tugged on her forelock if she'd known what one was. Not that they weren't nice. Both of them had been boomingly friendly and assured her they were delighted to have Joe back on the estate. Lady Langham had even asked her about herself.

'Manchester!' she'd exclaimed, when Nancy had told her where she came from. 'Heavens – isn't that all factories?'

Nancy had tried to explain that Chester was a different place and that not everyone worked in factories, even in the city, but it had been clear that Lady Langham's ideas about the north were fixed, so she'd very quickly given up trying to change them and just agreed that, yes, Langham was beautiful.

'They'll not stay at the party long,' Meredith was saying now. 'They don't want to inhibit people's fun, but they've come down with a few bottles of claret Daddy brought back from France.'

'From France?'

'That's right. Apparently half the big houses were abandoned when Fritz fled. They'd drunk most of the cellars dry, swine, but there was still some to mop up.'

Nancy looked at Meredith for irony but found not a trace of it; clearly the English stealing the French wine was warranted in her mind. She supposed at least Lord Langham was sharing it out, which was generous of him.

'Your father fought, then?' she asked.

'Lord no. Far too old. Just sat in an HQ somewhere ordering other people to get stuck in. Still, he's got a half-decent tactical mind, I'm told, so hopefully he helped a bit.'

Joe leaned in to Nancy and whispered in her ear. 'Lord Langham was one of the masterminds behind D-Day.'

'Really?'

'Really. He just doesn't like to shout about it. Lost his son at Dunkirk, God bless him, and was on a mission for revenge from that moment onwards.'

Nancy looked to Lord Langham, gaily pouring French claret into glasses for a few bemused-looking villagers. The war had changed them all one way or another; it would take a lot of adjusting for everyone.

'That's so sad.'

Joe nodded.

'Yep. For Lady Langham too. She opened up the house as a hospital for convalescing soldiers after James died. Had over a hundred here at the height of the conflict.'

'Oh, I know,' Nancy agreed. 'I volunteered there for a bit.'

Joe looked at her, surprised.

'Did you? You never mentioned it.'

Nancy felt herself colour. Damn – she shouldn't have said anything but it was too late now.

'Just at the end of the war, when there were no German planes to watch out for. We had time to spare, you know, so it seemed a good use of it.'

'Right. So you know Lady Langham then?'

'Oh, no,' Nancy said hastily. 'I was a lowly minion.'

And working in one particular area, she thought to herself, but Joe was still looking at her curiously and she turned hastily to Meredith.

'Do you still have injured men at the house?'

Meredith, who had been beckoning her father over, turned back to them and nodded.

'About thirty of them, yes. Mainly Americans from various Norfolk bases, convalescing and waiting for a boat home. Mother's tried to keep the officers. I think I'm meant to fall for one, but there's a few regulars hanging in there so I flirt most with them, just to worry my parents.'

'Merry! Isn't that a bit unkind?' Joe protested.

'Well, they shouldn't be such snobs then, should you, Daddy?'

Lord Langham had reached them and frowned at his daughter.

'What's that?'

'You and Ma, all set on an officer for me.'

'Oh, yes. Absolutely. That would be splendid. Though not an American one, please.'

'God forbid!'

'Can't have you disappearing off across the Atlantic, can we. Especially not now that…'

His words caught in his throat and Meredith threw her arms around him.

'Don't worry, Daddy, I'm going nowhere. It's good old Langham for me now.'

'Should hope so too,' Lord Langham said gruffly. 'Prettiest place in the world.'

At Nancy's side, Joe stiffened and, turning to him, she saw his neck tighten. He cleared his throat.

'It is that, my lord, and should stay that way.'

Lord Langham looked at him curiously. Joe coloured but stood his ground. 'The Gamekeeper's Cottage, my lord – it's a beautiful building, do you not think?'

'Oh, I do, son, I do. One of the finest.'

'But it won't be, will it, if it loses its roof?'

'Ah, I see.' Lord Langham looked at Joe for what felt like a very long time. Nancy slipped her hand into his and felt him clutch it gratefully. 'I'd love to restore the roof, Joe,' he said eventually. 'Truly I would, but it's so expensive. We're running on a shoestring here. A new house would be far more economical, as well as leaving us money for improved hatcheries, more workers, even a replacement tractor – all offering ways to earn more going forward.'

Joe shuffled his feet miserably.

'I do see that, my lord, but—'

'But it's your home, I know, and my offer to gift it to you still stands if you can manage the renovations yourself.'

Joe looked miserable and Nancy hated to see it.

'I'll help,' she said to him.

'*You* will?' Lord Langham looked amused. 'How?'

'In every way I can.'

'Which is many ways, I bet,' Merry said stoutly. 'The world's changed, Daddy. Everyone's been working together in the war – rich and poor, Yanks and Brits, blacks and whites, men and women. You can't expect them all to go back into their separate boxes afterwards. It doesn't work like that.'

'I don't see why not,' Lord Langham mumbled. 'I liked my box.'

'But don't you see, Daddy, there *are* no boxes any more. They've been blown sky-high, along with half our houses and far too many of our young men. Bombs don't discriminate, so neither should we.'

Nancy's heart soared. She couldn't have put it better herself and certainly wouldn't have dared to, but nothing seemed to faze Meredith Langham. 'Women are more than kitchen maids now and we can't waste them. Oh!' She clutched Nancy's arm. 'I've had a marvellous idea. You should come up to the house, shouldn't she, Daddy? We could really do with you there.'

'Really?'

Nancy looked keenly at her new friend. This could be her way into the estate. Surely even Ted wouldn't dare refuse an order from Lord Langham.

'Absolutely. Mummy!' She waved Lady Langham over. 'This is Nancy. She's super talented.'

'Well now…'

'Been in the ATS. Ack-Ack girl.'

'Lovely,' Lady Langham said, looking slightly bemused and no wonder.

'So,' Meredith said with exaggerated patience, 'she can come up and help us with the convalescents. She can come up and nurse.'

'Nurse?' Nancy spluttered.

All around her, people were nodding and expressing delight.

'She's done it before, earlier this year.'

Earlier this year, Nancy thought, amazed that was all it had been. It felt like forever.

'Isn't that great, Nance?' Joe was saying to her. 'Isn't that what you wanted – to get out of the house?'

'Well, yes, but…' Joe's face fell and the protest died in her throat.

They all looked so pleased with the idea; how could she possibly explain that she didn't want to give up tending to one set of men just to go to another? She'd only volunteered before because… Well, that didn't matter now. The bottom line was that she was rubbish at looking after people. The ATS had seen that straight away. She'd been rapidly bypassed for nursing or cooking or even admin work and put straight onto the guns. And she'd loved it. How come the army could see who she was and these people – her new family and neighbours – were totally blind to it?

She looked helplessly to Meredith who bit her lip.

'Not really your bag?' she mouthed. Nancy gave a little shudder. 'Sorry. Still, at least we can do it together?'

Nancy smiled at her. That much was true. It was a step forward of sorts, and she'd have to try and take it on as enthusiastically as it had been offered.

'Sounds good,' she managed.

'There are perks,' Meredith told her. 'Like this dress, for example.'

'It's amazing,' Nancy said, eyeing up the flowing skirt. 'How on earth did you get all the fabric?'

'Perks, I told you. There's a rather gorgeous GI in convalescence with us who had his sister send it over from America. Seems it's just the thing there, and it's been so long since anyone has even begun to think about fashion that I thought I'd snatch at the chance to bag it.'

'It's lovely.'

'It is,' Joe agreed. 'You'd look beautiful in a dress like that, Nance. I'm going to get you one.'

'Joe, you don't—'

'No, I am. You deserve it, putting up with me and Ma and Pa, and little old Langham.'

Nancy took his hand and they wandered away from Meredith and her parents.

'Don't be silly, Joe. Everyone's been lovely. *Life* is lovely.'

And looking round the green, it really did seem as if it was. She should stop mithering about wanting more and count her blessings. She loved Joe so much. Even a hint that he might have been up to something in the woods with Meredith ten years ago had made her prickle with jealousy.

She watched as several men carefully carried the piano out of the pub and set it on the green, near to the hog roast. Someone struck up 'We'll Meet Again' and instantly people gathered, raising their voices in song to acknowledge that their happy few had made it through the war alive. Nancy owed it to all those who had not survived to enjoy every day as best as she could.

Chapter Nine

Volunteer day – those two words had most people running for the hills, and very sensible of them too. Lorna, however, seemed to have found herself parking in a muddy field outside the Langham Dome on one of England's dampest summer mornings, wearing her scruffiest clothes and with a selection of gardening tools in the boot. It wasn't the most glamorous start to a day out but, despite that, she found herself quietly pleased to be here.

David was with her and Charlie had come along too, enticed, perhaps misleadingly, by the promise of exploring the 'gun place'. Lorna felt a little guilty about that as Lilian had been quite clear that the aim of the day was to tidy up the area around the dome, but Charlie had been clingy since the trip to the park and Mary had been very happy having Stan to herself, so she'd taken the chance to keep him close.

'It's raining,' Charlie said, peering out of the window as they pulled up.

'Drizzling,' Lorna corrected him, though she could already see that it was the sort of persistent shower that would soak you more effectively than any dramatic downpour. 'And you have Grandpa's waterproof.'

It was far too large for him of course, but it was in a brand he deemed acceptable so he'd agreed to bring it along. Now, though, he looked out as the next car along disgorged a boy and a girl about his own age, and folded his arms.

'I'm not wearing that.'

'Charlie…'

'I don't need it. It's not cold.'

'No, but—'

'They're not wearing coats, so why should I?'

Then, to Lorna's surprise, he was out of the car and gone, strolling super casually after the other kids whose own mum, Lorna noticed, was standing at the boot of their car holding two coats uselessly in her hands. She got out and looked across.

'Why won't they ever wear them?' she asked.

The other woman shrugged.

'Lord knows. It drives me mad, but my mum tells me I was the same at their age. Ah, look – they're making friends.' Lorna looked and, sure enough, Charlie was talking to the other two. As they watched, the boys separated themselves off a little. 'How old's your son?' the woman asked.

'Nine.'

'George is too. He'll be delighted to have another boy. He hates kicking around with Annie.'

'But what about Annie?'

'Oh, don't worry about her. She's got other friends turning up any minute. That's one of the reasons George hates it. I'm Rachel, by the way.'

She stuck out a hand and Lorna took it.

'Lorna. You here to volunteer?'

''Fraid so. My dad roped us in.'

She nodded across the field to the man greeting the kids, and Lorna smiled.

'Richard is your dad?' Lorna asked.

'You know him?'

'He roped me in too.'

Rachel grinned.

'He's very persuasive. Shall we enter the fray then?'

'Let's,' Lorna agreed, turning to help David get the tools out of the boot and feeling even better about the day ahead.

She'd been restless this week and it would be good to do something physical, so she gladly stuck her hand up when Lilian, looking like a sweet gnome in dungarees and a stripy T-shirt, asked for people to help dig out a vegetable bed.

'It's going to be a Dig for Victory' exhibit,' she told her little band, which included Lorna, Rachel and nominally their children, although the boys were already eyeing up a very climbable tree nearby. 'We've got some old railway sleepers to put around the edge, but we need the grass out and the topsoil turning. It'll be hard work.'

'Good,' Lorna said and picked up her spade, ready to get stuck in.

'You were right,' Lorna told Lilian ruefully two hours later, as the volunteers were called together for tea and sandwiches, 'this *is* hard work.'

Lilian laughed.

'Victory doesn't come easily you know, Lorna. Are you OK?'

'Fine. Just aching in muscles I didn't even realise were there. Nothing a bath won't sort out later. And it looks good.'

Somehow, she and Rachel had dug out a six-by-three-metre bed with next to no help, and Lorna felt a rush of satisfaction as she looked over it.

'It does indeed,' Richard agreed, coming across. 'And the other two will look even better.'

'Other two?!' Lorna wailed, and he clapped her heartily on her sore back.

'Don't worry, you've got all afternoon.'

Lorna looked at him, horrified, but Lilian gave him a gentle punch on the shoulder.

'Nonsense, Richard. These two have done more than enough digging for now. We can swap jobs after the cakes are gone. Flapjack, Lorna?'

'I think I love you, Lilian,' Lorna told her and she giggled.

'Don't want to scare you off on your first time, do we? More tea? Lovely. Now, tell me about this diary you've found.'

'Diary?' Rachel asked, so Lorna filled her in on her treasured discovery. Several others gathered round to listen, and Lorna found herself at the heart of a lively discussion about the ATS girls.

'They were a great lot, by all accounts,' one older man said. 'I used to hear stories about them in the Blue Bell.'

Lorna pictured the pretty pub she'd eaten chips opposite the other day. Others, then, remembered the gunner girls drinking in there. The connection gave her a thrill – this history was just about in touching distance, and perhaps these local stories would tell her why Nancy hadn't been keen on the pub.

'The gunner girls used to go there, did they?' she asked him.

'On their nights off, yes. Made themselves very popular with the locals.'

'Though not the locals' wives, hey, Brian?' Richard said.

'I'm sure they weren't like that,' Rachel put in quickly.

'Oh, I dunno,' Brian said. 'Not with the locals, perhaps, but I reckon they got up to a few things with the airmen. Not that I'm complaining, and I bet the airmen weren't either.'

Lorna looked at Brian crossly.

'You're assuming that just because there were a few women in a barracks full of men that they, they…' She looked self-consciously around for Charlie, but he was a little way off with George. 'That they you-know-whatted the lot of them.'

Brian smiled.

'Perhaps not the lot of them, but there was a great story about one of them for sure.'

Lorna looked to Rachel, uncertain if she should be encouraging this, but Rachel had no such qualms.

'What story?' she demanded.

Brian took a sip of his tea and smiled round at his rapt audience.

'I wasn't there, mind – I'm not *that* ancient – but the older blokes were talking about it over their ale for years after. Word was, there was a hut in the woods that one of the girls used to use for trysts. *Intimate* trysts, if you know what I mean!'

He winked and his audience chuckled.

'How did they know?' Rachel demanded.

'Because they were all out in the woods one night towards the end of the war and came across her in the act!'

'What were they doing out there?'

'No idea. They always fudged over that bit. Spot of poaching most likely; rabbits were a boon to any kitchen in wartime.'

'That's true,' Richard said keenly. 'Do you know—'

Rachel nudged her dad quiet.

'So what did they find this girl doing exactly?' she demanded of Brian.

'Well, the story goes that as they were romping around in the woods, they went into the shed, and there, naked as the day she was born and straddling some lucky bloke, was one of the girls.'

'Seriously?'

'So the story went, my love, but you know how these things can be exaggerated.'

'There has to be a grain of truth in it, though,' Richard said. 'And why not? Life's for living, right? And it must have felt far more that way during a war when you could die at any time. Especially airmen – their life expectancy was awful. There's a bit about it on one of the boards in the dome, actually, and...'

The groans of the little group told Lorna that Richard must hold forth often, and she suppressed a smile as he indignantly closed his lips. She turned to David.

'Do you think that was Nancy? She met your dad in the pub, you said.'

'True. Oh, I do hope so! Did the story ever include who the lucky man was, Brian?'

Brian frowned, fighting to remember.

'I think there was mention of someone called Hank. Funny name.'

'American,' Richard said sagely.

'Course. There were a few Yanks stationed here at various points so it could easily have been. Coming over taking our girls, hey? Shocking!'

Lorna looked to David again.

'Not your mum and dad then.'

'Nope. It was probably Dot. Mum and Peggy were always teasing her about being "wild" during the war.'

'Certainly sounds pretty wild,' Rachel said. 'And good on her. Does your diary say anything about it, Lorna?'

'Nothing so far, but I'm only about halfway through. I'm trying to ration it, to have something to look forward to. Does that sound silly?'

'Not at all. You've got all summer, so why rush?'

Lorna smiled gratefully at her new friend. This diary was one of the few things getting her through the days right now. It had been a welcome distraction from her own life and, in truth, she dreaded finishing it, however much she was intrigued by the secrets at its heart.

'Of course, it's from 1945, after the war, so it's not really about their life on the base – though Nancy does say how much she missed it.'

'Maybe it *was* her then,' Brian chuckled.

'Not because of *that*,' Lorna told him scornfully. 'Quite the reverse. From what I can gather, she loved it for the liberation it gave her, for being allowed to do something more than keeping home. I think she struggled with being expected to go back to that afterwards.'

'Don't blame her,' Lilian said firmly. 'We can cover that in our exhibition.'

'Exhibition?' Richard asked, frowning.

Lilian raised her eyebrows to Lorna and, taking the hint, she turned to Rachel's father.

'It was your idea, Richard, remember? And it's such a good one. People will love to hear about the gunner girls.'

'I certainly would,' Rachel agreed.

'And me,' Lilian threw in.

David laughed.

'Looks like you're doing an exhibition, Rich. Now, are we getting on with this work or what?'

Lorna was grateful to be released. The group were all really nice and it was fascinating to think that some of them could have drunk with Nancy and Joe later in their life, but she felt curiously possessive of Nancy and her friends, and she hadn't really enjoyed Brian's rather insalubrious story. It had set her thinking though – had one of them been having a liaison with a rich American? Did this Hank somehow fund the changes at the Gamekeeper's Cottage? She couldn't begin to imagine how, and suddenly wanted to go home to the annex and talk to Nancy about it, but that was a nonsense. Nancy had been dead for years.

'No such thing as ghosts, hey, Matt?' she muttered under her breath, realising she was now talking to two dead people.

Lilian came over with a litter picker for her afternoon's assignment and she took it, grateful to have something practical to focus on. Charlie, she noticed, had given up all pretence of working and was running around with George, a pair of sticks for guns as they rolled dramatically into pretend trenches and fired off rounds of imaginary bullets. Seeing the dome didn't seem to have put him off the idea of war, unfortunately, but at least he was happy, so she took her giant pincers and started work.

When she reached the edge of the fenced-off land, where it bordered what had once been the airfield, she paused, looking out and trying to picture the Nissen huts, control tower and long runways of yesteryear. There was a map inside the dome and she fought to try and remember it, to work out where everything had been. The turkey farmers had made changes, of course, not least the big birds that were pecking around in the grass, but it was still possible to imagine planes coming flying in from the east, grateful to be safely home from yet another dangerous mission into enemy territory.

Focusing on a patch of land beyond the one-time control tower – now a farm office – where she'd been told the anti-aircraft gun had been situated, Lorna tried to imagine Nancy and the others setting it up night after night, preparing to bring down any German planes foolish enough to enter their territory. She'd always been captivated by the imprint of the past on the present and she'd rarely felt it more keenly than here.

'Isn't it fascinating, Matt?' she murmured.

'If you say so, gorgeous.'

The reply came to her clearly, because that was what he'd always said when she'd started off on one of her 'historical ding-dongs'. But he'd always listened anyway and always been prepared to diverge off their planned path, if a castle or a monument caught her eye. Their very first trip away had been to walk Hadrian's Wall, as she'd been covering it with her Year Sevens and had been dying to see it for ages. If she remembered rightly, mind you, she'd been a little too distracted by the wonderful man at her side to pay as much attention as she should have done to the stones of the ancient Roman edifice.

'I miss you, Matt. I miss you so much.'

Her legs felt weak with longing and she leaned heavily against the fence. She thought about Nancy and her friends, stuck in a hideous war with their lives on the line every single day. So many women must have lost husbands and sweethearts, sons and fathers – but that didn't mean that any one of them was any less sad than

Lorna was right now. She clutched at the tops of the little pickets to stop herself dropping to the ground, trying to think of the women working on the guns, of the planes flying safely in, of Dot getting 'intimate' in the woods – anything from the past that pervaded this place to stop her losing herself in her own, spiralling present.

'Mum?' Charlie came out of nowhere. She felt his hand under her elbow, small but surprisingly strong. 'Mum, are you OK?'

She blinked away her tears and looked down at him.

'Fine, sweetie. I'm fine, thank you.'

'A bit grumpy?'

She nodded slowly.

'A bit grumpy, yes.'

'You're allowed to feel whatever you want,' he told her solemnly, and she stared at him, stunned to hear her own words of so-called wisdom. 'Here.' He beckoned her down close to his face and, looking from left to right, whispered, 'You should talk to the worms about it.'

'The worms?'

'In Grandpa's garden. They're very good listeners and they know about Daddy now, so they'd get it – the grumpiness.'

Lorna crushed him to her, not caring about his squeals of protest.

'You, Charlie Haynes, are the cleverest, wisest, kindest boy I know.'

'Mum! Let go.'

'I will do, in a minute.'

He harrumphed but then flung his arms around her and cuddled her back.

'The worms, Mum,' he said sternly.

'The worms. I promise. Thanks, Charlie.'

'No sweat.'

Then he was wriggling away and running back to his new friends. Lorna leaned on the fence, feeling the spiral of despair recede as she watched the happy crowd slaving away around the Langham Dome. Then, on a deep breath in, she picked up her litter picker and set back to work, her thoughts turning to Nancy and her intriguing diary once more.

Chapter Ten

Monday, 1 October 1945

So, at last the Open Season is upon us, which means, as far as I can gather, that everyone is allowed to shoot the pheasants we've been carefully breeding for so long. It seems a bit sad but it's the way of the world, I suppose, and Ted's been so excited that I'd never dare say a word against it. I can't believe this sort of thing's been going on for hundreds of years and I never even knew.

Life's different in the country. More raw. In Chester we used to get our meat from the butcher, cut up and wrapped in paper. Down here, we often as not get it straight from the field. Ted and Joe will come in with a rabbit in their sack, and by nightfall Betty's skinned it and got it into the pot. Sometimes I can't help picturing the little creatures peering up out of the long grass, all curious about the world around them, but I try to push it away. I don't want Ted thinking I'm soft. Well, any softer than he already does, by dint of being a woman.

Joe keeps telling me to 'wait till you taste venison, Nance'. That's deer, apparently. I worry that I'll never be able to eat one of those beautiful, gentle hinds, or the magnificent stags. They've grown their antlers now and, my, they look something! Don't they know it, mind. They're strutting around like they own the place – which I suppose, in their heads at least, they do.

Joe says that soon the 'rut' will start and I'll hear them bellowing out their manliness to attract the best girls. One night he tried to demonstrate. Ooh, he looked cute with his chest bare and his head back, roaring, but then Betty banged on the door to see if everything was all right and we both dissolved into laughter, so it didn't really have the desired effect. Let's hope the stags are more successful.

For today, though, it's all about the pheasants – and, my, there's quite the to-do!

Nancy stood staring at the mass of people gathered on the sweeping drive outside Langham Hall, chattering nineteen to the dozen as men dressed in earthy colours gathered in important little groups with guns and dogs.

'Opening Day,' Nancy had called it over tea a few weeks back, and Ted had frowned at her.

'It's not Opening Day, Nancy.'

'Isn't it?'

'No.'

Joe had stepped in.

'You're sort of right, love. That's just not the expression we use. We say, "the Open Season starts".'

'But…' She'd bit back her objections at the pedantic distinction between what were surely the same basic words, and asked, 'Why?'

'Because that's how it's always been,' Ted had said.

'Oh.'

Silence had fallen and Joe had rushed to fill it.

'Up in grouse country they start much earlier, on the "glorious twelfth" of August.'

'That sounds good,' Nancy had said.

'That sounds duzzy,' Ted had corrected her gruffly. 'They're so full of themselves, grousers. So showy.'

Nancy had hidden a smile.

'We don't have a glorious first here, then?'

'No! We just get on with it without all the poncing about.'

Betty had safely steered that conversation into smoother waters but now they were here, on 1 October, and it seemed to Nancy that quite a bit of poncing was going on. She might even – out of Ted's hearing, obviously – call it 'showy'.

The great and the good of the area were gathered on the gracious driveway in front of Langham Hall, warming themselves in the autumn sunshine and partaking of a magnificent array of pies, pastries and cakes that Betty had put together. She seemed to be the go-to cook in the village and, although several times a waiter had brought a platter to Nancy, she'd waved them away, unable to face eating any of the delicacies after what had felt like endless days making them all. Now she'd taken refuge behind a large bush to survey the scene uninterrupted. The First of October Feast, whilst not, apparently, 'glorious', was Betty's pride and joy, and after six long years without it, she'd gone to town.

'Last time we celebrated the start of the Open Season, that Hitler had not long started up his own bloody hunt,' she'd said to Nancy over her rolling pin the previous week. 'We were at war by then, but it didn't feel like it out here in quiet old Langham. Lovely time we had. Sunny as midsummer and with some of the best shooting ever. Ted came home laden with birds. Laden. Said it was going to be a fine autumn. I can remember it so clearly. "A fine autumn," he said, and then that night Mr Churchill was on the radio telling us we had to be "defenders of civilisation and freedom". Me and Ted, we don't really understand all that grand stuff, but we knew one thing – we had to stop shooting birds and start shooting each other instead. Terrible!'

Nancy had been unable to dispute the tragedy of it all and she'd tried to throw herself into Betty's exuberant preparations for the big day, but there was only so much pastry she could roll out before her arms started to ache and she went mad with boredom. The only way

Nancy had got through those long days in the Gamekeeper's Cottage kitchen had been to daydream about her time on the gun. Ridiculous, really, to take your mind off peace and prosperity by recalling danger and fear, but at least in the face of possible death she'd felt alive. And at least Peggy, Connie and Dot had had more to talk about than whether the men would like redcurrant in the venison tarts.

Standing in the fug of pastry production, Nancy had sent herself back there – up the road to the end of the airfield in the cold and the dark and the wind. She'd relived her night-time conversations – Peggy's dirty jokes, Connie's lively stories of debutantes' antics, and Dot's reports of her never-ending adventures with men. There had been quite a few other women on the base, working in the offices and kitchens, but the four of them had been the only ones on the gun and that had bonded them tightly. Thinking back from the safety of the cottage kitchen, she'd felt again the heady mix of fear and excitement when a plane had come into view, recalled the sharp concentration of working the finder, the visceral burst of triumph at a hit, and the ongoing sense of sheer importance.

She'd been doing something vital up there – vital to the villagers gathered so carelessly here now, and vital to the whole of Britain. She'd been saving lives, not filling stomachs, and she missed it. Oh God, she missed it! She was an ungrateful, contrary cow, she knew, but that didn't make the feelings go away, and they felt strong this morning as she lurked in the bushes, watching the hunt ready to head out without her.

'Nancy! I thought I'd lost you.' Joe came flying between the foliage and wrapped his arms around her waist. 'I love that dress.'

She looked down at the soft yellow fabric sprigged with little blue flowers and smiled. Her mam had made it for her the summer before she'd signed up to the ATS, and she loved it too. It was getting a little chill for summer dresses as the leaves began to fall, but today the sun was shining and with a good cardigan she was plenty warm enough.

'Thanks, Joe.'

He spun her round to face him.

'Have you tried the venison tarts? Delicious! I love the redcurrant in them.'

Nancy gave him a stiff smile.

'Your mother will be delighted to hear that.'

'Nancy?'

'She agonised over whether to include it.'

'Right.' He looked at her more closely. 'Are you feeling quite well?'

She shrugged.

'I'm OK.'

'OK?!' He took a step back. 'What does "OK" mean?'

She blushed.

'Good, you know. All right. The GIs on the ward say it all the time, and I guess I've caught it off them.'

Joe's eyes darkened slightly. Despite his initial enthusiasm for her helping out here at Langham Hall, he wasn't really keen on her nursing the soldiers. If she was honest, she rather liked his jealousy; it made for very enjoyable nights in their lurid pink bedroom. She'd had to give up her hopes of him using protection, instead trying to avoid what Merry had told her were the 'problem days' and keeping her fingers crossed.

'The Yanks really don't know how to talk properly, do they?' he said now.

Nancy laughed.

'Maybe not, but they certainly know how to fight.' Joe's brow darkened further. Everyone knew they'd needed the US troops to win the war, but it still rankled and, feeling suddenly mean, Nancy reached for his hand. 'Apparently the last men might be going next week. There's a ship at Liverpool can take them home.'

'All of them?'

'So Merry says.'

Joe's eyes lit up but he controlled himself impressively.

'That'll be nice for them.'

'Yes.'

'Will they not need you up here any more, then?'

'I guess not.'

Nancy looked up at the Hall and along to the windows of the west wing, where the once beautiful ballroom had been turned into a hospital. She'd been coming up twice a week, sometimes more, to help out. The work wasn't much more exciting than at the Gamekeeper's Cottage, but the company had at least been livelier. Mind you, there'd been one hairy moment with a long-term convalescent.

'Don't I recognise you?' he'd asked Nancy, grabbing her arm when she'd been checking his blood pressure one day.

'I don't think so.'

'I do. I remember all the pretty ones. You were here when I first came in, when that top-secret chap was holed up in the far room. In and out of there, you were.'

'They had to have military to tend him,' she'd said stiffly. 'For safety.'

'Right. Important, was he?'

'I've no idea. I was nursing him, soldier, not talking politics.'

He'd grunted but the topic had, thankfully, been dropped. She'd kept a careful eye on him for a few days all the same. The last thing she needed was him blabbering to the others, but he'd seemed to keep himself to himself, and she'd relaxed again and got on with the job. Most of the soldiers were well enough to joke about with, and Merry was great fun and very frank.

'I'm not the son Daddy thought would be running the old place but, fair play to him, he's making the most of it. I'm permanently worn out, learning everything he spent the last twenty years drumming into James at super-quick speed, but we're getting there. He'd be happier, I think, if I found myself a husband, but how am I meant to do that while I'm up to my eyes in bookkeeping and estate management? Mummy suggested they send me off to London with a suitcase full of pretty dresses to bag myself a second son who'd be delighted to take this place on but, all credit to Daddy, he says Langham's in the blood and will be better cared for by me – girl though I am – than some stranger.'

'God, you're lucky,' Nancy had told her. 'Ted doesn't believe women are up to anything more than cooking, cleaning and making babies. I honestly don't know how he thinks I managed a bloody great big gun.'

'Blocked it out, no doubt. Doesn't want to know so doesn't even try.'

'I guess. It's just so frustrating, Merry. I could do so much to help them on the estate but they won't let me. They've run themselves ragged getting ready for Open Season, and all I've been allowed to help with is the bleeding pastries.'

'Give it time,' Merry had suggested, and that's what Joe always said too, but Nancy wasn't convinced. All time was doing was grinding them safely into their preconceived little ruts. Soon they'd be so deep, there'd be no getting out at all.

'If I'm free from nursing,' she said to Joe now, looking up at him through her eyelashes, 'perhaps we can start my training on the estate?'

'Perhaps,' he agreed, but with no conviction. 'More importantly, we should talk to these Yanks about getting you a dress like that one Merry wore to the fete. Will you introduce me?'

Nancy sighed, then nodded and led him back out into the chattering crowds and towards Chuck and Marvin, her two favourite GIs. Joe's steps faltered a little as they approached, but Nancy tugged him firmly forward.

'Boys, this is Joe, my husband. Joe, this is Chuck.'

'Hey, Joe! You're a lucky guy, you know, having this amazing little gal all your own.'

'I know I am,' Joe agreed, squeezing Nancy's waist as he shook Chuck's hand. 'Thanks, Chuck.'

'And this is Marvin,' Nancy said, turning him to the second of the soldiers.

Marvin stuck out a hand, and Nancy saw Joe's fingers flinch only the tiniest bit before he clasped the dark skin in his own.

'Nice to meet you, Marvin. I hear you boys might be heading home soon?'

'Yes, siree. Can't wait. Everyone's been so kind to us here but there's no place like home, is there?'

'Not at all,' Joe agreed heartily. 'I was born and bred right here in Langham, and I dreamed of this place every single day I was away at sea.'

'It's pretty,' Marvin said, 'with the fields and trees, and those great big antlered deer of yours, not to mention the handsome orangey birds y'all are about to go shoot. And it's quiet. Very quiet.'

Joe laughed. 'Too quiet?'

'Sometimes. I want to get back to New York and take my girl dancing all damned night long.'

Joe drew Nancy closer.

'I bet you do,' he said softly. 'There's no greater joy than holding your girl in your arms.'

The two men shared a look of deep understanding, and for a moment Nancy had to blink and look around her at the soft Norfolk countryside that had not, until so recently, seen anything more exotic than a pheasant, yet was now host to a dark-skinned American – a dark-skinned American who felt exactly the same as their own pale soldiers. If that divide could be bridged, then why not the one between men and women as well?

Suddenly a horn sounded out, low and clear, and everyone spun round to look up at Lord Langham, standing at the top of the steps. A tweed-clad Meredith was at his right shoulder and a proud Ted at his left.

'A toast!' he cried. 'To peace, prosperity and pheasant hunting!'

The cry was taken up loudly by all, and now Ted headed down to join the men with the gundogs as those who were off on the hunt began to muster.

'I'd better go to Pa,' Joe said, giving Nancy a quick kiss. 'See you later, sweetheart. Chuck, Marvin, are you hunting?'

'Not me,' Chuck said, indicating his heavily bandaged arm, but Marvin nodded.

'Thought I'd give it a go. Beats shooting Boche, hey?'

'Come on then. This way.'

Nancy watched Joe lead the big, black soldier towards his father and didn't know whether to feel proud or jealous. She watched Joe introduce Marvin and saw Ted, like Joe before him, hesitate but then welcome him in. In the gruff gamekeeper's world, it seemed that men were men whatever their colour, and as she watched Ted find Marvin a gun and explain the finer parts of its mechanism, she had to swallow back an unpleasant bile in her throat. She longed to be included.

The big group had more or less separated out now into murky-clad hunters and floral wives. Pastries and wine goblets were discarded all over the place and the dogs were straining at their leashes, keen to be off. Lord Langham came down the steps to join them.

'Are we all set, gents?' he asked in a booming voice, but then Merry nudged him in the ribs and he hastily added, 'And ladies?'

Nancy stared as Merry lifted a gun and nodded approvingly.

'Ready, Father.'

Nancy looked to Joe, but he was studiously avoiding her eye. Fury rose up inside her. Merry was going on the hunt? Merry, who was every bit as much a woman as she was? Merry, who'd spent the war driving supplies around whilst she'd fired guns? That wasn't fair. She'd specifically asked Ted if she could go along weeks ago and he'd just told her, 'No women on the shoot.' He'd added a grudging, 'It's not safe,' and tried to pat her hand, but she'd pulled away.

'It wasn't safe for me to fire at German planes, Ted, but I did it. I did it well.'

'And now you don't have to, dear.'

'But I want to.'

He'd looked at her curiously.

'Why?'

It had been all she could do not to scream.

'Why do *you* want to?'

There'd been an awkward pause and then he'd stiffly offered: 'Tradition.'

'Tradition?! Fair enough, but it's also because you love it, isn't it? Because it takes skill and nerve? Because it's thrilling and exhilarating and satisfying?'

'Well, yes,' he'd conceded. 'But that's because I'm a man.'

She *had* screamed then. Not until she'd fled the house and stumbled, half blind with fury, into the woods, but she had screamed. It had felt good but had achieved nothing. Betty had had a nervous word with her the next day about how 'it really isn't fun out there in the cold with the nasty, dirty guns', and Ted had simply never mentioned it again. It had been clear it was non-negotiable, so Nancy had buckled down and made the pastries and put on her pretty dress and gone to see them all off like a good girl. And now this.

She marched up to her friend.

'You're going on the hunt, Merry?'

All eyes turned her way. She sensed Joe sidling round to her and that only made her angrier. All he'd want was to shut her up, to hustle her away before she could, God forbid, make waves in his precious village. Where had the brave, bold, exciting Joe she'd fallen in love with gone? How could a man who'd leaped from a sinking ship into churning waters, brow bleeding and ears ringing with the cries of dying friends, not be capable of standing up to his own father? He'd hated the war, she knew – they all had – but he couldn't just act as if it had never happened. He'd been in awe of her bravery, he'd told her, when they were courting in the snatched moments between both their duties. He'd loved her 'spark', been excited by her 'free spirit', so how come he was now doing his very best to stamp it all out?

'I'm hunting, yes,' Merry agreed easily.

'That's good. Can I come?'

Merry shrugged.

'Of course you can.'

'Now, Merry,' Lord Langham said, 'let's be sensible. Nancy is hardly dressed for shooting. The birds would see her from a mile off.'

He attempted a little laugh but it rang hollowly around the terse group of hunters. Nancy looked down at her favourite dress and hated it suddenly.

'I can change.'

'Into what?' Joe asked at her side.

She rounded on him.

'Perhaps into the "country clothes" you promised me, Joe?'

He shrank back, looking nervously around.

'There hasn't been time to make them, Nance.'

'No? Seems to me there's been plenty of time.' She waved to the piles of food still stacked high on the trestle tables. 'I could have made half the pastries and had ample time to run something up. It wasn't time that was the problem, was it?'

'Nancy, please.'

Joe looked pained and she hated it, but for too long she'd given in to that little 'please'. For too long she'd let him fob her off. She looked to Ted.

'You said there were no women on the shoot, Ted. That's what you, the gamekeeper himself, said.'

Ted shifted his feet, his face scarlet. The men around were looking down as if to spare him the humiliation of a nagging woman. It was pathetic. She stood before him, hands on hips, waiting for an answer.

'Meredith is different,' Ted mumbled eventually.

'Because?'

'Nancy, please!' Joe's voice was urgent, but she didn't care any more.

'Because what?' she demanded.

'Because she's aristocracy,' Ted said, lifting his head up defiantly so that his voice rang out, suddenly loud.

'Because she's aristocracy,' Nancy repeated slowly. She looked around the crowd of men, desperate to get off to their sport, and across to the women, ready to wave them off and clear up in their wake. This wasn't what she'd fought for. This wasn't the life she'd been promised or the new beginning she wanted. She stuck her head up high and faced them all. 'I see,' she said clearly. 'I see now – having a title is the only thing that could possibly make up for not having a cock.'

And then, to a shocked gasp from the crowd and a bark of a laugh from Meredith, she fled, off down the hill to the Gamekeeper's Cottage, to lock herself in the annex and pour her heaving heart out into her diary.

Monday, 1 October 1945

I've really done it now! Joe is going to hate me. He's going to wish he'd never married me and almost certainly ask me for a divorce. Mam will die of shame if I have to go crawling back to her a cast-out woman. Yet why should it be like that? Why should I be punished for standing up for what I want in life? What I was promised in life. 'You'll help out on the estate, Nancy,' that's what Joe told me. 'You'll be brilliant at it,' he said. 'With your bravery and your skill and your energy, you'll be just what we need to take the estate forward.' Well, where's all that gone, hey? So who's the shamed one? Him, that's who. Not that anyone will see it that way.

What do I do? No one's come after me. Betty will be mopping up pastries and crying to her floral friends about how ungrateful I am. Ted will be striding out at the head of the hunt, all tight-jawed and hoping that if he ignores me, I'll go away. And Joe? Joe's clearly made his choice, gone with his pa and his precious hunt. I'm not the woman he wanted. I excited him when we were at war, at risk of our lives, but now that all is stable – horribly, horribly stable – it turns out excitement is the last thing my husband wants.

It might be best if I go now. Just pack my bag, leave my wedding ring on the side, and sneak out to the train station. I'll be gone by the time they get home and they can all get on as if the war never happened, as if I never happened. Yes, it might well be best if I go now, and if my heart breaks, well, it will mend. In time, I hope, it will mend...

Chapter Eleven

'A green one, Stan. Are you sure? Only, the whole rest of this wall is red and… fine.'

Lorna sat back as Stanley carefully slotted his green Lego brick into her nicely uniform red wall and tried not to let it bother her. Matt would have laughed at her 'OCD' and suggested that Stan throw a pink one in too, to really wind her up. Later though, when the kids had gone to bed, he would have put the house on the floor and said, 'Go on then, break it up – you know you want to!' then handed her the red bricks to rebuild it the way she liked it. He'd always teased her – and she him – but in a loving way. She missed that so much.

'Mum! Window! You said you'd do the window.'

'Right, yes. Of course.'

She delved into the box for the right-sized window, loving the cheery rattle of the little bricks against her fingers. It reminded her of her own childhood, which was hardly surprising as it was her original set they were playing with. She'd been obsessed with Lego for years and had topped up her collection at every birthday and Christmas. With only her mum and her maternal grandparents to buy for her, however, it had been slow going until her mum had come rushing home from a jumble sale in the village with a big box she'd picked up 'for an absolute bargain'.

That had been a happy day indeed, and Lorna looked fondly across to Mary as she worked on a tricky Jeep with Charlie. Actually, Charlie had moved on to a structure of his own while Mary was still focused on fixing the wheels to the vehicle. Lorna smiled.

'That's looking good, Mum.'

'Yes, Charlie and I… Oh. What are you building, Charlie?'

'A gun battery,' Charlie said promptly.

Lorna jumped.

'Really?' She'd been showing him pictures of the gunner girls on the internet last night, but she hadn't realised he'd taken it in. A gun battery was tricky to construct with Lego, but he was giving it a damn good go. 'What's that bit?'

'That's the range finder, of course, and this is the predictor, and this is going to be a store for the shells.'

'You listened well last night.'

He shrugged.

'It's interesting. I'd have liked to be a gunner girl, I reckon. Well, not a girl, of course. I don't want to be a girl.'

'God forbid,' Lorna said drily.

'But I'd like to have manned the guns. In Germany boys did it.'

'Really? How do you know that?'

'I read the article you showed me.'

Lorna blinked at her son, amazed. She'd only searched the images for him but clearly he'd gone deeper. Perhaps she'd bred a little historian after all?

'What did it tell you?'

'About how many people it took to fire the gun, and about how they calculated where to shoot – like Richard showed us in the dome. It said that women had to do it in this country because all the men had gone to fight, but in Germany they had the… the Hitler Youth?'

'That's right,' Lorna said. 'Did they not have women in their forces then?'

'Not really. Hitler didn't like it. He thought women should be cooking.'

'Not the worst thing Hitler thought, admittedly, but pretty rubbish all the same.'

'Yes,' Stan put in solemnly, 'Daddy was a far better cook than you.'

'What?!' Lorna looked at him indignantly. 'When did Daddy cook?'

'Daddy did barbecues. Barbecues are the best cooking.'

Lorna rolled her eyes at her mum.

'Matt did barbecues about ten times a year, tops.'

Her mum laughed.

'I remember the ones I was lucky enough to share though, and they were very good.'

'They were,' Stan agreed earnestly.

They all laughed, and suddenly Lorna realised that for the first time they were talking about Matt naturally. It was both a relief and a sadness. She thought of what David had said to her on her first day here, about feeling as if moving on was a betrayal. 'If it had been you,' he'd asked her, 'how would you have wanted Matt to be?' And, of course, she'd have wanted him to be happy – the thought of him in pain was horrible – so perhaps she had to embrace this and honour him with the good memories.

'They were, Stan,' she said, 'but maybe Mummy can barbecue too.'

Stan looked sideways at her.

'I'm not sure about that. Daddy said you were too easily disfractured.'

'Distracted,' Lorna corrected him, laughing again. That was so true. If she'd ever been put in charge of the meat, she'd do a good job at first then spot someone to talk to or a game to play, and think, *It'll be all right for a bit.* Ten minutes later there'd be a cry of despair from Matt, and she'd turn to see ominous smoke rising off the coals. 'I would do my very best not to be, Stan, I promise.'

'I'm a dab hand with a barbecue,' Mary put in. 'I don't get distracted as long as I have a G&T with me. Tell you what, how about we give it a go tonight?'

'Yes please, Granny!'

'I'll go and see if we've got coals. Charlie, can you finish my Jeep?'

'Course I can. I can't do any more on my gun battery anyway, because we don't have any guns.'

'We do actually,' Lorna said, digging around and turning up a hand-held gun from a soldier set that had come in the jumble-sale box.

'It's a bit small,' Charlie said, but he took it anyway and set about mounting it onto his battery.

Lorna went back to helping Stan with his house as Mary headed out to find the barbecue, and a contented peace fell. Lorna soaked it in gratefully. She'd taken Charlie's advice and the evening of the volunteer day, she'd wandered down the garden, ostensibly to admire David's vegetables but actually to consult with the worms. Her son had been right – they'd been very good listeners.

She'd told them what she'd not dared to admit to anyone else – that she was sad, yes, but also eaten up with anger that this had happened. 'Why us?' Charlie had wailed, and she'd asked the same of the worms. They hadn't answered (of course, she wasn't going mad yet), but just saying it out loud had taken some of the sting out of her jumbled feelings and therefore removed some of the 'grumpiness'. Knowing they were there if she needed to get things off her chest again also helped. Her mum was pretty smart. Thank heavens she'd had the sense to come to her for the summer. Or, rather, Aki had had the sense to send her.

She glanced up at the calendar as she and Stan began the roof work on their Lego house. Time had lost all meaning in the quiet peace of Langham, but term must be finished now so Aki would be free. Perhaps she could suggest that she came and stayed for a few days? Though, now she thought about it, David had mentioned his daughter might be flying in. She looked up as he came into the living room.

'Did you say Tilly was coming to visit, David?'

'Maybe. Some time. You can never tell with Tilly until she actually turns up. Why?'

'I was wondering if I might, maybe, invite my friend Aki over for a few days? She could sleep in with me and—'

'Of course you can, Lorna,' David interrupted her. 'I want you to think of this as your home.'

She flushed.

'You're very kind, David.'

'Not at all. I like having you around. I miss youngsters in the place and I know your mum loves it.'

'Even so, thank you.'

'No problem. Besides – you've got me very interested in Mum's time here after the war. I've been doing a bit of research into the cottage.'

'Found anything out on the roof?' Lorna asked, handing Stan another tile. It was so easy constructing a Lego roof, but a thatched one must have been something else altogether.

'I dug out the papers from when the work was done. It was the back end of 1946 so they must have found the money from somewhere. A lot of money it was too – a thousand pounds. A fortune back then. No more clues in the diary?'

'Just talk of some important patient up at Langham Hall. An American perhaps? I'm wondering if he had anything to do with Hank.'

'Of naked-girl-in-the-hut fame?'

'Exactly.'

'Intriguing idea. The roof was paid for by the Wilsons and Lord Langham was true to his word about gifting it to them. I found the deed signing ownership over to the family from the same period with a nice little patch of land and shares in the estate. It certainly seems the family came into some money from somewhere but I'm afraid I can't tell you anything more. Oh, but I've been on at Richard to dig out the RAF Langham records, and guess what…'

There was a twinkle in his eye and Lorna leaped up eagerly.

'What?'

'I've got the list of the ATS girls on site during the war. There were a few in the kitchens and the offices, but then there's four girls listed on the gun battery.'

'And they are?' Lorna asked eagerly.

'They are: Nancy Jones...'

'Jones?'

'Her maiden name. She didn't marry Dad until 1944.'

'Of course, sorry. Nancy Jones...'

'Margaret Bradford, Dorothy Lewis and... Constance Marshall.'

'Connie!' Lorna gave an inadvertent little skip. 'I told you there was a Connie.'

'So what happened to her?'

That stopped her skipping.

'Do you think she died?'

David frowned.

'I guess it's the most likely explanation. Does the diary not say anything?'

'No. I'm nearly at the end – sadly – and they're all still very much friends.'

'Well, we have a full name now so perhaps the internet will turn something up. I'll set about it this afternoon. Oh, and I hear we're having a barbecue later!' He aimed this at the boys who cheered obligingly. 'Who wants to come with me to buy coals then?' Only Stan took this bait. 'And maybe some new Lego?'

'New Lego?' Charlie was on his feet straight away. 'Do you think they'll have a gun, Grandpa, a proper sized one for my battery?'

'We could certainly have a look,' David agreed. 'Get your shoes on, boys.' He looked to Lorna. 'If that's OK, of course?'

'Very OK,' she smiled.

It had been a lovely morning but a little time to herself would be good. Perhaps she could read some more of the diary and see if it gave any clue about what had happened to Connie. At that moment, however, the doorbell rang out and Mary came bustling inside with a man in tow – a young, smiling, exceedingly hot man. Lorna blinked.

'Lorna, this is Kyle,' Mary said. 'He's a builder.'

She gave Lorna what looked horribly like a nod towards Kyle's – to be fair, considerable – muscles as he stepped forward to shake her hand. Lorna frowned at her.

'Nice to meet you, Kyle.'

'You too. Mary tells me you're living in the annex.'

'Er, yes.'

'Great little place, isn't it? I've done a few jobs on it over the years to keep it intact. Fantastic excuse to meet the film crews.'

'Film crews?' Charlie asked.

Kyle turned and, as soon as he saw him, bent down to his level and stuck out his hand.

'Hi there. I'm Kyle, and you are?'

'Charlie,' Charlie supplied, shaking the hand without hesitation. 'Did you say film crews?'

'Oh, yes, David here has had all sorts filming in the annex over the years.'

'Anything good?'

Kyle gave him a conspiratorial look.

'Not properly good. Not like *Star Wars* or *Harry Potter* or anything. Historical dramas mainly.'

'Oh.' Charlie looked disappointed.

'I love a historical drama,' Lorna said.

'Oh, me too,' Kyle agreed, deadpanning Charlie a wink.

Charlie laughed and Lorna shook her head, amused despite herself. Kyle was a natural with kids. But why was he here? She looked to David.

'Have you got another film crew wanting the annex? Do you need us to move out? Because we can, of course, if—'

'No, no, no,' David assured her. 'Nothing like that. Quite the opposite in fact. Your mum and I are thinking of renovating the place. Modernising.'

'You're going to take out the period stuff?'

'We're thinking about it. That Bakelite stove is dangerous so no one can cook in there, and the armchairs are falling apart.'

That much was true. Lorna had nearly gone through the seat when she'd sat down the other morning. Even so…

'It seems rather sad, to wipe out all that history.'

'It's the wallpaper, isn't it?' Kyle laughed. 'You don't want to lose that amazing pink wallpaper.'

Lorna shook her head.

'OK, so perhaps I could lose that, and perhaps a modern kitchen would be more practical, but it still seems a shame.'

'We have to move forward, darling,' Mary said.

Lorna sucked in her breath.

'I guess so,' she agreed tightly.

'And we can keep some key bits – the fireplace, the wireless.'

'The wireless doesn't work.'

Mary gave a little shrug.

'Well, there you go then. So – will you show Kyle through to the annex?'

Lorna stared, wondering why this had become her job.

'Me?'

'If you don't mind. I've got to go with David to get the barbecue stuff.'

'Now?'

'If that's OK?'

She could hardly say no without looking like an idiot, but as she watched Mary shepherding the others off, leaving her to take the hot builder through to the annex, she cursed her mother. This was not fair, not right. She'd thought her mum had loved Matt, but he'd only been gone two months and already she was setting her up with someone else.

'I'm guessing you know the way,' she said tightly to Kyle.

'Sure do,' he agreed. 'I can just get on with it if you're busy.'

He smiled easily at her and she felt instantly churlish.

'No, it's fine. Looks like I'm not busy at all.'

She nodded to the front door, where Mary was pushing shoes onto the boys' feet with unseemly haste.

'Must be good to have a break?'

'I guess, yes. Here we are.'

She showed Kyle into the annex, wishing her mum had warned her so she could have tidied up. The boys' pyjamas were flung in the general vicinity of the unmade bunk beds, with Stan's miniature Superman top hanging off the funny dark painting over the mantelpiece. She suspected her own bedroom was in a similar state and was glad the door had swung closed.

'Did Mum tell you what she wanted before she rushed off?'

'She's given me a very comprehensive list, yes.'

Lorna smiled.

'That would be right. She loves a list, does Mum. To be fair, I do too.'

'Can't beat a list!' Kyle said, waving a piece of paper with Mary's distinctive looping handwriting on it. 'I'll get measuring up then.'

'Great. I'll just, er…'

She waved vaguely towards the bedroom and made a dive for it as Kyle bent to take a tape measure out of his bag. She couldn't resist pausing, however, to watch as his T-shirt came untucked from his shorts, revealing a beautifully muscled back. She might be cross with her mum for shoving this man at her, but Aki would love him! She took her phone out of her pocket to take a surreptitious snap, then dived into the bedroom to send it to her mate with the message: *North Norfolk not as dull as you might think.*

Aki came straight back.

Wow! What are you up to, you lucky girl?!

Lorna's insides curled.

Nothing. I couldn't. Just thought you'd like the view.

Of course. Sorry. I didn't mean anything. Lorna could almost hear the panic in her friend's tone and started to type out a reply assuring her it was OK, but then Aki added, *I do like the view, btw.* Lorna smiled.

Why don't you come and see it for yourself?

When?

Whenever you want. Mum and David are happy for you to stay and I'd like to see you.

Great. I'll see if I can fit you into my schedule of hot men waiting to take me to tropical islands. Oh wait…

Lorna laughed.

Hot man here…

Why exactly?

He's a builder. That's all I know. Think Mum's trying to set me up with him.

Bit too soon?

LOT too soon. I'll kill her later.

'Erm, Lorna? Can I come in?'

'Course,' she called, realising too late that she'd spent all her time texting Aki and none of it tidying up.

Got to go, Aki. Hot man coming into bedroom...

Don't leave me this way!

She laughed and stuffed her old nightie hastily under her pillow as Kyle came in.

'What do they want to change in here?' she asked him.

'Apart from the wallpaper?'

'Obviously – though I admit I've got rather fond of it.'

'It's pretty cool, in a kitsch sort of a way. Dazzling though. Glad I don't have to sleep in here.'

'Yes, well, you don't, do you.' She sounded ridiculously starchy even to herself.

'Sorry,' Kyle said easily. 'That came out wrong. I just meant the wallpaper.'

'I know.'

God, this was excruciating. Would she have to do this – to date again? Not now, obviously, but at some point. She wasn't sure she could bear all the flirting and the waxing and the nerves. It had been hard enough in her twenties, but now... Not to mention, of course, the fact that she would never, ever, ever find anyone she loved as much as Matt ever again. Tears threatened and she stumbled out of the bedroom, muttering something to Kyle about leaving him to it.

Her eyes were misted, and she felt dizzy and short of breath. The smell of chlorine seemed to fill the air and, fumbling for the arm of the nearest chair, she sank into it – and fell straight through. Pain sliced up her back and the sheer shock of it sent the tears spilling out.

'Lorna! Oh God, poor you.' Kyle's voice was kind and his arms strong as he lifted her gently out of the wreckage of the art deco armchair.

'It's not the chair,' she gasped, sucking in oxygen, feeling as if the air didn't have enough of it.

'Here.' He tested the other chair with his hand and lowered her gently down. 'Lean back to open up your airways. Slow, deep breaths. That's good. That's better. Does it feel better?'

Her breathing did, yes, but the sadness was still spiralling relentlessly inside her.

'I don't want to date,' she burst out.

'What?'

'Sorry. I don't mean you. That is, I don't want to date you—'

'Which is a good job as—'

'I just don't want to date at all. *Ever.* I just want Matt back.' The oxygen was going again and the dizziness was returning. She thought she might be sick and pushed herself up to make for the loo, but her legs felt wobbly and her vision was swimming. 'Oh God, what's happening to me? I can't die. I can't die too. The boys. They need me.'

'Lorna – shhh. It's OK. May I?' Kyle held out his arms and she stumbled blindly into them. They closed around her, warm and sure, and he patted her back as her mum might. 'There, there. It's OK. Relax, breathe, take your time.'

'I'm sorry, I—'

'Don't apologise. It's my fault. I intruded. But none of that matters. Let's focus on you. Breathe, Lorna – in through your nose and out through your mouth. That's it, that's good.'

His voice was so soft and assured that she did as he instructed. Slowly her heart rate seemed to steady and the room came back into focus. Once she could trust herself, she stepped back.

'I'm OK now. Thanks, Kyle. I really am sorry. I've no idea what came over me.'

'Panic attack. Perfectly normal, especially after all you've been though.'

'Mum told you?'

That didn't surprise her. Mary had never really worried about privacy. It had been excruciating when Lorna was a teen and had to put up with her discussing her piles in the supermarket queue or the quality of M&S knickers in the ladies' or, on one particularly awful day, the problems of period pains with Lorna's new boyfriend. Or, as he'd very rapidly become, ex-boyfriend.

'Do you mind?'

'What's to hide? My husband died. End of.'

'Except it's not really, is it – it's the start of all sorts of pain and heartache. I've been there. Well, not a husband, but you know… Anyway, it was horrible. Took me two years to start dating again. There's no rush, you know, and you don't have to do it if you don't want to. Not ever.'

Lorna looked at him. He was really ridiculously handsome. And very kind too.

'But then I'd have to be alone for the rest of my life.'

'Bummer, isn't it?'

It was such a mad understatement that Lorna couldn't help laughing.

'Bummer,' she agreed. 'You know what, Kyle, you're almost as good as the worms.'

'The what?'

'Doesn't matter. Now, look, can I help you measure up? Then you can tell me Mum's plans for this lovely place, as I have to admit that the idea of modernising all the history out of it seems rather sad to me.'

'You sure?' Kyle asked, with a pointed look at the broken armchair.

Lorna rubbed her back.

'Well, maybe not all of it. Now – give me the end of that tape measure.'

Kyle had been gone for some time when Mary, David and the boys finally came back.

'How long does it take to buy a few burgers?' Lorna asked.

'Oh, the boys were peckish and the supermarket café does a marvellous lunch deal, so we couldn't resist grabbing a bite to eat. We thought you'd be glad of the peace.'

Lorna frowned at her mother.

'That's not what you thought though, was it, Mum?'

'What?'

'Leaving me alone with the hot builder.'

'Hang on a minute, Lorna…'

'What did you expect? That I'd jump him on the pink eider-down?'

'Lorna! I expected nothing of the sort.'

'It's been two months, Mum. Just two months. I'm not ready for a new man.'

'I know that. Lorna, shhh, please. That wasn't what I meant at all.'

'So why rush out?'

'I had my shopping head on, that's all. I'd forgotten I'd asked Kyle over.'

'Yeah, right! It's not on, Mum. I don't want to be fixed up with anyone.'

'Lorna—' David started, but she was too cross to listen.

'And I certainly don't want to be fixed up with some calendar-boy builder.'

'Which is a good job,' Mary shot back at her.

'Are you saying I'm not good enough for him?'

'I'm saying, idiot daughter, that he's gay.'

That stopped Lorna in her tracks.

'Gay?' she stuttered.

'Did you not guess?'

'Erm…' Lorna felt herself flush.

'Did the gym-perfect muscles and the immaculate hair and the totally comfortable way he was around you and the boys not give it away?'

'Mum! That's gross stereotyping.'

'True, sorry, but the fact still remains that Kyle—'

'Is gay!' Lorna clapped a hand to her forehead. 'I feel a right idiot now.'

'That's because you *are* a right idiot,' Mary agreed cheerfully. 'But don't worry about it. Here – we brought you a nice sausage roll.'

Lorna took the snack, still feeling rather bemused.

'You looked so pleased with yourself when you showed him in,' she said to Mary.

'Did I, darling? Perhaps because he's pretty hard to get hold of. He's very popular around these parts and, let's face it, he *is* very easy on the eye.'

'He is,' Lorna agreed, letting her mum off the hook.

There was still something suspicious about this, but if she knew her mother, it would be very hard to winkle out what she was up to. She'd just have to keep an eye on her and hope for the best. In the meantime, Kyle had at least helped her to get through a difficult moment, and for that she could only be grateful.

Chapter Twelve

That's it. I'm going. Sorry, diary. I know I should be writing down my exciting adventures as a married woman, but it turns out I'm awful at being married. I'm awful at compromising and I'm awful at putting my husband first. I don't even see why I should, that's how awful I am at it. So, I'm off. Now. Well, as soon as I can stop crying...

Nancy made for the bus stop, head down and hat pulled low over her brow to hide her tear-stained face from curious onlookers. There were bound to be a few. Many of the villagers had been up at the Hall, enjoying the spectacle of the hunt heading out, so they'd all have heard her outburst. Tongues would be wagging about how coarse she was, how forward, how little she understood country ways, and how terribly she'd treated poor Ted and Betty. And she supposed she had, if you looked at it through their eyes, but they hadn't tried to look through hers once.

On several occasions, Betty had invited her to tell her about life during the war, but every time she'd started, her mother-in-law had shut her down with exclamations about how awful it all sounded and what a relief that it was over. She'd closed her ears to Nancy's descriptions of the skills needed to accurately locate the enemy planes, or how much she'd enjoyed the rigours of the physical training, or even the camaraderie between the girls.

It was odd because, as it turned out, others had done war work around here. She'd found out that a number of local women had made the daily trip into Norwich to manufacture vital aircraft components at the Boulton and Paul factory, so although she was perhaps the only 'soldier wife', she wasn't the only one who'd done her bit. Still, though, Betty didn't want to hear.

'It's not natural, is it, girls with guns,' she'd said once and, fed up, Nancy had challenged her.

'If someone had threatened Joe when he was little, would you have shot them?'

'Oh, yes!' Betty had said, straight from the heart, but then she'd thought about it and added, 'But I'd have called Ted first, obviously.'

'Why obviously?' Nancy had demanded, though she'd known the answer before Betty had spoken it.

'Because he's a man.'

Every time she tried to talk to her parents-in-law, she hit these brick walls of belief: men do this and women do that. They understood, just about, that both were capable of each other's roles if they had to be, but to them it wasn't 'right'. The war had tipped the world off its axis, and for Ted and Betty, and many like them, the best possible thing they could do now was to nudge it back into exactly the same place it had been before. They couldn't see that there might be another way; a better way.

And Joe? Even hearing his dear name inside her head sent shards of pain all across Nancy's body, as if she'd been grenaded. She'd not known him long but she'd known him deeply. Or she'd thought she had. They'd met in such extreme circumstances that they'd both felt that if it was right in this madness, it would be right anywhere. It seemed, however, that the most dangerous thing for them had been stability. Had the whole relationship been an illusion, a cheap thrill with no real substance to hold it together when, ironically, the going got less tough?

They'd rejoiced in how similar they were, but in truth they couldn't be more different. Nancy couldn't stay here to be stifled and crushed into a role she hated. It would only end in bitterness and she couldn't bear that. Joe would be better off without her. There were several lovely village girls who'd be only too glad to cook his meals, and wave him off to hunt, and turn his damned mangle for him. Ending their marriage would hurt. It would hurt a lot. But better a quick, clean death than a slow, grinding one; her work up at the hospital had taught her that.

Sobbing again, Nancy pulled her scarf up so that only her red eyes were showing. It was far too hot for such a get-up and she'd be fooling no one about her identity around here, but she needed the protection all the same. She reached the bus stop on the green and scanned the board. She could go to Dot. Dot would be there for her. Or Connie. Perhaps there would be a space in this house she was sharing with the other trainee teachers? Nancy's heart twisted at the thought of going back to single life, but there was nothing else for it.

There was a bus to Norwich due but, unsurprisingly, not for twenty minutes and she couldn't stand here all that time, exposed to everyone. She could already see Mrs Runcie coming to the doorway of the shop to eye her up. Word would be flying around the village in moments. Look, there were Miss Snales and Miss Richardson pausing to chat with the grocer, looking in her direction. She turned away and the Blue Bell caught her eye, sitting white and innocent-looking in the autumn sunshine. Only she knew it wasn't so innocent.

Nancy shivered. The memorial donation box was sitting on the window sill, amongst the well-tended flowers, prissily arranged to show the villagers' honour for the dead. Or, rather, for *their own* dead. No, she'd never fit into this village. She'd been mad to think she would with what she knew of the locals. They were too old-fashioned, too set in their dark little ways. She had to get out of here.

Pulling her suitcase against her like a shield, Nancy spun on her heel and made off down the Norwich road. She'd wait at a stop further up, outside Langham. It might be cheaper from there anyway, which would be as well since she only had a half-crown coin to her name and no idea if that would be enough to get her anywhere near Chester. When she'd tentatively asked Joe about money after her trip to Norwich with the girls, he'd told her not to worry, everything she needed would be provided. He presumably hadn't expected her to need an escape plan.

Tears blurring her eyes again, she marched off out of Langham, not daring to look either side to wish goodbye to the little village that had so briefly been her home. The leaves were starting to turn but she'd never see autumn here now, let alone winter. The duck pond froze, or so Merry had told her, and everyone went out and skated beneath the stars. On Christmas Eve they decorated the old oak with bunting and sang carols around it, warmed by the pub's mulled wine, before processing to Midnight Mass. She'd been so looking forward to being a part of it, and now she'd be seeing Christmas in down a grubby back street of Chester once more. Not that she didn't love home, or at least the dear people there, but she'd been ready for something new, something of her own.

But Langham wasn't her own, was it? Langham was—

'Nancy!' She froze, then scuttled forward again, head down and suitcase banging against her legs as she rushed to get out of the village. She couldn't face him. Not now. 'Nancy, wait! Please.' The voice pierced her fragile heart and she almost looked back, but she couldn't. She'd made up her mind to go and she had to see it through. 'Nancy, don't go!'

Now she did look back, in time to see the bus cresting the rise on the far side of Langham. The next bus stop was still a few minutes' walk away. She broke into a run. Out of the corner of her eye she saw Joe haring down the field from the woods, waving his arms frantically at her. She turned her head away.

She was almost at the stop now; she'd forgotten how fast she could run since the army had drilled her to fitness. She looked to the village, desperate for the old coach to reach her, but it had stopped at the green and Miss Snales and Miss Richardson were slowly climbing on. Nancy willed them to hurry up. Not that Joe could stop her if she wanted to leave. And she did, she really did, but seeing her husband before her, she might weaken. She might lose her nerve. If, of course, he even wanted her to stay.

'Come on, bus,' she said under her breath.

The doors were closing and it was moving again, heading towards her. One more minute and…

'Nancy, I love you!' Her whole body juddered and her red eyes turned magnetically towards Joe. 'I love you, Nancy!' He was shouting so loud that all of Langham would surely hear him. Mrs Runcie was watching intently but he didn't seem to care. 'I love you and I want to be with you, whatever it takes.'

The bus wheezed up and pulled to a stop. The door cranked open and the driver looked at Nancy.

'Where to, miss?'

She opened her mouth to tell him but nothing came out.

'Nancy! You can't go, not without taking me with you.'

Joe bowled onto the road and stood there, arms and legs wide apart in a big, gangly cross. The driver looked at him and then back to Nancy.

'Joe! What on earth are you doing?' she asked.

'Seems he's keen for you to stay, miss,' the driver said helpfully.

'Course he is,' someone said from inside the bus, and Nancy saw Miss Snales beaming at her. 'It's not every girl can say "cock" to Langham!'

At her side Miss Richardson gleefully chorused 'cock', and the others on the bus tittered and pushed forward to see Nancy.

'Good effort, I reckon,' one woman with a baby on her lap said. 'I didn't lollop out to that bloomin' factory in Norwich every day of this war just to come home and wash pants. He washed his own fine whilst he was poncing around in North Africa taking pot-shots at Italians, so he can damn well carry on back home.'

Nancy stared at the woman incredulously. It seemed that, even in Langham, she wasn't the only one facing challenges at home.

'Nancy!' Joe cried a little weakly, and she looked back to see his raised arms wobbling unhappily.

'Joe?'

'What's it to be, miss?' the driver asked, looking at his watch.

'Give him a chance,' Miss Snales suggested.

'Just one more, mind,' Miss Richardson added.

'One more's all I need,' Joe said. 'I promise.'

It was too much. He looked so gorgeous standing there, his arms shaking and his big, brown eyes pleading with her. She gave the driver a small nod, then stepped away from the bus stop and out into the road. Joe swept her into his arms.

'Oh, Nancy! I can't believe you were about to leave. I was about to lose you. I couldn't bear to—'

The driver sounded his horn and, almost laughing, Nancy dragged her husband off the road to let the bus pass. It sailed off, Miss Snales and Miss Richardson waving merrily from the window, and suddenly they were alone.

'Cock,' Joe said, tenderly pushing the scarf off her face. 'You said cock to them all.'

'I know. I'm sorry, Joe. I don't know what—'

'Don't apologise. You looked amazing, eyes ablaze and your whole gorgeous body bristling with anger.'

'What?'

'You looked magnificent, darling. I was so proud.'

'Proud? You were trying to shut me up, Joe.'

He hung his head.

'I was and I'm sorry. I've been trying to shut you up ever since you arrived and it's been wrong of me. I was so pleased to be back, so happy everything was still as I remembered it, that I forgot it shouldn't be. It's actually all different because you're here now.'

'Not *all* different, Joe.'

'But intrinsically different. I've been so used to being Pa's right-hand man that I forgot you come first now, not him. I only stayed to make sure everything was organised with the shoot, then I was coming to find you and promise to tell him that. Now. Well, tonight.'

'Steady, Joe. It's not really his fault. It's a lot of change for him.'

'It is, but it's a good change. An extra pair of hands will help him loads, and such beautiful ones too.'

He took both her hands in his and pulled her close. Nancy felt every part of her melt against him, just as it had the first time she'd ever kissed him outside the Blue Bell. But time had moved on; it was more complicated now.

'I don't know if we can do this, Joe,' she whispered.

He took her chin in his hand and tilted her face up to him.

'We can, darling. I know we can. I want you on the estate, really I do. I just need to talk to Ma and Pa.'

He sounded so fired up, so like the bold young sailor she'd fallen in love with, but he couldn't take a torpedo to his parents' protests. This wasn't war any more.

'I'm not sure it'll do any good, Joe. They've been so kind, so welcoming, but I'm not what they expected – or what they want.'

'That's not true. You're exactly what they want, need even, they just can't see it yet, and I've been useless at telling them. Useless!'

He kicked out angrily at the bus stop post and it shook in the ground.

'Joe…'

'Well, I have. I promised you there'd be a Nancy-shaped space at the Gamekeeper's Cottage and it's my job to carve it out for you.'

'No!'

He jumped.

'No?'

Nancy softened her voice.

'No, Joe. It's *our* job. That's what this is all about; that's the whole point. We fought for our country side by side, and now we

have to fight for our future the same way. I don't want you to do
it for me, but *with* me.'

'With you. Right.' This time he hit his poor forehead to the
post. 'I'm sorry, Nancy. I'm rubbish at this.'

Her heart went out to him. Up on the hill she could hear guns
going off as Open Season truly started for the first time in six years.
He should have been there with his dad and Lord Langham and
the rest of the shoot, but instead he was here, with her.

'Not rubbish, Joe, and I'm no expert either. I don't think swear-
ing is exactly the best way to go about ingratiating myself, is it?'

Joe gave a small smile.

'Oh, I don't know. It certainly got you noticed, darling.'

'Cock,' she said softly, shaking her head at herself. 'My mam
would be horrified.'

'But it's not up to her now. Nor to my parents neither. The
future is ours, Nance, to make of it what we wish, and we're going
to claim it together.'

'Thanks, Joe. Maybe not quite in the way I tried today, though?'

'Not in public perhaps.'

She looked up and saw his eyes were dark with desire. Her body
pulsed instantly. It was weak with fear and anger and tears, and
the rush of lust was a welcome strength.

'No?' she asked archly.

'But maybe in private. In our own little annex. In our own
bedroom.'

'Our own, unbelievably pink bedroom?'

'You mean you don't like it either?'

She shook her head and then raised an eyebrow up at him.

'But I reckon I could put up with it right now.'

'Me too,' he agreed, clutching her close and crushing his mouth
against hers. 'God, me too, Nance. Let's go.'

As he tugged her at top speed back up the road down which
she had trodden so brokenly a short time ago, she felt her heart

race with desire and joy and excitement. It wouldn't be easy, she knew that now. Changing Ted's mind about the ways of the world would be like trying to shift a tank with your bare hands, but at least Joe wanted to try.

Betty was in the kitchen of the Gamekeeper's Cottage when they tumbled inside.

'Joe…?' she started. 'Nancy, I—'

But Joe put up a hand.

'Later, Ma,' he said. 'Let's talk later. For now, my wife and I need a little time alone.'

'You do? Right. Of course. I'll, er…'

But they were into the annex, door firmly closed behind them, and falling onto the lurid bed in a tangle of tears and kisses, their need for each other even fiercer today than it had ever been because now, they both knew, there was so much more to lose.

Chapter Thirteen

'Cooee! Anyone home?'

Lorna looked up from playing with the boys in a newly acquired paddling pool to see a young woman appearing down the side of the house. She had blonde hair in braids, wore a daisy-patterned dress and Doc Martens, and had a huge rucksack on her back.

'Tilly? Tilly!' David leaped up from his weeding and went bounding across the garden to sweep her into his arms. 'How on earth did you get here? Why didn't you call? I'd have picked you up.'

Tilly laughed.

'I've spent the last six months trekking around South America, Dad. I think I can handle Norfolk!'

'I don't doubt it,' he shot back, kissing her, 'but the point is that you don't have to. Besides, I suspect that the public transport system in darkest Peru beat ours in dear old Langham.'

'You're not wrong there. We had to wait ages in Norwich but it was fine. Xavier hasn't seen an English city before so he was fascinated.'

'Xavier?'

Tilly turned and waved down the side passage, magicking up a small, dark-skinned young man who scuttled to her side.

'Xavier is Brazilian,' Tilly told them.

Xavier nodded proudly.

'First trip to UK,' he said in heavily accented English.

'Then welcome. We're honoured to have you.'

'Honour is mine. Is hot.'

He gestured to the sun in some confusion. Clearly this version of English weather had not been widely reported in Brazil.

'Don't get used to it,' Lorna said. 'It isn't very often like this. That's why it's so green.'

She swept a hand around the lush lawn and flowers of David and Mary's pretty cottage garden, and Xavier nodded keenly.

'Green, yes.' He pointed to the sunflowers. 'Green and yellow. Like Brazilian flag. Very kind of you to make them for me.'

He beamed round and they all gave an obliging laugh.

'Can we throw the bags inside, Dad?' Tilly asked.

'Of course. I haven't prepared a room though. Or, er, rooms?'

'Room,' Tilly said firmly. 'And don't worry about it. We got a last-minute flight so there wasn't really time to let you know.'

'A flight from Brazil is, what, twelve hours, Till?'

'Well, yes, but you can't make calls, can you? Anyway, I wanted to surprise you.'

David hugged her.

'It's a lovely surprise, darling. Come on in.'

He led the new arrivals into the house, and Charlie and Stan, who'd been staring at them from the pool, came running to Lorna.

'Who are they, Mum?'

'Well,' Lorna said, thinking about it, 'I guess Tilly is sort of your aunty.'

'Really? Cool!'

'Isn't it?'

'And the man?'

'The man is… is Xavier. Tilly's friend. He's from Brazil.'

'Epic,' Charlie said. 'I bet he's brilliant at football.'

'I'm not sure all Brazilians play foot—'

But Xavier was back out already and heading straight for Charlie.

'Did someone say football? Bring it on! I got skills, boys. Big ball skills.'

Charlie eagerly ran to fetch a ball, and Xavier kicked off his shoes and began to demonstrate what certainly looked like some pretty good moves.

'It seems he does have big ball skills,' Lorna laughed to Mary.

'You better believe it!' Tilly said, reappearing at their side with a dirty laugh. 'And he's not bad with his hands either.'

Lorna watched as Xavier flicked the ball over Stan's head with one foot and caught it on the other side of the excited little lad with the other.

'And it looks like he might save me hours of being battered by a football,' Lorna said happily. 'Drink, Tilly?'

'Yes, please! I feel like I've been travelling forever. My poor body has no idea what time of day it is.'

'Must be cocktail hour then?'

'Must be! Lead the way.'

Lorna glanced to her mum who nodded her on.

'You're Lorna, right?' Tilly asked her, as they headed inside and opened up David's exceptionally well-stocked drinks cabinet.

'Right.'

'I was so, so sorry to hear about your husband. It must be awful for you.'

She was open and easy with her sympathy and Lorna appreciated it. Too many people tiptoed around the subject, trying to find a way of saying they were sorry without actually saying it. She was sick of bland expressions like 'passed away' and 'gone to a better place'.

'That's nice of you,' she said. 'Thank you. It has been pretty pants, but it's been good to escape here to Mum, and your dad's been so kind.'

'He knows what it's like. I do too, sort of. I was devastated when we lost Mum. I was eighteen and all over the shop. I stuck around here making a hash of my A-levels for a few months and then took off. I've barely been back, which is mean really as I love seeing Dad, but I found it too hard being here without her. Does that make sense?'

'God, yes,' Lorna agreed. 'That's partly why I came to Langham. Seeing all the places where Matt and I had been so happy was driving me mad.'

'It's like water torture, isn't it? Drip, drip, drip on your poor mind until you think you're going crazy.'

Lorna nodded – that was it exactly.

'It's great here, though. I mean, I still think about Matt all the damn time, but at least there's fresh places to see and people to meet. I need the distractions.'

'I'll drink to that,' Tilly said. 'Talking of which – what d'you fancy?'

Lorna stared at the array of spirits.

'I've no idea. Matt was the cocktail maker in our house. I'm not up to much more than a G&T.'

'Good job I am then,' Tilly said with a grin. 'Cosmopolitans?'

'Lovely!'

She watched as Tilly expertly assembled the ingredients and shook up a beautiful red cocktail. David had a set of six crystal glasses and, as Tilly took five of them down, Lorna couldn't help staring at the empty one left on the shelf – Matt's one.

'Cheers, sister!' Tilly cried, and Lorna dragged her eyes away.

'Sister?'

Tilly grimaced.

'Sorry, bit presumptuous. I'm always going crashing in like a bull in a china shop.'

'Not at all. I like bulls.'

Tilly laughed.

'Is it OK to call you that, then?'

'Of course it is. It's great. I've just never been called it before.'

'Never? God, I guess not. You're an only child, aren't you?'

'Afraid so.'

'Well, not any more. So cheers, sister!'

'Cheers… sister.'

They smiled at each other and drank. The cocktail was delicious and Lorna already had a feeling it would slip down far too easily.

'Don't worry,' Tilly said, 'we can make ourselves another before we take these out for everyone.'

'You read my mind.'

'It's my greatest talent. Well, that and cocktail making.'

'You'll be a rich woman then.'

'Hardly. Not like my high-earning brother and sister. I'm the black sheep of this particular family, I'm afraid.'

'I like black sheep nearly as much as bulls. Does it matter what you do, if you're happy?'

'Not at the moment certainly.'

'That's OK then. Xavier seems nice.'

Tilly thought about this.

'I'm not sure we've been together long enough for me to know how nice he is, but he's sexy as hell. God – the things that man can do to a girl!'

Lorna giggled and took another sip of her cocktail.

'I'm glad I'm safely in the annex tonight.'

'Oh, I couldn't do it with Dad in the room next door. I might have to sneak down to the bottom of the garden.'

'With the worms.'

'Oi! Xavier's is definitely not a worm.'

Lorna giggled, then was suddenly reminded of something.

'Matt and I used to go to the bottom of the garden when we stayed with his parents before we were married. They were a bit puritanical and didn't like us sharing a bed. Fair enough, I guess, but we didn't see it that way at the time. His dad had this shed – a proper man-shed, you know, with his tools in it, plus a kettle and a little chair. Oh, the things we did on that chair!'

She flushed at the memory, then thought of the story about Dot in the hut in the woods back in 1944. Some things never changed.

'My dad hasn't got a shed,' Tilly said, frowning. 'Just one of those plastic tool-store things. I don't reckon even Xavier would fit in there.'

'And his worm certainly wouldn't!'

They both squealed with laughter, and David came inside and looked them up and down.

'What are the pair of you talking about?'

'You don't want to know, Dad,' Tilly said, wiping her eyes. 'You really don't want to know. Cosmopolitan?'

'Lovely,' David said mildly. 'I'll, er, wait outside.'

He retreated and they burst into laughter again. Lorna felt her sides ache pleasurably and drank down the last of her cocktail to hand her glass over for a refill. It was a long time since she'd talked about the early days of her relationship with Matt and it was nice to remember. Painful, but nice. She looked again to the empty cocktail glass stuck up on the shelf, then impulsively stretched up and brought it down.

'Could you make another one, Tilly?'

'For Matt?'

She nodded shyly. 'Is that stupid?'

'Not at all. Come on, Matt – Cosmopolitans all round.' Lorna reached out and gave her a hug. 'What was that for?'

'Getting it.'

Tilly laughed.

'There's not much to "get", Lorna. You loved him, he's gone: that's really, really sad. You have to do whatever you can to deal with it. And, of course, to celebrate what you had. Now come on – let's get these out into the garden.'

She dropped a kiss onto Lorna's forehead and headed out to the garden with four glasses on a silver tray. Lorna picked up the remaining two.

'Cheers, darling,' she whispered to the bright blue sky, then, taking a sip from both drinks, she followed her exuberant new-found sister back to the others.

Chapter Fourteen

Saturday, 15 December 1945

Just over a week to Christmas and, oh, everything's so perfect. Thanks to the new arrangements, I'm getting out and about on the estate, and with the air so fresh I feel healthier than I ever have. Hungrier too – and not just for food. Joe and I have been using these dark nights as an excuse to retire earlier and earlier, but I can't say we've exactly been sleeping. Not sure how I'm not pregnant yet, but thank heavens for that! They'd all want me to stop gamekeeping if I had a bun in the oven, so it's best not, for now at least.

A few days ago the ice came in hard, and last night Joe took me skating on the duck pond. Lord, those blade things are crazy! Joe strapped them onto my boots – my new 'country' boots that are meant to be my Christmas present but that he said I could have early, just for this. He tied them up tight so I'd 'be safe', but I tell you I've never felt less safe. I was tipping around all over the place and that's before I even got on the ice.

Everyone else was SO good at it. For a bit I stood on the side and watched them whipping round the pond, laughing and calling to each other and chatting away as if it was ground beneath their feet and not this cold, slippy stuff. Merry was amazing, of course. She had actual ice-skating boots, white and shiny and beautiful, and she could skate backwards and on one foot and even do jumps. She looked stunning in a big fur coat and black slacks, cut so tight I

swear you could almost see the shape of her beneath them.
Just goes to show what money can buy – not only good clothes
but the confidence to wear them.

Still, I had my new boots too, and eventually I let Joe
take me out on the ice. I was useless at first but I picked it
up. Slowly, I admit, but I stuck at it and worked my way
round and round the pond, and eventually, well, I wouldn't
say I've mastered it, but I did a complete circuit unaided
and it felt fantastic. And tonight – tonight I'm off to see the
girls! This is going to be a lovely Christmas indeed.

Nancy picked up her blusher but then, looking at herself in the
grand triple mirror over her dressing table, she set it down again.
Her cheeks were a natural pink already and her eyes white and
clear. Country life was doing her good and she smiled, recalling
the feel of that final, unaided lap of the pond last night. She'd still
been ridiculously wobbly and far from in control of herself, but
she'd done it. Ted and Betty had clapped her and Joe had swept
her into his arms and kissed her, and she'd felt as if she'd turned
twenty loops and jumps.

Ice skating, it seemed, was a bit like life here in Langham
these days. She and Joe had sat down with Ted and Betty after the
'incident', and the four of them had squirmed their way to a few
conclusions. In summary, they'd agreed that Nancy wasn't Betty and
needed a chance to do things her own way; the estate was run-down
and needed all the help it could get to become profitable again;
and Ted and Betty were getting on and both needed to rest – just
a little – to stay healthy and well.

The result was a new pattern to life at the Gamekeeper's Cottage.
In the mornings, Nancy went out with Ted and Joe to learn about
estate management whilst Betty sorted lunch. At midday they sat
down together to eat, and in the afternoons Ted and Joe went out
again whilst Nancy helped Betty with chores around the house,

save on Wednesdays when Joe and Nancy swapped roles. That had been a big concession from both Ted and Betty, and Nancy had been terrified about how the first Wednesday would go, but it had been fine.

Ted had taken her to the pheasant hatchery – presumably the girliest part of the job he could think of – and Nancy had been rapt by the whole process. Ted was surprisingly eloquent, especially when he wasn't trying to be manly, and the afternoon had flown by. They'd headed home together, still chatting away about the improvements they could make if they had the money, to find Betty and Joe in fits of laughter as Joe tried to change the beds. Tea that night had been the jolliest since Nancy had arrived, and although no one had actually been foolish enough to say they'd enjoyed the role reversal, the success of it had sat warmly between them.

The third part of the new pattern was that everyone was in by four, and Ted and Betty put their feet up whilst Nancy and Joe sorted tea. Betty had found that really hard at first and had been forever appearing at the kitchen door 'just checking you've got everything you need', but she was slowly getting used to it, and two days ago she'd even let Ted take her down the Blue Bell for Christmas drinks.

Now, as Nancy glanced at Joe, fiddling with the wireless to find them some festive tunes, she thanked God he'd got to her in time the day of the hunt. She wasn't skating expertly around life on the Langham estate yet, but she was definitely getting there and it was paying off; not just in her satisfaction, but in the profitability of the estate. Ted had started a 'roof fund' and, although they knew they were unlikely ever to find a way to raise the amount of cash needed, it helped them all to try.

She stood up and reached for the dress her parents had sent her as a Christmas gift. Her mum had made it and they must have saved up half the family's clothing coupons to get the beautiful dark green velvet. She'd nearly cried when she'd opened it ('Don't save this for Christmas Day,' the card had urged. 'You'll want it before, I hope.'), and had worried that the box of chocolates she'd specially chosen for them was nowhere near enough in return. She'd managed a rare call from Langham Hall to a friend of the family who'd recently had a telephone installed, and they'd all tumbled round to talk to her.

'It's too much, Mam,' she'd said, but her mum had just laughed.

'Nancy, my love, you spent three years in scratchy khaki to defend this country, so the least we can manage is something a little more luxurious to reward you.'

She remembered that now as she stepped into the dress and pulled it up over her hips. It wasn't quite the full-skirted sweep of Merry's American frock, but it was the grandest thing she'd worn in a long, long time and felt wonderful on. It only just fastened up – country life was making her plumper, as well as brighter-skinned – but even she had to admit it looked pretty good. Joe's eyes had certainly widened.

'You look utterly gorgeous, Nance. I can't believe you're going out in that without me.'

She giggled and squirmed away from his roving hands.

'It's a girls' night, Joe – I can hardly take you with me.' He pouted his lips and she stood on tiptoe to kiss them. 'I'll wear it on Christmas Day too, I promise.'

'Keep it nice then, won't you?'

'Of course. I told you, it's a—'

'Girls' night, I know. You forget that I know your girls, my love. Dot will have you all dancing the night away.'

'In Peggy's rooms! That'll hardly be riotous.'

He smiled in acknowledgement. Peggy and her husband were staying at RAF Langham for a few days, and Peggy had suggested that the gunner girls took the chance to revisit their old haunt before 1945 – the last year of the war that had brought them all together – unwound. Harry had some stuffy dinner in the officers' mess but Peggy had managed to get out of it and talked the cook, who remembered them fondly, into making the four of them something in her rooms. Nancy couldn't wait.

'Come on then, my love,' Joe said, as she slid on her shoes. 'I'll walk you up the road.'

'Just like the old days?' she suggested.

His eyes darkened.

'Now *that* would definitely not be good for the dress!'

She batted her eyelashes up at him.

'Well, maybe if you bring me a scruffier one when you come to pick me up…'

'Now you're talking. Oh, but…' They both looked out of the annex window to where a few flakes of snow were falling onto the already frozen ground. 'Perhaps we'll have to wait till spring.'

'Perhaps,' Nancy agreed. 'But at least, this time, we know we'll have spring together.'

He kissed her.

'How about a quick dance before you go instead then, beautiful?'

Nancy blushed.

'Of course.'

Taking her into his arms, he danced her around the little living room to the strains of Bing Crosby's 'White Christmas' from the wireless. Pressing herself tight against him, she thanked God for this first Christmas of peace in a long, long time, and that she had this wonderful man to share it with.

'Ooh, our Nance, you look beautiful!' Betty said, when they finally moved through to the main house to head out. 'But will you be warm enough?'

'She'll be fine, Mum,' Joe said. 'She's got a big wool coat.'

'Scarf? Gloves?'

She fussed around as if Nancy were a child and, touched, Nancy let herself be bundled up then leaned over to kiss Betty's cheek. 'Thanks for caring.'

Betty flushed.

'There now, get away with you – of course we care, don't we, Ted love?'

Ted offered an affirmative grunt and a 'Have fun, lass,' and finally they could escape.

Nancy headed out into the snow feeling a warm rush of love for her parents-in-law. Her arrival had certainly disrupted their lives, but they were doing their best to meet her halfway and she hoped it was paying off for all of them. The only sticking point was that Ted remained adamant Nancy wasn't to shoot a gun.

'But I won't be a proper gamekeeper if I don't go shooting,' Nancy had protested. 'And, besides, I did it in the war.'

'The war was a terrible thing,' had been Ted's tight retort, and there'd been no arguing with that.

With all the other concessions he'd made, Nancy hadn't wanted to push him any further. Still, though, she'd hankered to learn, and as she and Joe set off up the road, she glanced guiltily across the fields to the big, disused barn on the far side of the estate. On her birthday in the middle of November, Joe had surprised her by blindfolding her and leading her across to it.

'Is this some naughty experiment?' she'd demanded.

'No,' he'd answered, 'although it could be!'

In fact, that night in the annex they'd got the blindfold out again and it had released new and very welcome sensations in Nancy, but the gift in the barn had been better, even, than that. Joe had set up a makeshift firing range and there, in private, he had started teaching her to shoot. Every week they'd been up there, even when the ice had bitten, and it often reminded her of her hours in the amazing little dome at the airfield.

She could see the dome up ahead of them now, gleaming white at the side of the road, like some sort of igloo in the Norfolk snow. She'd not been able to believe it the first time she'd seen the virtual plane fly across the ceiling of that funny structure. In fact, she'd ducked, setting the men at the projector laughing away – though they'd soon shut up when she'd got on the machines and proved herself accurate to well within the defined parameters every single damned time.

It had been the same with Joe. After all that training, lining up the sights had been second nature to her; simply pulling the trigger was only a small step on, although learning to take the recoil had been challenging.

'You're a natural, darling,' Joe had told her, with awe in his voice.

'Just like you,' she'd said, but he'd shaken his head vehemently at that.

'Not like me at all. I can handle a gun, Nance, but I don't like them. That's partly why I went for the navy rather than the army – more radar and keeping watch than hand-to-hand combat.'

'Oh, Joe – don't do yourself down. You were so brave out on those ships.'

'So scared, more like. I got on with my job, but there's little more nerve-racking than a submarine alert – knowing that you could be blown sky-high at any minute and without ever even seeing your enemy.'

He'd shuddered and she'd clutched him close, hating the horrors they'd both had to endure. But the war was over now and she was longing for new challenges, so she could make her own mark on the world.

She could hit the bullseye eight times out of ten, and Joe had promised he'd take her out to try live targets when the time was right – by which he meant when Ted was well out of the way. Nancy felt guilty about the subterfuge sometimes, but Joe was certain that when his father saw how competent she was, he'd change his mind and she could become a full gamekeeper-in-training like him.

They just had to be patient. At least, for now, the festive season was upon them.

'It'll be our first Christmas Day together,' she said as they turned onto the airfield.

'And I cannot wait. I've been hoarding mistletoe for weeks.'

He kissed her, long and slow, and she wrapped her arms around his neck, drawing him closer until an amused voice cried, 'Oi! Unhand my gunner girl, sailor,' and he pulled away with a groan.

Nancy turned to see Dot come running towards her, Connie and Peggy hot on her heels.

'You coming in, Joe?' Peggy offered. 'I've got a lovely mulled wine on.'

For a second Joe looked tempted, but then he glanced around and shook his head.

'Girls' night,' he said with a smile. 'I'm out of here.'

'Chicken,' Connie teased and they all watched, laughing together, as Joe headed off down the road, flapping imaginary wings and squawking into the night sky.

The girls tumbled into Peggy's rooms together, grateful for the high fire in the grate so they could throw off their winter coats. The others had dressed up too, Nancy saw. Dot was in a dark red dress, daringly skimming her knees, Peggy in a wide-belted dusky pink polka dot, and Connie in the most stunning white evening dress Nancy had ever seen.

'That must have cost a fortune,' she gasped, hardly daring to touch her friend in case she stained the beautiful silk.

Connie just shrugged.

'It was part of my debutante wardrobe. A nonsense really – so impractical. But it seemed a waste not to wear it again, so here I am.'

'Looking stunning, Con. If there were any men here, they'd be all over you.'

'And I wouldn't give them a second glance,' she said. 'Not now…' She cut herself off, blushing furiously, and they all leaped on her.

'Connie Marshall – are you courting?' Nancy demanded.

'No!' She blushed. 'That is, maybe.'

Dot laughed.

'It's one or the other, girl. You can usually tell.'

'It's complicated.' Connie shifted awkwardly, and Nancy saw that even her shoulders had turned pink against the white straps of her gown. She reached for her hand.

'Are you all right, Con?'

The youngest of the four turned to her, her hazel eyes unnaturally bright. Nancy wondered if the others had been drinking before she arrived, but when she spoke Connie's voice sounded steady enough.

'I'm good, Nancy, really. Never been better. I feel, well, wonderful actually. It's just…'

'Complicated,' Nancy finished gently. 'Well, I'm sure you'll figure it out, because I tell you what's simple – you're a great girl with a great brain and a great future ahead of her. Who you choose to spend it with is entirely up to you.'

'You think so?'

'I know so. Our worlds, our ways, remember?'

'Our worlds, our ways,' Connie repeated almost dreamily, then added, 'Anyway, tonight I'm here to see you lot, my gunner girls, so men can wait. Now, hug me, won't you, please?'

Nancy obliged and the girls settled into their chairs, chattering nineteen to the dozen. Peggy's mulled wine was delicious, especially once Dot had added 'a little plum-liqueur magic' from a silver hip flask, and Cook provided a delicious homity pie and a small plum pudding to get them in the festive spirit. Everyone had good news to report. Peggy's work on establishing a permanent women's army was going slowly but steadily, Connie was loving her teaching course, and Dot had been made a supervisor in Tony's handbag factory. The wireless was playing carols and they all sang along merrily.

'Peace on earth and goodwill to all men!' Dot said, beaming round at them.

'*All* men?' Peggy asked.

'Absolutely. It's Christmas.'

'Including the Germans?'

'Why not the Germans?' Connie snapped, making everyone jump. 'What?' she demanded, leaping to her feet. 'Hitler and his cronies are dead, so surely we can afford to be nice to everyone else? A life is a life, wherever it's come from.'

'That's not what they taught us on the guns,' Peggy said drily.

'But we're not on the guns any more!' Connie shouted, stamping one foot.

They all froze, looking nervously at each other. Then Dot pushed herself up and gave Connie a hug.

'Sadly that's true, Con.' The younger girl squirmed a little but she persisted. 'And it *is* what they taught us when we were nursing.'

Nancy pictured the hospital up at Langham Hall, remembering her first stint there with the gunner girls and then her more recent work.

'I was nursing in the hospital again recently,' she confided.

Everyone turned her way.

'At Langham Hall?'

'That's right.'

'Was it all right?' Peggy asked. 'Are you safe?'

'Quite safe,' Nancy assured her, 'though one man did recognise me. Even mentioned the top-secret patient.'

'Nancy!' Peggy pleaded, looking as upset as Connie had a moment ago. 'We said we wouldn't speak of this.'

She jumped up and checked at the door, though they could hear the sounds of merriment drifting across from the officers' mess. She looked very agitated and Nancy felt bad, but she'd been bottling this up inside her these last few months and at least here she was with the three people she could trust.

'Sorry, Peg. I just, you know, feel the secret weighing on me sometimes.'

Peggy nodded. 'I know, but that's war for you. We have to keep it. We agreed to keep it. Right?'

She looked desperately around at the others, who shifted in their chairs. All the light seemed to have gone out of the evening and Nancy hated this awkwardness between her dearest friends.

'Sorry,' she said, hopping up to join Dot, who still had her arms around Connie, and pulling Peggy insistently with her. 'I'm sorry, really. Forget it, girls. It doesn't matter. Of course we should keep the secret – I'm the one still living in Langham after all.' She hugged them tight and, feeling their arms go around her in return, drew in the love of her crew like the finest mulled wine. 'Come on,' she said, 'who's for more pudding?'

They snatched at this, taking the chance to fill their bowls and calm their thoughts. As they settled again, Dot, always first to defuse any tension, smiled around at them.

'I tell you what – it's lively in my factory. I thought *I* was bad, but those girls know how to party! We went out for Christmas drinks last week and I swear I was the tamest one there.'

'Not possible, Dot,' Nancy laughed.

Dot screwed up her nose.

'Looks like it is. Mind you, I had to be a bit careful with, you know, being a supervisor.'

'Ooh! Look at you, boss lady,' Peggy teased fondly.

'It does feel a bit mad,' Dot said. 'But good mad. Tony and I talk plans for the factory all the time now. I'm sure it's not the sort of pillow talk I used to have, but I love it. We want to extend, to improve the facilities, especially the loos – they're awful, girls, you should see them. I told Tony they won't do. Blokes might be all right with stinky loos but women don't like it. To attract the best workers, you've got to offer the best conditions.' Nancy stared at Dot. 'What?' she said self-consciously.

'Nothing. That is, I think it's marvellous. You sound so focused.'

Dot gave a little shrug of her shoulders.

'The factory's starting to matter a lot to me. I want to see it do well. Mind you – we need money to do that. Sales are good, but it'll take a long time to gain the sort of cash we're looking for and I'm not the most patient girl around.'

'We're struggling for cash too,' Nancy told her. 'I have loads of ideas for the estate, but Ted and even Joe don't seem to want to hear them. Sometimes I think they're using not having the money as an excuse to ignore me.'

'Money, hey?' Peggy said. 'The root of all evil.'

'Only if you don't have any!' Dot shot back.

'I don't,' Peggy said indignantly. 'At least not enough.'

'For what?'

'Oh, nothing in particular.'

She looked away and Connie regarded her curiously.

'You must have a salary though, right, Peg? That's why I want to be a teacher – to pay my own way. If I can afford to make it to the end of the course, that is!'

'A wage is freedom,' Nancy agreed. 'I'd love to work, but Joe wants me to have a baby and settle into cosy domesticity like his mum. Mind you, I'm doing everything I can to prevent that.'

'Prevent a baby?' Peggy asked, turning back to her.

'Yep. It's hard though, especially without letting him know. Merry – that's Lord Langham's daughter – says I have to avoid certain days.'

'How do you do that?'

'Oh, you know, headaches and suchlike.'

'Is that fair on Joe?'

Nancy stared at Peggy in amazement.

'Of course it's fair on blinking Joe. He gets to do what he likes whilst I have to fight for every tiny bit of space on the estate. Honestly, I spent the war being so, so…'

'Useful?' Connie supplied.

Nancy nodded.

'Useful – exactly. I'm not saying looking after a house isn't useful, of course it is, but surely it doesn't have to be all I do? Our worlds, our ways – right?'

'Right!' Dot and Connie agreed firmly, but Peggy seemed miles away.

'Peggy?' The older girl blinked dazedly at her. 'Isn't that right, Peggy?'

'What?'

'Our worlds, our ways,' Dot repeated a little impatiently.

'Oh. Yes. Of course. We should do whatever we want with our lives.'

Her voice was strained again and Nancy reached for her hand. 'Is everything all right, Peggy?'

Peggy sighed and, to Nancy's astonishment, brushed a tear from her eye. She'd never seen Peggy cry before, not even when their favourite pilot at RAF Langham had made it all the way back across the sea with his tail on fire, and then crashed onto the beach less than a mile from base. They'd all gone to his funeral and the church had been a mass of tears, but not Peggy. To Nancy, she'd been the big sister of their group, the calmest, bossiest, strongest one – or so she'd thought.

'Peg?' she prompted gently.

'I'd love a baby,' she said, so low they only just caught the words. 'We've been trying for, oh, ages. Ever since the war ended, but so far…'

Nancy squeezed her hand tight, feeling instantly awful.

'It'll happen, Peg. It can take time.'

'Yeah,' Dot agreed. 'My parents didn't have me till ten years after they got married. Mam told me once that they tried everything – that was a painful conversation, I can tell you. But then one day, when they'd all but given up, there I was!'

Peggy turned filmy eyes to her.

'Ten years?' she whimpered.

Dot bit her lip and looked to the other two.

'I meant that to be a hopeful story.'

Nancy smiled at her.

'It is. Dot's parents were an extreme example, Peggy, but proof it can still happen.' Peggy was twisting her hands round and round in her lap, and Nancy leaned in to take one. 'Is something else bothering you?'

'No. No, it's just… there's a treatment in America. Someone told me about it in the hospital when we were… you know.'

'Nursing,' Nancy said firmly.

'Yes. It's a "hormone treatment", whatever that means. They don't do it here – just tell you to think welcoming thoughts and pander to your husband and give up work! This man, though, he said pregnancy is physical not psychological, and these hormone things work wonders. It costs a fortune, though, and that's after you've paid to get out there.'

She looked so miserable that Nancy's heart went out to her. Here she was, battling to avoid a baby when it was Peggy's dearest wish.

'You don't need miracle treatments, Peg, honest, especially not from the Yanks. You just need to stay strong and eat well and, and…'

'And do it all the time!' Dot finished, and they all squealed with shocked laughter.

Peggy wiped the tears from her eyes and smiled at them.

'You're right. Thank you, girls. I don't know what I'd do without you lot.'

'You'll never have to find out,' Nancy told her firmly. 'Us gunner girls, we stick together. Now, Dot – put on some music and let's kick up our heels like we used to.'

Dot needed no second urging and they danced what was left of the night away, glad to throw their troubles into the music. Nancy was happily worn out when Joe turned up at midnight to escort her back to the Gamekeeper's Cottage.

'I'm tired, Joe,' she said, leaning gratefully in against his solid frame.

'I'm not surprised, sweetheart. 1945 has been a hell of a year.'

Nancy smiled and twisted her fingers into his.

'It has that.'

Her body ached and her head was spinning and something, maybe Dot's plum liqueur, was making her feel sick. It had been a strange night, with Peggy's sad admission and Connie acting oddly, and right now she couldn't wait to be tucked up in her own bedroom at the Gamekeeper's Cottage, beneath her own lurid pink roses.

'It'll be nice to get home,' she said.

Joe twisted to look into her face.

'Home?' he asked.

She nodded sleepily. 'Home.'

Then she gripped his hand tighter and set her steps down the road towards the first houses of Langham on the horizon.

Chapter Fifteen

Someone was shaking Lorna. She pushed them away but a hand closed round her arm again and shook harder.

'Mum! Mum, wake up.'

Her eyes shot open. It was still dark, the only light creeping in from the living area and pinging off the pink roses.

'Charlie! What is it? Is it Stan? Is he OK?'

'He's fine, Mum. He's ready and so am I. You need to get up.'

'Ready for what?'

Even in the half-light she could see him roll his eyes.

'Ready for the dew, of course. It's the first of August.'

Lorna groaned.

'Seriously? We're really doing this?'

'Of course we are. Aunty Tilly says it's the best way to stay "healthy and youthful", remember? Don't you want to be healthy, Mum?'

'Of course I do, Charlie, I'm just not sure—'

'Or youthful? Tilly is very youthful.'

'Tilly doesn't have kids,' Lorna muttered, but Charlie was still tugging on her arm so she reluctantly pushed back the covers and forced herself out of bed.

Tilly had been full of some morning-dew ritual at tea last night and the boys had lapped it up. They were all to get up and be in the garden ready for sunrise so that they could wash their faces and hands in the first dew, to make themselves, as Charlie had rightly remembered, 'healthy and youthful'. David and Mary had firmly said that it was far too late for them to manage that, but Lorna had laughingly agreed that it sounded wonderful. She hadn't thought it would actually come to anything but here they

174 ANNA STUART

were at – she glanced at her phone – 5 a.m., apparently heading out into the garden.

'Come on, Mum. If we don't get out before the sun, it won't work.'

'OK, OK.'

Lorna grabbed her dressing gown and let herself be pulled by her two excited sons into the main house and through to the kitchen.

'Tilly better be up,' she grumbled.

'Tilly certainly is,' chirped her stepsister, looking ridiculously perky. 'Come on – Xavier's put chairs out ready.'

'We're allowed to sit on chairs?'

'Course we are, Lorna. Well, until the sun comes up, when we have to roll naked in the grass.'

'Naked?!'

Tilly winked at her.

'You're so gullible – though don't let me stop you if you want to.'

'*I'm* going to roll naked,' Stan announced, already stripping off his pyjamas.

'Me too,' Xavier agreed, loosening his already tiny kaftan.

Lorna thought longingly of her nice warm bed, but as she took a seat in the semicircle of chairs with a naked Stan on her knee, and looked to the horizon, she felt a small thrill creep across her skin. The skies were clear and the faintest tinge of pink was starting to run up and along the horizon. Then, as the sky turned rosy above the roofs of Langham, the rays hit a thin line of cloud and turned it purest gold. They all gasped.

'That's one big helping of health and youthfulness,' Tilly said softly.

'Is it time?' Charlie asked.

Stan squirmed to get down but Tilly held up a hand.

'Just a minute more.'

She was right because now the colours were deepening, morphing luxuriously into the rich pinks of the roses in Lorna's bedroom, run through with ambers and reds. Lorna glanced at

Charlie and saw his upturned face glowing, as if he were staring at a stained-glass window, and blessed her crazy new stepsister for this strange little ritual.

'Now!' Tilly said.

Xavier was first, flinging off his kaftan and diving onto the lawn, taut brown buttocks glowing. Stan shot after him and, with a self-conscious look around, Charlie also cast off his pyjamas and hit the grass.

Tilly looked at Lorna and shrugged.

'If you can't beat 'em, join 'em,' she said and scampered off, naked as the day she was born, to her dewy baptism.

'It's all right for you,' Lorna muttered, 'you've not had two children.'

She glanced to the gloriously burning sky and sighed.

'Go on, Lor,' she could almost hear Matt saying. He'd have been straight in there, she knew, revelling in the impetuousness of it. She'd never been very good at that. Well, except for all those times in his parents' shed…

'Oh, sod it!'

She shrugged off her dressing gown and T-shirt and hit the lawn too. It was cold, that was her first thought, but the dew did tickle quite nicely at her skin, and the sheer rush of the crazy roll was energising. Stan flung himself delightedly onto her, his eyes astonishingly blue in his rosy face as he rolled his muddy body against hers and she kissed him.

'Do you feel more useful, Mummy?' he asked and she laughed.

'Youthful, Stan. And yes, strangely enough, I do.'

Thankfully the boys got cold quickly, and she was able to leave Tilly and Xavier to their own little rituals and pull her sons inside for a shower, before tucking them back into bed. She worried that the excitement of it all would make it impossible for them to go back to sleep, but thankfully the reverse seemed to be true and they both drifted off again within minutes. Lorna curled back up in her own sunrise-coloured bedroom, relishing the warmth against her still-tingling skin. Sleep, however, did not come as easily to her.

She thought of Tilly and Xavier outside and felt a rush of searing envy. Ever since Stan had gone to school last year, she and Matt had been rediscovering each other. After several years of broken nights and early mornings, things had finally stabilised and they'd been having what Matt had called a 'glorious renaissance'. At times it had been almost like the rush of meeting someone new, and now that had all been taken from her.

It was August, so she'd gone three months without him. She supposed day-to-day living had got a little easier, but she sometimes feared that her time here in Langham was a sort of illusion, an easily lived pretence that she could go along with, but not real life. Real life was back in Norwich, looming on a not-so-rosy horizon with a September that would involve going back to school for all three of them. There would be no excuses, no leeway. However kind people were, she would be expected to 'get on', and quite right too. She just didn't know if she could do it.

Even thinking about the comprehensive she taught in made her feel panicked. She loved her job. The kids were great, even the naughty ones, but you had to be on top of your game to keep in charge and she was nowhere near that. It wasn't that they were cruel, just that they were finely tuned in to exploitable weaknesses and if they sensed there was a chance of messing about, they would most certainly take it. What if she burst into tears, or forgot what to teach, or had a panic attack, like she had with Kyle the other day?

Don't think about it, she urged herself, opening her eyes to focus on the cerise roses. These were the very same flowers that Nancy would have stared at. Had she liked them? she wondered. She must remember to ask David. He was taking her to see Dot's twin girls,

May and June, later on this morning, so she tried to focus on what they might be able to tell her. Dot, sadly, was dead now, the same as Nancy and Peggy. Peggy's son, William, had followed his parents into the army and retired to Hong Kong, so there would be no meeting up with him, but Dot's daughters, now in their seventies, were still in Norwich and keen to get together.

They lived in a retirement village on the outskirts of the city; May with her husband, and widowed June with three dachshunds. They'd suggested a café called the Wonky Sunflower for tea and cakes, and Lorna was looking forward to it. She closed her eyes again and tried to think through all the questions she wanted to ask them, hoping to lull herself to sleep, but it only made her more alert. All the gunner girls, it seemed, had been in need of money and all of them – or at least the three that they knew of – had found it, and in large sums. How had they done that? Why had they sworn each other to secrecy? And what did it have to do with the top-secret patient in Langham Hall?

Lorna's brain was spinning and the inevitable tears sprung to her eyes. She wanted to be able to roll over and cuddle up to Matt. She wanted to feel his arms go round her and know that, whatever else was going on, she was safe in his love. Her whole body ached for him and on a sudden impulse she fumbled for the red leather book on her bedside table. The cover was soft, the pages giving and the comfort of the old book seemed to reach out to her like a gift.

'Thank you, Matt,' she murmured into the dawn and, hugging it to her like a teddy bear, she finally slept.

It was a shock, therefore, when Stan came running in what felt like mere moments later and launched himself with his customary vigour onto her tummy.

'What's that?' he asked, tugging at the diary.

'History, Stan.'

He wrinkled up his little nose.

'Put it away,' he commanded and, when she obeyed, burrowed himself determinedly into its place.

'We did naked rolling!' he said gleefully.

'We did, Stan,' she agreed, squeezing him tight but, having established first place in her affections, he was off into the main house to tell Granny and Grandpa about his sunrise adventure.

Smiling, Lorna followed him.

'Naked rolling, hey?' Mary said, kissing her.

'It was Tilly's idea.'

'Of course it was,' David laughed. 'We could barely keep clothes on that girl for the first five years of her life.'

'Really?' Stan was agog. 'Even in the snow?'

'Perhaps not in the snow – though there was the time we visited Sue's cousins in Finland and had our first sauna. We went rolling in the snow then.'

Stan sighed wistfully.

'When will it snow, Mummy?'

'Not for ages – I hope. It's only August, Stan.'

'Oh. When's Christmas? At Christmas can we do that? Can we have a sore knee and roll in the snow?'

'A sauna, Stan.'

'OK, but can we?'

'Maybe.'

He huffed, old enough now to recognise an adult 'maybe' for the fraud it often was, but Mary got out the Cheerios and he was happily distracted.

'Ready to go and see May and June?' David asked Lorna, handing her a coffee.

'Are they really called that?'

'They really are. They were born either side of midnight at the end of May and Dot, being Dot, chose to mark that out in the most obvious way possible.'

'Brilliant.'

'I'm born in March,' Stan said. 'So does that mean I should be called March?'

'I suppose so.'

He frowned.

'That's a bit silly though, isn't it? No one's called March. 'Cept soldiers.'

'Soldiers aren't called March, Stanley,' Charlie said, wandering in. 'That's just what they do.'

'Even in January?'

'In any month, stupid.'

'I am not stupid. I'm not the one called after a month. Or a dot. Why's she called Dot?'

David took a deep sip of his coffee.

'Lively in the mornings, aren't they?'

'Very,' Lorna agreed, taking a big gulp of her own.

'Shall we head to Norwich sooner rather than later?'

'Let's!'

The Wonky Sunflower was, as its name might suggest, bright yellow and bursting with flowers though not, thankfully, at all wonky. May and June were already there when Lorna and David arrived and got up eagerly to greet them. David had told her that they'd been born identical twins, and even seventy-four years later they were hard to tell apart. June, thankfully, had chosen to tint her white hair with a very pretty lilac, and May had a small scar above her carefully plucked eyebrows, but other than that they seemed to have aged in amazingly identical ways.

'David! So good to see you. It's been far too long.' They hugged him in turn, then happily did the same to Lorna. 'And you're the little gem who found Aunty Nancy's diary. Is it full of juicy stuff?'

'Not really, I'm afraid,' Lorna said, taking a seat as the twins waved a waitress over.

'More tea, please,' May said, gesturing to the pot they'd clearly already polished off between them. 'And can we have the cake platter?'

'Cake platter?' Lorna queried.

'That's right,' June said, rubbing her hands. 'It's like tapas but with cakes. Genius!'

'No more fretting over which one to choose,' May added. 'You get a little bit of them all.'

It did sound pretty genius, and Lorna settled back and let the three older people chatter as she enjoyed a moment to herself. It was clear from their banter that they'd known each other well growing up, and the talk was all of trees they'd fallen out of, graveyards they'd dared each other to enter, and disgusting foodstuffs they'd cooked up and apparently eaten.

'David was the worst for that,' June told Lorna gleefully. 'When I had grandkids, I discovered the *Horrid Henry* books and there's a story in those that always reminds me of him – he mixes ketchup and milk and spice and baked beans, all in one horrible gloop.'

'I never actually poisoned anyone,' David protested.

'I don't know,' May said. 'Once we got into our teens and you started doing the same thing with spirits, you nearly did for me once or twice. You could have knocked me over with a feather when Mum told us you'd got a place at medical school. "They're not going to know what's hit them," I said to June, but in fact you turned out OK.'

'Cheers, May!'

'My pleasure. Ah, cakes!'

The cake platter looked every bit as delicious as promised. Dainty morsels of five different types of cake were arranged on a three-tiered stand and Lorna's mouth watered. She'd cleared out of the kitchen without any breakfast this morning, and after her early morning dew-rolling she was starving. She needed no second urging to tuck in, and swiftly decided the Wonky Sunflower was her favourite café ever. In truth, it would be easy to come again, as she was closer to home here than she was to Langham. The thought made her feel light-headed and she swiftly chose another cake.

'Did you bring the diary along?' May asked.

Lorna nodded through a mouthful of Battenberg and dived to fetch it from her bag. She set the small book on the table and the twins stared at the red leather cover. May put out a finger to trace the 1945 on the cream plaque, then looked to her sister.

'I think I'd feel odd reading it,' she said.

'Me too,' June agreed. 'Have you read it, David?'

He shook his head.

'Feels a bit intrusive somehow. I've been getting the good bits from Lorna.'

'Very wise. Are there good bits, Lorna?'

'Depends what you mean by "good", I suppose. I find the whole thing totally fascinating. I've worked for years as a history teacher and I've never had the privilege of reading such an intimate primary source as this one. I feel a bit like a toddler being held up to peek in a window – a window into 1945.' She flushed and bit at her lip. 'Listen to me – I sound like some sort of voyeur.'

'Not at all,' May said with a smile. 'Surely that's exactly what history is – a window into the past? And it's lovely to see someone so enthused by their subject.'

'Thanks, May. I've needed it this summer, to be honest, and the fact that you all knew Nancy makes it extra special. I've read a bit before about women having trouble with being expected to go back to domesticity after their war work, but to actually see one woman's struggles on a day-to-day basis really brings it home.'

'Struggles?' June asked. 'How funny. Aunty Nancy always seemed such a powerhouse to me. Well, all the gunner girls did. How could you not be, after that sort of experience?'

'I think that's what Nancy felt too, but her in-laws seem to have had a harder time accepting it. I get the sense she maybe bought her way into their favour.'

'Bought? How?'

Lorna shifted.

'I'm not sure, but the roof on the Gamekeeper's Cottage was falling down, and the diary is full of how expensive it was going to be and how they couldn't possibly afford it. Yet, somehow, it was redone in 1946 and the family acquired the house and some land at the same time. There are suggestions that the other women needed money too – Connie for her teaching degree, Peggy for fertility treatment, and your mum to improve the factory. Did she do that?'

'Oh, yes,' May agreed. 'When we were little it was one improvement or extension after another. Could that not just have come from normal business profits though?'

'It could,' Lorna agreed. 'And I've no idea if Peggy ever went to America to conceive or it happened naturally.'

May cleared her throat.

'Peggy did go to America one summer – remember, June? We were about seven and were very jealous. If I remember rightly, her William came along the following year so that would make sense.'

Lorna stared at them – so Nancy, Peggy and Dot had all needed substantial sums of cash. And found them.

'What about Connie, then?' she asked. 'I've no idea what happened to her at all.'

'Connie?' June asked, looking confused.

'Connie?' May repeated, frowning. 'Who's Connie?'

Lorna stared, then turned slowly to David. What was going on here? In the diary the four gunner girls seemed such a solid team, so how had one of their members been effectively wiped out of history? It seemed so sad.

'You two didn't know her either?' David said. 'I'm so glad. I thought maybe I was going mad!'

May frowned.

'The name does ring a bell. Let me think – more cake might help.'

She reached for a mini scone.

'Does the diary not say anything?' June asked.

Lorna lifted it up, stroking the soft leather.

'Not so far. Nancy talks about a "secret" every so often but even in the diary she's really careful about not revealing it. Maybe it'll come out in the remaining entries.'

She patted the book, already longing to dive back in.

'Hope it's nothing too raunchy,' June said.

'It'd be *your* mum's diary you'd need for that,' David told her.

Lorna looked askance at him but the twins just laughed.

'True enough. Mum's war diary would be a read and a half. By all accounts she was… friendly with a fair few lads.'

'That was unusual back then, right?' Lorna asked, unsure how to put it.

'Perhaps not as unusual as we think, especially in the war. If you didn't grab your chance with someone, it might never come again, especially if you were dating a pilot. D'you know their average life expectancy was four weeks?'

Lorna remembered Richard starting on something like that before the others at the dome had shut him up, but she hadn't realised it had been that bad.

'Why on earth did anyone sign up with odds like that?'

May laughed.

'Well, they didn't know it at the time. It was only worked out afterwards.'

'They'd have seen how many people didn't come home, though.'

'They would, yes, but they were young men, conditioned to believe it would never be them, and of course the uniform was fantastic. All the girls love a bomber jacket, right?'

'Right, though that's not much use if you're dead.'

'Hence why they were at it any chance they got. I'd say that prim-and-proper manners start to look a little ridiculous in the face of death, wouldn't you?'

'Absolutely,' Lorna agreed. 'Talking of which, I heard a story—'

'That Mum was caught getting jiggy in the hut in the woods?'

'You know about that?'

'Everyone knows about that. Even Dad.'

'He didn't mind?'

The twins looked at each other.

'He didn't seem to,' May said.

'But then, there always seemed to be something else to that story.'

'Something they wouldn't tell us.'

'Maybe it was your dad who was with her?' Lorna suggested.

'Nah. They didn't meet till after the war. It wasn't that. Something more… secret.'

Lorna and David looked at each other. Lorna leaned in.

'The gunner girls were definitely hiding something. They swore an oath about it. It could be to do with that man – Hank, I think he was called.'

'Hank?!' June exclaimed. 'Mum never mentioned a Hank. American?'

'Got to be,' May agreed. 'Is that how Peggy got hold of the fertility treatment idea?'

'I don't know!' Lorna wailed. It suddenly felt desperately frustrating. She reminded herself that it didn't really matter, that the past was the past and clearly it had turned out all right for them all, so why was it important how that had come about? But the historian in her was burning to know, and right now that burn was keeping her going. There had to be a way to find out more.

'Connie!' May suddenly said, spraying crumbs. 'Goodness, I'm so sorry, but I've just remembered why I know the name Connie.'

'You have?' Lorna asked eagerly.

May looked to June. 'Was it not Connie that Mum asked about at the end?'

June threw her hands up.

'It was, yes! Well remembered, May. She wanted to see someone called Connie before she was too frail to do so.'

'But in the end she couldn't.'

'Why not?' Lorna asked.

'Because Connie was frail herself and it was too far to travel.'

'Too far? From where?'

May and June looked at each other, and it seemed to Lorna as if all the pretty flowers in the quirky little café leaned in to hear.

'From Germany, Lorna. Connie lived in Germany and had done ever since just after the war.'

'Germany,' Lorna echoed, stunned. She hadn't been expecting that. What on earth had those women been up to out on their gun in rural Norfolk, both during the war and, it seemed, after it? Now she really couldn't wait to get reading again.

Chapter Sixteen

Saturday, 9 March 1946

I'm pregnant. I have to be. I've known it for ages, really, but haven't wanted to actually write it down in case that made it true. Ridiculous. As if words on a page could be a clearer indicator than my monthlies disappearing and feeling bloomin' sick all the time. What an idiot!

At least the sickness has stopped now, which is a relief, but has to mean the baby is well and truly lodged. Which in turn means I'm really going to have to tell Joe. I don't know how he's believed I have a tummy bug for so long! Yesterday he told me country life is 'filling you out'. I was right indignant but he said it was a compliment, said he loved having a bit more of me in his hands.

He hasn't put the signs together yet though. Why would he? Betty's the only one who might notice, but with us spending less time together these days, I've managed to hide it from her too. That can't last. I've got to tell them. Joe'll be proper pleased so I don't know why I'm putting it off really. I just had to be sure before I got his hopes up. Plus, of course, I don't want him to stop me shooting.

I'm getting so good after all my secret lessons. Not perfect, but I can hit the target at least 80 per cent of the time. It's not so different from the big gun, except that this time I get to pull the trigger myself. I reckon even Ted would be impressed if we ever dare actually show him what I can do.

If they don't all stop me the minute I tell them about the baby, of course. Maybe one more week…

'It's time,' Joe told her, as they walked home on the second Saturday in March with two rabbits for the pot, both bagged by Nancy.

'Time for what?'

'Time to show Pa what you're capable of.'

Nancy swallowed, instantly nervous. She was happy shooting with Joe, but Ted was another matter altogether. On Saturdays her father-in-law often went out for supplies, taking Betty with him, and it had become Nancy and Joe's time in the woods. Live birds and rabbits were, Nancy had discovered, far, far harder to shoot than a straw target. No surprise there, perhaps, but it was more than just the fact that they moved about. It was the sense of duty to them; the need to make the shot clean and the death instant. The pests had to be kept down so the estate could thrive but no one, least of all Nancy, wanted to cause suffering.

There was little more distressing than catching a wing, or a hind leg. The first time she'd done it, in mid-January, she'd been sick in the bushes. Joe had dispatched the flapping crow within moments of her own bungled shot, but seeing it crash about in the treetops had turned her stomach and she'd heaved up her breakfast at their feet. Mind you, it had turned out there'd been another reason for her sickness around then. The smell of coffee had done it, or a bit of gristle in the meat or, at one point, just getting out of bed.

It was terrible timing, really. She'd just got everyone here to let her out on the estate and her shooting had improved so much. With Joe's encouragement she'd focused on perfecting her skills and now, with the spring thaws upon them and vermin increasing at an alarming rate, she could dispatch anything with one sharp shot. But that was in private.

'I don't know, Joe,' she said. 'Ted's been so good about all the changes. I don't want to upset him.'

'He only objects because he thinks it's not safe.'

'Are you sure? I think it's more about dignity or maybe pride.'

'He'll be dead proud of you when he sees what you can do. Just like I am.'

Her heart melted.

'Are you? Really?'

'Really, Nancy. I reckon we'll have you taking down a stag by autumn.'

Nancy shivered.

'Not a stag, Joe. They scare me.'

He laughed.

'They scare everyone. What d'you think those great big antlers are for?! But you could do it, I know you could. You're a better shot than me now.'

'And you don't mind that?'

'God, no. As I said before, I don't really like guns. You're welcome to them as far as I'm concerned; I saw enough death in the war to last me forever, thank you very much.'

Nancy reached up and kissed him.

'I'm sorry, Joe.'

'What for?'

'That you had to go through that. You told me once that you were sorry I'd had to take up the guns, but what about you? What about all our men? No one should have to go to war, whatever sex they are.'

'No,' he agreed, 'they shouldn't, and I just hope the damned politicians get it right this time and put a stop to it forever.'

'They better,' Nancy said darkly, 'or we'll all be annihilated by an atom bomb.'

They both shivered. The true horror of the atomic bombs over Japan was still coming out. The mushroom-like explosion had looked bad enough at the time, but new footage was reaching the cinemas now – pictures of thousands of Japanese civilians in crowded hospitals, physically rotting away, their skin a mass of burns and blotches, their hair falling out in clumps and their guts spewing from them in vile brown vomit. The bomb, it seemed, had carried on exploding inside people long after the great mushroom cloud had dispersed, and only now were even the scientists who'd developed it realising quite how deadly their weapon was – or so they claimed. If this was the new technology of war then it must, surely, be avoided at all costs.

'The United Nations won't let that happen,' Joe said firmly, as they turned up the driveway of the Gamekeeper's Cottage. 'It can't. We have to make the world safe for our children.' He looked at her sadly and she so nearly told him of the new life growing within her, but then he marched up to the door and said, 'And if you want to do that with me, Nancy, then I'm proud to let you,' and the moment passed.

Soon, she told herself, as they went inside to the smell of lunch bubbling in the pot. *Tonight maybe, when the Dancing Club is on the wireless and we can dance together.* She hugged herself at the thought of how pleased he'd be. As for the rest, she'd sort it. Hadn't her own mam been out and about right up to the first birthing pains with every one of them? It was good for you to stay active and she'd just have to find a midwife who could convince Ted and Betty of that. And Joe, of course. He might be proud of her shooting ability now, but she was pretty sure that once he knew his son or daughter was growing inside her he'd be even prouder of that. And even more cautious about it. Maybe Joe was right – though he didn't know why yet – and it was time to show Ted what she could do before she told them about the baby. But how?

She followed Joe into the kitchen to find her parents-in-law in a good mood. They delightedly accepted the two rabbits, and told Joe and Nancy how Lord Langham and Merry had come to the gun shop with them and then taken them for morning coffee afterwards.

'Morning coffee!' Betty crowed in glee. 'In this beautiful hotel. So swanky, Nance. They brought us cakes on a trolley, all sorts of different ones to choose from. They looked so delicious that I got in a tizz about which one to pick, so Merry ordered four and cut them up into quarters so we could try every single one. Wasn't that kind of her?'

'Very kind,' Nancy agreed.

'She's a good girl, that one,' Ted grunted. 'A bit wild growing up, but she's knuckling down now she's the heir. Goodness, you should have seen her negotiating with the bullet supplier. Putty in her hands, he was. We've never had a lower price. Never.'

Nancy focused on her food and forced herself not to say anything. There was surely no need? Ted could see for himself what women could do given half a chance, and she only hoped that he didn't still think it was all down to Merry's aristocratic blood.

'What have you two been up to then?' Ted asked, when talks of cakes had run their course.

They both flushed.

'We were up in the woods,' Joe managed. 'Checking the grain distributors.'

'All well?'

'Yes, but the thaws are really on us now. There's mice everywhere, Pa, and you know what that means.'

'Crows everywhere too.'

''Fraid so. We need to cull before they start laying.'

'We do, son, we do.' Ted looked out of the window. 'Well, it's a fine day for sure.'

'Today, Pa?'

'Why not? Perhaps a few of the village lads would be up for joining us? They can keep the spoils.'

'They don't eat crows?' Nancy asked, horrified.

Ted laughed.

'They don't, lass, but their dogs do. They're good to hang over the veg patch too – deters the others.'

'Does it really?'

'Seems to. Clever creatures, crows. Shame to kill them really, but the farmers will thank us for it when the grain starts to ripen.'

Joe stood up.

'Tell you what, Pa. I'll head down to the village to recruit a few lads and I'll bring them up to the woods to meet you.'

'You will?'

'Of course. My legs are younger than yours.'

'Cheeky!' Ted said, but he looked pleased all the same.

'And how about we make it a competition? Ten bob for whoever bags the most.'

'That'll be me, lad.'

'Then it won't cost you, will it?'

Ted grinned.

'Fair enough. Ten bob it is, and may the best man win. We'll start at two.'

'See you then. Oh and Nancy, didn't you say you were feeling a bit gippy?'

Nancy looked up. 'Gippy?'

'Poorly, you know. You mentioned it in the woods earlier, remember. A bit dizzy.'

He was looking at her urgently so she nodded.

'Dizzy?' Betty asked, on instant alert. 'We can't have that. Go you and lie down, Nance.'

'Good idea, Ma. Nancy didn't sleep well last night, did you?' Again the look. Nancy shook her head. Was Joe up to what she thought he was? And if so, could she do it? He pulled her to her feet. 'Come on, I'll tuck you up and close the curtains. You've got time for a good couple of hours' rest before we get back, hasn't she, Ma?'

'Of course,' Betty agreed. 'Run along straight away, Nancy. I'll tidy this up.'

'I'll clean the guns,' Ted said.

'And I'll find the competitors,' Joe added. 'Should be a good afternoon.'

He hustled Nancy through to the annex and began bundling clothes down the middle of the bed.

'Joe! What on earth are you doing?'

'This is sleeping you, in case Ma looks in. And these' – he rifled in the wardrobe and pulled out a pair of khaki trousers – 'are your shooting trews.'

'You're joking?'

'I'm not. In these and a big coat with a hat over your hair, you'll look like any one of the lads. Get into the woods, bag some birds, and then we'll tell Pa.'

'Isn't that a bit underhand, Joe?'

He frowned.

'It is a bit, but I reckon it's the only way. He knows how good you are with the pheasants and the hedgerows and the books. Now we're going to show him how good you are with a gun. Can you do it?'

Could she? Nancy thought of Peggy setting up a permanent women's army, of Dot climbing up the ranks at MacLaren's, and of Connie training to teach. Her fellow gunner girls were taking their lives in both hands and making something of them, so she owed it to them to do the same.

'I can do it, Joe,' she said, and reached for the trousers.

Nancy had never concentrated so hard in her life. Even on the big finder with a German killing machine in her sights, she'd never been as tightly focused as she was that afternoon. She'd sneaked into the back of the woods as Joe, Ted and three lads from the village had set off from the front, and had made a start as soon as she'd heard the first of their guns go off.

They'd divided up the woods for safety so it was easy to avoid detection, and being alone also gave her time to let the crows settle fully before she shot again. It took patience and nerve, but it meant that she bagged one almost every time and bagged it cleanly too. Twice she passed near Ted and sensed him watching her, and her focus notched up even further. She heard a grunt of approval as first one bird and then a second hit the woodland floor, but when she dared to look round, he was gone. Did he know who she was? The clothes were bulky, yes, but he'd surely lived with her long enough to recognise her now? She desperately hoped so, but as Joe's voice called out the end of the impromptu shoot at half past three and they all began to make their way to join him, her heart started racing.

Her bag was heavy on her back and her arm and shoulder were, she suddenly realised, aching badly. She stopped behind a tree to watch the others gathering and felt a sudden urge to drop her bag and flee, but Joe had seen her and was beckoning her forward. Head low, she went. The others looked at her curiously but were too busy counting out their catches to ask any questions. Nancy hefted her own bag off her back and, pulling back the drawstrings, emptied her clutch onto the ground in front of her.

'Cor!' Tom, the lad next to her, looked over. 'That's a fair lot you've bagged there, boy.' He bent to see her face as the others looked her way. 'Is that…? Nah!'

Joe came to Nancy's side and counted out her crows.

'Fifteen. Nice work!'

Tom had twelve, as did Joe. Ray had eleven, and Donnie declared he had thirteen and a half.

'And a half?' the others jeered.

'I think it was dead already,' Donnie admitted. 'But I bagged it. Not that it matters anyway – he got more than me.'

He pointed to Nancy and they all looked at her again. She felt as if her heart were going to batter its way out of her swollen breasts and suddenly feared for the baby. For the first time she knew, with searing certainty, that she wanted this child, this product of her and Joe's love for each other. What was she doing here?'

'Not he,' Joe said, reaching for her hat and removing it with a flourish. 'She.'

Her dark hair was in a tight bun so didn't exactly cascade down her back, but it might as well have done for the gasps from the boys.

'Nancy!'

'God, girl, where did you learn to shoot like that?'

'Soldier wife, ain't she? Nice one, Nance – you put us all to shame.'

She was touched by their ready acceptance and gave them a tentative smile.

'You won the prize too,' Tom said.

'Not quite,' Joe told him. 'Dad got sixteen, didn't you, Dad? Dad?'

They all fell silent. Ted Wilson was scarlet in the face and visibly quivering.

'You,' he said, pointing at Nancy, his voice like ice.

Nancy dropped her gun and took a step back.

'I just wanted to show you I can do it, Ted,' she stuttered. 'I just wanted you to see that you could trust me.'

'Trust you?! You sneak out here, telling my poor Betty that you're ill, dress up like a man, steal a gun and take part in this shoot under totally false pretences, and you want me to *trust* you?'

Nancy swallowed. Joe stepped hastily forward.

'It was my idea, Pa, not Nancy's.'

'Was it indeed?' He rounded on Joe. 'That's worse. I tell you, son, she's bewitched you.'

The village boys huddled nervously together and one of them crossed himself. Nancy looked at him in disgust.

'I'm not a witch. That's ridiculous. I'm just a normal person who's good with a gun and happens to be a girl.'

Ted shook his head vehemently.

'It's not natural. It's not right. You've betrayed me, both of you. I welcomed you in, Nancy, made you a part of my family. I let you onto my estate, against my better judgement, and I even took you out alone. I did everything you asked of me, everything. I had one small condition, one request and you couldn't respect it, could you? You couldn't just be grateful and work with me? Oh no! You had to go behind my back and betray me.'

'No!' Nancy cried.

'Yes,' Ted snarled, then slowly, horrifically slowly, he picked up his gun and began to raise it to his shoulder.

'Dad, no!' Joe threw himself in front of Nancy.

Ted shook his head.

'Get out of here, Nancy. You're a wrong'un and no mistake. You've bewitched my son and bewitched my crows, but you're not going to bewitch me.'

'Pa, please.'

Joe took a step towards Ted, hands held high, but Nancy had had enough. Turning on her heel, she fled off down the field so fast her feet almost fell from under her. She came out in the village, just behind the Blue Bell, and paused, hand on its white wall to catch her breath. The little memorial-fund box sat jauntily on the window sill, with a note exhorting people to give what they could for the memory of Langham's dear, lost sons.

Scum! Boche scum!

The words ghosted through her as her emotions ran high. Had the men been right that dark night near this very pub, or had the gunner girls? And what would it cost her if the secret got out now? It wasn't the first time she'd run contrary to what the men of Langham wanted, and unwelcome memories were flooding her mind. She pulled her hand from the pub wall as if stung and picked up her feet again.

Shooting up the track, past an astonished Betty tending the roses over the door of the Gamekeeper's Cottage, she flung herself down the corridor into the annex. There she threw herself on the stupid bundle of clothes masquerading as her sleeping self and wept until she thought her pounding heart might break. She'd ruined everything. Ted was right. She'd betrayed his trust and disrespected his views on his own land. This village was no place for the likes of her, and this time there was nothing else for it; baby or no baby, she had to go.

Chapter Seventeen

'Sambuca!'

Tilly leaned back in her chair and waved to a nearby waitress. Lorna looked across to Aki, sitting at her side.

'Sambuca?'

Aki laughed. 'Why not, Lor? We're on holiday!'

'I suppose so.'

Lorna looked around the Blue Bell, transformed with bunting, streamers and even a big piñata for 'Mexican night', and smiled at Aki, glad her friend was here. She'd been delighted when she'd rung up to say she was coming to stay, and had welcomed her with open arms when she'd arrived two days ago. It had been great to have time to talk, not just about the weighty stuff but the sort of nonsense they'd always enjoyed jabbering over. Aki had chosen to bunk in with Lorna in the pink bedroom, and it had been lovely to have someone to chat to before she drifted off to sleep. Not that it looked as if there was going to be much sleep tonight.

'Hey, Mia!' Tilly called to the waitress, apparently an old school pal of hers. 'Can we have three sambucas, please? Flaming, of course.'

'Of course,' Mia agreed with a grin, and headed for the bar.

Lorna looked at her stepsister across the two empty wine bottles already gracing their table.

'Are you sure this is wise, Tilly?'

'Wise?' Tilly looked horrified. 'Of course it's not wise. It's a girls' night out, Lorna, my lovely – we're not meant to be wise.'

'Of course not. Sorry! It's been a while since I went out.'

'All the more reason not to mess around being "wise".' Tilly chucked back the last of her wine. 'My big sister is "wise". Wise and composed and… and sensible.' She spat the words out as if they were some sort of curse, and Lorna laughed.

'Is that so bad?'

Tilly made a face.

'I guess not, and Helena's lovely, really, just so…'

'Wise?' the other two chimed in at the same time, laughing.

'Exactly. Did you meet her at the wedding, Lorna? Tall, elegant, immaculate, matching husband.'

Lorna nodded, picturing the couple. She'd been introduced and exchanged small talk with them both. They'd been very polite but it had been a struggle to find much to say, and she'd been almost grateful when Stan had smudged a canapé into her dress and she'd had to excuse herself to go and sort it out.

'She doesn't seem at all like you.'

'You can say that again! Helena is the most driven person I know. She wanted to be a doctor from the moment she could hold a stethoscope. All she'd ever do as a child was play with her toy medical kits and beg Dad to be taken into the surgery with him. God, she was a daddy's girl, that one. Perhaps that's why Mum's death didn't seem to hit her as hard as me.'

'Isn't she older too?' Lorna asked.

'Quite a bit, yeah. She was in her last year of her precious medical degree when Mum died, so she hardly had time to grieve.' Tilly shook herself. 'Sorry, that's mean. I'm not usually mean. I know Helena was devastated but she'd left home, she was getting on with her life, so maybe it was easier not to let it, I dunno, get to her as much.'

'That sounds likely,' Aki said. 'Do you have any other siblings?'

'A brother – Rob. He's a good laugh. Bit over-keen on money though. He's in Singapore now, happily making millions. Not that Helena's exactly poor. No idea how I missed that particular gene.'

She grimaced again and Lorna reached across to squeeze her hand, seeing for the first time that lively Tilly was a bit more vulnerable than she usually let on.

'Money isn't everything. We should know – right, Aki? – we're teachers!'

'And you like it?'

'Love it,' Lorna answered automatically, because she did, didn't she? Even if the thought of walking into school again still made her insides turn to *Horrid Henry*-style gloop.

'Me too,' Aki agreed. 'You should think about it, Tilly, if you ever want to settle down.'

'Settle down! That's nearly as bad as being wise. Ah – sambucas, thank goodness!'

She watched happily as the waitress set down three shot glasses, filled with the clear spirit and topped with coffee beans, then pulled out a lighter.

'Ready?'

'Absolutely.'

Mia flicked on the flame and set fire to all three in a practised swipe. Lorna gasped as the flames flared up from the glasses.

'You want me to drink that?!'

'Yep,' Tilly laughed. 'It's delicious.'

'But how?'

'Just knock it back. Here we go, girls: three, two…' Lorna took her glass and looked to the others as they lifted theirs up. 'One. Down the hatch!'

Lorna closed her eyes, lifted the glass to her lips and threw the liquid into her mouth. It filled it with a rush of warm aniseed, and she felt her eyes widen as it seemed to warm through her before she swallowed and the sensation was chased all the way down her throat.

'Wow!' she said. 'That was amazing.'

'Wasn't it?' Aki beamed.

'My lips don't half tingle though.' She put her fingers to them. 'What?' she asked as the other two looked at her with concern. 'What's wrong?'

'Lorna,' Aki said, 'did you put the glass to your lips?'

'Of course. How else am I meant to drink it?'

'You tip it in from above. The glass is hot.'

'I know! It hurts a bit actually.'

'I'm not surprised, sweetie, you've burned the side of your lips. Here.' She grabbed some ice from the untouched water jug and handed it to her. 'Put that on and I'm sure it'll be fine in a minute. Another one?'

'Too right!' Tilly agreed.

'Maybe some ice cream?' Lorna suggested faintly, dabbing at her poor lips with the ice.

The others laughed.

'Let's compromise on a Baileys, shall we? And then, look – the band is starting up.'

'Band?'

'Oh, yes! That's the joy of Mexican night. Norfolk isn't exactly blessed with nightclubs, but once a month you can dance the night away right here in good old Langham. They come from far and wide for it.' She swept an arm around the pub, which was certainly impressively crowded. 'It won't be a rave but it's a laugh all the same.' Lorna glanced at her watch but Tilly swiped her arm down again. 'Don't fret, Lorna. I've already told Dad that babysitting duties include tomorrow morning, so relax and enjoy yourself. You deserve it. We all do.'

Lorna supposed that was true and sipped gratefully at her Baileys, as the other two knocked back second sambucas, expertly tipping the liquid through the flames and into their mouths from well above their lips.

'To the girls!' she toasted, and they gladly took up the cry.

'It's so good to have escaped Xavier for a few days,' Tilly said. 'He's a sweetheart but, goodness, he's worn me out. That man is insatiable!'

Xavier had some friends living in London, and yesterday Tilly had sent him off to see them without her.

'Is it serious between you?' Lorna asked.

'Serious? Nah. Xavier is great, but I couldn't spend the rest of my life with him. He's fun but he's not interesting enough.'

'Tilly!'

'What? It's true. Even I'm not fool enough to believe that a marriage can be built on sex alone.'

'It'd be a start though,' Aki said wistfully, and Tilly turned her sharp stare on her.

'Man troubles, Aki?'

'*Lack of man* troubles, more like. I'm hopeless.'

'Internet dating?'

'Tried it. Over and over. I'm the wrong age. People are either desperately looking for a first wife or already onto a second. They're either in a rush to move in or determined never to do so again. No one seems to want to just get to know each other. It's hell.'

Lorna shivered. Would that be her now? What would her profile say: *Lorna Haynes, 35, widow and mother of two, looking for someone who's never going to match up to the man she lost.* That ought to bring them flocking in! She shuddered, horrified at even the whisper of a thought of dating again.

'But hey,' Aki said swiftly, 'who needs men? We've got each other, right?'

On cue, the band struck up with a ukulele version of 'Girls Just Want To Have Fun' – slightly peculiar but catchy all the same. Aki grabbed Lorna's hand and made for the dance floor, Tilly hot on their heels. The band had picked well, and other women were joining them as the lights dimmed and the cosy little place morphed from restaurant into cheesy nightclub. Lorna threw herself into the music, feeling the dance chasing the alcohol through her veins. Aki was right – she didn't need a man, not right now at least. Even if Matt were here, he'd be propping up the bar with a lager and staying well clear of the oestrogen-rich dance floor, so she could relax and enjoy herself for once.

'Girls!' she bellowed with the rest. 'Girls just wanna have fuuun!'

Was it too much to ask?

The band, perfectly bonkers in ponchos and sombreros, certainly knew how to work a crowd. Despite the apparent limitations of their instruments – an accordion, a ukulele, pan pipes and some bongos – they rocked their way through lively versions of all the pop classics. Lorna found herself perpetually going to sit down, then being caught by the next song and dancing on. An hour later her feet were sore, her face was unbecomingly sweaty, and she felt great.

'We're going to take a break now!' the singer called into the mike, and she sighed with relief.

'Thank God! I need water.'

'And tequila!' Tilly added.

Lorna groaned. 'Do you never stop, Till?'

'Never!'

'Did someone say tequila?' a voice said behind them, and Lorna spun round to see a certain handsome builder standing before her.

'Kyle! Tilly, do you know—?'

'Kyle! Certainly do. We were at school together. Kyle, gorgeous – how the hell are you?'

Lorna saw Aki's eyes widen and gave her a small shake of the head.

'Gay?' Aki whispered. Lorna nodded. 'Thought so.'

Lorna cursed herself again for not spotting it before – though to be fair to her, Kyle had been in his builder's clothes and not in the spray-on jeans and muscle shirt he was now sporting. He also hadn't had a topless man draped around him last time.

'Meet Spenser,' he said, giving the man an affectionate squeeze. 'And these are Raj, Marcus and Dan.'

The other three men in his party leaned in to shake hands. It felt a little incongruous in the fairy-lit bar area, but now someone was ordering more tequilas and the conversation flowed.

'Good to see you looking so well,' Kyle said to Lorna, and she clenched her teeth.

'Sorry for going all pathetic on you the other day.'

'No problem. I imagine staring at those cerise roses day in, day out can do that to anyone!'

She smiled gratefully and took her tequila, though she couldn't help noticing Kyle was still staring rather intently at her.

'What's wrong?'

'Are your lips OK?'

Lorna put a hand up to them and felt the skin raw at either side. 'Sambuca accident.'

'Right. Could happen to anyone! Cheers!'

They all drank. Lorna's head spun. She really ought to get some water, but now Spenser was talking to her.

'Are you the history teacher Kyle's told me about?'

'I am,' she agreed cautiously.

'Cool. What periods do you teach?' She must have looked at him askance because he laughed and added, 'I'm a professor at UEA. An Egyptologist. Surprise, right?'

Lorna tried not to look at his bare chest.

'Of course not.'

He laughed.

'I don't look quite like this when I teach. I've got a tweed jacket and everything. I just like to let my hair down at the weekends.'

She smiled.

'And why not? I teach various periods, to be honest, but I've been looking into the Second World War a lot recently. I found this diary, you see…'

'No way! An actual diary? From the war?'

She looked at him for sarcasm but could find none; he was genuinely fascinated.

'From just after it. She was a gunner girl right here at RAF Langham, and married a local boy. Her name was Nancy Wilson.'

'I knew Nancy.'

'You did?'

'I grew up in the next village; you get to know everyone around here. Plus, David Wilson was the GP. The things he's treated me for!' He raised an eyebrow and she laughed, but then he looked serious again. 'Nancy's diary though – that's great. What a shame she's not still alive to talk to about it.'

'When did she die?' Lorna asked, suddenly realising that she'd never even asked David this.

Spenser considered.

'About ten years ago, I think. I was away at university so I didn't make it to the funeral, but I heard the church was rammed. Are any of the other gunner girls still around?'

'As far as I can tell, three of them are dead. I can't locate the fourth, but I've just found out she may have gone to Germany.'

Lorna had spent hours on the internet ever since May and June had told her about Connie being in Germany, but marvellous as Google was, it was only as good as the search you typed into it and a first name, maiden name and country were not quite enough to track down her subject. It was very frustrating.

'Germany!' Spenser said. 'After the war? Interesting choice.'

'Isn't it? I think something odd might have gone on, Spenser. The gunner girls all seem to have come into money shortly after the war ended and…'

'And you think that was by nefarious means?'

Lorna bit her swollen lip.

'Maybe. I hope not. I'd hate to have to tell David his mum was a crook.'

Spenser rubbed her arm.

'I'm sure she wasn't. People loved Nancy Wilson around here, especially women. She did all sorts to help Lady Merry shake up equality issues in the House of Lords and, closer to home, the two of them headed a group setting up nurseries around Norfolk. Plus, she paid for the war memorial.'

'Which war memorial?'

'The one out there.' Spenser pulled her to the window and pointed across to the smart marble cross on the green, shining in the moonlight.

'Nancy paid for *that*? As well as the cottage roof and the new hatcheries?'

Spenser shrugged.

'Look at it this way, Lorna – if Nancy did come into money in an… unorthodox way, at least she spent it well. Does the rest matter?'

'I keep telling myself that,' Lorna agreed, 'but…'

'But no historian can resist a mystery. I know! I'm sure something will come up if you keep looking. Tell you what, I've got a mate at the uni who's a military historian. I'd be happy to ask him to help if you like?'

'Really? That would be fantastic.'

'Just text Kyle your number and I'll get onto it on Monday. For now, though, the band are coming back!'

'Already?' Lorna gasped. She hadn't even had that water yet, but everyone was piling back onto the dance floor and she was carried along with them. Aki, she noticed, was dancing close up to Dan and looked very happy. Tilly threw herself into the fray with Kyle and Spenser, and the three of them started up some sort of warped

Macarena to a pan-piped 'Uptown Funk'. Lorna tried to dance but her head was spinning even more, and then the band segued into 'Sweet Caroline' and the whole room turned.

She and Matt had danced to this song on their honeymoon. His parents had paid for them to have a beautiful beach chalet in the Seychelles, and it had been impossibly romantic in all the most Instagram-worthy ways. They'd eaten a number of times in a bar right down at the edge of the surf and danced to soft, crooning tunes with others in the holiday resort, but on Saturday night a guest band had come in and the place had been flooded with locals. Much like these quirky Mexicans, the band had gone for their own take on popular tunes, and towards the end of an amazing night, they'd struck up with 'Sweet Caroline'.

As the Blue Bell's makeshift dance floor rocked around Lorna, she pushed her way through the sweaty bodies and stumbled for the loos. All she could see was Matt, holding her hands and bouncing up and down with her, both of them shouting the words at the top of their voices, high on life – high on each other. She would never, ever feel that way again.

'Matt,' she moaned, as she made it into the loos and threw herself at one of the basins, splashing water onto her face, not caring that it would streak her make-up.

Her legs felt weak and her whole body was starting to shake. She looked into the mirror and saw herself – a black-eyed clown with a mocking sambuca smile burned onto her face.

'Why?' she screamed. 'Why did you leave me, Matt? Why did you have to drive on that bloody road at that bloody time? Why not five minutes later? Two hours later. I'd have forgiven you. I'd have forgiven you anything, but now I can't forgive you this, can I? I can't forgive you this because you aren't bloody well here to forgive!'

Her legs buckled and she sank to the floor, burying her head in her hands as the tap mercilessly sprayed water onto her. Let it. Let it fill the whole room up and take her away because she couldn't cope with this. She just couldn't.

'Lorna! Oh darling, come here.'

She felt arms go round her and a hand stroke her wet hair from her face. She felt lips touch her forehead.

'Mum?'

'It's me, Lor. It's Tilly. I've got you. I've got you safe. I'm sorry. A girls' night out was a stupid idea.'

'It was a brilliant idea,' she choked. 'I'm rubbish, that's all. I've forgotten how to enjoy myself. I've forgotten how to live because half the time, Tilly, I just don't want to do it.' She sucked in a shaky breath. 'Oh God, that's awful. I'm awful. I don't mean it, not really. I'd never leave the boys. I just… it's just *so* bloody hard!'

Then she was crying again but Tilly sank down next to her, held her tight and let her sob against her chest until, finally, the tears ran dry. Faint strains of 'I Will Survive' floated through the door and Lorna groaned.

'That band sure knows how to pick its tunes. Sorry, Tilly, I've been no fun.'

'Oh, Lorna,' Tilly said softly. 'I know I may act like I need non-stop fun, but I think I can handle a few tears in the loo, and you'll hardly be the first.'

'Is it ever going to go away? The sadness, I mean.'

Tilly shook her head.

'Not totally, I don't think, but it will fade, I promise. When Mum died, I felt as if someone was sticking red-hot needles in me at least twenty times a day. Now, it's only maybe once a month, when something reminds me of her.'

'Once a month?' Lorna sighed. 'Fantastic.'

'But Lorna, listen – you don't have to do this alone. I'm here for you. Always. I'm your sister now and that's never going to go away.'

Lorna stared at her.

'Never?'

'Never, ever. I'm going to be there for you, Lorna Haynes, whether you like it or not.'

Lorna looked into Tilly's hazel eyes and saw real care there, real love. Fate had taken Matt from her, but she was handing over little compensations and Lorna had to grab them with both hands.

'I like it,' she said, and then Tilly was hugging her again, and it might not be fun but it was something so, so much more. Thank heavens she'd come to Langham this summer – she was getting fonder of the place every day.

Chapter Eighteen

Saturday, 9 March 1946

Oh God, I've really done it this time. I can't stay in Langham now. This is far, far worse than saying some rude word in front of a few villagers. Ted was so angry, so hurt, and he was right to be. He's been nothing but kind to me. He's turned his way of life upside down to accommodate me, and what do I do? Disobey him on the one little thing he asked of me. He's right – I'm disrespectful and mean and downright bad. But I'm not a witch. How can he even think that I'm a witch?

'Nancy? Nancy, are you in there?'

Nancy froze at the sound of her mother-in-law's tentative calls and then shoved the diary under her pillow. Not Betty! Not now. Bleary-eyed, she looked around for escape, but there was only one way into the annex and that was through the house. Betty appeared in the bedroom doorway and looked down at her.

'Oh Nancy, whatever is the matter?'

She came rushing to her side and, however complicated her relationship with this family might be, right now Nancy was miserable and lonely, and the soft arms Betty was holding out to her were impossible to resist. She flung herself into her gentle embrace and drew in comfort like a little girl. She wanted her own mam. She wanted her sisters and her big, easy dad, and even her scamp of a brother. She didn't know what she was doing here in

Norfolk, where life was so very different and she seemed to make mistakes at every turn.

'There, there, lass. Cry it out. It can't be that bad.'

Nancy gulped down her tears. It *was* that bad! Wait until Ted got home and Betty heard what she'd done. She wouldn't be cuddling Nancy then; she'd be showing her the door quick-smart and possibly Joe with her. Her ridiculous cravings to shoot a gun might split him up from his beloved parents, and she couldn't bear that.

'I've been so stupid,' she gasped into Betty's comforting bosom.

'Oh, we're all stupid sometimes, lass. What have you done?'

Nancy pulled back a little to look up into Betty's kind face.

'I can't tell you.'

'Why?'

'Because you'll hate me.'

Betty gave a soft laugh.

'I doubt it, lass. I don't have it in me to hate anyone. That Hitler, maybe, but surely you've not done anything quite as bad as him?'

Despite herself, Nancy gave a little hiccup of a laugh.

'No, not as bad as him, but that leaves a lot of scope, Betty.'

Betty stroked her hair back from her wet face.

'So tell me.'

Nancy sighed.

'I guess you'll find out soon enough. Any minute maybe. Ted's furious.'

'Ah.' Betty gave a sage nod. 'He has a temper on him, my husband. Allus has done. If it helps, lass, it usually dampens down as quickly as it flares up.'

'Not this time. I've really upset him, Betty. I'm sorry. I think he'll ask me to leave.'

'Leave?! Lordie, I doubt it, Nancy. He thinks you're the bees' knees.'

'What? No, he doesn't.'

'He does. Tells me how good you are with the estate, how quickly you've picked up everything he's taught you, what an asset you're going to be to us all.'

Nancy stared at Betty incredulously.

'No, he doesn't,' she repeated, stupefied.

'He does! Oh, I know he can be a bit gruff, lass, and he's not been brought up to believe girls can do these things, but he's picking it up faster than you'd imagine.'

'He's never said anything.'

'No. That's not Ted's way.'

Nancy felt sorrow well up inside her; this was worse than she thought.

'Well, take it from me, I've really blown it now. He won't want me anywhere near the estate after today. He thinks I'm a witch.'

'A witch?! Goodness, Nancy, Norfolk may be a bit backwards but we're not that soft.'

Nancy didn't bother replying. Ted's words were still ringing in her ears: *You've bewitched my son and bewitched my crows, but you're not going to bewitch me.*

'I think perhaps I should go before he gets back.'

'Over my dead body!'

'What?'

'You're not leaving me here with that pair of boys. I love having another woman around, lass, even one who likes lolloping out in the grounds, and d'you know what – those Wednesday afternoons with my Joe are the best gift you could ever have brought me. We have so much fun. I'd never have guessed you could do baking with a man, or flower arranging or embroidery, but he's given it all a go and it's such a joy to be with him, the two of us. You youngsters, you've a very different way of viewing the world and it's hard for us old lot to keep up, but we're doing our best, really we are. Now, please, Nancy, tell me what you've done before Ted comes blustering in and I get some garbled version. Please.'

Nancy looked into her mother-in-law's eyes and saw real compassion there. There was more to Betty than just floral pinnies, and she had to trust her now. She drew in a deep breath.

'Joe's been teaching me to shoot.'

'Ah.'

'And this afternoon I went out with the men in disguise and I shot down a whole lot of crows – more than any of the others, bar Ted, thank heavens. I was good at it, really I was – careful and safe and all of that – but when Joe revealed who I was, Ted was furious. I mean, really furious. I don't blame him, either. He said I'd disrespected his wishes and I had. He said we'd betrayed him, Joe and me, and we had. Really, Betty, I've ruined everything.'

And then she began to cry again. It was pathetic and not at all in keeping with the competent gunwoman she'd been trying to be, but she couldn't help it. It was as if the pressure of keeping it secret was pushing the tears out of her like a pump, and she couldn't hold them in. Betty stroked her hair and said 'there, there' over and over, and Nancy supposed she should be grateful she hadn't run screaming from the annex, but neither did she seem to have anything helpful to suggest.

'Nancy,' she said eventually, 'this seems to have hit you very hard.'

'He's furious, Betty.'

'Yes, but even so. Is there something else you want to tell me?'

Nancy looked up at her again. Betty's head was on one side and a faint smile was playing on her lips. It wasn't what Nancy had expected.

'You know?'

'I wondered, that's all. I, er, heard you being sick a while back and had my hopes, but then you didn't say anything so I thought maybe it had really been a bug. But you've been looking a little... fuller. In a good way. I mean, it suits you. So I suppose I started wondering again. Is it true, Nancy? Are you in the family way?'

Nancy smiled at the quaint phrase.

'I believe so.'

'Oh! Oh, I'm so pleased. Does Joe know?' She shook her head. 'No? Goodness, the man must be blind. They are though, men. He'll know now and—'

'Know what?'

They both looked up guiltily to see Joe standing in the doorway, Ted a dark shadow behind him.

'Nancy?' Betty said.

Nancy sat up on the vivid pink bed and brushed her hair back. She must have looked a right state, all red-eyed and blotchy, but both men were staring at her and Betty's hand was in the small of her back as if propping her up, and it seemed there was only one thing to say.

'I think I'm pregnant.'

It was as if she had uttered some sort of spell. The fear fell away from Joe's face as fast as the anger from Ted's, and they both tumbled forward into the room, smiling and falling over themselves to congratulate her. Maybe she was, indeed, a witch? Or perhaps just possessed of the feminine magic so mysterious to all men. However equal they might become with a gun, they would never be able to bear life, and for perhaps the first time since she'd arrived at the Gamekeeper's Cottage, Nancy felt suffused with pride at being a woman.

'Nancy! Darling, that's amazing. Are you sure? Are you well? Are you happy?' The questions tumbled out of Joe as he sat down on the bed and took her into his arms. 'A baby!' he cried, as if she was the first woman ever to produce one. '*Our* baby. Oh Nancy, I couldn't be happier.'

'A new little gamekeeper,' Ted said, hovering close but not daring to approach her. 'Oh Nancy, no wonder you were a bit, a bit...'

He stalled and no one filled in a word for him. It didn't matter. What they had here, as if, indeed, by magic, was a way of healing the rift without ever having to probe it. This second 'incident' could be explained away as a product of 'hormones', a rush of blood to the womb that had made Nancy in some way 'not herself'. Nancy hated that. She put a hand to her stomach, wanting the baby so much now but still resenting that it could define her so easily. She longed to stand up and yell, 'This has nothing whatsoever to do with shooting crows.' But what was the point? Ted had been upset (an understatement if ever there was one), and that had made Joe upset, and that had made Nancy upset, and here was a chance to wipe that all away and 'get on'.

'When do you think you're due?' Betty asked, taking Ted's hand.

'Late summer?' Nancy hazarded. 'I need to see a doctor to be sure.'

'Of course you do,' Ted said. 'Of course. We can sort that. Only the best, Nancy, for our baby.'

'Hey, maybe by the time it's born they'll have that health service up and running like they keep promising,' Joe said. 'It might be born for free, Nance.'

'Wouldn't that be something!'

'Now come on,' Ted said. 'Joe, you take a pot to the Blue Bell for a drop of ale, and Betty, you whip up a cake. We've to celebrate.'

'Ted…' Nancy felt she should say something but had no idea what it was. 'Ted, I'm sorry.'

He waved her quiet, then leaned over and gave her a quick, whiskery kiss on the top of her head.

'All forgotten, Nancy.'

'But—'

'Don't worry yourself about it. You'll be needing to take care of yourself now, won't you?'

So you won't be going anywhere near a gun, Nancy finished despondently in her head. Everyone else was in the mood to party and she mustn't be churlish, but it didn't feel like such a cause for celebration to her. Now she'd got used to the idea, she was longing to have this precious baby, but she still couldn't help wondering what its arrival might change for her. She had to do something before it was too late; she had to talk to the gunner girls.

Chapter Nineteen

Lorna prised the tin open and groaned. Normally she liked the smell of fresh paint but this morning, with sambuca and tequila still swilling around her system, it wasn't doing anything for her. Why on earth had she agreed to come along to help repaint the outside of the Langham Dome? She must be mad.

They hadn't got in until almost 3 a.m. last night, and then Lorna had had to listen to Aki waxing lyrical about Dan for at least another half an hour. It had been rather sweet at the time, but she'd kill for that extra bit of sleep right now. In theory she'd had a lie-in, but years of waking at six thirty had worn a groove in her mind that had pinged her awake. Although she'd stayed in bed for as long as she could, she hadn't slept again, and had given up and gone for a cup of tea at eight. Three cups and a Full English later and she'd been feeling up to the second volunteer day, but now she was actually here she wasn't so sure it had been a good idea.

'Does that paint smell odd to you?' she asked Aki.

'Everything smells odd to me,' she groaned. 'And that sun is way too bright!' She adjusted her sunglasses and reached for a bottle of water. 'How's Tilly?'

They looked over to where the younger woman was chasing Charlie and Stan around, brandishing her own paintbrush and looking as fresh as a daisy.

'Disgusting,' Lorna said.

'Unfair,' Aki agreed.

They grinned at each other.

'Are we getting too old for nights out, Aki?'

'Nah. We just need a bit longer to recover. And it was worth it.'

'To meet the lovely Dan?'

She flushed.

'Maybe. Doubt it'll come to anything. The nice ones never do. He's probably married, or kinky or—'

'Aki?'

'Dan!' Aki shot upwards as two men ambled towards them, and Lorna suppressed a smile as her friend tried to arrange her hungover body into a welcoming pose. 'You came.'

'It sounded a worthy cause when you told me about it last night, so I thought why not.'

'Fantastic. Nice day for it too.'

'Lovely. Although it's a bit hot. Don't know about you two, but we're hungover as hell.'

Aki laughed.

'I am so glad you said that. I feel awful.'

'You certainly don't look it,' Dan said, and the pair of them smiled at each other. 'Maybe a coffee would help?' he suggested, waving to the stand Lilian had set up across the field.

'It's worth a try,' Aki agreed, and they were off instantly, chattering away, hangovers apparently cured before they even got near the caffeine.

Lorna looked to the other man.

'You're Raj, right?'

'Right.'

'You got dragged along by Dan?'

'Certainly did. He was too nervous to come on his own. It was very funny. Kind of sweet too, I guess. He's been on his own for far too long, so it's nice to see him actually interested in someone.'

'Is he single?'

'Single, solvent and – as far as I know – not especially kinky.'

Lorna blushed.

'You heard us?'

'Sorry. I don't think it's going to matter though, do you?'

He gestured to where Aki and Dan were sitting at a picnic bench, so close as to look almost like one.

'No, but now you're stuck here with us.'

'Guess so, but hey, my wife's doing the girls' ballet class so at least I got out of that! Have you got another paintbrush? I might as well make myself useful until lover-boy is done.'

Lorna found him one as Lilian called the volunteers together to make a start on repainting the dome. She looked around at the kind little group while Lilian gave out jobs, and felt warmed to see them. Tilly had talked Kyle into coming along, and now he was fastening a harness to the top of the dome and hitching them both up to do the top section. Charlie and Stan were begging Mary to be allowed to join them, but when Rachel arrived with George and Annie they were thankfully distracted. David was chatting to Richard and Brian, the three of them waving paintbrushes to punctuate their conversation, though they stopped obediently as Lilian directed everyone to space out around the dome, ready for the assault. They almost looked, Lorna thought, like a line of soldiers preparing themselves to go over the top, and she brandished her own brush as Lilian called for them to 'Start painting!'

There was something mesmerising about covering the stained old paint with pristine white, and Lorna happily focused on her little patch of curved wall, trying to reach as high as she could to spare Kyle and Tilly from having to drop down on their harnesses. The kids helped for a few half-hearted minutes, then dropped their brushes and chased off into the trees together. Lorna smiled to see them go. Charlie seemed much better these days. He was chatting again and playing more naturally. Every so often she would look out of the window and see him sitting beneath the runner-bean frames, talking earnestly to the worms, but it seemed to be working for him so she tried to leave him to it. He deserved privacy to mourn as much as she did, and she blessed her mother for the simple idea.

'Aha – the diary girl!'

Lorna turned to see that Brian had made his way round so that his section came up against hers. She stifled a groan; she wasn't sure she was quite on form to deal with him today.

'Morning, Brian. Lovely day.'

'Isn't it just. Kirstie and I were up and at it bright and early this morning.'

Lorna blinked.

'Kirstie?'

'My Labrador.' He indicated a squat dog sitting quietly to one side. 'She loves a sunrise walk, bless her, and it's good for me to get up and on. I could spend all day in bed if it wasn't for her.'

'Could you?'

He wrinkled his nose.

'Not really. I'm an active sort, you know, but some days it's quite hard to be bothered.' She looked at him curiously and he gave a self-conscious shrug. 'I never used to be like this. It was only after my Janice died that I got lazy. Well, not lazy – just struggling to see the point.'

Lorna swallowed.

'Someone told you about Matt?'

He screwed up his face.

'David did. Sorry. Not my place to say anything, probably. I just thought—'

'No, no. It's lovely of you, really. Nice to have someone who understands. It's my boys who get me out of bed in the morning.'

Brian looked over to where Charlie and Stan were chasing George around the trees.

'More persistent than even a Labrador, I imagine.'

'Afraid so, but you're right, it's probably a good job or I'd huddle in my own misery all day long.'

Brian reached out an awkward hand and patted her shoulder.

'It does get better. It's a slow process, but it honestly does get better.'

'Thanks, Brian.'

'And it helps to have people around you.'

He waved to the happy painters and Lorna nodded.

'It certainly does. And projects like this one to spark your interest. Ooh, talking of which – you know those stories in the pub, Brian, did they ever involve a girl called Connie?'

'Connie?' He frowned. 'Not that I recall. They weren't my stories, you understand.'

She smiled at him.

'I get that, Brian – you're not nearly old enough.'

'Feel it some mornings, but still, thanks. Connie?' He swirled his paintbrush thoughtfully across the dome. 'I don't remember anyone mentioning that name, but they tended to talk about the gunner girls as if they were, you know, all one.'

'I can imagine. I'm interested in this particular girl because it seems that she moved to Germany after the war.'

'Germany?! Odd choice back then.'

'Isn't it? I guess I wondered if there were any POWs around here or anything?'

'POWs?' He looked at her. 'Well, yes – there was the German pilot.'

Lorna's stomach lurched.

'What German pilot?'

'The one who crashed his plane in the fields outside the village. You could see pieces of the wreckage for years. Even when I was a kid, you could turn up bits of metal if you dug around. Quite the story, it was. Seems he must have done very well to get himself out of the plane as it was fully on fire. His radar operator was killed straight out, but somehow he made it to the airfield and turned himself in to the authorities.'

Lorna's head spun. Could there be a connection to Connie and the other gunner girls?

'Do we know what happened to him, Brian?'

'No idea. I think maybe he was treated at the hospital up in Langham Hall. It was mainly British and American soldiers in there so a German would have stood out, poor bloke.'

Lorna had to stop herself reaching up and giving Brian a great big kiss. It all made sense now – this German pilot must have been the top-secret prisoner that the gunner girls were nursing. But who was he? And what happened next? Did it have anything to do with the money they all apparently came into?

'Are there records, do you know?'

'Bound to be, but I've no idea where. You need a historian.'

Lorna's heart jumped again as she remembered Spenser saying he had a mate at the university who might help her. Really, all this excitement was not good for her hangover, but she didn't care.

'Hey, Kyle!' she called up. 'If I send you my number, would you pass it on to Spenser?'

'Spenser?' Kyle squinted down at her from his harness. 'You want me to give Spenser your number? Lorna, you do know…'

She laughed.

'Not like that, Kyle! It's a history thing.'

'Ah! No problem then. Fire it over and I'll send it straight on. Oi!'

He ducked as Tilly came swinging in from the side, out of control on her harness and with her paintbrush waving wildly. Lorna watched, open-mouthed, as the loaded brush caught Kyle smack on the side of his face, sending a long white streak up his defined cheek.

'Sorry, Kyle!' Tilly giggled.

'You little minx!'

'I didn't do it on purpose, honest. I… Oh!' She gasped as Kyle streaked paint down the back of her blonde hair. 'Right, builder-boy, you're for it!'

She dipped her brush into the pot attached to her waist, but before she could attack him Kyle had put his strong arms around her, pinning her to the dome. Lorna giggled and looked around for Aki but she'd disappeared, probably into the trees with the lovely Dan. She had a fleeting moment to hope she didn't bump into Charlie and Stan before a roar split the air.

'How dare you!' Everyone spun round to see a small, dark and very irate figure come storming across the field. 'Hands off my woman!'

'Xavier!' Tilly called from Kyle's arms. 'It's not what you think.'

But Xavier wasn't listening. He flung his arms in the air and looked at the little crowd.

'I am gone three days. Just three days and already someone has put his filthy hands on my Tilly.'

His accent was thickening with his anger and the effect was dangerously comic. Lorna looked from Tilly and Kyle, suspended on the side of the dome together, to Xavier strutting about below, with the great and good of Langham watching on, and it was too much for her. She burst out laughing and Xavier turned on her, stalking forward.

'You think this funny, Miss Lorna? My heart, it break. Break wide open. I come halfway across world with this woman and she betray me – and in front of whole town.'

The small group of volunteers looked at each other, clearly unsure what to do next. Lorna took Xavier's hands and fought to control her laughter.

'Like Tilly said, Xavier, it's not what you think. Kyle is gay.'

'Gay? He like men?' Xavier looked uncertainly up at Kyle, then spat. 'Nonsense! Look at him, han-mandling my lady like a professional.'

Now it wasn't just Lorna who was laughing. Rachel turned away to hide a splutter and Brian went to bury his face in his dog's neck. Tilly was trying to lower herself down the dome but was no expert on the harness and had got herself stuck in Kyle's clip. Thankfully, David remained calm and strode over to the poor Brazilian as he looked desperately around at the chaos he'd created.

'I can assure you that Kyle has no interest in my daughter, Xavier. Nor she in him. She speaks only of you. She's been pining since you left.'

'Pining?' Xavier questioned.

It was the word that had confused him, Lorna was sure, but it might as well have been the concept, for Tilly had most certainly not been pining. Finally, though, she had made it down to the ground and ran to Xavier, leaning in to kiss him and inadvertently smearing him with paint.

'My jacket!' he wailed, but then their lips met and he didn't seem to mind too much any more. His hands went around Tilly, reaching openly for her bum and pulling her tight in against him and, eyebrows raised, David turned away.

'Coffee, anyone?'

'Good idea,' Lilian said, hurrying her little group across to the drinks stand. 'And after that, Richard has got hold of some old camera equipment and is going to show us how the range finder really worked.'

'Fantastic!' Lorna said, following her.

With first Aki and now Tilly heading for the trees, she was fast running out of friends, but as Richard proudly unveiled the ancient camera she didn't care. Charlie came loping in, magnetically pulled by the promise of guns, and, coffees in hand, those not romantically entangled crowded into the dome and watched Richard set it up. It took a while and quite a lot of long-winded explanation but Lorna enjoyed it, drawn in by one thought above all – Nancy could have been here, in this very dome, learning how to shoot planes. Richard finally dimmed the lights and, with a creak and a whirr, the wheels of the machine spun into life and a genuine Messerschmitt was projected across the ceiling, so close that Lorna actually ducked to avoid it.

Was this what it had been like the night the plane had come down over the village? she wondered. Feeling it via World War II technology made her feel closer than ever to her roommate from across the ages. If this thrill of life-and-death urgency had been Nancy's experience of the war, was it any wonder she'd found peacetime dull? But what on earth had it led her to do that was so bad she'd had to rip up her precious diary? And what did it have to do with this German pilot? Lorna was more determined than ever to find out.

Chapter Twenty

This pregnancy lark isn't as bad as I feared. I haven't been able to see any of the girls, but Dot says she has something planned for very soon and, to be honest, I don't feel so bad now. I've got loads of energy, my hair's gone proper glossy, my tits are the sort of glorious mounds I've always been jealous of, and I can't get enough of my Joe. Bless him, he's worn out. He's not complaining though! Well, not about that bit.

I cannot believe that this time last year we'd just declared victory in Europe. I was still in the barracks with the girls. It had been a normal sort of day. We'd been cleaning out the machines in the morning and we'd got a netball game in the afternoon. Lord, I loved those netball games. We didn't have enough ATS girls on site to make two full teams, so some of the lads used to play. They joked about it at first, laughing at the restrictions on movement compared to football – well, they soon found out it's not as easy as it looks and were clamouring to play. That day, though, our game was cut short.

We'd heard rumours, of course, but there were rumours all the time around then. Our lads had been advancing so fast we'd been expecting a surrender for months, but Hitler was a stubborn old bugger. That day though – that day it was finally over. We gathered around the wireless in the mess hall to listen to Churchill announce the victory, and I remember us all glued to his words. I remember them sort of swelling in my heart.

There was this sense of awe, of relief, of unspeakable pride. Churchill talked about how long Britain had stood alone against the Nazis and how brave we'd been. He talked about a 'bird of freedom' chirping in human hearts and I remember thinking how lovely that was. He's a gruff man, but he has a way with words for sure. When he'd finished, we partied. Of course we did. I think Dot was the first up on the tables, but the rest of us weren't far behind. All I could think was 'Joe will be safe now. Joe can come home and we can be together.' And look now – here we are! And with a baby on the way.

Everything seems to be bursting into life around here. There are lambs in every field, chicks in every hedgerow, calves at their mothers' sides and the most beautiful, shy fawns with the deer herd. They're just like Bambi. Joe took me to see that film on our third date. Didn't see much of it, if I'm honest, but I remember the poor little thing's big eyes, and I can't help thinking about it every time I spot another of our own lovely fawns in the long grass.

But anyway, our own baby was rolling around and kicking out like a good'un in bed last night and I lay there, feeling it having its little party inside me, and had this sense of, well, of wonder I suppose, that I was growing another human being inside me. Joe loves that too. He lies for hours with his hand on my belly, waiting for the little'un to move. He talks to it sometimes too, soft stuff about how well he's going to look after it and what a great world he's going to make for it. It's very sweet, really it is, but he hasn't half got protective. I wasn't allowed to dance on the tables this VE Day, that's for sure!

'Letter for you, Nance.'

Nancy looked up surprised as Betty handed an envelope over the breakfast table. It couldn't be from her family as she'd heard from them just a few days ago, brimming over with excitement about the baby. And the handwriting didn't look like it belonged to either Peggy or Connie, her other correspondents. Dot always preferred to phone, saying she couldn't get words down fast enough on paper, so who could this be from?

'You going to open it?' Joe teased and, blushing, she reached for her knife, slid it carefully under the flap, and drew out a cream card.

You're invited to a hen party

Nancy stared at the rich copperplate in confusion.

'What's a hen party?' she asked.

Ted, Betty and Joe looked up from their own letters. Betty laughed.

'Nothing special, Nance. Just a get-together that's all girls. Hens, you know?'

'Hens? Right. Is that like the GIs calling us chicks?'

'No,' Joe said firmly, 'it's not like that. Hens is a fond term. Chicks is more, more…'

Nancy looked at him, amused.

'More what, Joe?'

'More salacious,' he said, pursing his lips amusingly primly. 'Who's inviting you to this "hen" party anyway?'

'Dot,' she said happily. 'It's in Norwich this Saturday. Tea and cakes at her mum's house. We don't have anything on, do we?'

'Saturday?' Betty asked. 'No. Saturday's free. Sounds lovely, Nance.'

'Norwich, though,' Joe said. 'It's a way.'

Nancy looked at him.

'It's forty minutes on the bus, Joe. I've been a few times, remember?'

'I don't want you out late.'

She laughed.

'It's tea and cakes, darling. At eleven in the morning. It would have to really kick off to keep me out late.'

'Right. Tell you what, I've got a few things I need from Norwich. We can go together.'

'It's a hen party, Joe.'

'Not to the party! You can go off to your tea and cakes and I'll do my business, and then we can meet up to come home together.'

'What do you need?' Ted asked.

'Oh, a few bits and pieces.'

'For the estate?'

Joe coloured.

'No, Pa, for me. Is that allowed?'

'Course, son. Course it is. Why not?'

Nancy sighed. There was nothing Joe wanted from town and they all knew it. He was only coming to be sure that she was looked after, and that was very sweet of him, if totally unnecessary. The doctor had put her due date in early September, so only four months away now, and Nancy swore that if he could keep her tucked up in bed all that time, he would.

All credit to him, mind, he'd given in to her insistence that she could still do work on the estate, albeit light tasks. She had Merry to thank for that. When she'd heard the happy news, she'd turned up at the Gamekeeper's Cottage with a gorgeous hamper full of treats for Nancy – lemon drops, scented bath salts, chocolate and lavender oil.

'To rub on your stomach,' she'd told Nancy as she'd unwrapped these wonders. 'To stop stretch marks. We don't want the little bugger ruining your gorgeous figure, do we?'

'Merry!' Joe had objected, but Nancy had laughed and agreed.

'That's why I need to keep going out and about too,' she'd said.

'Quite right, quite right. There's all sorts of studies into how beneficial exercise is for pregnant women. Goodness, some of the Langham girls were working in Boulton and Paul's right up until the day they popped. Young Rose Fowler gave birth on the factory floor, right there among the fuselages with the other girls cheering her on. Marvellous!'

Joe had looked as if he might be sick at the thought, but Nancy had found it very cheering.

'Is there any way of reading those studies, Merry?'

'Oh, yes! My mate Flopsy's a nurse in Norwich General. She's stepping out with one of the senior maternity consultants. Bound to be able to bag a copy. I'll ask her.'

And, true to her word, she'd come round again a week or so later with ten pages of densely written script, complete with graphs and pie charts. Joe had blenched when she'd shown it to him and been content to rely on the title: 'A Treatise Advising Exercise During Pregnancy' by Dr Sebastian T. Myers. Ted had been even more horrified – and impressed – by it, and Nancy had let it sit on the coffee table for several days before she'd spirited it away.

She'd read it all the way through, though, and been delighted to see her own instincts confirmed by the good doctor. She didn't blame her new family for being cautious, especially if Betty had lost a baby, but going into Norwich to see her friends was surely not a problem.

'It would be lovely if you could come too, Joe,' she said and saw his shoulders relax. 'Perhaps we could even stay a night?'

They all looked horrified.

'Stay a night? In Norwich? In a hotel?'

Betty said the last word as she might have done 'concentration camp'. Not that she would ever utter those words aloud. None of them would. Bit by bit more stories were leaking out about the horrors of places like Auschwitz and Dachau, but even down the

Blue Bell they were whispered. No one could believe any man was capable of such inhumanity to his fellows, and no one wanted to give it validity by talking about it.

'It was just an idea,' Nancy said limply.

Betty's nose wrinkled.

'Goodness, why stay in some mouldy hotel bed, slept in by who knows who, getting up to who knows what, when you can come home to your own nice, clean, comfortable one?'

'Quite right,' Nancy agreed. 'Silly idea. Now, haven't we got feeders to fill?'

The moment had passed, but later that night she spoke to Joe about it.

'I was just thinking of our honeymoon, Joe, remember?'

His eyes darkened instantly.

'How could I forget, gorgeous?'

'I thought we could, you know, recapture a bit of that, that...'

'Excitement?' He pulled her close. 'I reckon we could manage that here, don't you?'

'God, do I?!'

This middle stage of her pregnancy was doing funny things to her body, making her crave sex at peculiar times of the day. Last week she'd have taken her husband to bed every damned lunchtime if his parents hadn't been there, and on Friday she'd firmly closed the door to the annex before tea, put some lively tunes on the wireless, and forcibly stripped him.

'Are you sure it's safe?' he'd kept asking, stroking her swollen belly.

'Quite sure,' she'd told him. 'I checked with Merry and she asked her friend, and apparently it's totally fine. Baby's a long way up inside, Joe – further than you'll ever get.'

'Cheeky!' he'd cried, but he hadn't objected any further.

Yes, he'd definitely keep her in bed for the next three months if he could! Instead, he was stuck with a bus trip to Norwich.

*

Nancy and Joe turned down the street to Dot's mum's house, arm in arm, and stopped to stare, horrified anew at the ravages of war. Why did it still continue to surprise? Nancy wondered. They all knew the figures, they'd all seen the pictures on the newsreels, but somehow being faced with the damage in person hit you harder. Dot's house was tucked behind the cathedral down what must once have been a pretty little street, but was now blighted by bomb damage.

The Luftwaffe had been trying to hit the cathedral in some sort of twisted cultural wipe-out, using their own Baedeker tourist guides to pick the prettiest cities to target. Somehow they'd missed the beautiful church, but they'd sure as hell wreaked havoc on the homes all around. Dot's house was one of only five still standing amongst the rubble of the rest of the street, and they approached it sadly.

'How will the country ever find the time to repair all this?' Nancy asked Joe, as they stepped over splintered beams and broken bricks.

'Or the money,' he said.

They both looked uneasily at each other. A leak had formed in the roof of the Gamekeeper's Cottage last week, and they'd had to place a bucket in the hall to catch the drips. Joe had tried to plug it with lime plaster but it wouldn't last long, and if the hole grew, they were in trouble – the cottage would fall down and they'd have no choice but to move into Lord Langham's new build. The problem was that they were as poor as the rest of the country at the moment, and Nancy was still racking her brain for ways of raising some cash. Looking at the ruins of the city, however, reminded her how lucky they were to even be alive.

'Thank God we won, Joe.'

He held her tight against him and they stood there, frozen amongst the rubble of so many people's homes, and tried to imagine what life might be like now if the Germans had made it onto their little island. It had been close, they both knew. Closer than anyone had ever admitted over the wireless, or on the cheery posters stuck to every telegraph pole and bus stop.

'Thank the Lord for the Russians,' Joe said darkly.

'The Russians?' She peered at him. 'Don't you mean the Americans?'

He shrugged.

'Them too. They helped us win the war, perhaps, but Russia made sure Germany lost it. If they'd stuck on the German side, we'd all be saluting Hitler now.' Nancy shivered and he gave her a hug. 'But what are we talking like this for, sweetheart? We *did* win. We *did* see off the bastards and we are safe. Our baby will be born into a peaceful world, so let's look forward to that, not back to the dark days, hey?'

She nodded.

'You're right, Joe. Now, do come in and say hello to Dot and the others.'

But at that Joe pulled back.

'No way!'

'Why not? Peggy's going to be there, Connie too. I'm sure they'd love to talk to you.'

'And I to them, but Nancy, it's a "hen party", remember? Strictly no men allowed.'

'I'm sure you can come in for a minute,' she said, but at that moment a peal of girlish laughter floated out of the window at the front of the house and Joe shook his head vehemently.

'I'll leave you to it, thank you very much. I'll come back around one, shall I?'

'Thanks, Joe.'

He bent and kissed her.

'My pleasure. If it runs over, you'll find me in there.'

He indicated a pub called the Wig and Pen just down the street, and Nancy laughed.

'What hardship, darling.'

'The things I do for you!' he agreed, tipping his hat at her, before turning and sauntering back down the wrecked street towards the cathedral. Nancy watched him go a moment, then turned and knocked at Dot's door.

'Nancy! Oh my golly goodness, look at you!'

Dot dragged her inside and she was instantly surrounded by girls, ushering her into the best seat and cooing over her bump.

'You look so well,' Peggy said. 'Pregnancy suits you, Nancy.'

Nancy looked at her friend for signs of sadness. She knew from Peggy's letters that she was still battling to conceive but, to her relief, her friend seemed genuinely pleased for her.

'I'm as fat as a pig!'

'Nonsense,' Connie said. 'You look just the same but with a football smuggled up your dress. Your hair's so glossy and your skin's amazing.'

'It wasn't at the start,' Nancy assured her. 'I was green and sick and half asleep most of the time.'

'Well, you look fabulous now,' Peggy said, unable to keep a wistful note from creeping into her voice.

Nancy hugged her.

'How's the women's army corps, Peg?'

'Slow to non-existent. It's such an uphill fight, Nance, and now my Harry's been posted to the north and I'm going to have to go with him. I've no idea how I'll get anything done up there.'

Nancy laughed.

'It's not all wilderness outside London, you know, Peg. Where in the north?'

'Not sure. Manchester, I think, wherever that is.'

Nancy nudged her.

'That's more or less where I come from, and it's a great city. Far less bombed than London or poor old Norwich.'

'Wouldn't be hard! It's a long way away though, Nance.'

'Not that far. It's near my home town, so when I go up to visit my mam I can come and see you too.' Peggy still looked down, so she leaned close and added, 'You know what – people have loads of babies in the north. Something in the air maybe, or the water.'

'Really?'

Peggy's eyes lit up. Nancy felt a bit guilty. She had no idea where she'd got that from, but if Peggy was positive it was more likely to happen, of that she was sure.

'Really,' she said firmly, and was rewarded by a smile.

An older lady joined them. She had to be Dot's mum, Sandra, for she was the spit of her – the same bright face and twinkling eyes, just with a few added wrinkles.

'Welcome, ladies, to my miraculously still standing home.'

'The bombing must have been awful for you,' Peggy said, all charm again.

'Terrible,' Sandra agreed. 'One week, that's all it took. One damned week for those bloody Germans to wipe out half the city. First night it happened, I swear I thought the world was ending. Oh, we'd heard about it from London, of course we had, and felt wholly sorry for the poor people stuck there, but we'd never imagined it would come to sleepy old Norwich. Such lummoxes, we were!'

'Were you here?' Nancy asked. 'In this house?'

They looked out at the wreckage either side.

'Not after the first night,' Sandra said. 'Grabbed the littlies and ran for my mother's out in the Broads. Came back a week later to this – couldn't believe the house was still here.'

'You must have felt blessed,' Peggy said.

Sandra looked at her and smiled sadly.

'Mainly, my lovely, I felt guilty. All those people with nowhere to go, and my place stood there unharmed. We slept near on twenty of us in here for weeks until everyone could find places to stay.'

'Twenty? That must have been dreadful.'

Sandra smiled again.

'My house had survived and I'd happily have shared every last inch of it. Now, tea. And cakes. We've made lots of cakes, so you all have to eat up!'

They needed no second asking. Connie and Peggy sat on the arms of Nancy's chair as a gaggle of other women gathered round. Dot introduced her sisters, her childhood friends, and her colleagues from MacLaren's. There were so many names that they soon jumbled in Nancy's head, but it didn't seem to matter. It was enough just to be here, together. The atmosphere reminded her a little of the barracks in Langham, and for a fleeting moment she envied Dot her factory job with these loud, loving women.

'Ladies,' Dot said. The chatter died down but not by much, so she clambered onto the coffee table, balancing precariously amongst the plates of cakes as her mum fluttered at her feet. 'Ladies!' All faces turned her way and she grinned. 'Better! I have a few words to say.'

Nancy looked to Peggy and Connie as they watched their friend address the room. She seemed to have grown since the war. She'd always had plenty of confidence but in a giggly, party-girl sort of a way. Now she was more commanding. That, Nancy supposed, was what being a supervisor had done for her.

'Get on then, lass,' one of her workmates called out. 'Me tea's going cold.'

'Watch it, Cathy Johnson, or I'll have you on press-studs on Monday.' They all groaned; it seemed press-studs were not a coveted job. 'But anyway, I will get on with it. I wanted to say thank you all for coming and for making it to the house – tricky to find round here, I know.' She gestured out of the window at the lack of other buildings and they all laughed at the dark humour. 'Where was I? Oh, yes. Thank you for coming and I'll get straight to the point of this "hen party".'

'Is it you saying we're chicken, Dot?' Cathy called.

'Not at all. It's a Yank thing – you get your girls together to support you in, you know, important life changes.'

They looked at each other, puzzled. Dot looked round at them gleefully and suddenly Nancy knew what was going on.

'What life changes, Dot?' another girl demanded. 'Stop being so damned mysterious.'

It was too much for Dot to hold in any longer. Clapping her hands and bouncing perilously amongst the cakes, she said, 'Marriage,' and then, as everyone stared open-mouthed, she jumped up and down on the table and cried, 'I'm inviting you all to my wedding!' The room went wild. Dot produced a very large diamond ring and everyone fell on it.

'Come on then, our Dot,' Cathy exclaimed, 'how did he propose?'

Dot needed little urging. She sat herself on the table and beamed round at her eager audience.

'It was so romantic, girls. He took me on a picnic out on the Broads in this cute little rowing boat. We found this lovely island and he laid out a proper rug and plates and all that. So posh! He even had a big hamper full of goodies, and when I opened it up and saw the champagne, I said, "Ooh, what are we celebrating?" Then I looked up and there he was on one knee with this little box held out in front of him, and he said, "I very much hope, my beautiful Dorothy, that we are celebrating you agreeing to be my wife!"'

The girls squealed in glee.

'What did you say?' someone asked.

'I said yes, of course, you duzzy, or we wouldn't be here now, would we?!'

There were general catcalls in the poor girl's direction, and Nancy looked around at these boisterous factory women and smiled.

'Dot's landed on her feet, hasn't she?' Connie whispered to her.

'Dot was always going to do that,' Nancy said fondly.

'What do his family reckon about their fancy manager son marrying one of the factory girls, Dot?' someone else asked.

'Factory *supervisor*,' Dot corrected her haughtily, but then grinned. 'They don't seem to mind at all. Tony took me to meet them after he'd proposed. Ooh I was nervous, especially when I saw their house. Dead big it is, over in Thorpe St Andrew, but they were lovely to me.'

'Where's Thorpe St Andrew?' Nancy asked.

'It's the nice part of Norwich,' Sandra told her, but at that, Dot shot over and threw her arms around her mother.

'It's nice here, Mum.'

'It was,' Sandra said sadly.

'And it will be again. Tony says there are big plans to regenerate Norwich. His brother's on the council and he's told him all about it. We just need to raise a little cash and then we're going to make this city beautiful again.'

More cheers. Nancy reached out and linked arms with Peggy and Connie either side of her. It seemed Dot had found not just the man for her but her place in life, and it was wonderful to see. They all, mind you, could do with a little cash right now.

Later, when the cake was gone and the tea was drunk, as well as the lethal homebrew Sandra had produced to toast the bride-to-be, the local guests made for home and only Peggy, Nancy and Connie were left.

'Let's help you clear, Sandra,' Connie said, leaping up, but Sandra waved them away.

'Don't you dare. I know how much you girls meant to our Dot during the war, and that means a lot to me too. Friends are everything in hard times – and in good ones too. So you four sit there and chat while you can, and Daisy here'll help me, won't you, Dais?'

Dot's youngest sister got up reluctantly, and the others needed little encouragement to settle down again.

'When's Baby due?' Dot asked, sinking down at Nancy's feet.

'September.' Nancy had a sudden horrible thought. 'When's the wedding, Dot?'

'The tenth of August, so don't you be early, girl. I want you there. In fact...' She drew in a breath and looked round at them all. 'I want you three to be my bridesmaids.'

'Us?' they squealed.

'Of course you. My gunner crew. You were at my side when it counted in the war, so I want you there again at my wedding. Only not in that ghastly khaki uniform. I've got something far more stylish in mind.'

Nancy looked down at her bump.

'I'll be an elephant, Dot.'

Dot winked at her.

'But a stylish one! And who cares, Nance. You look amazing. I'm so jealous. I want babies, lots of them, and as soon as I can. Tony does too.'

'But what about work?' Connie asked. 'I thought you loved it at MacLaren's?'

'I do. And I still will.'

'Dot! You can't work if you have a baby.'

'Why not? Loads of women did in the war. If we could make it work then, we can make it work now. Peacetime's meant to be easier, not harder.'

'You'd still go into the factory?'

'That's the plan. Not when they're babies, like, but from maybe six months old. Loads of Minister Bevin's wartime Day Nurseries are staying open, and I have this idea to set up one of our own, right on site. Not all women want to give up work any more to kick around at home with a child.' Nancy stared at Dot. 'What?' she demanded.

'Nothing. That is, everything. I think it's amazing, Dot. Brilliant. It's everything I've been telling Joe about wanting to learn to be a gamekeeper. Looks like we're all moving on in the world.'

'Leaving the war behind.'

'And all its secrets with it,' Peggy agreed.

Silence fell. The girls looked awkwardly at each other.

'I wonder what happened to him,' Dot said eventually.

'He's not just a "him",' Connie snapped.

'What?'

The others turned to stare at her. She looked flushed, though the temperature in the cosy room seemed, to Nancy, to have dropped.

'He had a name,' Connie said fiercely. '*Has* a name. I mean, I assume he still has it.'

'Connie?'

Now the younger girl had definitely gone pink.

'Ernst,' she said, sticking her chin up defiantly. 'He's called Ernst.' Peggy and Dot looked uneasily at each other. Connie turned to Nancy. 'Don't you remember? You should. You were the one who—'

'Connie!'

Now it was Peggy's voice that was sharp. Connie's lip wobbled and Nancy looked unhappily around at her friends. Just like at Christmas time, Dot's jolly party had suddenly turned tense at the mention of the secret that bound them. She put an arm around Connie and gave her a squeeze.

'Do you know where he is, Connie? Where Ernst is?'

'Nancy...' Peggy begged, but Dot came over and knelt close in, and eventually Peggy did too.

'It's just us,' Nancy said. 'Just the four of us. We're safe.'

Connie looked uncertainly around but Sandra and Daisy were in the kitchen, singing over the dishes, and there was no one else in the house. A tear dropped from her right eye, and Peggy reached out and wiped it softly away.

'Nancy's right, Con. I'm sorry I shouted. You can talk to us, you know you can.'

Connie gave a weak smile.

'He's in a POW camp in Norwich,' she whispered. 'I... I see him sometimes. Just in the field, you know, working. I say hello. I'm allowed, aren't I? I'm allowed to say hello. He's not just a German; he's a man. A nice man. A man that we—'

'A man that we nursed,' Peggy finished firmly.

Connie opened her mouth to protest, but then her shoulders sagged and she nodded again.

'A man that we nursed,' she echoed.

'Well, I don't see any harm in you saying hello,' Nancy told her. 'And, let's face it, he'll be repatriated soon, so you might as well be kind to him until then.' Connie's face set mulishly and Nancy felt her stomach churn. 'Connie?'

'Quite right, Nancy,' she shot back, her voice barbed. 'Soon he'll be gone, out of the way where none of us have to think about anything as inconvenient as an enemy.'

Nancy drew back at her sharp tone.

'You know I don't think like that, Connie. We talked about this when we were working in the hospital. An injured man suffers wherever he's come from or whatever side he's fighting on – and so does his family.'

Connie rubbed her hand across her face.

'Sorry. I do know that. I'm just sick of secrets.'

They all tensed.

'What are you saying, Connie?' Peggy asked.

'Nothing. That is, I don't know. I turn twenty-one in three weeks and come into my trust fund. Once I've got that, there's nothing my parents can do to stop me running my life however I wish, and I suppose that's got me thinking – would it matter so much if what happened came out? Like Nancy said, we're all moving on.'

They stared at her.

'No one will care in Manchester,' Peggy said slowly.

'Or at MacLaren's,' Dot agreed.

But then they both turned and looked at Nancy.

'I live in Langham,' she said, panic churning in her swollen belly. She grabbed for Connie's hands. 'I'm still in Langham, Connie. I drink in the Blue Bell.'

'Perhaps you shouldn't,' was Connie's tight answer.

Nancy thought of that moment when she'd stood against the pub after the terrible crow-shooting, feeling the deceptively white walls pulsing with the blackness of what had happened. She'd known it was dangerous to live there, but she'd never expected the danger to come from one of her very own gunner girls.

'You may soon be free of *your* family, Connie, but I live with mine. Well, Joe's. This coming out could ruin all the progress I've made with them. Would you really do that to me?'

Connie's hazel eyes widened. For a long, long moment no one spoke, and then she pulled Nancy into a hug.

'Of course not. Oh Nancy, of course I wouldn't. I wouldn't put you in danger for anything. I'm sorry. Don't listen to me. I've had too much of Sandra's homebrew. I'm emotional, irrational. Forget it – please. Our secret is safe with me, I swear it.'

Nancy could only pray that was true, but later, leaning against Joe as the bus rumbled its way back to Langham, the fear returned. The baby, after being quiet all day, seemed to be taking the chance to practise somersaults, and Joe placed a hand over her belly, giving a little chuckle of delight every time he felt it kick against him. It was a lovely sound but a terrifying one too, because it was the sound of what she had to lose. She'd just started to truly feel that Langham was home, and now the secret at the heart of her war years was threatening to take everything from her.

Chapter Twenty-One

Lorna's eyes moved so fast across the pages of Nancy's diary that the words started to blur. There were probably a hundred jobs she should be doing around the Gamekeeper's cottage but everything seemed to be coming to a head back in 1946 and she just couldn't stop reading.

'Lorna?!' Tilly called suddenly. 'Lorna? Are you in there? Lunch is ready.'

'Be through in a minute!' she called guiltily. 'I'm just, er, popping to the loo.'

'OK. No rush.'

Lorna heard her stepsister head out into the garden to summon the boys from the den they'd been building all morning and her eyes pulled inexorably back to the diary. She was so close to the end…

'Just a tiny bit more,' she muttered and turned the page, then gasped at the sight that met her eager eyes. 'No!'

There were just two pages left and then a gaping hole where someone had ripped the final sheets out of the notebook. The remains lay rough and almost scarred-looking against the leather spine, and Lorna ran a finger tenderly down their ripped edges.

'Why did Nancy do this to you?' she asked them, shocked, then heard herself and tutted.

First she'd chatted to dead people, then she'd progressed to worms, and now she was talking to inanimate objects. She had to get a grip but the loss of the last pages felt devastating. She sat staring at the damage, as frozen in time as the little annex.

'Lorna?' Tilly's head appeared around the door. 'Oh God, are you OK?'

Lorna looked up at her, dazed.

'They're gone.'

'What are? What are gone, Lor?'

She held out the diary. 'The final entries.'

Tilly put a hand to her chest. 'You gave me a heart attack there! Is that all?'

'All?!' Lorna wept. 'Nancy was getting less and less discreet and I was so hoping I'd find out the gunner girls' secret.'

'Right.'

'And now...' She pointed to the torn spine.

'Now they're gone,' Tilly finished for her. 'I'm sorry.'

Lorna sighed. Through in the house she could hear the boys chattering excitedly about some game they'd invented, but she could barely even face them. This was silly. She shouldn't be getting so ridiculously caught up in the past, but as she pushed herself out of the chair, her heart felt heavy.

'Ooh,' Tilly said suddenly. 'I've just remembered, I've got a message for you from Spenser. He says can you call him. Something about military records?'

Lorna blinked. Spenser had been in touch to say his mate Laurence at the university was 'intrigued' by the diary, and in exchange for a look at it, he was happy to do some digging. Had he found something? Setting the torn diary down on the coffee table, she picked up her phone and called his number.

'Lorna!' Spenser's voice bubbled down the line. 'Have I got something for you, honey!'

'What?' she asked eagerly. She needed this.

'A possible name. Laurence has turned up the patient records from when Langham Hall was a hospital, and it seems there was a German pilot in there for several months in 1944.'

'And you have his name?'

'Sure do! What's it worth?'

Lorna considered as she straightened the Turner picture that had, as usual, gone squint.

'A round of tequilas?' she suggested.

'Done! He was called Ernst Schneider. He was a pilot, and it seems he had to be guarded quite carefully whilst he was being treated. He went to a POW camp in Norwich once he'd recovered and was repatriated after the war.'

'Did he by any chance marry?'

'No idea about that, sorry. You could google it.'

'I will!' Lorna said, her voice squeaking ridiculously with excitement. 'Thanks so much, Spenser. That's worth *two* rounds of tequilas!'

'Hooray. This Saturday?'

'Why not?!' Lorna said, then remembered her hangover last week. 'That is, let me see if I can get Mum to babysit.'

Spenser laughed.

'Anytime, Lorna, honestly. Don't worry about the tequilas, except that it would be fun to go out again. Don't forget, I'm a history nerd too, so the best reward will be to find out if you get to the bottom of the mystery.'

'Oh, I will,' Lorna assured him. 'I definitely will.'

She clicked off the call and switched across to Google. She could hear the others gathering around the table in the main house, but she just had to see. This might just make up for the missing pages and, deciding to go straight for the historical jugular, she carefully typed in 'Connie Schneider'. Google thought about it for a moment and then delivered her a wealth of text. Lorna stared at her screen in disbelief. It was in German, but one click and Google gave her a near-instant translation.

Much-Loved Headteacher Retires, the top hit read, and Lorna scanned eagerly down an article from the *Münchner Merkur* – the

Munich Mercury – in 1991. It described Connie Schneider as a dedicated and devoted teacher in a local secondary school, and detailed a career that had started with her teaching English in 1950, progressing to head of the English department, deputy head and finally headmistress, a role she'd held since 1966 – an impressive twenty-five years' service. It even obligingly mentioned her husband, Ernst Schneider, a local businessman who had served as Bürgermeister of Germering, a borough of Munich.

Lorna stared and stared.

'So, Connie Marshall – you married him,' she said softly. 'You married your German POW.'

Ernst Schneider, it seemed, had crashed his plane outside Langham, turned himself in at the base and been nursed at the Hall, kept under strict guard and with military care – military care provided by the gunner girls. Connie must have fallen in love with him then, but it still didn't explain what was so dangerous about the situation for Nancy.

'Lorna! Are you coming to eat?' her mum called.

She looked up, momentarily dazed. 'Coming!' Pausing only to give the poor, torn diary a quick pat, she ran into the kitchen, brandishing the phone. 'I've found her.'

'Who?'

'Connie, of course. I've found Connie!'

Mary looked at her as if she were mad, but David jumped to his feet.

'Really? Where?'

Lorna grinned at him. 'Munich.'

It took a little explaining to the rest, but they were all intrigued and Lorna was permitted to use her phone at the table – a privilege pounced on by the boys.

'If Mum has her phone, I should be allowed my tablet,' Charlie said.

'Are you looking up lost German prisoners of war?' Mary asked him.

Charlie frowned. 'Sort of.'

'In what way?'

'We have prisoners of war in *Clash of Clans*, Granny.'

'Doesn't count, I'm afraid. It's got to be real ones.'

'Mummy's looking up prisoners?' Stan asked, gazing at her in some concern.

'From a long, long time ago, sweetie,' she assured him. 'And he wasn't a prisoner because he did anything bad.'

'Just tried to blow up Norwich,' David said drily.

'David!' Mary snapped, and he went back to his soup.

'I suppose that's true,' Lorna said, 'but I guess our pilots were doing the same over there so, you know, all's fair in love and war. Anyway, it's forever ago now and he clearly went on to be a very good man. This article says he was a Bürgermeister.'

'Really?' Charlie's eyes lit up. 'Is that an actual job? Does it mean you get to eat burgers every day?'

The adults laughed and Charlie tensed up immediately. Lorna reached a hand across to him.

'It's the German word for mayor, Charlie. It means you're in charge of a city.'

Charlie considered. 'That's pretty decent too.'

'And knowing the Germans, it would have involved a fair few burgers,' David told him kindly, 'or hot dogs at least.'

'Cool!'

It *was* cool, Lorna thought as she flicked through the various pages. Connie seemed to come up all over the place, mainly in features on the school. She'd clearly been a very active headmistress and there were pictures of her getting stuck in on the sports field, or in fancy dress for charity events, or even being pelted with sponges at fundraisers. German school fairs, it seemed, were very like British ones, and Lorna felt a rush of fellowship for this kindred spirit of a teacher. For perhaps the first time since Matt's death, she thought of her own school with fondness and peered intently at the photos, trying to see into the eyes of the woman who – if they'd got her right – had fired guns at the Germans and then become one of them.

'Moving to Germany after the war can't have been a popular move?' Tilly asked.

'It might explain why no one ever spoke about her,' Lorna agreed. 'Though it seems a bit sad. I hope they didn't fall out over it.' She looked around the table. 'How are we ever going to find out?'

'Is she dead?' Charlie asked.

'Well, of course…' Lorna started, then stopped herself. She was reading an article about a community service medal that Connie had been awarded, and now her eyes moved to the date at the top of the piece: 2018. Connie Schneider had been alive in 2018, so there was a good chance she was still alive now. She read on and saw that she was listed as widowed and living in a care home in Munich. She looked to the others.

'How many care homes do you reckon there are in Munich?' she asked.

David grimaced.

'There must be hundreds, Lorna.'

She nodded forlornly.

'But worth checking out,' Tilly said, giving her hand a squeeze. 'What's to lose?'

'Hours and hours?' Lorna suggested.

Tilly laughed.

'Good job we've got hours and hours then. If her husband was Bürgermeister of a particular area, that might be a good place to start, right?'

'Right,' Lorna agreed, cheered.

'So, let's make a list and get cracking.'

'With what?'

'With phoning them and asking for Connie Schneider, of course.'

Lorna hopped up and kissed her.

'You are a star, Tilly! A total star.'

It was a curious afternoon. The boys were allowed to take biscuits and fruit out to their den whilst the adults manned their phones like some sort of peculiar telethon. Even Xavier joined in, though his brand of English was fairly hard to understand even for a native speaker, so they soon sent him to supervise a football game in the garden – a job to which he was far better suited. Lorna sat in the sunshine flooding through the French windows, watching her boys chase a ball around after a Brazilian whilst she politely asked care homes in Bavaria for a woman who may or may not still be alive, and wondered at the bizarreness of life.

It was mid-August now, and if it had not been for the terrible accident, she and the boys would be sunning themselves on a campsite in the south of France with Matt. It was a thought that tore her up if she allowed it too much rein in her mind and it was, at least, a relief to have this historical mystery to distract her. Not that they seemed to be making much progress.

'Ah, sorry. I must have the wrong home.'

'My apologies for disturbing you. My information is obviously wrong.'

'What a shame. I was told she was here.'

They made their apologies over and over to the various homes on their lists, and Lorna began to think this was a wild goose chase (or, at least, a wild gunner-girl chase), when suddenly Tilly said, 'Yes, yes, that's right. She is very old, yes, but wonderful. An inspiration to me.'

They all stopped and stared at Tilly, who was loving her role.

'She taught me years ago. I was so fond of her. Michael? Oh, yes – yes, Michael told me to call, bless him. He is, yes, very devoted. I know, amazing. Your oldest resident, really? How lovely. Sorry?'

She looked around at the others. 'When do I want to come and visit? Good question.' She shot a quizzical look at Lorna, who swallowed. Visit? Could they do that?

'Next week,' David said suddenly.

'What?' Lorna stuttered.

'Next week,' Tilly said firmly into the phone. 'Maybe Wednesday? Four o'clock? Perfect. Thank you so much. My name? Of course, sorry – it's Lorna Haynes.'

'Tilly!' Lorna squeaked, but Tilly was too busy saying an effusive goodbye to pay her any attention. She switched off the phone and looked smugly round at them all. 'We found her. She's expecting us next Wednesday!'

'Tilly,' Lorna said, as calmly as she could manage, 'Connie lives in Munich.'

'So? That's what flights are for, surely?'

'Well, yes, but the boys—'

'Will love a trip to Germany.'

Lorna felt panic rise inside her. She couldn't do that. She couldn't take the boys on a plane without Matt. She couldn't trek them across Germany to see some poor woman who had no idea who she was, and who wouldn't necessarily remember anything about Nancy or the war or being a damned gunner girl. She sucked in air, and Mary was up and by her side instantly.

'Breathe, Lorna. You're fine. You're safe. You don't have to go to Germany just because Tilly had fun pretending to be you.'

Tilly's eyes widened, and she was on her knees at Lorna's side in an instant.

'No, of course you don't. Sorry, Lorna, really. Tell you what – I'll go. Xavier wants to get to Europe, so why not start in Munich? I hear it's beautiful.'

'That's very kind, Tilly, but…'

But what? she asked herself. In truth, now that the prospect of seeing Connie was there before her, it was hard to resist. She turned her eyes to her boys, screaming with laughter as they both piled into their makeshift goal, to try and save Xavier's shots. Could she take them?

'I'd like to go,' David said quietly.

'I would too,' Mary agreed. 'We could get a little chalet together and see the area, and then I could watch the boys whilst you go to see this Connie lady.'

'Seriously?' Lorna asked, staring at her mum.

Mary took her hand.

'Seriously, Lor, if you think you're up to it. You've done so well these last few weeks and it's clear this diary is part of that. Why not follow it all the way through?'

Still Lorna stared at her. An already bizarre afternoon had shot off the scale. Was this really happening? Had her ripped-out pages been replaced with a real, live gunner girl? It seemed so.

'Why not?' she agreed.

'Yay!' Tilly called, hugging her. 'I'll start googling flights right away. Oh, and I'll see if I can find this Michael Schneider on Facebook and make contact. Perhaps he could be there too so that we don't overwhelm Connie.'

'Good idea,' Lorna agreed. The last thing they wanted was to descend on this poor woman asking difficult questions about the past, if she was frail. She must be in her nineties, so they had to tread carefully.

'I'll look at accommodation,' David said.

'And I'll call Kyle,' Mary added. 'Hopefully he can get the renovations done whilst we're away.'

'Not the wallpaper!' Lorna said.

Mary looked at her sideways.

'You want to save *that* wallpaper, darling?'

'It's sort of cool.'

'It's sort of psychedelic! But don't worry, it's more the living area that needs Kyle's attention.'

She was looking shifty and Lorna frowned at her, keen to know more, but at that point Tilly cried out, 'Cracking deal from Stansted here. Cheap flights leaving in… ooh, two days.'

'Two days?' Lorna echoed faintly, instantly forgetting the annex.

Could she really take the boys halfway across Europe in two days? It all felt very fast, and she was grateful when her mum put an arm around her shoulders.

'Slow down, everyone! We'll only go if you want to, darling.'

Lorna leaned appreciatively into her. 'I wish Matt could come.'

'I know. I wish it too, with all my heart, but I also think he'd want you to do it – if you're up to it, that is.'

Lorna nodded slowly. She longed to have her husband here to run the plan past, to discuss it and cost it and agree that it was a good idea. But Matt wasn't here any more; the decision was hers and hers alone. She closed her eyes, breathing deeply. Her husband would have loved this, she reminded herself. He'd been the spontaneous one, ready to try anything at the drop of a hat. She'd always been the voice of caution but, really, where had that got her? And this was her chance to put the final pieces of the gunner girls' jigsaw into place. She opened her eyes and looked at the others.

'Family holiday in Munich,' she said. 'Let's do it!'

Chapter Twenty-Two

Saturday, 10 August 1946

Today Dot gets married! Who'd have thought it? All those times we lay in barracks as she clambered back in the window to wake us up, and tell us about her current GI or sailor or even, once, an officer. She seemed like she'd never settle down, but then along comes Tony and, bang, she's all loved up. Perhaps it's peacetime – lets you believe in a future enough to actually go for it?

Anyway, it's going to be a hell of a day. Tony's insisted on paying for the whole thing. Sandra's mortified, poor love, but we told her just to let him and enjoy it, and I think she will once we actually get to the church. He's really gone to town. We had a 'rehearsal' last night, would you believe, and the church was full of hundreds of flowers. So beautiful. After the service we're off to the Royal Hotel for the wedding breakfast. It's a right swanky place and, somehow, he's got around rationing to arrange for beef stew and dumplings, with a giant fruit cake for afters and real champagne to propose the toasts. I just hope Joe lets me have some!

The only thing Dot and Sandra have provided are our dresses but, oh, they've done a wonderful job. Sandra's adjusted her own wedding dress for Dot, adding the most exquisite embroidery around the hem and down the slim sleeves. It's as white as a summer cloud, mind. Peg, Connie and I couldn't resist a few jokes about that! Sandra deliberately ignored us, and who cares anyway. Dot loves Tony and

*she's going up the aisle to him looking that beautiful I'm sure
he won't give two hoots what happened before.*

*For us bridesmaids, Peggy got hold of some parachute
silk, and Sandra's sewn us up three right elegant knee-length
frocks in the prettiest pale green. That's to say, two of them
are elegant. Mine's more of a sack, pulled in over my huge
belly with a sash, but at least the colour suits me, so maybe
the resemblance to an elephant doesn't matter so very much.*

*Ooh, got to go – the car's here to take us to church. Details
to follow tomorrow.*

'You may kiss the bride!'

A cheer rippled around the church as Tony took Dot's beaming
face in his hands and kissed her, then the noise grew as she wrapped
her hands around his neck and kissed him back. Two small patches
of pink appeared on the vicar's cheeks, and Nancy looked to Peggy
and Connie and smiled. *Typical Dot!*

'She's got no decorum,' Connie whispered.

'And good on her,' Peggy added. 'It's her day, so let her enjoy it.'

Dot certainly looked set to do that.

'Enough now, Dot,' Connie whispered, tugging on the bride's
dress.

Dot surfaced, looked around and said loudly, 'Ooh sorry, forgot
where I was for a minute,' and the whole church laughed.

Even pinker in the face, the vicar hastened them into the vestry
to sign the register, thankfully missing the very lewd wink that
Dot turned back to offer the congregation at the door. Nancy let
Connie and Peggy through before her and her eyes sought Joe's.
He blew her a kiss, looking gorgeous in his demob suit, and she
wondered if he was thinking the same as her – how very different
this grand affair was to their own wedding.

Of course, they'd only had twenty-four hours to arrange theirs,
so fancy frocks and flowers had been out of the question. Besides,

as serving personnel, they'd both had to wear their uniforms, so Nancy had gone up the aisle in murky khaki. Not that she'd cared; she'd have walked up there in her undies to get to Joe. Joe's lieutenant, Tinker Johnson, had stood as his best man because he'd lost his closest mate to the Anzio sinking. Tinker had reluctantly signed the register as Reginald, causing much merriment to Joe and the others of his crew who'd made it, and they'd all burst out of the registry office into a blustery March day in gales of laughter.

The wedding breakfast had been at a café in the middle of Portsmouth. Sausage and eggs all round with iced buns as a wedding cake. Someone had piled them up in a pyramid to make it look grander for the cutting, but as soon as they'd put the knife in, they'd gone tumbling down all over the place. Guests had scrambled to snatch them off the floor but no one had cared. They'd just brushed off any dust and eaten them anyway. Nancy remembered it as a day of non-stop joy, but looking around the beautiful church as Dot and Tony posed for a photo, her huge bouquet laid out on the table before them, she felt a small twinge that they'd not had all this. Even her gunner girls hadn't been there.

It's not important, she told herself sternly. *It's the union that counts, not the flowers or the frocks.*

She flushed darkly at the word 'union', recalling their brief honeymoon – two nights in a boarding house just down the coast with a very lewd landlady who'd conjured up huge meals from somewhere, telling them they 'needed their strength'. She hadn't been wrong either. With only forty-eight hours together before Joe's ship sailed back to the Mediterranean to prepare for a southerly D-Day invasion of France, they'd made the most of every minute. And then… Then Joe had sailed and Nancy had been back to RAF Langham. She'd been miserable at being parted from her husband so soon after their wedding day, and without the girls she might never have got through the agony of waiting for him to come back.

'Are we ready, ladies?'

The vicar's voice interrupted her reverie and she snapped guiltily back into the present. This was Dot's wedding, not her own, and she should pay attention to her friend. She busied herself making sure Dot's bouquet was hanging nicely, leaving the other two to arrange the small train on her dress as she most definitely could not bend down that low. She had three weeks to go and was dreading getting any bigger. She hadn't seen her toes for ages and was having to have her shoes fastened for her like a little girl.

The organ struck up a lusty tune and Dot sallied out from the vestry on Tony's arm, taking her time and waving to almost everyone in the church as they made for the door, the photographer dashing ahead of them. Outside, the sun had broken through the early clouds and Nancy could see a crowd gathering on the street, keen to share in anyone's joy. Dot smiled and waved some more, and Tony stood proud as punch at her side as the rest of them gathered around her and smiled for the photographer. Nancy did her best to hide her bump behind young Daisy who was acting as flower-girl, and then the rest of the congregation were flocking out and she could, with relief, take Joe's arm for the short walk to the Royal Hotel.

'You look beautiful, darling,' he told her.

'I look like a lump.'

'A beautiful lump.'

She batted at him playfully.

'Watch it! These shoes are killing me, so if you're not careful you'll be carrying this lump to the reception.'

'Willingly, my lady,' he said, bowing and reaching out to lift her.

She hastily side-stepped him.

'Lord no, Joe. It's me who's heading for the hospital to have this baby, not you with a broken back.'

'Not today, I hope?' he said in alarm.

'I hope not too. Now come on, Dot says there's French champagne!'

They followed the happy crowd down to the hotel where they found not only champagne, but a real live swing band. Nancy couldn't manage more than one dance in three, and that only with a lot of heavy panting, but she was very happy sitting watching the others fling themselves around the dance floor. Joe sat patiently at her side, but she could see him itching to dance and nudged him forward.

'Take Connie out for a turn,' she said. 'She's got no one to dance with.'

'That's not true,' Joe said, 'she just keeps turning them down.'

Nancy watched her young friend and saw that she did indeed refuse the attentions of several men. Heaving herself to her feet, she sidled over to her.

'Why aren't you dancing, Con?'

'I'm useless at it.'

'You are not. I've seen you.'

'In the barracks with you lot. That's fine, but put me in the arms of a man and I lose all sense of balance.'

'Isn't that part of the fun?' Nancy teased, but she saw Connie's face close up and instantly regretted it. 'Sorry, Connie. How's' – she sought the right word but couldn't for the life of her find it – 'things?' she finished in the end.

Connie looked nervously around the grand room, but everyone was busy dancing and chatting, and no one was paying them any attention. She straightened her back and looked straight at Nancy.

'Things are good, Nance. I'm courting properly now.'

Nancy swallowed.

'You're courting' – she dropped her voice – 'the pilot?'

'Ernst,' Connie said straight away, her face lighting up at just the use of his name. 'Yes. I'm being very discreet, Nancy, honest. No one at Langham need know.'

Nancy drew a long breath into her congested lungs.

'I'm sorry if you can't shout your love from the rooftops, Con.'

Connie smiled shyly.

'Oh, don't worry about that. I've never been a rooftops type of girl anyway.'

'But your folks…'

'Don't have a clue. No one does.'

'But what about if…?'

'If we want to spend our lives together?' She shuffled her feet. 'Well, we'll just have to cross that bridge when we come to it, won't we?'

'Connie, are you sure about this? Isn't it dangerous?'

'For you, you mean?'

'No, Con – for you.'

'Maybe, but right now it feels like it might be more dangerous to lose him. And why should I? He's a good man, really he is. He's younger than me – only nineteen. He joined up as soon as he could because he wanted to do his bit for his country, just like our lads did. Is it his fault which country he comes from?'

'I suppose not.'

Connie's voice was rising and Nancy looked around nervously. She didn't mind her friend courting a German, but she was pretty sure there'd be a lot of people who would.

'It might be tricky though, Con.'

'I know! God, Nance, I know. He's still a prisoner but he's proved himself trustworthy, so when they're sent to work in the city, his supervisor gives him plenty of freedom. We can meet when he stops for his lunch, but not for long and never alone. It's not enough.'

'Connie! You're not thinking of doing anything illegal?'

'No. Not illegal…'

'Connie?'

Connie leaped up, drawing herself to her full height.

'I'd have thought you, Nancy, of all people would understand. Now, I really must go to the ladies'. Excuse me.'

'Connie!'

But she was gone, slipping through the happy dancers and away. Nancy wanted to follow her and demand to know her friend's plans, but what gave her that right?

I'd have thought you, Nancy, of all people would understand.

The words haunted her because Connie was right. She should understand. Hadn't she been fighting to use all she'd learned in the war now that peace had come? Shouldn't that extend not just to earning a living, or firing damn guns, but also to showing compassion to all men?

'Are you well, Nancy?'

She looked round to see Joe.

'Fine. I just… No, it's fine. Fancy a dance?'

'With you, gorgeous, any time.'

The music, thankfully, had dropped in pace, and Joe took her in his arms and led her sedately around the dance floor.

'You didn't talk Connie into dancing then?' he asked.

'Sadly not.' Nancy was bursting with Connie's secret – with their shared secret – and she longed to talk to someone. She looked up into Joe's caring eyes. He was her husband, father of her child, her partner in life – if she couldn't trust him with this, then who could she trust? 'She's courting.'

'That's nice.'

'Yes.'

'She doesn't look very happy about it.'

'No.' Nancy drew in a deep breath. 'He's German, Joe.'

'What?!'

Joe stopped dead and another couple went tumbling into them.

'Sorry. So sorry.' He resumed his movements but they were stiff now. 'You're not serious, Nancy?'

'Why would I make that up?'

'I hope you told her to end it straight away.'

Nancy squinted up at him.

'She loves him, Joe.'

'She can't. She can't love a German.' He spat it out like poison.

'Shhh! You might get her in trouble.'

'Get her in trouble?!' Joe shuffled her towards the edge of the dance floor. 'She's already in trouble, Nancy – lots of trouble.'

Nancy felt herself bristle at his attitude. It echoed with other voices from another night at the back end of the war when this had all started. *Scum! Boche scum.* She frowned. Connie was correct – what right did anyone have to make those sorts of judgements?

'Surely Germans are people just like us?' she said, but Joe shook his head violently.

'No. No, Nancy, they're not. They invaded every country in the name of fascism. They robbed millions of people of their lives for their poisonous brand of elitism. They put Jews into concentration camps, starved them and then shoved them into chambers and bloody well gassed them! And you say they're like us?'

His face had turned purple and his voice was rising dangerously. People were looking round.

'That was the Nazis, Joe. Not all Germans are Nazis. Don't be such a boor.'

He stared at her, mouth agape.

'You're calling me a boor?'

Her heart quivered but this was important. What he was saying went to the core of that dark night in the woods and she had to stand firm.

'Yes,' she said. 'You need to think about it more.'

He looked down on her, his face cold and dark.

'Oh, I've thought about it, Nancy. I thought about it a lot as I was thrown into the oily surface of the Med with men screaming for their mothers all around me and my own life flashing before my eyes. I thought about those Germans who'd torpedoed my boat, and then I thought of you and how I might never see you again. Let me tell you, it wasn't the Germans I was feeling sorry for. And now – now you ask me to think of them as being "just like us". That's cruel, Nancy – cruel.'

Tears shimmered in his eyes and she swallowed.

'Joe, I'm sorry. I only meant…' But he was gone, off the dance floor and pushing through the crowds towards the exit. 'Joe! Joe, wait.' She rushed after him, her feet crying out in her tightening heels and her body swaying with the unaccustomed bulk of the baby. 'Joe!'

He was at the door now and she tried to pick up her pace, but her foot caught on a scarf left dangling from one of the chairs and she felt herself start to fall. She clutched desperately for something to steady herself. Her fingers closed around a chair back and for a moment she thought she was safe, but it was a flimsy thing and tipped beneath her flailing weight, sending her crashing to the floor. She heard gasps, and a cry from someone – possibly Connie – but her head was spinning and her ankle was hurting and, worst of all, her belly was pulsing with sudden pain.

'Joe,' she whimpered, and then all went black.

The next thing Nancy knew, she was being wheeled on a trolley past a beautiful red-brick building, pockmarked with bomb damage. She put a hand to her head and struggled to sit up. What had happened? Had they been hit? Had they missed the plane? And where were the other gunner girls?

'Lie back, miss,' a kindly voice said, and she looked into the eyes of a young orderly. He didn't look like army.

'Where am I?'

'In the very best place for you – the hospital.'

'Was it a plane?'

'A plane?'

The man looked confused. Nancy closed her eyes and fought to remember. As clear as day she could see the plane coming towards her, veering all over the place, left engine on fire as it came down fast – too fast to avoid.

'Did it hit us? Where's Peggy? Or Connie, or Dot?'

'I'm here, Nance.'

She glanced round and saw Connie's face staring down at her.

'Connie! Where are the others? Are they hurt?'

Her body was aching all over, a steady pain that seemed suddenly to be spiking. Shrapnel? She lifted a hand to try and feel for her wounds, but someone grasped hold of it and a low voice said, 'Nancy. Nancy, darling, I'm here. You're safe.'

There was a figure next to Connie, a handsome man with worry etched across his lovely face.

'Joe! How have you got back?'

He rubbed her hand.

'You're confused, Nancy. We're not at war any more.'

'What?'

'It's 1946. It's all over.'

'Is it? Did we win?'

She heard the orderly give a low chuckle.

'We sure did, miss. Hitler's dead and the Boche hounded out like the dogs they are.'

Nancy's head swirled at the word 'Boche' and she looked back to Joe. They'd argued. Something about Germans.

'Where am I?'

'Norwich hospital. We were at Dot's wedding, remember?'

Did she? Nancy fought to clear the fuzz from her brain. She thought she could remember flowers, lots of flowers. And dancing. Only she hadn't done much of it. Why was that? She loved dancing.

'Then what happened?' she demanded.

'You fell, darling. Chasing me. I was… being an idiot.'

'You, Joe? Surely not. What have I done? It hurts. Actually, it hurts like hell.'

She doubled up on the trolley as pain spiked across her. Joe's hand tightened around hers and she clutched at it, fighting the agony. After a little time, it subsided slightly and she looked to him again.

'It's the baby, Nancy.'

'What baby?'

'*Our* baby. Nancy, you're having our baby.'

Time swirled crazily around in her head and snatches came back to her an image at a time: Ted and Betty, the Gamekeeper's Cottage and the pub, the woods and the guns, and then Dot in a ridiculously white dress and herself like a pale green elephant.

'The baby!' she cried, as it all came flooding back. 'Oh Lord, Joe, it's early. It's too early.'

'Not *too* early, Nancy. It might just need a little bit of extra care. The most important thing is to deliver it safely, yes?'

Nancy looked at him as she was wheeled into the hospital and the cracked red bricks gave way to bright, scrubbed corridors. This wasn't how she'd envisioned giving birth. She'd wanted it to be in the Gamekeeper's Cottage with the local midwife in attendance, but the war had taught her never to rely too heavily on any plans. She was here now and she had to get on with it.

It would have been nice to be able to say that her unplanned labour proceeded as swiftly as it started, but it didn't turn out that way. Baby, it seemed, wasn't any keener on this early birth than his or her parents, and as the birthing pains ripped through Nancy time and again, she had to grasp on to Connie, who'd been allowed in to help as poor Joe paced outside. Bit by bit, as the skies darkened outside the big window and Dot, presumably, headed off on her honeymoon to Cromer, the labour did progress.

'Not much longer,' the midwife assured her. 'You'll soon be holding your little one in your arms, I promise you.'

Right now, Nancy wasn't sure her arms would support her 'little one', but she gripped onto the iron bedstead and fought the next pain. She thought of poor Joe pacing the corridors, not knowing what was going on, but there was little time to worry about him now because suddenly the midwife was telling her she could push.

'Thank heavens!' Nancy cried. It hurt, oh Lord it hurt, but at least she could do something, at least she could make something happen. She pushed down with all her might.

'Brilliant, lass!' the midwife encouraged.

'You can do it, Nancy,' Connie told her, grasping at her hands. 'Again, gunner girl. Go again.'

So Nancy did. She felt as if it was a boulder not a baby coming out of her, but whatever it was, she wanted it out and she drove down with a cry of intent.

'Come on!'

And then, suddenly, through the pain and the noise, she heard a little cry. Plaintive at first and then growing in strength into a full-blown wail.

'Lungs are healthy then,' the midwife said with satisfaction. 'It's a boy, Nancy. You have a beautiful baby boy.'

She cut the cord and handed the baby to Nancy, and it seemed her arms did work. It seemed, indeed, that however heavy this precious boy was, they would always be able to hold him.

'My son,' she breathed and then, as Connie ushered a breathless Joe inside, '*our* son.'

Joe came to her side and looked down at the baby as it rootled for the breast. He was small but healthy, and as he found the nipple and latched on, Nancy felt the most amazing calm descend upon her.

'Oh darling, he's just… just beautiful.' Tears sparkled in Joe's eyes as he kissed first the baby and then Nancy. 'You're so clever, so strong. I thought from all the noise that you must be tearing apart in here.'

Nancy smiled up at him.

'So did I at one point, Joe, but it was all worth it.'

She stroked her baby's downy head as Joe put an arm around them both, and Connie backed carefully out of the room.

'I'm sorry, Nancy,' he said, kissing her again. 'I shouldn't have got so worked up. I should have listened. War has made everything far too black and white, and that's not a world I want to bring this little one up in. I want him to stand up for all that's good and human and right.'

'He will,' Nancy said, 'with you as a role model.'

Joe shook his head.

'I think you're the role model here, Nancy, my beautiful, strong, caring wife – and thank heavens for that.'

Nancy blessed him for his kindness but it was undeserved. She'd resisted motherhood for far too long and now her baby was here, in her arms, it was impossible to see what all her worrying had been about. She would care for this child with every breath she had, now and for always.

'David,' she said to Joe. 'David was a man who stood up against the bullies of this world. I think we should call him David.'

Joe smiled and kissed her.

'David, yes – I like it. Welcome to the world, David. I hope it treats you well, wherever you end up.'

'Even Germany?' Nancy dared to ask.

Joe shook his head but bent and kissed her.

'Even Germany.'

Chapter Twenty-Three

Was that David? Lorna looked out across the sloping meadows below her as someone jogged down towards the lake in the soft light of the sun rising behind the purple mountains beyond. It *was* David! She watched as he dived gracefully into the blue-green waters and blessed whoever had sent this lovely man into her and her mum's lives.

A pretty sound echoed up the hillside and she glanced around. Cow bells! Actual cow bells! She still couldn't quite believe she was here in Bavaria, or how very beautiful it was. David had found them the most perfect chalet above the stunning Tegernsee lake, and Lorna genuinely felt as if she'd been transported to another reality. She'd escaped to Langham to avoid the sorrow of home, but she'd never expected to find herself watching the sun rise to the sound of cow bells.

'I wish you could see this, Matt,' she muttered into the rapidly warming morning air.

They'd talked, every so often, about doing a 'European tour' one day. It had always been off in a hazy distance, beyond the clamour of life with small children and jobs, but it had been there – an ambition, a plan, a dream. They would buy a camper van, throw in some provisions, and head off for a long summer pottering around the backroads of France, Italy and Greece. They hadn't really considered Germany, and now that Lorna was here, she felt bad about that.

'You'd love it,' she told Matt. She'd decided to give up on her self-imposed restriction on talking to the dead. She knew he wasn't there. She didn't think some ghost was going to put its arms around her or find a way to answer her, but for so long she'd shared her thoughts with her husband and having to stop doing that had been so hard. Besides, the worms hadn't come to Germany with them, though she bet cows were good listeners if you gave them a chance.

She leaned over the balcony of the chalet, drinking in the hollow clang of the bells echoing softly up the slope. Below her, long grasses waved in a welcome breeze, and to her right the sun was throwing its first rays across the lake, sending diamonds dancing along the ripples of David's figure swimming out towards its centre. Any minute now, Julie Andrews would come running over the horizon and the scene would be complete. She smiled. She loved that film. She'd watched it every Christmas and, although Matt had whinged about it at first, he'd soon got into it, making Glühwein and apple pastries to go with. She sighed.

'Mummy, what's that noise?'

Lorna turned to see Stan hovering in her bedroom doorway, his blond curls bed-ruffled, his eyes half open and his teddy dangling from his hand. Her heart turned over with love and she swept him into her arms.

'It's cow bells, Stan, down in the meadows.'

'Cow bells?'

'Yes. They go round their neck so you can hear them.'

'Why?'

It was a good question.

'Because there's so much land, I suppose. They can maybe go wherever they want, and their owner can find them if they need to.'

Stan thought about it.

'Like Find My iPhone?' he suggested.

Lorna laughed.

'Just like that, Stan – only a nicer sound.'

'It *is* nice,' he agreed, and snuggled against her as they looked out over the landscape together.

Lorna held him close, drawing in the sweet smell of him. He was growing fast and was heavy in her arms, but she propped him against the balcony and held on tight, relishing his easy love. She didn't have Matt here and that still hurt like an ever-twisting dagger in her guts, but she had Stan and she had Charlie, she had Mum and David and Tilly, and that was amazing.

'Mummy,' Stan said, in his sweetest voice. Lorna braced herself for whatever was coming. 'David says they have lots of cows here to make chocolate.'

'Well, yes – to make milk to make chocolate.'

'So probably, here, people have chocolate for breakfast, don't they?' Lorna smiled. 'Sooo – can *we* have chocolate for breakfast?'

'Why not?' she agreed.

'Really?' He put his soft little hands either side of her face and looked intently at her. 'Really, really?'

'Really, really,' she agreed because, let's face it, she'd love chocolate for breakfast too and they were on holiday. Not the holiday she'd thought the summer would bring her, but a holiday all the same.

Tilly was very keen on the idea of chocolate for breakfast, and offered to run down to the little shop in the village to buy a selection. She was full of energy this morning. Xavier was off to Berlin on the train today – less impressed by rural Bavaria than the rest of them – and Lorna couldn't tell if Tilly was lively because he was going or because of whatever he'd done to her to say goodbye. Maybe a bit of both.

Tilly had confided in her yesterday, when they'd gone swimming in the lake, that Xavier had asked her to join him in northern Europe, but that she'd had an offer of a job on a vineyard in Italy that was a much more attractive prospect. She was going to wait until Xavier was set up in Berlin to break the news, presumably to lessen the chance of him joining her.

'He's great fun, Lor, but I'm ready to move on now. I think he is too – he just doesn't realise it yet. He'll soon hook up with some other people in Berlin and we'll quietly drift away from each other.'

'And that's OK?'

'That's how it should be.'

'Don't you want to meet, you know…'

'The one? I honestly don't think there is such a thing. That's to say, I think there are lots and lots of possible "ones", and it's up to you to grab the chance when you're ready.'

Lorna had shaken her head at her.

'Maybe, but I'd say you haven't been struck yet, not properly. From the first conversation I had with Matt, I knew he was special. I don't know why but it was like we were two pieces of a jigsaw, fitting together to make a full picture. Does that sound really cheesy?'

'It sounds lovely.' She'd put out a hand to her. 'I guess you're lucky you had that, and, you never know, you might get it again.'

'I can't see it.'

'Of course you can't. You're drifting at the moment too, just for different reasons from me. It happened to Dad, though. He and Mum were so happy and he swore he was done with romance when we lost her, but then along came your mum and look at them. Lightning can strike twice and all that.'

Lorna wasn't so sure but had promised Tilly she'd stay open to life, and if right now that included eating chocolate for breakfast, then she was fully on board. Plus, Charlie's eyes were a picture when he came down to see six large Milka bars in the toast rack.

'Is that for us?'

'Sure is!' Lorna agreed. 'Let's dig in.'

She was full of nervous energy herself this morning. It was Wednesday, and after three lazy days of Alpine luxury, it was time to head to Munich and see Connie. Mary had booked herself and the boys onto a trip on the lake, leaving David, Lorna and Tilly free to take the car the hour's journey into the city. They would meet Connie at the St Gisela care home at 4 p.m. and there, she prayed, the mystery of what had happened to the fourth gunner girl would finally be unveiled.

Michael Schneider had responded promptly to Tilly's Facebook message, and had turned out to be not Connie's son but her grandson.

'Did you not think it was a bit odd that a man with a ninety-four-year-old mother was abseiling and surfing?' Lorna had laughed when Tilly had shown her the profile picture of a young man in sporting gear. 'It says here that he's thirty-three, Tilly, which would have meant Connie had given birth to him when she was over sixty.'

'I didn't think, to be honest,' Tilly had breezed. 'I guess he is a bit young, but he seems nice and he says he visits his grandma a lot, so he's very happy to meet us there.'

'That's good of him.'

'He says she's very lively.'

That had been the best news of the lot, as it must mean Connie still had all her faculties. Lorna had to admit she'd been nervous that they'd come so far, only to find her unable to remember anything. Now, as she ate her way through an obscene amount of breakfast chocolate, she was only hours off finding out.

'OK?' Mary asked her.

She looked fondly over.

'I'm good, Mum, really. Thank you so much for sorting this. I thought I was going to have a totally miserable summer and instead it's been…'

'Only partially miserable?'

She smiled.

'Yes.'

'That will do for now. I, for one, have had a lovely time. I'm sad, of course I am, but it's been wonderful spending more time with you and the boys. I've loved having you in the annex. In fact—'

'Ready, Lorna?' David stood up, jangling the hire-car keys. 'Only we have to get Xavier to the train station for midday.'

'Right, yes, I suppose so. Mum?'

'It'll keep, darling. Off you go.'

So off they went.

The care home was a bright, clean, welcoming place. Set on the outskirts of Munich, it had pretty gardens and well-proportioned rooms with large windows to let in the sunlight. Lorna was relieved to see that Connie was in a nice place, then reminded herself that this woman was actually nothing to do with her. All she'd done was find a diary in a hidden drawer and latch onto Nancy's life to keep her from tumbling into the hole of her own. She hung back as they approached the door and David looked at her in concern.

'OK, Lorna?'

'Perhaps I should leave this to you and Tilly.'

'Why?'

'Because Nancy was, you know, your relation.'

David stared at her, but Tilly seized her arm.

'Absolute nonsense, Lorna. You found the diary, you pursued the details, you tracked Connie down. Stop dithering like an idiot and lead the hell on!'

Put like that, it was hard to argue, so Lorna gritted her teeth and rang the doorbell. It was answered by a young woman with a wide smile.

'You're the family here to see Connie Schneider?' she said in perfect English.

'That's right,' Tilly agreed firmly.

'We all love Connie. Her grandson, Michael, is here to greet you.'

She led them down an open corridor and into a wide lounge, decorated in crisp colours.

'This is lovely,' Tilly was saying to her. 'Much nicer than I imagined a care home would be. Do you have…? Oh.' Tilly stopped abruptly, her chatter dying on her lips, as a tall, broad-shouldered man with a shock of sun-streaked curls and aquamarine eyes came towards them. 'Oh,' she said again.

'Tilly Wilson?' he asked.

'Yes,' she said. 'That is, absolutely, that's me. Michael? Lovely to meet you. Thank you so much for coming. We're so grateful, we… Oh.' She stopped again as he shook her hand and leaned easily forward to place a kiss on each cheek. She put a hand up to her face. 'I thought it was the French that did that.'

He laughed.

'They cornered the PR on it, but we're all quite keen on kissing in Europe.'

'Are you?'

Lorna glanced to David and they shared an amused smile as Tilly gazed up at Michael Schneider, uncharacteristically floored. David waited a moment longer, then stepped up at her side to offer his hand to Michael.

'I'm David Wilson. And this is Lorna Haynes. We're pleased to meet you too.'

Michael shook their hands – though did not, Lorna noted, kiss them.

'Tilly's been messaging me all about this amazing diary,' he said. 'Do you have it with you?'

Lorna nodded, and took the leather volume from her bag. Michael smiled.

'I'm sure Oma will love to see such a tangible link to her past. She speaks of her "gunner girls" often, even now. Oh, but listen to me talking on when it is not me you are here to meet. My apologies. This way, please.'

He ushered them over to the window and there, sitting upright in a chair, was an old lady. She was small and very wrinkled, with snow-white hair and hands a little gnarled with age, but she was dressed smartly in trousers and a brightly patterned blouse and, most noticeable of all, she was smiling fit to burst.

'Connie Schneider?' Lorna asked.

'That's me.' She waved them forward. 'Pardon me for not getting up – my limbs don't obey me as I would like these days – but please, come in. Sit.'

Her voice had a slight German accent but it was underpinned by a distinctly Home Counties one, and Lorna smiled to hear it. They settled themselves and Michael called for coffee, then Connie looked around them all and said, 'So, my grandson tells me you found Nancy's diary?'

'Lorna did,' Tilly said. 'In a secret drawer.'

'How marvellous.' Lorna lifted up the little volume and Connie looked at her, hazel eyes shining. 'And you are…?'

Lorna swallowed. Who was she?

'I'm Lorna,' she started stupidly. 'I'm…'

David put a light hand on her shoulder.

'She's Nancy's granddaughter,' he said firmly.

Lorna felt tears well at his kindness but blinked them back.

'But never mind me,' she said to Connie. 'You and Nancy were good friends in the war, yes?'

'Oh, yes. The best. Peggy and Dot too. I was so lucky with those girls. We were very different, really, but we made the best team. Peggy was a Londoner and a military wife, Dot was a wild child from Norwich, Nancy a down-to-earth lass from Chester, and me? I was a Sussex debutante with a trust fund and no aspirations beyond finding a handsome husband. If it hadn't been for the war, we'd probably all have stayed right where we started out, but working that gun – it changed us.'

Connie looked out of the window a moment, her eyes fixed on something only she could see. Lorna thought of the diary – of Nancy's tales of the girls meeting up in Norwich and at the barracks and Dot's hen party in the days before hen parties were even a thing – and wondered if this bright-eyed old lady was seeing those events in her still lively mind's eye. Moved at this living connection to all she had recently learned, she leaned over and gently touched Connie's hand.

'We've been helping with the restoration of the Langham Dome,' she told her.

Connie instantly laid her other hand over the top of Lorna's.

'The dome? How marvellous. I remember training there. I'd never seen anything like it. I'd been to the pictures of course, but the dome was something else – a projection that felt so very real and that you could interact with. I remember standing in it for the first time, Nancy, Peggy and Dot at my side, and thinking, "I can't do this." But of course, I could. And I did. After that, I wasn't going to let anything stop me. None of us were.'

'Nancy certainly seems to have been intent on working as part of the estate rather than just in the kitchen.'

'Oh, yes,' Connie agreed with a chuckle. 'Joe had promised her she could be a gamekeeper and she wasn't going to stop until he fulfilled that promise.'

'From what the diary says, it nearly cost her her marriage,' Lorna said.

Connie nodded.

'That's true, but in the end, it made it even stronger. I sometimes think that so many of us gunner girls – and all the other service-women and factory workers and land girls – fought harder after the war than we did during it. Society wanted to slot us conveniently back into our kitchen-shaped holes, but we'd grown and we weren't going to shrink ourselves to fit back inside.

'It was the same all over Europe. We think of feminism as starting with the bra-burnings in the seventies but, let me tell you, it was the second half of the forties that got things moving. We may not have gone on parades, but we were fighting daily battles on our own hearths to build the platform to let that happen.' She stopped, worn out by her own eloquence. 'Sorry.'

'Please don't be.' Lorna pressed her hand tightly. 'We girls today owe a huge debt of gratitude to you, Nancy, Peggy, Dot and everyone like you.'

'Bless you.' Connie sat back, drawing in slow breaths. Michael leaped up to tend to her, watched intently by Tilly, but Connie waved him away. 'I'm fine, *Liebchen*, really. Maybe something a little stronger than coffee?'

She winked at him, and he grinned and reached into a bag at his side.

'Schnapps, Oma?'

'You're a good boy.' She looked to the others. 'Michael always brings me schnapps. A different flavour every time. What do we have today?'

'Apple.'

'Lovely! You'll join me?' They all nodded. 'Drink up then. We'll never get proper glasses out of this lot.'

'Is it forbidden?' Tilly asked, looking nervously around.

'Not forbidden, no, but frowned upon. It might make us "raucous", God forbid!' She checked for nurses and then gleefully waved Michael to pour them all a little measure of schnapps into their hastily drained coffee cups. '*Prost!*'

'To the gunner girls!' David suggested.

'To the gunner girls!' Connie drank, closing her eyes and savouring the taste for a moment. When she opened them again, she looked around a little sadly. 'How is England?'

'Fine, I suppose,' Lorna told her. 'Lots of rain and fields and tea, you know.'

Connie smiled. 'I don't really, not any more. I guess I'll never see the old place again now.'

'But you've been back?' Tilly asked.

Connie shook her head. 'Never.'

'Why?'

'People wouldn't have liked it. I'd signed myself over to the enemy and there was no going back after that.'

'But surely your family didn't feel that way?' Lorna asked tentatively.

It was wonderful to talk to Connie about the past, but the old lady looked to be tiring and she needed to work out how to get the conversation round to whatever secret had bound the gunner girls. Connie looked at her.

'Bless you for thinking so but, believe me, they did. There was a lot of bombing where I grew up. Not like London perhaps, but enough to wipe out far too many loved ones. I was marrying their murderer.'

Lorna gasped at the harsh word.

'Isn't war different?'

Connie smiled kindly at her.

'Only if you haven't experienced it, *Liebchen.*'

'But Nancy didn't refuse to see you, surely?'

Connie shook her head.

'No, Nancy was wonderful. We wrote for years. She told me all about you, David, and your younger sisters. I told her about Ernst and Michael and my own Nancy – named for her.'

David jumped.

'You have a Nancy too?' he asked, looking to Tilly. 'Did you hear that, Tilly – you and Michael are virtually cousins.'

'No, we are not,' Tilly said, horrified, then caught herself. 'But it's a lovely link between our two families all the same. Perhaps we can meet her some time?'

'Oh, I do hope so,' Connie said. 'I spent too long without Nancy properly in my life, so it would be a joy to see more of her family. And I know my Nancy would be keen to meet you all.'

'You talked to your family about the other gunner girls?' David asked.

'Oh, yes. Quite a joke it was, that Mama could have shot Papa out of the sky.'

'So why, then,' David asked, looking to Lorna and Tilly, 'didn't they talk to me of you? I knew Peggy and Dot well, but you – I never even knew you existed.'

Connie smiled sadly.

'Please don't blame your mother, David. It was for the best. It was what we agreed, to protect us all.'

'But why?'

Connie took another drink of her schnapps.

'Because of what happened on October the sixth, 1944 in the woods between Langham village and the air base.'

She drew in a breath and they all leaned eagerly forward.

Chapter Twenty-Four

Friday, 6 October 1944

'Cheers, girlies!'

'Yeah, cheers to you all – keep on shooting those damned Boche out of the sky, won't you?'

'And if you could bring one down over our way, we'd be grateful. We'd show the scum what we think of them, coming over here bombing our cities and our factories and our blinking families.'

'Scum!'

'Boche scum.'

Nancy, Peggy, Dot and Connie looked at each other nervously. The Langham locals were always very welcoming, but the level of animosity in the Blue Bell was dangerously high tonight. They understood it, of course they did. These were older men who'd fought in the Great War, facing down the German war machine from the trenches and seeing friend after friend sacrificed to enemy guns. Now they were seeing their sons facing the same horrors and, worse, were stuck at home powerless to help them. It was no wonder their hatred was so strong, but the girls didn't feel quite the same way.

It was disturbing, sometimes, sending your own young men out in planes with waves and cheers, and then turning your guns mercilessly on those coming in the other direction. They tried to focus on taking out the planes, rather than the humans at the controls. It was probably cowardly, but it was the only way they'd found to deal with the inherent violence of their task. Now they sipped at their gin and lemons and tried to relax, but it was hard.

'I've kept my gun in tip-top condition,' one of the blokes was telling his mates. 'Any German comes down around here, I'm having him, right through the heart.'

'That's too good for him, Ron. You gotta make him suffer first.'

'Yeah. Good old-fashioned bayonet.'

'Or kitchen knife.'

'Or rusty hoe!'

They clinked glasses vigorously and the girls sat a little further back into the corner.

'I think maybe I've had enough for one night,' Peggy said.

'Me too,' Connie agreed.

'I've got a bottle of vermouth in the dorm,' Dot offered. 'We could have a nightcap in bed?'

'Lovely,' Nancy agreed. 'Just don't tell us where you got it, Dot.' Dot winked.

'You've got to find the Yanks, Nance. Your Joe's very sweet 'n' all, but he's not got a hotline to the best booze in Norfolk, has he?'

'Honestly, Dot! You're incorrigible.'

'And thank heavens for that. Come on, girls, down the hatch, it's home time.'

They drank back their gin and got up.

'Going already, girlies?' the men asked, pausing in their torture fantasies to watch them head for the door.

''Fraid so, gents,' Peggy told them. 'Early duties tomorrow. Got to keep our trigger fingers steady.'

'Too right! Keep up the good work and remember – send one our way.'

They tumbled gratefully out into the night. The leaves were starting to turn and the air was cool, but it was welcome after the heat of the pub.

'Don't they realise that if we shoot a plane it will come down miles away? It's the crews further down the coast they need to be canvassing for their revenge plans, not us "girlies"!'

Nancy shivered.

'I hope the poor gits have the sense to come down over the sea if that lot are typical of what awaits them on land. Haven't they heard of the Geneva Convention?'

'If they have, they don't care,' Peggy said.

'But then, old Ron there lost both his dad and his uncle in the Great War, so I suppose you can sort of see where he's coming from.'

'Twisting bayonets into young men's guts though, Dot?'

'I know, I know. Oh, it's all horrible and I wish it was over.'

'It will be. Soon. The troops are storming towards Berlin.'

'And don't the Germans know it. Our job's not done yet, girls.'

'Home then?'

'Home,' they all agreed, linking arms and heading up the road out towards the airfield. It wasn't much over a mile and they had big coats and sturdy shoes on, so they set out happily enough, but they'd barely left the outskirts of the village before they heard a strange noise above them.

'That sounds like an angel whining,' Connie said, looking up to the stars.

'An angel, Con? Do angels whine?'

'Course not,' Peggy said, 'it's nice in heaven.'

The noise was getting louder now and they searched the skies.

'There!' Nancy cried, pointing to the east.

It looked like just another star at first, burning out its light miles away in a far-off galaxy, but it grew rapidly and suddenly it was lurching towards them, and they knew that was no star, but a plane – a plane with flames spewing from the left engine.

'Is it one of our boys? Is he going to make it?'

They watched anxiously as the plane wobbled in towards the land. It cleared the sea, but seemed to keep coming, faster and faster.

'It's going to hit us,' Connie gasped.

Instinctively they threw themselves to the ground as the plane veered overhead, swaying drunkenly, and then crashed into the trees beyond with a horrible shriek of torn metal and cracked wood. A ball of flame flew up, so hot they could feel it scorching across their skin, and they clutched at each other as they scrabbled in the mud. For maybe a minute the plane hung, suspended in the canopy just fifty feet from where they lay.

'It's a Messerschmitt,' Dot breathed. 'Those are Germans inside.'

'And they're in trouble,' Nancy said curtly.

Suddenly the branches gave and the enemy plane fell to the ground with a curiously dull thud, skidding a little way across the ground below.

'The cockpit's still intact,' Connie shouted. 'Look – someone's trying to get out.'

The glass over the pilot's seat shook furiously. Finally the clasps released, it broke away and a gloved hand shoved it off. A man appeared, pushing his goggles up onto his helmet. He leaned over, shaking his unresponsive radar operator, but the flames were engulfing the tail of the plane and he wrenched away. A hand went to his forehead in clear grief, but then there was an ominous bang from the engine. Horror flashed across his blue eyes and he put one foot up onto the edge of the cockpit to jump. Just as he did so, however, something exploded in the dashboard in front of him and he was flung out like a doll. His body hit the ground and he lay there, unmoving.

'Is he dead?' Nancy asked, standing up and moving towards him.

Peggy grabbed her skirt.

'Bound to be. Leave him, Nance.'

'But what if he's not?'

'He soon will be. Let's go.'

'It's too dangerous,' Dot agreed. 'That whole plane might explode any minute. We need to get away.'

Connie tugged on Nancy's arm, but then the pilot twitched and Nancy yanked away.

'He's alive.'

'Nancy!'

The pilot lifted his head, and his eyes were clear in the flickering light of the burning plane. He looked dazed and frightened and very, very young, and for a moment she saw something of her little brother in his face.

'Nancy, please,' Dot begged. 'He's not one of ours.'

'He's still someone's brother,' she retorted, 'someone's son, maybe someone's *husband*.'

'Nancy…'

But she was gone, running to the man, hand up in a useless attempt to ward off the flames.

'Bugger,' Dot said, but now Connie was running after Nancy, and with a groan Peggy and Dot joined them.

They grabbed at the man, clutching him roughly into their arms and bundling him away from the plane, breathing heavily, not so much from the exertion of carrying the slim pilot as from fear, but the plane burned steadily and they made it clear.

'He's safe,' Nancy gasped.

'Hardly,' Dot said drily. 'He's German. You heard the blokes in the pub. They'll have heard the plane come down in the village and they'll be on their way any minute.'

Sure enough, furious shouts rang out on the evening air. The girls looked at each other.

'We can't let them get him,' Nancy said. 'Look at him – he's a boy.'

She peered down at the now barely conscious pilot. His blond curls were thick with smoke, and his broad chest was heaving beneath his flying jacket as he fought to breathe.

'What can we do? It's a mile to the airfield and we can't carry him all that way before they reach us.'

They looked wildly around.

'The hut,' Dot said.

'What?'

'There's a hut in the woods.'

'How do you know?'

'Does it matter? Come on!'

The shouts were getting louder and, with a desperate look back down the road, the girls heaved the pilot to his feet and half carried, half dragged him into the trees.

'This way,' Dot urged.

The man moaned and Nancy cursed.

'I'm sorry. You were right, I should have left him.'

'Rubbish,' Connie said. 'You did the right thing – the Christian thing. We were the cowards, Nance, but not any more.'

'There!'

The hut was thankfully close. Peggy shoved on the door and, to their relief, it gave. They tumbled inside.

'There's a bed!' Connie cried, looking down on a rough assortment of blankets and cushions at the side of the little wooden room.

'Course there is,' Dot said.

'Dorothy Lewis!'

'Oh, shut up and get him laid down, will you?'

They obligingly spread out the man on the blankets. He peered up at them, fear in his blue eyes.

'Don't hurt me,' he begged in heavily accented English.

'We won't,' Connie said, dropping to her knees at his side. 'But you need to be quiet – *ruhig. Verstehen?*'

He nodded anxiously.

'Do you speak German, Con?' Peggy asked.

Connie flushed in the low light filtering in through the broken window.

'I had a German nanny, if you must know. Very nice she was too.'

'Right. You never said.'

'Not exactly a badge of honour at the moment, is it, speaking German?'

'I suppose not, but—'

'Hush!' Nancy said. 'They're coming.'

They looked at each other in horror. From outside the hut came the sound of men crashing around, calling to each other, bloodlust rippling through the air.

'He's not safe here either,' Peggy said. 'This is the first place they'll look.'

Sure enough, a rough voice outside cried, 'The hut! I bet the bastard's in the hut!'

'Behind the door, girls,' Dot barked, taking off her coat.

'But—'

'Behind the door – now!'

The others scrambled back, obediently cramming themselves into the space behind the door as, to their astonishment, Dot flung off her top and straddled the injured German, pulling the blanket up over them both to hide his uniform.

'*Mein Gott*,' he gasped, but she put her hand over his mouth and began moving rhythmically up and down just as the door flew open.

'Christ!'

Dot turned and glared at the intruders.

'What the hell do you think you're doing?'

They looked at each other, thrown.

'Sorry, miss. We, er…'

'Get out!'

'Right. Yes.' It was the bluff landlord speaking, but he was rapidly losing all his usual confidence. 'This is why you left the pub in such a hurry?'

'Do you blame me?'

'Erm, no. Course not. Only, have you seen any Germans on the run?'

Dot tossed her head.

'Do I look like I've got time for hunting down Germans?'

'No, but, er…'

'Hank?' she said, looking downwards. Nancy saw her thighs squeeze the poor pilot and he gave a game shake of his head. 'Thought not. Now, if you don't mind…'

Dot glared at the men again and, wide-eyed, they backed away. The door slammed shut. The girls all stayed frozen, but the sounds of the hunt moved further into the woods and it seemed that they had, somehow, got away with it.

'Dot, you peach!'

Connie flung herself on her friend as Dot climbed sheepishly off the pilot and reached for her top.

'Sorry about that,' she said to the young man, who stared wordlessly up at her.

Connie knelt next to him again.

'Are you hurt? *Bist du verletzt?*'

'*Meine Seite,*' he said faintly. Connie undid his jacket and they could all see a nasty wound running down his side like a gaping red cavern, a sliver of metal protruding unpleasantly from it.

'That's right where I squeezed him,' Dot gasped.

'Never mind that, we need to get it out.'

'And we need to get him to safety,' Peggy said. 'Connie, you look like you know what you're doing there. Dot, you need to stay in case the men come back, but Nancy, you and I can head for the base, maybe get a truck?'

'A truck?'

'I'll use my influence. Well, Harry's. If I chuck his name around, I'm sure we can manage. We can say Connie's sprained her ankle or something.'

'Ow!' Connie said obligingly, clutching at her ankle. Then: 'That's just what we need, Peg. We can't let him die out here, not now.'

'Agreed,' Nancy said. 'But why can't we just tell them we've got a prisoner?'

'Because word will get out that we rescued him, and then the villagers will be after *us*.'

'Fair point. Come on then, but God, I wish I was drinking vermouth in the dorm right now.'

It was an hour before Dot could finally crack open the bottle, and they were all more than ready for it by then. Peggy and Nancy had talked the duty officer into loaning them the truck for poor injured Connie, and they'd driven back to the woods at top speed. The men, thankfully, had headed onto the beaches, apparently believing that would be a German's first port of call, and they'd been able to lift the poor airman into the Jeep and head back to the airfield unseen.

If he could turn himself in officially, he would be protected from the hot-blooded men from the pub. So, they'd dropped him just outside the gates, Connie telling him to hide a while and then turn himself in to the duty officer once they were safely away. Then she'd put on a fine performance, limping suitably pathetically and leaning gratefully on the shoulders of the guards as they'd helped her into the dorm. There, Peggy had bandaged up her fake sprained ankle whilst Dot opened the vermouth.

'We made it,' Nancy laughed.

'Let's hope *he* does,' Connie added, more grimly.

But even as they clinked glasses, they heard a shout go up from the gates and knew that the pilot had reached the guards. He would be a POW now but he would, at least, be safe from the lynch mob. As would they.

'We can't speak of this to anyone,' Peggy warned, as they knocked back their first drinks and shakily held out their glasses for more. 'Anyone at all. We need to swear it.'

They looked solemnly at each other and swore.

'It's been a hell of night,' Dot said. 'It's going to be hard locking this up in our hearts.'

ANNA STUART

'It is,' Peggy agreed, 'but with it, we can lock up the knowledge that if we can do this, we can do anything.'

'Too right,' Connie agreed. 'We're not "girlies", we're gunner girls.'

They clinked glasses again, and Nancy looked around at her friends in pride and relief. She knew she'd asked a lot of them saving a German pilot but, bless them, they'd thrown themselves into it with her, and now a young man was safe to live out his days with his family when all this madness was over. How could that ever be wrong?

'We're gunner girls,' she echoed proudly. 'And we're going to run our worlds, our ways from now on.'

Chapter Twenty-Five

'Our worlds, our ways,' David said, smiling at Connie when she'd finished her story. 'That's what Mum, Peggy and Dot always used to say when the going got tough.'

Connie nodded.

'That night was something of a defining moment for us all. I'm glad it helped them through life; it certainly helped me!'

'Because that pilot was Ernst?' Lorna clarified.

The old lady smiled softly.

'It was. Love, it seems, can come quite literally out of the sky sometimes. And it was all down to Nancy. She was the one who was determined to save him, despite the danger. The rest of us would have left him, scared of the burning plane, but Nancy never thought of her own safety once, just of Ernst's.' She shuddered. 'And thank God. If we'd left him to the mercy of the pub hunters, who knows how my darling would have died.'

'The airfield officers kept him safe then?'

'They did. Once he'd officially reported in, they had no choice. Geneva Convention – and quite right too. He went into the hospital at Langham Hall and was looked after by the wonderful nurses there. Word got out to the village, of course, and they were furious. Ernst had to stay in his own room with a guard on the door at all times. They even caught a volunteer nurse trying to open up his wound again, so they asked for help from the airfield.'

'And you volunteered, Connie?'

'All four of us did. The war was marching on to its conclusion by then, and there were few planes coming our way so we had plenty of time. We all did stints at the hospital but I was, perhaps, the most diligent in my duties. Oh – that was a happy time. Scary but happy.' She leaned in. 'Let me tell you that I wasn't too pleased with myself for falling in love with one of the enemy. I resisted it for quite some time, but in the end…'

'In the end love won?' Tilly asked.

Connie nodded at her.

'It usually does. It's the only thing really worth fighting for. I don't regret any of it. Oh, I wish it hadn't cost me my parents, but they were the distant sort anyway.'

'You told no one about the plane?'

'No one. It wasn't worth it. Those men in the Blue Bell that night, my dears… You weren't there so you won't understand, but it was venomous. Nancy paid for a war memorial, I believe, somewhere near the pub?'

'It's on the green just outside, yes.'

'So intent on honouring their dead, they were – and rightly so. To Nancy, though, it was a memorial to all who had died in the war. There's a name on there, she told me, right at the bottom – Ernest Taylor. That's Ernst Schneider in English. Her way of respecting what we did that night, and perhaps of getting one up on those Langham men who would have torn him apart without our intervention.'

Lorna pictured the names on the memorial and vaguely remembered an Ernest Taylor amongst the rest. She smiled at Nancy's cunning. Then she thought of Brian telling the story of Dot's hut adventures. He'd said the locals had been coy about what they'd been doing in the woods, so maybe, in time, they'd seen the inhumanity of their intentions. Connie was right about one thing though – no one who hadn't been there would understand, and was it really their place to judge?

'It just seems sad that you lost out, Connie.'

'Oh, believe me, I got so, so much out of moving here. Germany has been good to me.'

She sat back in her chair with a soft sigh, and Michael got up and went to her.

'You look tired, Oma.'

David was on his feet immediately.

'Yes, you must be. We've worn you out with our questions, I'm sorry.'

Connie smiled at him.

'Please don't be sorry, David. That story has been inside me for far too long. It feels good to have finally let it out.' She reached out her hands and he took them carefully in his own. 'I owe my happiness in life to your mother, and it's a pleasure to be able to tell you that. We should probably have told people years ago, but keeping secrets is a hard habit to break.'

'I'm so glad you have.'

Connie's old eyes were closing, but still she held on to David's hands.

'I could never thank her enough, you know. I just hope that the paintings went some way to expressing my gratitude.'

'Paintings?'

For a little time Connie said nothing, and they thought she'd gone to sleep.

'I'd better...' Michael started, but then her eyes fluttered open again.

'The Turners. Nasty dark little things, but hopefully worth a bit. I gave the others a painting too, but I wanted Nancy to have double. She deserved it – without her I would never have had Ernst.'

She smiled softly to herself and her eyes drooped again.

'Turners,' Lorna repeated, looking to David. 'Isn't the painting in the annex a Turner?'

He nodded.

'I assumed it was a copy. Was it not a copy?'

He, Lorna and Tilly looked at each other.

'It must be a copy,' Lorna said. 'Nancy must have sold the original to get the money for the roof and the hatcheries. It must be how Dot funded her nursery and Peggy her fertility treatment. Connie turned twenty-one, inherited her trust fund, and gave it all away – for love.'

She looked fondly at the old woman who'd kindly shared her life story with them. She'd been so worried about a dark secret at the heart of the gunner girls' time in Langham, and all along it had been something so simple and so beautiful.

She smiled but then Tilly spoke: '*Two* paintings, Dad. Connie said Nancy had *two* paintings.'

'You mean…'

'I mean, you need to get your arse back to the Gamekeeper's Cottage and get that baby out of the frame!'

'Home, sweet home.'

David slotted his key into the lock and let them into the Gamekeeper's Cottage. It was nearly 9 p.m. and they were tired. The boys were lolling sleepily against Lorna and her own bones felt weary, but there was no way she was sleeping yet – not until they'd checked out the painting.

'Come on, boys, let's tuck you up.'

'Hungry,' Charlie said, but not very convincingly, and he allowed himself to be steered towards the annex.

Mary and David came in behind them and Lorna instinctively looked around for Tilly, before remembering that they'd left her behind in Germany. In theory she was organising to travel on to her Italian vineyard, but yesterday she'd announced that she thought Munich was a 'surprisingly fascinating city' and that she might stay another few days.

'Weeks, more like,' Lorna had teased her.

'I don't know what you mean, Lor.'

'Course you don't, Tilly. This fascination for Munich wouldn't have anything to do with a certain Michael Schneider, would it?'

'No!' Tilly had insisted, but the colour flushing across her cheeks had betrayed her immediately. Michael had been out to see them at Tegernsee, and he and Tilly had been all but welded to each other throughout his stay. It had been very sweet to see. 'OK, maybe a little,' she'd admitted. 'That's allowed though, isn't it? I can drift where I want, remember?'

'I do remember,' Lorna had told her. 'Just don't, you know, feel that you have to. Bavaria seems a pretty nice part of the world to me.'

'It does, doesn't it?'

Tilly had been endearingly shy, and Lorna had left her with a huge hug and a strong suspicion that someone else was going to have to get those Italian grapes picked this autumn. Already she missed her newfound little sister, but really hoped Tilly might have found something worth holding on to. Besides which, she'd love an excuse to go back to Germany for her next holiday; she'd heard it was wonderful at Christmas time.

Smiling at the thought, Lorna pushed open the annex door and stepped inside, her eyes on the boys, but when she looked up, she gasped.

'Oh my God!'

The annex had been transformed. They'd only been away a week, but Kyle had been busy. A pretty shaker-style kitchen had replaced the worn-out units, complete with a mini range cooker and a new limestone floor. The walls throughout the living area were a fresh clotted cream colour, and the collapsed armchairs had been replaced by bright gingham ones that gave a nice nod to the original kitchen whilst still looking modern. The wireless, Lorna was glad to see, had survived, as had the fireplace, though the original grate had been replaced with a modern gas fire. She leaned over to press a button on the front and a warm glow spread through the room.

'It looks amazing,' Mary said, coming in behind her. 'The man's a genius.'

'You designed it, Mum,' Lorna said, hugging her. 'I was sad to see the original go, but I have to admit this is far better. Oh, but...'

She turned to where the bunk beds had previously stood against the right-hand wall to find that Kyle had installed a partition. The boys, wide awake now, raced round to an arched doorway leading into a boy-cave of a room, complete with LED stars on the dark blue ceiling and camouflage tents over the bunks.

'Cooooooolll!' Charlie squealed, throwing himself inside.

Lorna looked to Mary.

'Is that a good idea, Mum?'

'Sounds like it is,' Mary said mildly, as the boys continued to express their pleasure from inside their cave.

'But it's lost you a lot of space in the main room. What if you have guests who aren't under ten?'

'Well, that was sort of what I wanted to talk to you about in Germany, but we never quite had time.'

Lorna looked curiously at her but David was pacing the room, increasingly distraught, and now he came across to his wife.

'Where's the painting, Mary?'

Lorna instantly forgot the partitioned bedroom because David was right – the dark little Turner was gone from the freshly painted walls and was nowhere to be seen.

'It must be somewhere,' Mary said. 'I didn't tell Kyle to throw it away.'

'Did you tell him to keep it?'

She thought about it.

'Not in so many words,' she admitted. 'No one really liked it.'

'True,' David agreed, 'but what if...'

'It was the original,' they all said together.

David was doing his best to stay calm as he checked the cupboards and corners for a stray painting, but he was looking increasingly agitated – and no wonder. Lorna grabbed her case and went to put it into the bedroom, out of the way, but the moment she opened the door she laughed.

'It's here!' she cried. 'David, it's in here. Kyle must have stored it in the bedroom to keep it safe.'

David and Mary tumbled in and they all looked at the little painting, sitting on the old dressing table.

'Thank God!' David said. He carried it back out into the main room and turned it this way and that. 'Though, to be honest, I don't think this is an original. I'm no expert but it's got no, you know, texture.'

'Take it out of the frame,' Mary suggested.

'Carefully,' Lorna added.

David nodded and laid the picture upside down on the new coffee table. The frame had fold-back clips and Lorna frowned at it.

'Wouldn't an original come in a proper frame?' she asked.

'I'd have thought so,' Mary agreed. 'Don't get your hopes up, folks.'

David released the clips one by one and slowly lifted the back off. Placing his hand dead centre, he flipped the painting and expertly lifted off the frame and glass. They all stared. The picture was printed onto shiny paper, a little faded perhaps but most definitely not two hundred years old. David sighed.

'Mum must have sold both originals and then bought a replica of one of them to mark Connie's kind gift.' He gave the other two a grimace. 'Silly of us, really, to imagine some sort of lost treasure.'

'Not that silly,' Mary said. 'It happens on *Antiques Roadshow* all the time.'

They laughed, but weakly. David sank into one of the armchairs and put the picture down on the table. The backing shifted sideways, and a few sheets of old paper slid out and fluttered to the floor.

'Padding,' David said, 'to push the print up against the glass. Come on, Mary, we should get to bed. It's been a long day.'

He made to stand up again, but Lorna put out a hand to stop him before he trod on the sheets.

'That's not padding,' she said, scrambling to grab the papers and turning them over to reveal some very familiar handwriting. 'That's the missing pages from Nancy's diary.'

Eagerly, she sorted them into what she hoped was the right order and began to read.

Chapter Twenty-Six

Wednesday, 21 August 1946

Connie came to see me today. It was so, so lovely to see her and she brought such gorgeous little gifts for David. We had tea and chattered away just like old times, and then – oh goodness, then she told me she was going to Germany. Germany! Ernst has been released and is to be repatriated. He asked Connie to marry him, and she's said yes and she's moving to Munich. Next week.

I didn't know what to think. I mean, she was so clearly happy. Bubbling with it.

'Don't worry, Nance,' she said. 'No one need know what happened. I'm just slipping away. No fuss, no fanfare, just a one-way ticket to Munich.'

'But your folks—'

'Will find out soon enough, and what can they do? I'm twenty-one now – a grown woman, free to access my own money and make my own decisions.'

'Is that to protect me, Connie? Because you don't have to protect me if—'

'I do, Nancy. I do have to protect you, because you protected Ernst that night and transformed my life.'

'But, Connie, won't it be hard for you out there?' I objected, but she just said, 'Ernst says not. He says Bavaria is different. It's in the south, you know, and far away from central power. It has its own identity apparently, its own way of life. He says his family will love me. They hated

Hitler. Imagine that – having a ruler you don't agree with and then being pulled into war by him.'

'And having your son forced to fight for him.'

Connie gave this funny little smile then and said, 'He's so brave,' or something like that. She's got it bad. It's sweet, really, and if she wants to go to Germany then why shouldn't she? It's what we vowed, after all, that night we saved Ernst – that we'd run our worlds, our ways. If Connie's way leads her to this Bavaria place, then so be it. I told her that and she cried.

'I won't see you again, Nance. Any of you.'

'Not for a while,' I agreed. 'But perhaps when all the hate has settled down.'

I hope it's true, but Germany feels a long way away at the moment.

'I have another present, actually,' Connie said to me then. 'It's in the car. Will you come and see?'

So I did, and the car was beautiful. A little red sporty number. Must have cost a fortune. It looked very odd sitting in front of the Gamekeeper's Cottage, all shiny and smart. I forget, sometimes, that Connie's from money. Or I did. It will be hard to now.

'I want you to have these,' she said, getting two squares out of the boot and turning them round to show me. Well, I don't mind admitting, my heart sank. They were pictures. Clever ones, I'm sure, but funny and dark – not my thing at all.

'Oh, you don't need to,' I said, quick as you like, but Connie took one look at my face and laughed.

'I don't mean for you to keep them, Nance. They're ugly old things, but I'm told they're worth quite a bit. Came to me as part of my trust fund earlier in the year, but there's no way I'm hefting them to Bavaria, so I thought it might, you know, be a help to you. To you and Joe and David. I've

given Peggy and Dot a painting too, as a thank you to my glorious gunner girls for saving Ernst for me.'

Well, I had no idea what to say, but she pressed them on me, told me to get them to Horners in Norwich as soon as I had need, so I had no choice but to take them and to thank her in return. Then she was getting ready to go, and I was so caught up in hugging her goodbye and wishing her luck that I didn't think about them again until Joe came in and we looked at them together.

'What the hell are we going to do with those?' he said, but it didn't take the drip-drip of water into the bucket down the corridor to spell it out.

I looked up at the roof.

'We're going to sell them. We're going to sell them, then we're going to get this roof mended, claim the house as our own and get on with making this the best damned estate in Norfolk.'

Chapter Twenty-Seven

'No wonder she decided to hide these pages,' Lorna said, passing the first of them over to David. 'If anyone had read them, they'd have known about the gunner girls saving Ernst straight away.'

'And by the sounds of it, they wouldn't have been too happy,' David agreed. 'Such a shame, isn't it, that whole nations were set against each other when really, apart from a section of fanatics, people were just trying to do their best to defend themselves.'

'That's war for you,' Mary said sadly.

Lorna hugged her.

'Spot on, Mum. Now, why don't you put the kettle on and I'll get this pair to bed in their amazing new bedroom.'

'OK,' Mary agreed, dipping into the cave to kiss the boys goodnight. Lorna heard her cooing to them: 'Do you like it? Yes? Good. That's really good. Stars like in Germany? You're right, Stan. Sleep tight. See you in the morning. What? Aah. I love you too, gorgeous.' Mary emerged a little pink-cheeked but smiling broadly. 'They're such sweethearts. We really love having them here, Lorna. That's why—'

'Mummy!' Stan called from his bed, and Lorna gave her mum an apologetic shrug.

'Get that kettle on,' she said, blowing Mary a kiss as she handed David the rest of the diary pages and ducked into the cave. 'Hopefully I won't be long.'

She was longing to read the rest of the mystery pages but right now her sons needed her and, really, she'd waited most of the summer to find out what had happened to Nancy, so a few more minutes were nothing. Thankfully, the excitement of the boys' new room had settled a little and that, on top of the rigours of the long trip home, had them both yawning. One quick story and a kiss apiece and they were snuggling down. Lorna stood for a moment, counting her little pair of blessings, then crept out and, leaving the door wedged open, made for the kitchen.

'Tea?'

'Lovely.'

Lorna gratefully accepted the steaming mug and took a big glug. What was it about aeroplanes that always made you thirsty?

'So,' David said, 'that was quite a trip.'

'It was wonderful. Thank you, David, you've made me so welcome here. I was very touched when you told Connie I was Nancy's granddaughter.'

'Well, you are now. I know I'm not your actual dad, but—'

She leaped up and gave him a hug.

'You're the only dad I've ever had, David, and I'd say I've hit the jackpot.'

'Oh, now…'

He looked quite overcome, and she laughed and hugged him again.

'It's amazing to have found so much family, and I think it will really help the boys now that, you know, they don't have Matt.'

'We're always here for you, Lorna,' David assured her.

'In fact…' Mary said, but at that moment Lorna's phone rang out.

She glanced down at the screen and saw Aki's face smiling up at her.

'Sorry, Mum, I'd better take this. Aki's talking about coming up again next weekend. I'd like to think it was to see me, but I suspect it's far more for the lovely Dan.' Mary nodded and she tapped on the screen to take the call. 'Aki! Hi, how's things?'

'I'm not sure.' Aki's voice was unusually cold. 'Why don't you tell me how "things" are, Lorna?'

'Aki? What's wrong?'

Lorna's mind raced. Had she done something to offend her friend? She couldn't have done, surely – she'd been in Germany all week.

'When were you going to tell me, Lor?'

'Tell you what? Aki, you're not making any sense.'

'When were you going to tell me you're leaving?'

'Leaving?' Lorna pulled the phone back to stare down at it, as if she might see her friend, but it was only her icon, frozen in a smile. She certainly wasn't smiling now. 'Aki, I'm not leaving.'

'So why, then, have I received a reference alert for Charlie and Stan from Langham Primary?'

'Langham Primary?' Lorna echoed, astonished. Then she caught sight of the blush spreading across her mum's cheeks and it all clicked into place. 'Mum,' she growled.

'I've been trying to tell you,' Mary stuttered.

'Lorna?' Aki asked from down the phone.

'There's been a misunderstanding, Aki,' Lorna said, her eyes fixed on her mum. 'A big one. I think I need to go and talk to my mum now.'

'Oh.' Aki's voice lightened instantly. 'Oh, I see. Good luck then. And Lorna – be kind to her. I'm sure she's only trying to do her best for you.'

'Hmm,' Lorna said. 'Thanks, Aki.'

She switched off the phone and looked at Mary.

'I can explain, Lorna.'

'I really hope you can, Mum, because it sounds to me very much as if you put in a request to change my sons' school without even asking me.'

Mary swallowed. David got up and tactfully slid away.

'I suppose I sort of did,' she admitted. 'But I wouldn't have actually done anything, I swear. I just happened to bump into the headteacher down in the village the other day. A lovely lady, by the way, she's in my bridge club and—'

'Mum!'

'Right, yes. Well, I just happened to ask her if there might be room for Charlie and Stan in the school if they ever, you know, wanted it.'

'Wanted it because…'

Mary shuffled awkwardly on the sofa.

'You've seemed to be happier here these last few weeks, Lor. Not happy. I know you can't be happy, not properly, not yet, but happ*ier*, more relaxed.'

'I have been, Mum. It's been a huge help, but—'

'And you said that being around the places where you'd lived with Matt was hard, and you seemed to like the annex and I just thought that maybe, for a year or two, you might want to, to move here. Not like you're a kid or anything, just for, for support. So I asked the question. That's all. I tried to talk to you about it in Germany but it never seemed to be the right time, so I thought I'd wait till we got back. I didn't know it would get all official.'

Lorna looked at her mum, scarlet-cheeked and rubbing her hands miserably round and round in her lap.

'Oh, Mum!'

'I'm sorry. I wasn't trying to make your decisions for you.'

'I know that.' Lorna's mind was racing. 'That's why you were so keen to get the renovations done? That's why you wanted to get Kyle in here and why you wanted me to help him – so the annex would feel more like mine?'

'He's done a good job, right?'

'He's done a good job, Mum, but did you have to be so secretive about it?'

'I wasn't sure how much you could take. Not that you're not strong. You are, but you've been through so much. I thought perhaps if you could see the annex looking modern and, and liveable, you might…'

'Move in for good?'

Mary shrugged.

'It sounds rather calculated, put like that. I didn't mean it to be. I just so wanted to look after you, darling. I hate seeing you hurting and I wanted to help, and I thought maybe this was a way that I could.'

A tear dropped out of her eye and it set Lorna crying too. She threw herself down next to her mum, butting up against her as she used to do when she was a confused teen. Mary put a tentative arm around her, and when Lorna leaned into it, she felt her mum's hand clamp tight around her shoulders – fierce and safe.

'Thank you,' she said, drinking in L'Air du Temps. For her it would always be the smell of security, of care. 'I couldn't have got through this summer without you. You've been my rock – like always.'

Mary shifted at her side.

'Always? Are you sure, darling? Because I worry sometimes that, with it being just us when you were small, I was often more of a burden to you than a help.'

Lorna pulled back and stared at her, genuinely astonished.

'You thought that? Good God, Mum – no!' She jumped up, pulling Mary through to the hall where she stood her in front of the photo of the pair of them on the double swing, laughing to the skies. '*That* was my childhood, Mum, right there. You were there for me, always. Not physically, perhaps – I was the only one at the primary with their own door key, but I loved that. It made me feel independent, strong. I loved making you a cup of tea when you got in, hearing about your day and telling you about mine. You were my… well, my rock.'

Mary squeezed her hard.

'And you mine, darling. It was just, seeing how pleased you've been to have a dad in David and a sister in Tilly, I felt bad I hadn't given you that before.'

Lorna rolled her eyes through her tears.

'Oh, Mum – drop the guilt! I *am* pleased, but that doesn't mean I wasn't happy before. This is new for both of us, right? And it's great that we're enjoying it. I love it here at the Gamekeeper's Cottage.'

'Then…'

'But I can't move here.'

It was only as she spoke the words out loud that Lorna realised how very true they were. It had been good to escape home and the constant reminders of a life that couldn't now be hers, but it was still home. She didn't have Matt in Norwich any more but she did have a job she enjoyed, friends she loved, and places that were important to her. So did the boys.

'I have to get on with my life, Mum. I have to move forward. I don't want to, not without Matt, but I have to do it all the same.'

'And you have to do it in Norwich?'

Lorna swallowed. August was running out and September was so close she could almost touch it, but somehow the panic had gone. That wasn't to say that it wouldn't come back on the first day of term when she had to step into school and take on all those kids, but for the first time since that dreadful phone call, she felt a glimmer of anticipation at going back into the classroom she loved. She had a hell of a resource now, too – wait until she hit her Year Sevens with a real-life diary from 1945!

'I have to do it in Norwich, Mum, yes. It's going to be hard though, and coming here sometimes – often – would really, really help, if you don't mind?'

'Mind?! I'd love it, you know I would.'

'Then it's a deal?'

'It's a deal!'

Mary hugged her again and Lorna held on tight. She still missed Matt with every fibre of her being, but at least she had others to love her and help her, and somehow, with their support, she would get through this. She waved to David, hovering in the living room, and he came over and joined the hug.

'Thank heavens Nancy found a way to keep a roof over this lovely house of yours,' she said to him, as they finally disentangled and headed back through to the kitchen.

He nodded. 'Do you think that's what got her finally accepted by Ted and Betty?'

'I'm not sure. Have you read the rest of the entries?'

He shook his head. 'You should read them first. This has been your quest all along, Lorna, and it's only right that you finish it off. Here.'

He picked the pages up from the table and put them into her hand. Lorna smiled at him.

'Thanks. I'll take these to bed then, if that's OK? I feel I need Nancy's cerise wallpaper around me to fully appreciate her words.'

David smiled and put his arm around Mary as Lorna made for the annex.

'I hope the ending is as bright as the roses.'

'Me too,' Lorna agreed, glancing down at Nancy's words on the precious pages. 'Me too.'

Chapter Twenty-Eight

Monday, 16 September 1946

I'm unnatural, I swear I am. I honestly love baby David so much that my heart often feels too big to fit into my chest, but he doesn't do anything and – oh, I can't believe I'm writing this – sometimes he bores me. Joe says maybe my brain has been altered by the war. Well, not by the war itself but by my army training. He says maybe putting girls through all that has made our brains more male so that now we don't function the way we used to. He says it kindly but it's a horrible thought. Might it be true?

This morning a man came from Horners to see the paintings. I don't think they believed me about them being Turners on the phone. I think they thought I was imagining I had treasure. The man arrived, all supercilious, but within minutes of training his fancy looking-glass on Connie's gifts, his manner changed. Suddenly he was all obsequious, full of what Horners could do for us and calling me madam. It made me want to laugh.

I soon stopped laughing when he gave us an estimated sale price, though. If we sell the pair, they could raise thousands, he said – thousands! Enough for the roof and to invest in the estate besides. Lord Langham is promising us shares if we help him upgrade the pheasant hatchery and buy a new tractor, and we can maybe expand the garden at the back of the cottage too – not just the rough beds Ted dug out in the

*war, but proper, smart, sustainable ones for sending produce
into the city. There's money in that. Dot says Tony knows all
sorts of people dead keen to buy posh veg. We could even get
a van, with a logo on the side.*

*I wake up in the night with all these ideas, and then
David cries and I remember that I'm a mum now and I'm
not meant to have ideas, just milk. The thought of handing
over my precious plans – not to mention my money – to Ted
and Joe to make them happen drives me insane.*

Nancy plunged her hands into the bucket, scrubbing at the
nappies with all her might, as if she could force her fears and
uncertainties into the water that was rapidly turning as scummy and
brown as her thoughts. Behind her Betty was cooing over David
as he lay on a mat, naked as the wonderful day he was born, and
kicking his tiny limbs in all directions as the late summer sun shone
in through the window. It was a wonderful sight and, as usual,
Nancy's heart swelled with love for her son. She wasn't unnatural,
she knew she wasn't. Just… restless.

She scrubbed more.

'Careful, lass, or you'll have the fabric clean through,' Betty
laughed.

'I want to get them clean for him. He's got a bit of a rash and
I don't want it getting sore.'

'Fresh air,' Betty said, 'that's what'll sort that out. Lovely fresh
air on your little bum-bum, hey, Davey sweetie? Hey? Hey!'

She leaned over the little boy, pulling faces, and David gurgled
happily in response. Nancy smiled; a baby's laugh had to be the
sweetest sound in the world. So why did she sometimes feel this
terrible urge to get away from him? It was ridiculous. These last
five weeks with her son, she'd felt the happiest she'd ever been, so
why did being happy make her so damned miserable?

She lifted a nappy out and held it to the light.

'Clean as a whistle,' Betty pronounced, which was stupid when you thought about it because what was so clean about a whistle? Nancy kept her thoughts to herself and nodded.

'I'd better get them through the mangle and hung out whilst the sun's still bright.'

'Good idea. I just hope this weather holds for a few weeks more.' Betty glanced at the bucket still sitting in the middle of the hall. 'Until the, er, the sale can go through.'

She looked shyly at Nancy. She and Ted kept doing this. They'd been beside themselves when Nancy had told them about the paintings and suggested they might cover a new roof to save the cottage.

'You can't do that,' they'd kept saying. 'You can't spend your money on our house.'

'I can,' Nancy had told them, 'because it's my house too now, and I want to see it preserved.'

There'd been tears and hugs, not just from Betty but from Ted too, and Nancy had felt more a part of the Gamekeeper's Cottage than ever before. She was going to send some money up to her own folks in Chester, but it was important that she invested in her new family too. She just worried that once she'd paid for the roof to be restored, they'd still want her kept firmly underneath it.

'Are you all right with David for a minute?' she asked Betty now.

'Of course. I'd be all right with David every precious minute God sends.'

It was true, Nancy thought, as she grabbed the bucket and headed out to the kitchen. Betty had taken the baby to her bosom, and Nancy was grateful there was so much love in the house for her precious son. She fed the first nappy into the mangle and turned hard and fast. She had so much energy pushing around inside her with nowhere to go that at times her limbs physically itched.

Merry had come to see her the other day, bringing a bolt of fabric and a pattern for the most amazing dress. It seemed that

Joe, bless him, had been conspiring with her to get Nancy a new
frock for when her figure returned, and she couldn't wait to sew it
up. Or, better still, ask Betty to sew it up – her skills with a needle
were vastly superior to Nancy's, just like her skills with a baby.
Mind you, Merry had also brought a picture of a backpack some
woman in America had invented to carry your baby around with
you, which Nancy had thought would suit her down to the ground
once David was a little bigger. Betty had been less impressed.

'How would you see Baby?' she'd asked indignantly.

'You wouldn't need to,' Merry had said. 'He'd be on your back
so you'd know he was safe.'

'He might slide out.'

'I think you'd feel that.'

'But he'd be on the ground! And besides, babies like to see your
face. A pram, that's what you need. A nice big pram that you can
push David down to the village in so everyone can see him. I'll
see what I can find.'

Betty was resourceful, that was for sure, and within a day she'd
bought a pram from a lady in the village whose children had grown
out of it. It was a beautiful piece of work, Nancy had to admit, and
it did mean that she could get outside with David, but the great
big wheels were no use anywhere but down the road. She'd gone
out yesterday afternoon, Betty trotting proprietorially at her side,
and although they'd been out for over an hour, they'd only made
it to the green and back. They'd had to stop every three minutes
for some villager to come out and coo over him and ask about his
sleeping and his eating, as if it was the most interesting thing in
the world. Nancy had stood and forced a smile and tried not to
look too longingly out at the estate, bursting with late summer life
and a hundred and one jobs to be done.

'Well, wasn't that an adventure?' Betty had said as they'd finally
got back home, using the sing-song voice that she believed David
loved, and that, to be fair, the baby did seem to respond to.

'An adventure?' Nancy had echoed faintly, thinking of the night in the woods when she and the other gunner girls had rescued an enemy pilot from under the noses of the very villagers she now lived amongst.

Maybe Joe was right, and the war had spoiled her, robbed her of her natural maternal faculties? If so, was there a cure, or was she condemned to years of feeling trapped under her own, very costly roof?

The nappies wrung dry, Nancy let herself out of the little back door into the garden to hang them on the line. She paused to draw in several deep breaths of fresh air and looked yearningly across the fields. Joe was mending fences somewhere over towards the Hall and if she listened carefully, she could hear the ring of his hammer on the posts as it echoed across the still air. Her fingers burned to lift the tool and hammer something. Anything!

'Nancy!' Betty called through the open door. 'I think Baby wants feeding.'

David's little cries followed her words and Nancy's breasts ached. She put a hand to them. It was a wonderful miracle that David was growing from milk she produced, but it also meant she was irrevocably tied to him. In the war, many women had given their babies bottles of an amazing new formula milk so that someone else could feed them whilst they worked in the factories.

'Bottles!' Betty had said. 'Imagine!'

Nancy had tried hard not to imagine; it was far too tempting.

Now she pegged the last nappy to the line and went inside. David was grizzling in Betty's arms, and the poor woman was jiggling him and singing softly but to no avail. Nancy could see the frustration in her face and felt a sudden rush of power. David was her baby, not Betty's. She loved him to bits; she'd do anything for him.

'Here, sweetheart.'

She took him into her arms and the baby immediately squirmed to reach her breasts.

'Thank you, Betty,' she said, and retreated into the parlour to unbutton the front of her dress and let David feed.

As he latched on, Nancy felt a quiet peace descend. Here, just the two of them, being a mother felt right. She looked down at the tiny mouth suckling and stroked his downy hair. She felt her own body relax into the cushions of the sofa as weariness hit. David loved to feed. Every two hours, day and night, he was asking for milk and it took him quite some time to get his fill. Nancy couldn't remember the last time she had truly slept, and it left her feeling less sleepy than strangely tingly, as if someone had wired her up to the electricity.

The sun slanted in through the window, sending dust motes dancing before her, and Nancy watched them in a daze. David spluttered and fell off the nipple, thrashing his little head crossly as he sought for it again. Nancy cupped her hand gently around the back of his neck and guided him in, and the suckling began again. Lord, he was so tiny and so helpless and, just think, if it hadn't been for her accident at the wedding, he might not yet even be born.

Nancy felt a sudden surge of nostalgia for that magical moment when he'd first been put in her arms and everything had felt right with the world. Tears leaked out of her eyes and she flicked them crossly away, but more came. Now she was crying as if she'd never stop, the tears dropping onto poor David's head making her blink.

'Sorry,' she hiccupped. 'Oh Davey, sweetheart, I'm sorry. It's not you. You're perfect. It's me. I'm all anyhow at the moment, but I'll take care of you, I promise you that. I'll make sure you're safe. Always. I'll, I'll…'

What would she do? The sheer weight of love seemed to press down on Nancy, stopping her words and sending the tears flowing faster than ever. What was going on?

'Nancy?' Betty came cautiously into the room. 'Nancy, are you…? Oh, my poor dear.'

She came rushing across and rubbed Nancy's back.

'Sorry,' Nancy gulped again. 'Don't know what's the matter. I'm just so… so happy.'

Betty gave a soft laugh.

'Baby blues, that's what's the matter. It's perfectly normal.'

'It is?' Nancy looked hopefully up at her.

'Oh, yes. I was a mess after giving birth to Joe. Ted didn't know what to do with me. He kept saying, "All's well, Betty. Really. All's well." And I kept telling him I knew it was, that everything was wonderful, but I kept crying too. He was baffled, poor man.'

Nancy laughed, but the laugh caught on a sob and turned into another hiccup. David looked up irritably as her chest heaved, and that made her laugh and cry even more.

'You need your mam, lass,' Betty told her.

'Oh, no. I mean, it would be lovely to see her, but you've been amazing, Betty, like a mother to me.'

Betty clutched her chest.

'Ooh don't, lass, you'll set me off too and then where will we be?! Let's ask your mam for a visit. That painting money should give us plenty for a train fare for her to get down, shouldn't it?' Nancy gave a little nod, the thought of seeing her mother overwhelming her too much for words. 'And in the meantime, we need to take good care of you. It's not just Baby who's new in the world, you know, it's Mummy too. It's a lot to get used to.'

'I love him so much, Betty.'

'I know you do, lass. And he loves you.'

'I'm not sure he knows how to love yet, but he needs me. He needs me so much. Sometimes that feels a bit, well, scary. Is that stupid?'

'Of course not. We all feel like that. Even now I feel like that about Joe. When he was away fighting, I was scared for what felt like every single moment. Loving someone means putting at least part of your happiness in their hands, and when those hands are so tiny' – she indicated David's little fingers curling in and out as he fed – 'it's doubly hard.'

Nancy smiled up at her through her tears.

'You're very wise, Betty.'

'Ooh, get away with you! I'm just a daft old mawther, but I've learned a few things along the way – and one is that you need a rest. When you've finished feeding him, why not pop him in the pram for his nap and get yourself to bed too? I can watch him if you trust me?'

Nancy laughed.

'I trust you more than I trust myself.'

'Goodness, don't do that. Take the time for yourself, though.'

Nancy reached out for her hand.

'Thank you, Betty, I'd like that, but do you mind if, instead of going to bed, I go out for a walk?'

'A walk?!'

'It's such a lovely day and my legs are so twitchy. The pheasants will be everywhere and Joe says the deer have come in close to the wood. I'd love to see them, and I think it will do me more good than a sleep.'

Betty shook her head.

'You're a rum'un, you are, our Nance.'

Nancy noted the 'our' and it almost set the tears flowing again.

'I know,' she said softly. 'I promise you, I know.'

'But if a walk's what's best for you, then that's fine by me, lass.'

Nancy swallowed back the tears, shifted David to the other side, and watched the dust motes dance in the sunlight. Out of the window, the woods seemed almost to beckon to her and she smiled.

'I'm coming,' she whispered, and she swore they waved their leaves in joy.

Before long she was out in her walking boots, striding up the field towards the woods. It felt so good. The sun was starting to drop, casting long shadows across the golden fields, and birds were circling in the sky above. The tips of the leaves were turning red and yellow, as if taking in the last of the sun's heat to keep them on the trees a little longer, and Nancy could feel a nip in the air. Autumn was here. The antlers were all but grown on the stags and, as she turned onto the top slopes, she spotted the velvet coating of one lying, cast off, on the ground. Only two more weeks to Open Season.

She bit back a smile as she realised it would be exactly a year to her now infamous 'cock' comment. The villagers seemed to have, if not forgotten it, at least forgiven her for it. Some, especially the women, even seemed to admire her for it. She'd been asked to join the Women's Institute and the knitting circle, and whilst neither truly appealed, she'd said yes, grateful for the inclusion.

Merry had suggested to Mrs Palmer-Jones, the formidable head of the WI, that she invite Nancy to speak about her experiences as a gunner girl, but Mrs Palmer-Jones had just frowned and said, 'I think the sooner we forget about the war the better, don't you?'

'I think the more lessons we learn from it the better, actually,' Merry had retorted as only Merry could, and Nancy had pulled her hurriedly away.

'People want to put it behind them, Merry,' she'd told her.

'Which is all well and good, but we can't forget it. And neither should we. Didn't we learn anything last time? Everyone swept the Great War under the carpet and, surprise, surprise, it wriggled out again, twice as big as before.'

'I know, Merry, I know, but what can people do out here in Langham?'

'You'd be surprised. If we all leave it to someone else, things'll never get done. I tell you, once I'm Lady Langham, I'm going to be up in the House of Lords telling people what's what.'

Nancy had smiled at her fondly.

'I bet you are, Merry, and quite right too, but for now, how about a drink in the Blue Bell?'

It had been cowardly of her, she supposed. She should have stood at Merry's side and taken on Mrs Palmer-Jones, tried to change attitudes one person at a time instead of smoothing everything over with platitudes. But this wasn't her village, not yet, and she didn't want to alienate people. Plus, she had her own private idea planned. If Connie's painting sold for as much as the auctioneer had suggested, she'd make a big donation to the memorial fund. She loved the thought of the memorial to their lost sons coming from money gained by saving someone else's. No one needed to know who that someone had been – no one but Nancy, Connie, Peggy and Dot.

She paused at the top of the hill to turn and look east to the village. It sat, snuggled into what passed for a valley around here, the roofs of the cottages glowing in the sun. As she watched, a bus came over the hill, stopped at the green and let several people out. Nancy remembered her near flight from Langham and turned her eyes back to the Gamekeeper's Cottage. Its soft sandstone looked like pure gold, and the roses over the porch were a glorious haze of white. The roof was sinking more than ever, but not for long. If everything went to plan, they'd have it mended before Christmas and could celebrate in their very own, restored home. Her mum would be amazed by how pretty it was, she thought, and smiled, picturing her face. She'd send an invitation tomorrow.

She bent to pick some pretty harebells from the longer grass at the edge of the woods and that's when she noticed them – the deer. The herd of females was grazing just over the ridge and, as Nancy watched, she swore they looked at her. Their elegant bodies seemed to go rigid, as if poised for flight, and she stood very still, not wanting to frighten them away.

'You'll be mothers soon,' she whispered to them, wondering if they knew, if they sensed it. The older deer must have some retained memory, surely? The young ones, though, wouldn't know what had hit them. She smiled in their direction but they were still on alert, and now she saw the nearest ones leap back. In an instant, the whole herd was off.

'Don't go!' she called, and that's when she heard the noise.

It was a low bark of a call coming from within the trees, not quite the plaintive roar of the rut but something close, like a warm-up. Nancy thought of the velvet antler coating she'd seen back down the field and looked around nervously. If the stags were getting ready to mate, they would be on edge and aggressive. She could see nothing but the cry came again and, swift on its tail, something else. Something more human. Nancy crept towards the woods.

'Help!'

She gasped and, plunging into the woods, threaded her way between the trees. She could still hear the sound of Joe's hammer somewhere over by the Hall so it couldn't be him, but she had no idea where his father was.

'Ted?'

'Help!' The cry was closer now and there was no mistaking Ted's voice, though the fear within it was new to Nancy. She picked up her feet and ran.

She found him in a clearing, sprawled on the ground with sweat on his brow and blood trickling down his calf. His trouser was split open to reveal a gaping wound and his gun lay a short distance away, as if it had been knocked from his hand.

'Oh no, Ted. What happened?'

He looked up at her, eyes wild.

'Nancy? Get back! Don't come close.'

'What? Why on earth…?'

Her words dried up as she followed his gaze and saw, not ten feet away, a huge stag. Its feet were set wide and its nostrils flaring. Its big eyes were fixed on Ted and it was pawing the ground as if preparing for another attack. Ted tried to scramble back but his leg looked badly damaged, and he cried out in pain. The stag's eyes narrowed and it lowered its head to go in for the kill.

There was no time to think, no time to weigh up the pros and cons of the situation. Nancy acted on instinct, diving for Ted's gun and placing herself in front of him as the stag began its charge. As he came towards her, she lifted the gun, lined up the sight – an easy task with such a large target – and pulled the trigger.

The single shot rang out around the trees as the stag, with a look of shock in its dark eyes, fell to its knees and then quietly sank to the ground just a couple of feet from Nancy. Slowly, she lowered the gun and stared down at its magnificent body. The great antlers were clean of their velvet and sharp as knives. One second more and she would have been gored on their point.

But she wasn't.

'You… you saved me.'

She turned and dropped to her knees next to Ted, casting the gun aside.

'Not yet. That's a nasty wound, Ted. We need to get you to a doctor.'

'You saved me,' he said again, and then his eyes rolled back in his head and he passed out in her arms.

It was a long and terrifying night. Nancy had managed to fashion a basic tourniquet and bandage whilst she'd screamed for Joe's help but, even so, by the time he'd come running to get Ted down the hill and into the Gamekeeper's Cottage, her father-in-law had lost a lot of blood and had to be rushed to the hospital. Betty, Nancy and Joe paced the corridor, David asleep in his carry-cot, but as the first rays of the sun peeked through the big window at the far end, a doctor came out.

'Mrs Wilson?'

Betty rushed forward.

'That's me. How is he, doctor? Will he live?'

The doctor took her hands and smiled.

'He'll live. He won't be walking for a few weeks, but he'll most definitely live.'

'Oh, thank you. Thank you so much.'

Betty broke down and Joe took her in his arms, clutching her close.

'Nasty wound that,' the doctor said to him. 'Did someone say it was from a stag?'

'It was, yes.'

'He was lucky then that the beast didn't finish him off.'

Joe looked to Nancy.

'Not lucky,' he said.

'No?'

'No, doctor. My wife shot it dead.'

'Your wife did?' The doctor looked to Nancy and gave her a slow nod. 'That's some woman you've got there.'

'It certainly is,' Joe agreed proudly.

Nancy flushed. She had no idea where to put herself, and was grateful when Betty placed a hand on the doctor's arm and asked, 'Can I see him?'

The doctor looked back to her instantly.

'Of course. He's rather dopey I'm afraid, but I'm sure he'd be delighted to see his family.'

He stepped back to usher them into the ward, and Betty moved as fast as Nancy had ever seen, rushing to Ted's side and covering him in kisses.

'Oh Ted, I thought we'd lost you.'

Ted nodded solemnly.

'So did I, Bett love, so did I. When that stag lowered its head to charge, I was saying my prayers to God Almighty to take me up to our Rose without too much pain, but I'd reckoned without our Nancy.' He held out a hand to her and, placing David's little cot down, she went to take it. 'That was the bravest thing I've ever seen anyone do, lass,' he said solemnly.

'I didn't really think about it, Ted.'

'Exactly. It was some of the most skilful shooting too.'

'Hardly. He was filling my sight.'

'And coming full pelt. You were quick and you were accurate, and I'm sorry, Nancy, that I ever said you shouldn't handle a gun. You're far better with it than any man, myself included.'

A shocked silence followed this statement. Nancy shuffled her feet.

'Thank you,' she managed eventually. 'Now, you should rest, Ted, and—'

'I'm not done.'

'Sorry.'

He smiled at her.

'Don't be sorry, Nance, please, but hear me out, whilst this stupid, stubborn old lummox has the guts to say what he has to. I've been wrong about you. I could see from the start that you had fire in your belly and I guess that scared me. You understand the estate like any man and you've got the skills to be the best gamekeeper out there. Better even, maybe, than our Joe. Certainly, together you'll be astounding. I didn't like that. It made me uncomfortable but, you know what, not half as uncomfortable as crawling across the ground with a stag eyeing me up.

'I'm a coward really. I've spent two wars scared, not so much of death – though Lord knows that's scary enough – as of change. I'm a man of habits, Nancy. Ask our Bett, poor lass. I used to drive her mad when we were first married with my finnicky little routines. I ground her down, bless her, but there's no one going to grind you down, Nancy, and neither should they. I don't know what they taught you girls in the army, but it's made you strong and that's a good thing. Why shouldn't a man have a strong woman at his side? I saw that all too clearly in the woods.'

He squeezed Nancy's hand and she felt tears spring to her eyes again. This was too much.

'There's nothing wrong with routines, Ted,' she said softly.

'Nope,' he agreed, 'but sometimes, you maybe have to find new ones. Now, I need to ask you something, lass.'

'You do?'

He nodded.

'Doc says I'm not walking anywhere for a month or more.'

'Definitely not.'

'And Open Season is only two weeks off.' Nancy gaped at him. 'Joe can't run the shoot on his own so, Nancy, would you do it with him?'

'Me? Really?'

'I can't think of anyone better.'

'But, but what about David?'

'Betty?' Ted said, looking to his wife.

'I'll have David,' she said instantly. 'If need be we can get him a bottle. You do the shoot, Nancy, you do the shoot for the family.'

'For the family?'

'If you want to.'

Nancy looked around at them all: Ted in the bed looking earnestly at her for help, Betty nodding her on and Joe watching her with pride. Behind them baby David slept, oblivious to all the excitement.

'I'd be proud to, Ted,' she replied.

Chapter Twenty-Nine

Sunday, 1 October 1946

I did it! Lordy me, I'm worn out, but I did it – I helped Joe, Merry and Lord Langham run the first day of Open Season and it went so well. I mean, there were a few hiccups. Someone should really have checked that young dog was on his leash before Lord Langham started his speech, and someone should probably have told the beaters not to draw so much attention to that poor young couple in the undergrowth, but on the whole the hunt was a success. Someone did say the redcurrant in the tarts was a triumph, but I had no time to be part of any of the baking – and I loved it that way.

I cannot believe today is exactly a year from me shouting rude words at the village and trying to leave – it feels so much longer ago. I've learned so much, found my place, had a baby! Betty was so proud today, standing there with David in her arms and all her friends cooing around him, and it was lovely to see. Would I have been like that if Hitler hadn't torn the world apart with his megalomania, and pulled me out of a hairdressing salon in Chester and onto the guns? I guess we'll never know, but once you've changed, there's no going back, and I'm loving the new direction of my life with my gorgeous Joe.

England feels like a different place with the shadow of war falling away from us all. It lingers in places – in ration books, in the haunted looks on some poor men's faces, and in the women bringing up babes alone – but I think we are all starting to believe that the sunshine of peace might be here to stay, and we can relax and find a way to live again. We don't have to be afraid any more and that leaves room to start making improvements.

Believe it or not, I wasn't the only woman on the hunt. Merry was there and she'd brought in her nursing friend Flopsy, and another aristocratic type who's apparently helping her fight for increased women's freedoms in the House of Lords. Some of the men muttered about it, but then Ted stood up and told everyone about me saving his life by shooting the stag and that shut them up. Bless him, he went so pink. Speaking in public really isn't my father-in-law's thing, but he did it all the same and I'm so very grateful to him for embracing me as he has.

Most of the men were really friendly on the hunt after that – especially when they saw how well we could shoot. Next year I'll get Peggy and Dot to come along too. After all, my gunner girls were the ones who propped me up when I thought the fight was too hard to win, so they should be here to see the new world we're quietly creating in our little part of Norfolk. Standing on the drive of Langham Hall in trousers and a gun slip, instead of a floral frock and a tea urn, may not be the most dramatic of revolutions but it's a revolution all the same. And besides, I think we've all had enough of drama for now.

I wish I could invite Connie, but the shadow of war hasn't fallen back enough to allow people to see Germans as anything more than the enemy. Maybe it never will? That would be a great sadness, but we can only hope that time will heal. For now, wounds are raw and it's understandable that people will find it hard to trust. Connie's been so brave, going out there to live with Ernst. I assume her neighbours in Bavaria must see her as a potential enemy too and just pray that she is safe. She writes to me, at least, and seems happy – maybe losing a war makes a nation more forgiving? Or maybe, like Connie says, many of them hated Hitler too and are relieved to be free of him.

One thing I do know – Connie is strong enough to sort it out herself. Our worlds, our ways, as we said that long-ago night in the woods when we took a chance on humanity instead of war. Now I'm chasing pheasants in those woods instead, and doing it in style too. Did I mention how well today went?

It seems, though, that I must stop writing. The pages are running out, my son is fast asleep in his cradle, and my husband's arm is sneaking around my shoulders. Time, I think, to kiss goodbye to the past – both the war and this tricky year after it – and look to the future with my wonderful family, here in the Gamekeeper's Cottage that finally feels like a true home.

Epilogue

Lorna lifted the scraper to the wall, then hesitated. She looked to David who nodded her on, so, drawing in a deep breath, she slotted the blade under the newly steamed wallpaper and slid it upwards. An elegant curve of neon pink roses came away from the wall and fell to the floor at her feet.

'No turning back now,' she said.

'Mum would thank you if she were here. I imagine she's been pacing the heavens for years, waiting for someone to have the sense to finally do this.'

Lorna smiled and looked around the lurid room, trying to picture Nancy's face when she'd first walked in here, fresh off the train and facing her new life in the Gamekeeper's Cottage. She must have been so looking forward to being able to be with Joe, but the war ending had been only the start of her battles, and those of all the gunner girls. Thank heavens they'd had each other to help them get through. Friends, as Lorna had found out in the last month, were incredibly valuable.

Going back to Norwich had been hard, but at least she felt as if she was taking steps into the future again. They were very small, very tentative steps, but steps all the same. The other teachers at school had been wonderful, and the head had made a point of taking her aside and offering her help whenever she needed it. Mums and dads at Charlie's football matches had all offered support with lifts, and the boisterous togetherness of the touchline crowd was a comfort in itself. Parents in the playground had also rallied round and the boys had been inundated with playdates to stop them moping. She'd even been persuaded out on a mums' night to a new cocktail bar in town and had surprised herself by enjoying it – and, thankfully, by not crying in the toilets this time.

Aki had been especially wonderful, insisting on bringing round meals at least twice a week and staying to help Lorna see the boys to bed. She might be Aunty Aki, but she was also their headteacher and Charlie, for one, was not going to mess around with her even if he was desperate for another half-hour on his Xbox. Lorna had jokingly taken to calling her best mate 'the bedtime bomber' but she was also sure to let her know how much she appreciated the quiet routine of having someone else around. Aki was still seeing the lovely Dan, and Lorna blessed the Langham Dome for bringing what was starting to look very like love into her friend's life.

She still cried herself to sleep too many nights of the week, but she allowed herself that and slept the better for it. Her grief wasn't going to go away and all she could do was try to ration it out into manageable sections, so that in between she could cope with life for herself and the boys. They were slowly moving on – not from Matt, but at least from the raw pain of his loss.

'Bye-bye, roses,' she said, setting to with the scraper again.

It was sad but it was time. The annex was moving on too. Lorna came to stay here at least twice a month, hitting the road after school on a Friday and returning after one of David's amazing roast dinners on Sunday evening. It was her hideout, her retreat – a place to recharge her batteries for the rigours of the week ahead – and really, despite their kitsch joy, cerise roses were not especially restful. Hence the scraper.

'It's going to look so much bigger,' Mary said, joining in with her own tool.

She looked very sweet with her smart hair tied up, forties style, in a scarf. Clearly David thought so too, as he paused in his own work with the steamer to give her a kiss.

'Oi! Leave her alone, Dad.'

He glanced at her. It was the first time she'd called David that, and for a moment she was scared he was going to object, but instead he leaned over and kissed her cheek too.

'Apologies – daughter – I'm straight back to work.'

'Glad to hear it.'

They pushed on in companionable silence. Lorna felt the warmth of the steamer and, even more so, the warmth of her new family. Tilly had indeed stayed on in Munich, and last week Lorna had booked a trip for them all to go out to Bavaria once school broke up for Christmas. Tilly had been sending them pictures of the most amazing-looking festive markets, and Lorna couldn't wait to see them for real. Christmas, she already knew, was going to be impossibly hard this year, and having something new to do would really help.

She tore more and more strips off the wall, keeping an eye out for any places where Nancy might have hidden another diary, though she knew, really, that the one from the year the war ended had been a one-off. After all, what young mother had time to write a diary! Remembering her own sons, she glanced through to the living room, but they were happy with the Lego so she was free to work on, and within less than half an hour, the back wall was clear.

Lorna stood back and stared around in astonishment. As usual her mum was right – the room looked so much bigger, if perhaps a little stark. She bent and picked up a long, wide strip of the old paper from the piles littering the floor, running her fingers over the raised flowers.

'OK?' Mary asked.

'I'm OK, yes. It's just a bit sad, I suppose.'

Lorna looked over to the dressing table where she'd found the diary all those months ago. It had been a lifeline for her – a way out of the mire of Matt's death – and she owed Nancy a huge debt of gratitude for leaving it there for her. She and David had decided to donate the diary to the Langham Dome where it would be preserved in a special case for all to see, set at the heart of the ATS exhibition they were launching in two weeks.

Lilian had been over the moon with everything Lorna had turned up for her, and Lorna had loved the project and hoped that it would, in some way, honour Nancy. She'd kept the story of the pilot and the men from the Blue Bell out of it – those villagers were gone now and the secret was best kept that way for everyone. The focus of the exhibition should stay where it belonged – on all the brave gunner girls who'd fought to keep Britain's skies safe. Richard was already preparing a long speech on the subject, and Lilian had laughingly confided in Lorna the other weekend that she was wondering when to break it to him that she'd asked David, as Nancy's son, to publicly launch the project.

Before they'd handed the diary over, however, Lorna had typed it all out and had bound copies made for the family – and, of course, to use with her Year Sevens. She'd had to censor a few of the pages, but she'd written several lessons around Nancy's battle to keep the privileges of action and independence after the war, and other teachers had been clamouring to use them. The local paper had been in touch, and the other day the head had taken a call from *History Today* asking if Lorna might like to write an article. Even better, the local WI were keen to hear her speak, and Lorna was touched to finally be spreading the stories of these wonderful women that had been kept quiet for far too long.

'I feel a bit guilty for wiping out all this history,' she admitted to Mary now.

'We're not wiping out history, darling, just making way for new stories.'

'I suppose.'

'Look, why don't we keep a bit? We could put it in a nice frame and hang it over the bed as a nod to the past.'

Lorna smiled, instantly cheered.

'Great idea, Mum. Thank you.'

She selected a suitably intact piece and placed it carefully on the bed, then they stood there together, looking around the stripped-back room. Suddenly, a sound from the living area made them jump.

'What was that?' Lorna asked.

'Sounded like music.'

'Stan? Charlie?!'

Lorna shot through into the living room but both boys were still there, playing nicely. Charlie was making improvements to his gun battery with the new Lego kits David had been accumulating, but Stan was to one side, staring intently at the ancient wireless – and no wonder. From the old grille speaker came a run of finest jazz, as clear as day.

'Nancy?' Lorna whispered, looking around.

She shook herself; there was no such thing as ghosts. But as the music continued to play out through the old annex, she wondered if there was, at least, a spirit of a person that lingered in the things they'd loved. For a moment, she thought she saw Nancy and Joe dancing around this little room together, and her body ached to be held.

'Matt,' she whispered, but now Stan was reaching for her hands and Charlie's feet were twitching to join them, and as David swept Mary out across the carpet, Lorna gathered her two boys against her and danced – danced for the future that Nancy had found for herself and for the future that she, too, could finally see once more as something to be embraced.

A Letter from Anna

Dear Reader,

I want to say a huge thank you for choosing to read *The Secret Diary*. As soon as I found out about the many 'gunner girls' keeping Britain's skies safe during World War II, I knew I wanted to write about them, but what really gripped me when researching their amazing work was how hard they, and all the women working for the war effort, found returning to 'normal' life after 1945.

The war was a terrible, terrible time but it did so much to liberate women and allow them to discover just how brave, capable and clever they were. Clearly, being expected to go back into the kitchen after such challenging experiences was always going to be problematic and finding a happy balance is something that we are still working on today. I hope that Nancy's story was one way to explore this huge social shift and that you enjoyed discovering it with Lorna. If you did, and want to keep up to date with all my latest releases, just sign up at the following link. Your email address will never be shared and you can unsubscribe at any time.

www.bookouture.com/anna-stuart

If you get the chance, do pay a visit to the Langham Dome and see the amazing technology that was invented to practise anti-aircraft fire and that led to huge innovations in the film industry that we all love today. And if you enjoyed reading my story, I'd be very grateful if you could write a review. I'd love to hear what you think, and it makes such a difference helping new readers to discover one of my books for the first time.

I also love hearing from my readers – you can get in touch on my Facebook page, through Twitter, Goodreads or my website.

Thanks,
Anna x

 annastuartauthor

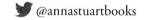 @annastuartbooks

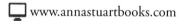 www.annastuartbooks.com

Acknowledgements

As always, there are so many people to thank in the bringing together of this book. I owe a huge debt to the fabulous team at Bookouture and especially to my brilliant editor, Natasha Harding, for believing in this story and helping me to shape it into something worthy of all the fantastic readers out there. Thanks are due, too, to my lovely agent Kate Shaw for her continued support and to my top writing support team of Julie Houston and Tracy Bloom who are always on standby with advice, encouragement and (when pandemics allow) glasses of wine!

I have dedicated this to my supper club friends – the local mums who I met a long, long time ago at a postnatal class with our first babies in which we all (we found out later) were convinced we were very much the worst mother there! This paranoia, it turns out, is one of the many joys of the roller-coaster ride that is parenthood and I've been so grateful to have these wonderful women in the carriage with me all of the way. Those first babies are now off to university and where, before, we met at toy-strewn coffee mornings, nowadays we can have far more civilised dinners. They are my gurus, my supporters and my friends and it seems right that this book about the challenges of fitting motherhood around a career should be dedicated to them.

On that note, it seems only fair to thank my family. One of the big joys of writing novels is getting the chance to tell the people close to you how much you appreciate that, so here's to you, Stuart, Hannah, Alec, Emily and Rory, as well as to my lovely wider family – parents, siblings, nieces and nephews – who are blessedly too numerous to name. A shout out, too, to Cookie – my loyal canine office companion and the one who gets me off my arse and out of it at least once a day!

Finally, the biggest thank you to my readers. The greatest joy of this crazy, frustrating, wonderful job is receiving messages from people who have enjoyed my books – they always light up the darkest day. So thank you and I really hope that you enjoy this one too.

Historical Notes

Women in the military

Britain was very quick to recruit women into the military – far quicker, for example, than America. At the start of the war it was female volunteers only but from 1941 all unmarried women between twenty and thirty were called up to join one of the auxiliary services:

- The Auxiliary Territorial Service (ATS)
- The Women's Royal Naval Service (WRNS)
- The Women's Auxiliary Air Force (WAAF)
- The Women's Transport Service (WTS)

Later, conscription was extended to some married women. They were never meant to serve in the front line of battle but, to be honest, for much of the war the front line was indistinguishable from the home front, especially with regard to anti-aircraft gunnery – a part of the ATS. 731 women died serving in these Auxiliary units during the war.

Gunner girls

In 1938, a year before the war had even started, a female engineer called Caroline Haslett suggested using female gun crews. Winston Churchill, luckily, was a staunch supporter of the idea, stating that, 'a gunner is a gunner', and his own daughter, Mary, served on a gun-site in Hyde Park. These talented women rapidly became known as 'gunner girls', or often 'ack-ack girls', for the sound of the gun firing.

The only problem with the whole scheme was that a Royal Proclamation forbade women from using deadly weapons! The workaround for this was that the girls were assigned to mixed-sex batteries, with the women doing all the technical preparatory work and the men actually loading and firing the guns. This must have been frustrating for the women at times and must also have created some tensions. Apparently, for the first crews the army chose fresh, young recruits rather than old hands who might have resented working with women. Nonetheless it was often a battle to convince the men that the girls were up to the job – which they most certainly were. The three vital roles the 'gunner girls' did were:

- **Spotter.** Sharp-eyed girls like Dot would search the skies for enemy planes using state-of-the-art binoculars, or an identification telescope.
- **Height-and-range operator.** The height-and-range machine, operated by girls like Nancy, calculated the distance a shell would have to travel through the air in order to hit the target. It was a large, cylindrical machine that worked rather like a horizontal periscope. They had to line up split images of a plane in their viewfinders to get a reading to call out to the predictors.
- **Predictor.** The Sperry Predictor was a complex device used to calculate the length of fuse required to ensure that the shell exploded at the right moment. Girls like Peg and Connie calculated this vital information and passed it to the male gunners who would load the shells into the gun and pull the trigger.

The whole procedure lasted seconds, so required a steady hand and a quick mind; only the sharpest and calmest of the ATS recruits were assigned to gunner duty. Scoring a direct hit was tricky, but scaring the pilot could at least put him off course and prevent him hitting his target. It was also an important morale boost to the civilians in the vicinity of the many gun crews up and down Britain to hear the sound of the ack-ack guns fighting back against the enemy and, as the girls proved their worth, most people – like those in the Blue Bell – were very proud of their local crews.

Langham Dome

The dome is an amazing piece of architecture. Bright white and almost perfectly cylindrical, it looks wonderfully like something aliens might have landed in and, to be fair, it was so technologically advanced in its time that you might almost have believed they had! The concept is simple – a film of an attacking aircraft is projected onto a mirror which then moves, sending the aircraft onto the dome's interior walls in a form of early 3D image.

The practising gunners could aim a gun in the centre of the dome and try and 'shoot' the image. A copy of the gun's sight could also be projected onto the wall so that the gunner could see how accurate he – or she – was.

The dome would also be filled with the noise of the plane and of bombs exploding and shells being fired to put the gunners under the sort of pressure they would experience when working the anti-aircraft guns for real. Forty-three of these dome teachers were built around England at the start of the war. Only six now remain and Langham is a beautifully restored version that is very well worth a visit. Find out more here: https://langhamdome.org

MacLaren's factory and Bevin nurseries

The MacLaren firm was founded by Douglas Colin MacLaren, who followed his father into the tailoring business in Attleborough. In 1940, he enlisted in the Royal Navy but on his return from the war, he decided to branch out from tailoring into ladies' handbags and, in partnership with John Pellegrini, bought up an old shoe factory with over 900 square feet of space in which to produce high quality leather bags. They were very successful and continued to produce quality handbags for another thirty years, employing over 200 full-time staff plus many more outworkers producing goods from home. MacLaren bags are still coveted on vintage sites today.

I could not find out if this specific factory had a day nursery for the children of female employees but many others like it did so it did not seem too much of a reach. Before the war there had been little provision for state-organised childcare, with women mainly being expected to stay in the home once married. There were a handful of nurseries for those on whose wage the family relied but they were far from widespread with most people relying on friends or family if needed.

During the 'phoney war' in 1939 many children were evacuated from the cities and their mothers went to work supporting the war effort. When a German invasion did not materialise and most children were released home, women had a problem with continuing the work that their employers – and the country – had rapidly come to rely on. Add to this a need to further mobilise the female workforce as more and more men went to war, and there was big pressure for childcare.

The man to truly grasp this and make it happen was the enlightened Minister for Labour, Ernest Bevin, who demanded in 1940 that nurseries be set up *before* married women were recruited. They were run by local authorities and funded by the Ministry of Health but, despite Bevin's efforts, there were only a few of them until various local campaigns, such as the Birmingham Day Nursery Campaign, brought pressure to bear on the government to increase provision.

Originally nurseries were just for women in government factories but increasingly they were expanded to private companies who were contributing vital supplies for the war. Women did pay for childcare but at a very subsidised cost and the nursery's place in society was cemented in the Education Act of 1944 that dictated that local education authorities were to have regard to the need to secure provision for children who had not attained the age of five years, by the provision of nursery schools or nursery classes in other schools.

After the war, inevitably, demand dropped away somewhat but never to pre-war levels as many women had enjoyed the camaraderie, sense of purpose and financial reward of working and wished to continue. Numerous nurseries remained open and new, private ones opened up, often attached to specific factories or workplaces. Dot's nursery at MacLaren's is a fictional part of this very important trend.

Boulton and Paul factory

Boulton and Paul, where many of the women of Langham are shown to have worked during the war, operated out of the huge Riverside works in Norwich. The company was a major supplier of aeroplane parts and prefab shelters during the war – almost all of which were made by women.

It was a fascinating business, started up by a young man called William Moore, who left his family's farm in Wareham to open an ironmonger's in Norwich. He soon branched out into making stoves and grates and his business turned more to manufacture than retail. It passed down to William Boulton in 1839 and he took on a visionary young apprentice called John Dawson Paul in 1853. They opened a small factory and foundry in Rose Lane in 1865 to start making horticultural supplies, including wire netting – supplying over 7500 miles of it to Australia to control wild rabbits!

They added structural steel and engineering departments to the factory in the early twentieth century, making coveted motor boats and the sledges for Scott's ill-fated expedition to the Antarctic.

Come the First World War, however, they started making prefab buildings for PoW camps and aircraft hangars, plus over 5000 miles of their core wire netting for the trenches in Flanders. They moved into making aeroplanes, at the government's request, in 1915 and relocated to the Riverside site to build more, having bought twelve acres of land from Colman's (the mustard firm). By the end of the war they had built more than 2500 planes and almost 8000 propellors!

They were well placed, therefore, to support the war effort when conflict came to Europe again. The Riverside works were attacked by the Luftwaffe in 1940 but continued to operate throughout the war, making wooden fuselages for planes and gliders, tank transporters and more than 85,000 Morrison air-raid shelters. Most of the workers in the war were, of course, women – both in the offices and on the shop floor. Apparently pressure on the ladies' loos (just twelve cubicles and six sinks) was so great that they had a strict rota, with just five minutes allowed to get twenty women through.

Between 1940 and 1944 many women worked seven days a week, till 4 p.m. on weekdays and 2 p.m. at weekends and as a lot of them also volunteered in the Civil Defence Service, they would go on duty in the evenings, or even all night, as ARP wardens, firefighters, first aiders and stretcher bearers, before returning to the factory the next morning. The end of the war must have been a great relief to these overworked women but it's also easy to see how much they must have missed the camaraderie and sense of purpose.

Baedeker bombings

This is a term coined for a series of air raids by the Luftwaffe against historic towns and cities across Britain in the spring of 1942. The decision to target these smaller, largely non-military, cities is thought to have been a retaliation for the Royal Air Force's bombing of Lubeck, Rostock and other historic towns in Germany. They are so-called because it is believed that the targets were selected by consulting the famous German Baedeker travel guides to find the most culturally impactful sites to weaken British morale. This was more or less admitted by the German propagandist, Gustav Braun von Stumm, a spokesman for the German Foreign Office, who reportedly said: 'We shall go out and bomb every building in Britain marked with three stars in the Baedeker Guide.' Goebbels was furious at this admission and it was never spoken of again but the name 'Baedeker bombings' stuck on both sides.

The major targets were the beautiful cathedral cities of Exeter, Bath, York, Canterbury and, as shown in the novel, Norwich. Norwich was badly raided on 27 and 29 April 1942, with the Luftwaffe taking 222 lives and bombing out many homes, though they miraculously missed both the cathedral and the town hall. Norwich was better placed than some of the other Baedeker cities because, due to its coastal position, it had been blitzed before and had air-raid precautions in place. These were now upped and the use of barrage balloons in particular prevented further serious damage when the Luftwaffe came again in May and for a final try in June.

Shooting season

Despite being a Derbyshire girl, the specific cycles of the shooting season were a mystery to me before I started researching this novel. I have long been used to seeing pheasant hatcheries on walks and was certainly aware of the increase in the beautiful birds around the autumn, but it was only when I wrote this book that I found out about the legal 'season' for shooting.

The Game Act of 1831 divided the year into an 'open' season, in which shooting is permitted, and a 'closed' season in which the game must be left alone to live and breed. In the UK the open seasons are:

Pheasant: 1 October–1 February
Partridge: 1 September–1 February
Grouse: 12 August–10 December

Deer are also protected by a closed season, which varies depending on species but for red, sika and fallow deer is 1 April–31 October for females and 1 May–31 July for the poor males. Strangely, you seem to be able to shoot male deer during their 'rut' in late September/October, which seems a little unfair to me and looks (without diving into it too deeply) to be a point of contention amongst the hunting – or, rather, 'stalking' – community.

Infertility treatment

In the novel, Peggy needs money to go to America for infertility treatment and whilst I had no specific drug or company in mind, the 1940s and 50s were certainly a vital era in finally understanding and treating infertility as a physical condition. Apologies for the length of this note, but I find it a fascinating subject and hope you do too.

The history of dealing with a couple struggling to get pregnant is as torrid and misogynistic as you might, sadly, imagine. For centuries, all such problems were laid squarely at the woman's door (look at Henry VIII, piling up wives in the hunt for an heir and totally ignoring the fact that it was almost certainly his own syphilis creating all the problems). The church would advise any childless woman to examine herself for sin and when the medical profession finally began to see past this, they came up with psychological theories that were every bit as damaging. It was suggested that infertility was the result of women's unconscious hatred of their husbands, fear of sex, neurotic loneliness or, as one paper concluded, of a woman 'resenting her role in society because she perceives restrictions'.

Some more enlightened scientists, though, were starting to probe the actual physical process of conceiving. Ova and eggs were discovered in 1827 and, although sperm had been identified as far back as 1677, the realisation that pregnancy was achieved by sperm entering the ovum wasn't cemented until 1843. In the late 1850s a couple of forward-thinking doctors started attempting artificial insemination with some success, which was largely random as he had no knowledge of the timing of the menstrual cycle (despite midwives and, indeed, most women, knowing the time to avoid for centuries – clearly they weren't consulted!).

Also, of course, no one dreamed to question whether sperm could be faulty, though in 1884, a brave doctor called William Pancoast inseminated the woman of a couple he was treating with sperm from another man without telling them. The result was a baby and a very happy couple – until he finally admitted to it a few years later. He was disciplined but a breakthrough had nonetheless been made and from then on male infertility was finally considered as a genuine possibility.

Alongside all this work, scientists and doctors were also starting to understand the role of hormones. The actual word 'hormone' wasn't even known until 1905 when Professor Ernest Starling used it in a lecture at the Royal College of Physicians in London. He coined the word from the Greek meaning 'to arouse or excite', and defined it as 'the chemical messengers which, speeding from cell to cell along the blood stream, may coordinate the activities and growth of different parts of the body'. From here on in scientists across the globe were working to discover more about these 'messengers'.

In the early 1920s Edgar Allen and Edward Doisy, researchers at the Washington University school of Medicine in St Louis, Missouri, identified oestrogen and began to develop the first therapeutic tests involving oestrogen injections. Edward Charles Dodds, in England, was the first to produce a synthetic oestrogen called diethylstilbestrol, which – against Dodds' own advice – was rapidly taken up by medics to reduce miscarriages in pregnant women. Sadly, Dodds was proved right when it was later discovered that the drug greatly upped the chances of cancer but it was still a step on the hormone-discovery ladder. Next to be identified were progesterone and testosterone and then their roles in conception could be explored. Chemical hormone substitutes, such as those I suggest Peggy took, could then be developed and they remain a standard part of infertility treatments today.

In a rather wonderful side story, an Italian scientist called Piero Donini was the first to extract and purify FSH and LH, the hormones that stimulate ovulation, in the late 1940s. He called his substance Pergonal (after the Italian 'per gonadi' or 'from the gonads'!) but could not get approval to manufacture it until the late 1950s. The project hit a stumbling block because they needed thousands of gallons of urine from post-menopausal women (as anyone who might be pregnant could contaminate the drug). As chance would have it, the head of the drug company knew an aristocrat who was nephew to Pope Pius XII and this pope gave his blessing for nuns across Italy to donate their urine! The drug was a success and the first birth directly attributed to it was in 1962 in Tel Aviv. Another twenty more pregnancies were achieved in the next two years and in the eighties it was so popular that the company were having to source 30,000 litres of urine a day! Luckily, the company found a way to synthesise the hormone, allowing the nuns to go back to weeing in peace.

The first IVF embryo was created in 1944, with the credit going to Dr John Rock of Harvard though it was in fact his lab assistant, the brilliant but very female Miriam Menkin, who performed the successful experiment! You have to suspect that if the scientists had used, or even just consulted, female experts they could have made such breakthroughs far earlier but as it stands the 1940s through to the 1960s were a vital time for progress in scientific treatment of infertility and I was glad to give Peggy a baby with the help of hard-working scientists like Miriam.